SHA

For a moment, S...
then the rage c...
She'd imagined...
was nothing compared to the loathing that gripped her
now. The monster had kept the poison—the poison with
which, he believed, he had once tried to murder her—
under the very bed where the two of them had lain
together and quite possibly conceived their children.

Had its proximity amused him? Had he laughed every
time he'd opened the chest and given her the chance
to spy the emerald glass glinting at the bottom? Had it
excited him to know that if he wished, he could caress
or kiss the venom onto her lips as she slept?

WIFE. MOTHER. NEMESIS.

She forswore any further hesitation or second
thoughts. Thamalon was going to die, and before the
month was out. All she needed was a plan.

FORGOTTEN REALMS

SEMBIA: GATEWAY TO THE REALMS

FORGOTTEN REALMS®

THE SHATTERED MASK

SEMBIA
GATEWAY TO THE REALMS

BOOK
III

RICHARD LEE BYERS

Wizards
OF THE COAST®

THE SHATTERED MASK
Sembia: Gateway to the Realms: Book III

Cover art by Raymond Swanland
Map by Dennis Kauth
First Printing: June 2001
This Edition First Printing: July 2007

9 8 7 6 5 4 3 2 1

ISBN: 978-0-7869-4266-4
620-95932740-001-EN

U.S., CANADA,
ASIA, PACIFIC, & LATIN AMERICA
Wizards of the Coast, Inc.
P.O. Box 707
Renton, WA 98057-0707
+1-800-324-6496

EUROPEAN HEADQUARTERS
Hasbro UK Ltd
Caswell Way
Newport, Gwent NP9 0YH
GREAT BRITAIN
Save this address for your records.

Visit our web site at www.wizards.com

DEDICATION

For Ann

ACKNOWLEDGEMENTS

Thanks to Lizz Baldwin and Phil Athans,
my editors in the FORGOTTEN REALMS®,
and to my fellow writers of the Sembia project,
Dave Gross, Ed Greenwood, Paul Kemp,
Clayton Emery, Lisa Smedman,
Voronica Whitney-Robinson, and Kij Johnson,
who created many of the characters
and settings in this story.

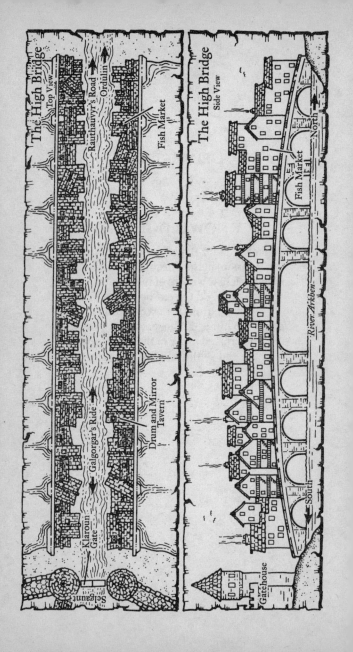

The High Bridge
Top View

Klaroun Gate

Galgorgar's Ride

Rauthauvyr's Road

Ordulin

Fish Market

Drum and Mirror Tavern

Selgaunt

The High Bridge
Side View

Gatehouse

South

River Arkhen

North

Fish Market

CHAPTER 1

25 Hammer, 1372DR,
The Year of Wild Magic

Shamur Uskevren was grateful that all three of her children were home. Even Talbot, who generally resided in a tallhouse across town, had moved back into Stormweather Towers, the Uskevren family mansion, for a day or two.

Shamur found her oldest child in the solarium, where shafts of afternoon sunlight fell through the many windows to nourish the potted plants. This winter it was fashionable for the merchant nobles of Selgaunt to exchange portraits, and Thamalon Uskevren II, Tamlin to his family and Deuce to his friends, was posing for a picture. A handsome young man with wavy black hair, he sat astride a red saddle which in turn rested on a trestle. He held a stirrup cup in one hand and wore a falconer's glove on the other, which he poised as if he actually were carrying a hawk upon his wrist. Presumably his favorite horse and bird would do their posing later in the stable and the mews.

Around the painter and easel milled a tailor and two apprentices, displaying samples of fabric: gleaming damask with designs woven in, shimmering sarcanet, and brocades embroidered with silver and gold. Tamlin winced at a hideous pattern of orange and mauve, whereupon the tailor smiled ruefully and congratulated him on his taste.

Regarding Tamlin from the doorway, Shamur remembered how his birth had brought a spark of happiness into her life after a year of utter misery. A sob welled up inside her, and she suppressed it. She'd worn her mask of lies for thirty years, and she must wear it for a few hours more. When she spoke, her voice was steady, her features, smiling and composed. "Hello, my son."

"Mother!" Tamlin replied.

He scrambled down from his wooden mount and strode to meet her. His father had once remarked that the Uskevren heir was too vapid and self-centered to truly care for anyone but himself, but now there was no mistaking the love in his deep green eyes. Behind him, the artist and tradesmen bowed respectfully to the mistress of the house.

Up close, Tamlin smelled of wine. Evidently the silver cup was more than just a prop. Shamur hugged the young man fiercely. So fiercely that, puzzled, he asked, "Is something wrong?"

"No." She forced herself to let him go. "Of course not. Can't a mother be happy to see her son?"

"She certainly can," he said, "for I'm delighted to see you as well. Especially since I'm having a beastly time deciding on colors. Gellie Malveen says that after Greengrass, everybody who counts will be wearing yellow, but I hate the way I look in yellow!"

They spent the next few minutes in consultation with the tailor, planning Tamlin's spring wardrobe. Ordinarily Shamur delighted in assisting her son with such endeavors. Now, as he chattered on and on about what to wear to balls, hunts, sailing parties, and cotillions, as if there were nothing more to life than revelry, she felt a vague disquiet, and wondered how he would fare in the days ahead.

"Have you paid attention to the negotiations with the emissaries from Tantras and Raven's Bluff?" she asked.

Tamlin blinked. "Excuse me?"

"The discussions are important," she said. "If we can convince their cartel to trade with House Uskevren exclusively, it will greatly augment our profits."

Tamlin peered at her uncertainly. "Well, that would be nice, I suppose, but you know I find all this buying and selling and dickering wearisome. Father is attending to it, surely?"

Shamur sighed. "Yes, of course." Let her perfect boy remain carefree for a little longer. Why not? One way or another, he'd have to become responsible soon enough. "Let's consider something of *true* import: the cut of your doublets."

They spoke for a few more minutes before she took her leave to seek out Talbot, her youngest. He was staying at Stormweather Towers to facilitate his use of the mansion's library, and that was where she found him.

The library was quite possibly the most unique in the land of Sembia. Most of the human inhabitants feared and distrusted elves, but Thamalon Uskevren found them fascinating. In consequence, the Old Owl, as people called him, had filled this room with an assortment of elven artifacts. Golden light from the enchanted sconces gleamed on bronze and wooden masks, a longbow carved from some unidentifiable substance white as alabaster, enigmatic sculptures of fused crystal, and, the pride of the merchant lord's collection, a set of ivory chessmen with a mahogany board. The volumes and scrolls shelved in the massive oak bookcases suffused the air with a musty odor that persisted no matter how often the servants cleaned and aired the chamber out.

Talbot sat at the table, hunched over a book. Like Tamlin, he'd inherited Thamalon's dark hair, but unlike his brother, not their father's trim build and middling height. Tal was a broad-shouldered giant, the only member of the family who towered over the willowy Shamur. He was so huge that people expected him to be awkward, but when he lost himself in his fencing, he displayed a grace worthy of a dancer in the Temple of Joy.

Shamur thought she'd entered the library silently, with neither a creak of hinges nor the brush of a footfall to announce her, but somehow Talbot sensed her anyway. He shot up from his chair and spun around, his teeth half bared in a snarl and a wild reddish light in the gray eyes that so resembled her own.

When he realized who she was, that feral radiance died, and his features rearranged themselves into a sheepish smile.

"You startled me," he said.

"Evidently," she said dryly. She took him in her arms, and though she wanted to clasp him to her as tightly and as desperately as she had Tamlin, this time she managed to control herself.

"How are your researches going?" she asked.

"Pretty well," he said. "I think Mistress Quickly will be pleased."

Like Tamlin, Tal showed scant interest in his father's mercantile enterprises. In contrast to his elegant sibling, who chose to wile away the days enjoying the diversions appropriate to a man of his station, Tal inexplicably delighted in performing with a troupe of common players, over which one Mistress Quickly presided as impresario and occasional playwright. Supposedly she now intended to compose a tragedy on the subject of Parex the Mad, fifth Overmaster of Sembia, and her young Uskevren protégé was trying to help her learn more about the deranged monarch's disastrous reign.

Shamur turned to glance at the books on the table. Talbot's hulking body jerked, almost as if he'd had to suppress an urge to interpose himself between the volumes and her.

To her surprise, most of the books appeared to deal with

magic, demonology, religion, and natural philosophy rather than history. "*The Speculum of Selûne?*" she asked, flipping the pages of a book whose covers were plates of polished silver. "*The Visage of the Beast*? You won't learn much about Parex from these."

"Oh, but I will!" Talbot exclaimed, too loudly. She raised an eyebrow, whereupon he grimaced, lowered his voice, and stumbled on. "I mean, there's reason to believe Parex read these very books. That he misunderstood the ideas inside them, and that misapprehension prompted him to perpetrate some of his follies and atrocities." He eyed his mother as if trying to determine whether she credited what he'd told her.

She peered back, trying to read him in return, wondering why he seemed so nervous. Over the past few months, she'd noticed a difference, a strangeness in him, even though he'd done his best to hide it. It struck her now that after this day, this hour, she'd never have another chance to understand, or to help him if, indeed, he needed it.

"Talbot," she said, "you know that if anything were ever wrong, you could come to me, don't you?"

He hesitated. "Of course."

"I mean it," she persisted. "There's nothing you could ever do and no misfortune that could befall you that could turn me against you."

He smiled, looking touched, puzzled, and embarrassed, with all of a player's artifice. "I do understand that, Mother, and I'm grateful. But I swear, everything's fine." His eyes narrowed. "Is this going to turn into another argument about my acting?"

Recognizing that he had no intention of confiding in her, she allowed him to divert the conversation into the old, familiar squabble. "I've always encouraged you to take an interest in the arts," she said, "theater included. But why must you lend your talents to vulgar claptrap devised for coarse and ignorant minds? Why not something more respectable? You could perform in the court masques for a refined audience of your fellow nobles."

"I could," he said, "if I wanted to act in the dullest plays ever written. Tragedies where everything happens offstage, and the characters just stand around lamenting it. But I'm afraid I'd keep falling asleep in the middle."

"You," she said, smiling, "are a perverse and willful boy, and I daresay we should have switched you more often when you were small."

They talked a bit longer, and as usual, she found herself bombarding the feckless lad with the advice he so sorely needed on virtually every aspect of his life. His shaggy hair and slovenly attire. His unsuitable friends. His curious reluctance to court the eligible daughters of other merchant-noble Houses. Meanwhile, his secret trouble went undiscussed.

She consoled herself with the reflection that it couldn't be so terrible. Talbot had too much of a mild and unassuming nature to have blundered into a genuinely desperate predicament, even if it seemed dire to him. One way or another, he'd flounder his way out again. He'd have to, because she'd run out of time to assist him.

When she ventured in search of Thazienne, her daughter and middle child, she heard her before she saw her. Tazi was practicing in the training hall, and the crunch and clatter of her sword, chopping apart a wooden dummy, echoed through the corridors of the great house.

Shamur hesitated at the sound. Some time ago, on one extraordinary night, Tazi had seen her mother perform feats of which the dignified, pacific mistress of Stormweather Towers was supposedly incapable. Though the girl still didn't understand how such a thing could be, she alone of all the household knew that Shamur was something other than she seemed. No doubt for that reason, the older woman now felt a pang of anxiety that Thazienne would somehow divine her present intent. The object hidden beneath Shamur's voluminous skirt, which had scarcely troubled her hitherto, suddenly felt heavy and awkward, likely to clank, trip her, or otherwise reveal itself at any moment.

But her trepidation notwithstanding, she couldn't bear to

depart without seeing Tazi. She'd just have to make sure she didn't give herself away.

The salle was a drafty, high-ceilinged room where a chill hinted at the winter cold outside. Concentric rings inlaid on the hardwood floor defined the dueling circles. Live blades, blunted practice weapons, ash and whalebone singlesticks, bucklers, targes, and kite shields hung on the walls, along with a row of battered wicker fencing masks.

Tall and slim, her short black hair sweat-plastered to her head, clad in a man's ratty tunic and hose, Tazi advanced and retreated at the far end of the room. Her long sword flashed in precise attacks, cutting wood every time and returning to a strong guard afterward. She'd nearly completed the task of hacking the upper half of the dummy into splinters.

"Thazienne," Shamur said.

The younger woman pivoted. "Mother," she said, sounding terse and impatient. "What is it?"

"I hadn't seen you today," Shamur said. "I wanted to, that's all." She advanced and took Tazi in her arms.

At first, surprised and discomfited by her mother's display of affection, Thazienne stood rigid in her embrace. It was scarcely surprising. The two had been at odds almost from the day Tazi was born, for all that Shamur loved her and believed that the girl reciprocated her affection. At last Thazienne relaxed and rather gingerly returned the hug.

It was only to be expected that Tazi stank of sweat. But Shamur could also feel that the girl's heart was pounding and that she was panting raggedly. Moreover, a grayish pallor underlay her tawny skin.

"You're pushing too hard," Shamur said.

Thazienne scowled. "I'm fine. I simply need to build up my stamina. Which is what I was doing when you interrupted me."

A year ago, undead creatures had attacked Stormweather Towers, one grievously wounding Tazi before the household guards destroyed it. The hoydenish girl, from the cradle possessed of an energetic and adventurous temperament, lay bedridden for months, an ordeal that nearly drove her mad.

Now that the healers had finally released her from the prison of her chamber, she exercised obsessively, fighting to cast off the last vestiges of her infirmity and regain the strength and agility she'd enjoyed before.

"I want you to be careful," Shamur said. "Pace yourself. Otherwise, your exertions are likely to do more harm than good."

Tazi rolled her sea-green eyes. "Of course, Mother," she said in a tone that made it clear that, as ever, she would do precisely as *she* chose. "Anything you say. Was that all?"

"No," Shamur said. "I know that when you feel ready, you'll resume stealing, if, indeed, you haven't already." She'd discovered that Tazi practiced burglary for sport on the same night that the girl had witnessed proof of her mother's secret talents. "Be careful then, too. I know you're adept at thieving. I know that as you catfoot through the shadows, or find some fat lord's hidden coffer and pick the lock in a trice, you feel untouchable. But you're not. Things could go horribly wrong in an instant. You could lose everything, even your life."

Shamur expected Tazi to jeer at her warning, so she was surprised when the sweat-soaked, black-haired girl frowned at her thoughtfully. "What's troubling you, Mother? Why are you saying this now?"

Shamur silently cursed. She'd resolved to make certain that Tazi wouldn't suspect anything was amiss, yet she'd failed almost immediately. Now she needed to shift the focus of the conversation. "What troubles me is your poor judgment."

"I don't have poor judgment!" Tazi snapped.

"Of course you do," Shamur said in the condescending voice that always infuriated the girl. "You're still a child, so I suppose I shouldn't blame you when you behave like one. But until you grow up, you'll need a mother's guidance, thankless task though it may be."

Tazi responded with a torrent of abuse. She'd never been able to resist a quarrel, particularly when her mother sought to instruct her, and this occasion was no exception. Shamur judged that within a minute or two, the girl had forgotten all about her murky suspicion that something unusual was afoot.

Strangely, this last quarrel, echoing all the others through the years, afforded Shamur a sort of bittersweet pleasure. She had to force herself to break it off.

Afterward, as she went to fetch her riding gloves and cloak, the three conversations came back to her in all their triviality. It seemed to her that she hadn't said anything meaningful. Not even *I love you*. Not even *good-bye*.

But however inadequate, the partings would have to do. For now it was time to put love aside and fan the fire of her hate.

Brom Selwick hated the cold. As the gangly young man with the wispy, patchy, and generally risible chestnut goatee waited in the courtyard, he shivered and, beneath his weather-stained gray woolen mantle, hugged himself for warmth. His eyes roamed over the complex roofline of Stormweather Towers, a hodgepodge of shapes and architectural styles that somehow managed to meld into a unified and graceful whole, and he tried not to think about the all the varieties of delicious warmth—crackling hearth fires, eiderdown comforters, hot tea, mulled cider—awaiting him inside the mansion.

It was difficult not to think of them, however, because he had no real need to linger out of doors. His master hadn't commanded his presence. Still, he couldn't quite bring himself to retire inside. Several months previously, Thamalon Uskevren had engaged Brom to be his household mage, and the young man felt a keen imperative to prove himself worthy of his new responsibilities. To that end, he tended to hover officiously near his employer whenever he had nothing else to do.

Bundled up in an ermine-trimmed cloak, his breath steaming and his cheeks ruddy, Thamalon waited by one of the ice-sealed horse troughs, chatting with Erevis Cale, his butler. The Uskevren lord was a man of average height with a slight stoop, still muscular and fit despite his more than sixty years. His arresting dark green eyes set off his white hair, but his brows were vivid black. He stood and moved rather stiffly and deliberately, in a manner that somehow conveyed a sense of his authority and strength of character

Pasty and bald, his severe garments too voluminous for his gaunt frame, Erevis loomed over his employer like some sort of apparition. He too carried himself stiffly, but in his case, the rigidity reminded one of a jointed wooden doll. Some of Thamalon's servants made fun of the butler behind his back, mocking his awkward appearance and somber demeanor, but Brom recognized just how competently Erevis performed his duties, and the high regard in which Thamalon held him. In consequence, he rather admired Cale.

Two grooms clad in white and gold Uskevren livery led a handsome pair of saddled horses forth from the passage that ran to the stable. The roan gelding was one of Thamalon's favorite mounts. The jet-black mare, an exemplar of the celebrated line of horses bred by the Foxmantle family, was one of Shamur's.

"Well," said Thamalon, smiling, "my wife's horse is ready. If she herself were here, we could get underway. Not that I'm such a fool as to expect a woman to arrive on time."

Erevis smiled ever so slightly in acknowledgment of his master's humor, and then, as if on cue, Shamur Uskevren appeared, the hem of her hooded russet mantle sweeping along just above the pavement.

Though half a century old, Thamalon's lady was one of the most striking women Brom had ever seen, tall and slender with long, ash-blonde hair, lustrous eyes, and a fine-boned, intelligent face. Her clear, unlined skin made her look younger than her years, though at the same time, her austere manner could make her seem older. In Brom's opinion, Shamur was a cold one, who, though courteous and often even kind, never shared her innermost self with anyone. Though she played the role of a grand dame of Selgaunt society with skill and seeming relish, the wizard suspected she was profoundly lonely and unhappy underneath.

Shamur greeted Thamalon and Erevis, thanked the groom who was holding her mare, then swung herself into the saddle. She was an expert rider, but it seemed to Brom that on this occasion, she didn't mount quite as nimbly as usual. He thought he detected a hitch, as if something had momentarily impeded the action of her legs.

Thamalon climbed onto the gelding, and two servants opened the sturdy, iron-bound gates. Someone had swept the hexagonal paving stones of the courtyard clean, but Rauncel's Ride, the thoroughfare outside, still wore a shroud of snow, its whiteness much defaced by footprints, hoof marks, and wheel ruts.

Brom had grown up a cooper's son and was still learning the ways of a great House of the Old Chauncel, as the nobility of Selgaunt called themselves. Thus, it only now occurred to him that, though he'd been informed that Lord and Lady Uskevren planned an excursion into the countryside, they evidently intended, in breach of the usual practice, to ride forth without an escort.

With the realization came a pang of unreasoning apprehension. He scurried out in front of the horses, slid on a stray patch of ice, and had to flail his arms to keep his balance. Thamalon's reddish gelding whickered and shied.

The Old Owl smiled wryly down at his retainer. "What is it now, Brom?" he asked in his pleasant bass voice.

"I don't think you should venture outside the city walls without a contingent of the guards."

Thamalon arched an eyebrow. "Why not?"

Brom hesitated, for in truth, he couldn't explain *why not*. He simply had a feeling, and he suspected that alone would carry very little weight with Thamalon, whose life was in large measure founded on logic and common sense. He was still trying to frame a persuasive reply when, rather to his surprise, Erevis shambled up to support him.

"Master Selwick does have a point, my lord," the butler said. "It might be prudent to take an escort."

Ever willing to consider advice, especially from Erevis, Thamalon tapped his chin with his forefinger, pondering. Shamur gave him a melancholy smile. "Perhaps they're right, my lord. I was hoping we could enjoy these next few hours alone together, but there will be other chances, I suppose." Her frosty breath veiled her mouth as she spoke.

Brom's brown eyes narrowed in puzzlement. Among the Uskevren retainers it was generally believed that if Shamur had ever loved Thamalon, that love had withered long ago. The wizard couldn't imagine why she suddenly seemed to crave her husband's company.

But apparently Thamalon, who, gossip held, still yearned for Shamur's affection, wasn't disposed to question his good fortune. Smiling, he said, "It's all right, love. We'll have our outing as planned." He gazed down at Brom and Erevis. "I appreciate your concern, but we'll be all right. Things have been peaceful ever since the city got rid of that infestation of ghouls. Perhaps our rivals have finally resigned themselves to the fact that the Uskevren have returned to Selgaunt to stay. And if Shamur and I should encounter any trouble, we both have fast horses, and I've got this." He tapped the scarred nickel crossguard of his long sword, a plain blade in a worn leather scabbard whose lack of ornamentation stood in contrast to the richness of his garments.

"As you wish, my lord," said Erevis. The butler stepped clear of the horses and Brom reluctantly did the same.

As his lord and lady rode out, Brom felt another upswelling of dread, this one even stronger than the first. He almost cried a warning, then realized that Thamalon and Shamur were already gone, and the servants already pushing shut the gates.

When she and Thamalon reached the street, Shamur breathed a sigh of relief. For a moment she'd feared that Brom and Erevis would ruin everything. But happily, her scheme was still on track, and, intending to keep it that way, she turned and gave her husband another smile.

"Well," he said, grinning back at her, "I hope we don't come to grief. Otherwise we'll look like proper fools."

"I know," she said, guiding her steed around an ox cart heavily laden with rolled carpets. "But I think you'll agree that what I've found is unusual. Unusual and possibly so valuable that for the time being, it might be wise to keep it a secret even from our own retainers."

She'd told Thamalon that on a social outing the previous day, when she'd momentarily strayed from her fellow gentlewomen, the lackeys, and the guards, she'd noticed a fallen pillar lying almost invisible within a thick tangle of brambles. The cracked, weathered column bore Elvish inscriptions, and when she'd curiously approached and touched the stone, she'd experienced a rapid, dizzying succession of visions. Though she hadn't truly understood them, it had seemed to her they might be glimpses of the future. If so, then who knew, perhaps the column could be induced to provide foreknowledge that a merchant lord, a speculator in grain, wine, olive oil, and other commodities, might exploit to his profit.

She fancied it was a clever lie, just the bait to lure the man riding along beside her. But now, rather wistfully, he said, "And that's why we truly set out alone, to safeguard a treasure. Not because my wife is eager to have me all to herself." He sounded as if the pleasure of her society, not the prize she'd dangled before him, was his primary reason for accompanying her.

She marveled anew at the skill with which he counterfeited love, kindness, and honor so convincingly that occasionally, down through the years, she'd found herself warming to him in spite of everything. How astonishing—and maddening—to discover that he was as adept a pretender as herself.

But she mustn't let him guess that she'd seen the cruel face lurking beneath his facade of decency. To the contrary, she must do everything in her power to maintain his trust. Even feign a desire for reconciliation, if that would please him, no matter how the pretense churned her stomach.

She smiled at him and said, "You don't give yourself enough credit. It *is* pleasant to have some time alone with you. I . . . I sometimes wish that we were closer."

"Indeed?" His green eyes brightened. "So do I."

She continued to cozen him as they traversed the busy streets of Selgaunt, the richest city in Sembia, and, in the opinion of its inhabitants at least, the grandest in all the world. Signs of wealth and commerce abounded on every side: Magnificent temples. The mansions of the nobility. The tallhouses of prosperous burghers and aristocrats like Talbot, who desired a refuge away from their kin. Taverns, theaters, and street performers. Open-air marketplaces, shops, manufactories, warehouses, and strolling vendors. A host of wagons and pack animals that, when loading, unloading, or simply creeping along, often slowed traffic to a crawl.

Just before turning off Rauncel's Ride, Shamur glanced back for one last look at Stormweather Towers, her home and prison for more than two decades. She felt a twinge of jumbled emotion, but didn't bother trying to understand it. It didn't matter. Nothing did, nothing but hate and the cold weight resting against her leg.

As the Uskevren neared the north wall, the homes and shops became more modest. Once they passed through Klaroun Gate, however, they found themselves atop the most imposing structure in all Selgaunt: the High Bridge. Arching far above the wide blue waters of the River Elzimmer, lined with houses, taverns, and emporia, including its famous fish market, the stone span was an important precinct of the city in its own right, and, for commoners, one of the more desirable addresses. People liked to live there for the view.

At the other end of the bridge lay Overwater, where

traders from other cities and lands stayed while conducting business with their counterparts in the city. It was a noisy confusion of inns, tents, and paddocks, of strange clothing, accents, smells, and customs. To most of the smug, sophisticated citizens of Selgaunt, Overwater was a pit of gaucherie if not outright barbarism. Shamur, however, had once wandered the Dalelands and the southern shores of the Moonsea, and she generally enjoyed the foreign sights and sounds to be found there. They reminded her of better times.

Yet that afternoon they didn't attract her in the slightest. She and Thamalon only had a little farther to ride, and that realization filled her with a feverish impatience. She touched her mount with her spurs, and the spirited black mare plunged forward, scattering a flock of squawking chickens that had wandered out into the road.

Thamalon cried, "Ho!" and galloped after her. In a trice they left the confines of Overwater, and thus, Shamur reflected, Selgaunt as well. She'd departed the city of her birth once before, and, against all expectation, eventually returned. This time, however, she was certain she would never see the place again.

She led Thamalon off the broad artery of trade that was Rauthauvyr's Road, across snowy fields shining almost painfully bright in the light of the westering sun. At last they came to a patch of woods. Stirred by a breeze, the leafless branches of the oaks and maples scratched feebly at the sky.

Shamur took a deep breath, steadying herself. Making sure her rage wouldn't seep into her voice, for it was becoming harder and harder to maintain control.

"Why don't we leave the horses here? They'd have a difficult time trying to move through the trees." In reality, she wanted to make sure Thamalon wouldn't have the opportunity to scramble onto the roan and flee.

"Whatever you say," he replied. "You're the guide on this expedition."

They dismounted and tied the animals. Cautious as usual,

her husband removed a horn lantern from his saddlebag, just on the off chance they might find themselves still in the woods when darkness fell. Shamur reflected that he was wiser than he knew. One of them would indeed remain there through the night and perhaps forever after.

She led Thamalon into the trees. The afternoon was colder and darker in their shadow. It seemed quieter as well, as if the snow crunching beneath their boots, the susurrus of their breath, and the occasional rustle or snap of a branch were the only sounds left in the world.

The sky was darkening by the time they entered the clearing she'd selected for her work. A hidden arena far removed from all his minions, where no one would see or interfere.

"We're here," she said.

Thamalon peered about. Standing behind him, Shamur unfastened her cumbersome cloak and let it drop to lay on the snow like a pool of drying blood. The winter chill bit into her flesh, but she reckoned exertion would warm her soon enough. She lifted her skirt, removed the broadsword she'd concealed beneath it, unsheathed the blade, and discarded the scabbard. It would have been child's play to drive the sword between her husband's shoulders, but that had never been her way. Besides, she wanted to watch his face as he perished.

"All right," he said, puzzlement in his voice, "where is the pillar?"

"There is no pillar," she replied, now making no attempt to keep her malice from sounding in her voice. What a joy to discard her mask at last. "Turn around and face me."

He turned, and his brows knit when he beheld the weapon. "Is this a joke?" he asked.

"Far from it," she replied. "I recommend you draw and do your best to kill me, because I certainly intend to kill you."

"I know you haven't loved me for a long while," he said, "if indeed you ever did. But still, why would you wish me dead?"

"Because I know," she said.

He shook his head. "I don't understand, and I don't believe you truly do either. Rather, you're ill and confused. Consider what you're doing. You have no idea how to wield a sword. Even if we did fight—"

She deftly cut him on the cheek. "Draw, old serpent. Draw, or die like a sheep at the butcher's."

For an instant he stared in amazement at her manifest skill with her weapon. Then he stepped back and reached for the hilt of his long sword.

CHAPTER 2

A tenday earlier

Bileworm passed one of his misty gray hands through the other, then inserted his long, gnarled fingers into the bulging brow of his wedge-shaped head. It was his way of fidgeting when he was bored.

Perhaps he ought not to be bored, for after all, he'd rarely visited the world of mortal men. The stars in the black sky were a wonder, and so was the air, which carried the scents of wood smoke, horse dung, and a hundred other novel aromas, but was entirely free of the tang of brimstone. Even the temperature was peculiarly mild. He'd been surprised to overhear humans complaining of the winter cold.

But Bileworm's was not a contemplative nature. He had a restless need for activity, and when the brown spaniel with the floppy ears came ambling down the street, stopping periodically to sniff at a gatepost or the base of a tree, the gaunt, shadowy creature with the slanted amber eyes couldn't resist the opportunity for a bit of sport.

The dog was handsomely groomed with a wavy, silken coat. It was well-nourished, and wore a black leather collar with a brass buckle. Evidently it had somehow gotten loose from one of the pleasant homes lining this quiet, horseshoe-shaped boulevard. Bileworm was glad that someone loved the animal. He hoped he could make the spaniel run so far away that its doting owner would never see it again.

The spirit was crouching behind the alabaster statue of a trio of weeping maidens that some householder graced with more money than taste had seen fit to place at the arched entrance to his property. The lachrymose damsels currently dripped icicles, as if their tears had frozen. Abandoning this hiding place, Bileworm crept stealthily along on his toes and fingertips, his belly a scant inch above the cobblestones. He wanted to see how close he could approach before the spaniel noticed him.

As it turned out, not very, even though he'd moved silently and was downwind of his quarry. Beasts could sometimes sense the presence of beings of his ilk, and the dog abruptly wheeled in his direction. The animal growled and bared its fangs.

Bileworm hissed, exposing his own black, needle-like teeth, and pounced six feet closer. The spaniel turned and fled.

When he gave chase, Bileworm discovered that a dog can run faster than a man. Or himself in his present shape, for that matter. He sprang upright and his legs stretched until he looked as if he were pacing along on the longest stilts ever fashioned.

Now a single stride carried him over the dog and set him down in front of it. Its nails clicking on the cobbles, the animal scrambled about and ran in the opposite direction. Bileworm stepped over it again and again, blocking its escape no matter which way it tried to run.

The trapped dog whimpered and piddled, tingeing the

air with the sharp stink of urine. To further heighten the spaniel's terror, Bileworm stretched his arms long enough to reach the ground and pretended to try to snatch the animal up. His ethereal hands were incapable of trapping a creature composed of such coarse matter, but happily, the spaniel didn't know that, and in any case it would find his touch abominably unpleasant.

Suddenly, agony blazed up Bileworm's leg. Toppling, he lost control of his form, whereupon his limbs shrank to their normal length. When he slammed down on the pavement, his shadowy flesh splashing, the spaniel bolted.

The pain faded sufficiently for Bileworm to pull his body back together into something approximating its normal shape, roll over, and see what had happened to him. As he'd suspected, his master had stalked up behind him and thrust the iron ferule of his long black staff into his familiar's ankle. Wisps of violet light still crawled on the magical weapon.

Master was a compactly built man of average height. In this world, he'd opted to dress plainly and unremarkably in a deep blue fustian cloak and buckram robe, as if he were nothing more than an itinerant spellcaster of no extraordinary talent. His hands were white and delicate, almost the hands of a lady, and he wore an iron ring on the thumb of each. He'd concealed his face behind a crescent-shaped papier-mâché mask of the Man in the Moon, such as revelers often wore at festival time, or when embarked on a night of mischief. Within the shadowed sockets of the false face shone his most unusual feature, deep-set eyes with irises so pearly gray they were virtually white.

Master prided himself on his self-control, and though he was manifestly angry now, it wasn't reflected in his tone. "I asked you to remain in hiding while I scouted ahead," he said in his soft, prim tenor voice. "What if someone had seen you?"

"No one did," said Bileworm. "It's very late. The humans are all sleeping."

"You don't know that," said the wizard. "You might have

spoiled everything." The spirit flinched in anticipation of another burst of pain, but the wizard merely sighed and lifted the staff away. "Sometimes I don't know why I put up with you."

"Because I found you when you were naught but a writhing grub in a hole," said Bileworm, drawing himself to his feet. "Because it was I who saw your potential, restored you to human form, and helped you prove your usefulness to the archduke." Afterward, of course, when Master had begun to rise in the service of his new liege, he had enslaved his benefactor with his magic, but Bileworm had long since stopped resenting that. It was the way of the universe for the strong to subjugate the weak.

"Come," said Master curtly, "we have work to do. He turned and led his minion back up the street. They halted in the shadow of an elm to regard the house called Argent Hall.

Argent Hall, Master had explained, was the residence of the Karn family and also one of the oldest merchant-noble homes in this peculiar human city of Selgaunt. The builders of many of the newer mansions had opted to encircle them with relatively low walls, a joke to an invading army but sufficient to inconvenience thieves and rioters. Argent Hall, on the other hand, was a true castle, albeit not a huge one. Its twenty-foot ramparts all but concealed the keep at their center. There were modest turrets at the four corners and wall-walks behind the crenels.

Master murmured words of power and turned widdershins in a circle, sweeping his staff in a mystic pass. The air grew warmer. Blue and silver sparks flickered along the granite battlements.

"I just dispelled the wards set to bar intruders like you," the pale-eyed wizard explained. "Now, there's only one sentry patrolling the wall, and he doesn't go round very often. I imagine he's spending most of his watch in one of turrets to avoid the cold." Bileworm snorted in contempt. In his world, a lord so poorly guarded could not have survived an hour. "As soon as he passes, we'll go over the wall."

"Why don't we just kill him?" asked the familiar, leering.

Master sighed. "Because I want to slip in and out without anyone being any the wiser. As you know very well, so stop trying to annoy me."

After a few minutes, a spearman tramped quickly along the alure, making his circuit as rapidly as possible. When he disappeared from view, the wizard and his minion trotted up the street to the foot of the wall.

Bileworm simply lengthened his legs to reach the embattlement. Master reached into one of the many pockets sewn into his robe, brought out a small leather loop, flourished it, and muttered under his breath. Power sighed and crackled around him, and he floated straight upward.

The wizard and his minion crouched on the parapet and studied the bailey below, which the latter-day Karns had turned into a garden. Paths of crushed white stone traced ghostly patterns in the gloom, winding among beds of silvery roses in full flower despite the season. At the center of a turnaround stood a dry fountain, whose creator had fashioned it to look as if the water, when flowing, were a spring bursting forth from a natural rock formation. A bronze archer knelt atop the boulders. One hand shielding its eyes, the statue peered intently into the distance.

Behind the turnaround rose the donjon. Broad stairs ascended to tall, carved double doors, while a green banner emblazoned with a silver cockatrice hung above them. The structure had begun as a fortress, and in its essence still displayed the stark, utilitarian lines of a stronghold designed first and foremost to withstand a siege. More recently, however, the occupants had attempted to transform it into a stylish, luxurious home to rival that of other merchant-noble families, widening the meutrières into windows bright with stained glass and affixing decorative molding to the facade.

"Do you see anyone?" Master whispered.

"No," Bileworm replied.

"Nor do I. Come on." Master simply stepped into space, and, his spell of levitation still operative, dropped slowly and gently to the ground. Lengthening then contracting his right leg, the spirit nimbly stepped down beside him.

Gleaming softly in the moonlight, the silver roses looked as if an artisan had cast them from metal, but evidently they truly were alive, for they exuded a sweet, heady perfume even in the depths of a winter night. Clearly a master enchanter had created them. They were uncommonly beautiful, and Bileworm wished he had the leisure to linger and cup one in his ghostly fingers. After several minutes the petals would wither and die.

The two intruders skulked toward the great house. There was no chance of Bileworm's gossamer footfalls making any noise, but he tiptoed anyway, burlesquing stealth like a clown in a pantomime, purely for his own amusement.

Then a low shape, more than seven feet long from the tip of its snout to the end of its scaly tail, lumbered out from behind a wrought-iron bench. The eight-legged watch beast swung its crocodilian head in their direction, and Bileworm discerned the sheen of a luminous emerald eye.

"Hide!" Master whispered, lunging behind a tree. Bileworm sprang after him. "Don't even peek at it."

"Why not?" the spirit asked.

"It's a basilisk."

"*What?*" Few powers in this mortal sphere were capable of harming Bileworm, but the gaze of a basilisk was one of them. It could turn the flesh of even an insubstantial creature to stone. "Kill it, Master!"

"I can't, or people will know we were here. Be silent and I'll try something else."

Master whispered the rhymed couplets of an incantation and rotated the knobbed head of his staff counterclockwise. Worms of phosphorescence crawled on the black wood. Meanwhile, Bileworm listened to the basilisk's hissing breath and its tail dragging and bumping along the frozen ground. The sounds were growing louder. He didn't think the monster had spotted him or Master. Otherwise, it would be more excited. But, just his luck, it was coming toward them anyway, and if it looked at him squarely, it wouldn't much matter whether it had been intentionally pursuing them or not.

In his present form, Bileworm couldn't even strike a blow in his own defense, and fervently wished he could bolt. But he didn't, for he was far more afraid of Master than of any watch beast.

The reptile grunted, sounding as if it was just on the other side of their tree. Bileworm trembled. Then, at last, Master completed his spell.

Off to the left, bubbles of golden light swelled and burst. The soft brassy notes of a glaur rippled through a fanfare. Then a white stallion, its bridle encrusted with silver and pearl, appeared in the center of the illusion. The horse whinnied, turned, and trotted into the night, whereupon the basilisk gave chase, waddling as fast as it was able.

"I hope no one in the house noticed that," Master said, "but I had to divert the creature somehow."

"Do you think there are any more of them?" Bileworm asked.

"It's possible," the wizard replied, "so perhaps you might try keeping an eye out instead of cutting capers and playing the fool."

In fact, they reached the donjon without encountering any more trouble. Turning, his mantle sweeping outward, Master cast a second abjuration, wiping away another set of wards. Sparks danced and sizzled on the facade of the mansion.

The spellcaster had already decided that they wouldn't attempt to enter at ground level. Despite the lateness of the hour, there might well be a porter tending the front door, or other servants laboring behind any of the lesser entries. So Master floated to a dark second-story window, and Bileworm stretched up beside him.

The casement's lead cames ran diagonally, dividing the glass into diamond-shaped panes. Most of the quarrels were clear, a couple, bottle green. Master spoke a word of power and inside the frame, the fastener unlatched itself. The window swung silently open.

Master climbed inside through the drawn velvet curtains, and Bileworm followed. On the other side was a gentleman's bedchamber, and the sharp-nosed, yellow-bearded young aristocrat himself snoring beneath a heap of eiderdowns. The handle of a warming pan protruded from beneath the bed, and a crystal decanter lay on its side on the carpet. The scent of the spilled brandy tinged the air.

Just as Bileworm had wished to poison a rose, so now he would have liked to crouch atop the sleeper and swirl his shadowy fingers through his brain. He knew he could give the human nightmares. Indeed, given sufficient time, and sufficient susceptibility on the part of his victim, he might even drive the fellow insane.

But he knew Master wouldn't allow him to linger and enjoy that pastime, either. The wizard closed the casement once again, then beckoned Bileworm to follow him through the door.

Beyond the bedchamber was a sitting room where a lackey slumbered tangled in a coarse blanket on the floor. From there the intruders passed into a shadowy corridor. Oil lamps, most of which had been extinguished, reposed in brazen fixtures along the wall.

"Do you know which way to go?" Bileworm whispered.

"Possibly," Master replied. "In the old days, I visited this house on occasion. I believe I've got my bearings, but it all depends on whether our friend is still occupying the same suite."

The pair skulked on and eventually found a door with a cockatrice carved on the keystone of the surrounding arch. Master tried the knob and the portal opened.

Across the threshold were the lavish apartments of a great nobleman. A suit of gilded tourney armor stood in the corner, the helm crowned with the withered brown chaplet the wearer had won for his jousting. A red silk cover embroidered with songbirds shrouded a large gold cage. Paintings and tapestries crowded the walls.

The bedchamber was a spacious room currently lit by a

single candle in a red glass bowl. On the high domed ceiling was a faded fresco depicting the gods at play. Another covered birdcage stood by the window, and a green velvet cord hung beside the enormous bed. No doubt the occupant had only to pull it to ring a bell and summon his valet.

That occupant was a withered old man with a prominent beak of a nose. He lay slumbering on his back, and a gurgling sound rose from his open, toothless mouth. He wore an embroidered cambric nightshirt and a striped woolen nightcap as well. His flesh smelled of liniment and sickness.

"That's our man," whispered Master. He stalked toward the sleeper in a way that conveyed to Bileworm that he meant to take care of his business as expeditiously as possible.

"You said you know him," the spirit said. "Don't you even want to wake him up and say hello?"

"You just want to see him cower," the wizard replied, a thread of distaste in his voice.

"I hail from a cruel realm, Master, as do you, now. Besides," Bileworm added, "it might help me to see how he moves and hear how he speaks."

"Indeed," said Master skeptically. "Well, I suppose it won't hurt to indulge you. Briefly." He leaned down, took hold of the old man's bony shoulder, and gave him a gentle shake. The sleeper merely mumbled and tried to roll over. Master shook him again, more vigorously. "Wake up, Lindrian Karn."

The old man's rheumy gray eyes fluttered open. When he took in the masked figure standing over him, he yelped and groped frantically for the bell pull. Master held him flat on his back with one hand and poised the head of his staff in front of the old man's face with the other. Motes of magenta light danced and sizzled on the polished surface of the wood.

"Stop struggling," advised the mage. "Otherwise I'll have to hurt you."

Lindrian obeyed. From the looks of him, he was afraid but trying hard not to show it. "What do you want?" he quavered.

"You'll find out presently," Master replied.

The old man suddenly jerked in surprise. "I know those eyes! Marance Talendar!"

Master stiffened. He hated giving up any secret or advantage, no matter how slight, but on this occasion, he must have reckoned it could do no harm to confirm his prisoner's guess. For he lifted off the Man in the Moon mask, revealing an ashen, patrician face with a high, broad forehead, narrow nose, thin lips, and a pointed chin, handsome in a cold, intellectual sort of way. Lindrian gaped in horror and astonishment.

"My compliments," the wizard said, setting the mask on the table beside the candle. "You're sharp. I never dreamed you'd recognize me after so many years, and disguised in dim light, no less."

"But you're dead!" Lindrian whispered.

"Fortunately," Master said, "for were I alive, I'd be as ancient and decrepit as you. No offense. Actually, to be precise, I suppose I'm neither alive nor dead at the moment, but somewhere in between. I *was* dead, but in recognition of services rendered, my liege lord in the netherworld granted me a boon: to walk the earth again while I attend to unfinished business."

Lindrian swallowed. "You can't mean business with me. I never did anything to you."

"Of course not," Master said. "It was always me doing things to you. I imagined that if I wrecked your business ventures, I could ruin you, whereupon we Talendar could pick up your silver mines at bargain prices. The ruination of the House of Karn was my chief preoccupation at one time. But you never figured out who was afflicting you, and thus you never retaliated."

"It was you?" Lindrian said. For a moment, his barely controlled fear gave way to anger. "Damn you!"

Bileworm sniggered. "Rest easy, that's already been taken care of."

Lindrian turned, saw the spirit for the first time, cringed, and hastily turned back toward Master, who at least looked like an ordinary human being. "Then what do you want?" the old man asked.

"Do you remember how I died?" Master asked.

Lindrian hesitated, then said, "Thamalon Uskevren."

"Yes. To be precise, I died of the Owl's long sword opening my belly. It can take a long, excruciating time to succumb to a wound like that. I staggered and crawled a long way in search of help, my hands clasping the wound to keep my bowels from escaping, but at last my strength ran out. I sprawled in the mud and bled to death."

"That . . . must have been hard," Lindrian said.

"No, please," said Master, "you mustn't grieve, for as you can see, it wasn't the end of me. But the memory did stick with me through all that followed, and now, at last, I have a chance to exact some measure of retribution."

"I understand why you've come to me," Lindrian said, "and yes, I'll help you in exchange for my life. I never liked Thamalon anyway! What do you want me to do? Lure him into an ambush?"

Master's thin white lips quirked upward. "You'd betray your own kinsman, the benefactor who saved your House, on my behalf? I'm touched, or at least I would be if I trusted you. But actually, I have another scheme in mind. Bileworm, have you seen all you need?"

"Yes, Master."

"Then farewell, Lindrian. May your soul find itself in more congenial surroundings than did mine." The wizard set down his staff, picked up a plump pillow, and pressed it over the mortal's face.

Lindrian's emaciated limbs thrashed uselessly, and Bileworm smirked in delight. Master's face, however, was set with the resolution of one performing a necessary but noisome task. Not that he was squeamish about slaughter. He often relished it, but only when it was accomplished at a distance, by his magic or warriors under his command. He didn't like giving even a feeble old man the opportunity to fight and paw at him. On this occasion, however, it was necessary to kill without leaving a mark.

All too soon, in Bileworm's opinion, Lindrian's struggles ceased. One of the dead man's arms flopped half off the bed and pointed straight to the birdcage. Master discarded the pillow and wiped his dainty hands on the bed linen. "Your turn," he said.

The spirit reared up until his head brushed the fresco on the ceiling. Every portion of his body stretched thinner. Finally, stooping, he poured himself into the corpse's sour-smelling mouth.

Once he was completely inside, he thrashed and turned in the thick darkness like a man drowning in quicksand, until at last his own substance, permeating the corpse's body like arsenic suspended in wine, came into proper alignment with it as well. He felt the soft mattress beneath his form. He could feel Lindrian's gnarled, arthritic hand at the end of his arm and make the fingers close, evoking a throb of pain from the swollen joints. He took control of the cadaver's eyes and saw Master gazing down at him.

For that was the special gift of his kind. As certain other spirits had the power to possess the living, Bileworm and his siblings could clothe themselves in the husks of the dead.

The only drawback was that while wearing these shells of meat and bone, they were more vulnerable than they were used to. He reflexively started to raise his hand to protect himself, then checked the motion. It wouldn't do for Lindrian to suddenly acquire a new mannerism.

Speaking of the old man's habits, Bileworm had best make sure he could employ the corpse's brain as well as its muscles. For that was the tricky part, and despite what he'd told Master, it was that capacity and not a few minutes of observation which would enable him to impersonate the nobleman successfully. He tried to call forth Lindrian's memories, and the images paraded before his inner eye.

"Well?" Master asked.

"The first time he took a riding lesson, he fell off the pony," Bileworm said. The initial three words were slurred, but the ones that followed were perfect, even with regard to their inflection. No one could have guessed that it wasn't

Lindrian himself speaking. "From that, he acquired a secret aversion to horses that vexed him all his life. He killed a man in a duel when he was seventeen and afterward, weeping, he threw his sword in the river. To keep his valet from nagging, he ate a bowl of chicken broth and half a slice of toasted bread, even though he had no appetite. In short, Master, I know everything he knew. For the moment, I *am* Lindrian Karn."

"Good," the wizard said. "Then the fall of the House of Uskevren has truly begun."

CHAPTER 3

Shamur seethed with impatience as she waited for Harric to hop down off the back of the carriage and open the door for her, but the proper lady she'd strived so doggedly to become wouldn't forgo such a courtesy under any circumstances, even the current ones.

Harric usually gave her a gap-toothed grin when performing a service for her, but this morning the footman's long, lantern-jawed face was grave, his brown eyes, soft with sympathy.

"I'm sorry, my lady," he said as he gave her his hand.

"Thank you," she replied, then started up the stairs to the tall front doors, their panels carved with scenes of miners mining, loggers logging, and weavers weaving, all, presumably, for the greater glory of the Karns. She climbed as briskly as dignity allowed.

Over the course of nearly a century, the lavish furnishings of Argent Hall had changed considerably, but it was still recognizably the home in which Shamur had spent her childhood. Today the great house had an air of desolation, as if loss had already paid it a visit. People whispered when they spoke at all, and the servants drifted pointlessly about as if they'd forgotten how to perform their duties.

Fendolac met her on the white marble staircase that led to the upper floors. As always, the rawboned scion of the House of Karn seemed a creature of angles and points, including a long spike of a nose, stiffly waxed mustachios, and a spade-shaped, straw-colored beard. His outfit carried on the motif, for he had a passion for blades and swordplay, and even on this somber morning, in the privacy of his own home, had taken the trouble to strap on a gold-hilted long sword, clip a matching poniard to his belt, and slip a stiletto into the top of his high doeskin boot.

Still, his expression was grim. Shamur had to give him that much credit.

"How is he?" she asked.

"Failing," Fendolac replied. "He says he had some sort of attack in the night, but he won't let us send to any of the temples for a healer. Perhaps you can persuade him. He's asked for you several times."

Side by side, they hurried to Lindrian's apartments. As they entered, it seemed to Shamur that this part of the converted donjon was even quieter than the rest, and after a moment, she realized why. At this time of day, the old man's pet warblers, goldfinches, canaries, and vireos ought to have been chirping and fluttering about, but someone had removed them and their cage as well.

When they reached Lindrian's bedchamber, she saw that the birds he'd kept there were missing also. The patriarch of the House of Karn himself looked shockingly ill. His wrinkled face was white as wax save for bruise-like discolorations under his clouded, sunken eyes. Even worse, a faint, rotten smell hung in the air, as if his flesh was already decaying from the inside.

At least he was awake and alert. Propped against a mound of pillows, he gave Shamur a sardonic smile and said, "You came. I wasn't certain you'd bother."

Shamur felt a twinge of guilt, for in truth, she hadn't often called at Argent Hall in recent years, even after Lindrian had fallen ill. It was strange, really. Nearly three decades before, she'd loved her kin enough to forfeit any chance of happiness on their behalf, yet once she'd made the sacrifice, she'd gradually lost any enthusiasm for their society.

"Of course I came," she said. "What happened to your birds?"

"I had to have them removed so I could rest," Lindrian said. He coughed convulsively, spattering the front of his nightshirt with tiny drops of blood. "They were making a terrible commotion. They saw Death's hand reaching out for me, I imagine."

"Death needn't take you yet," Shamur said. "Not if we send for a priest versed in the healing arts."

"I'm terrified you're right," Lindrian said, "and that's why we're not going to do it. I don't want to live in pain any longer. I want to rest." He gave Fendolac a bitter smile. "Besides, my son is impatient to be Lord Karn, aren't you, boy?"

Fendolac's bloodshot eyes widened in shock. "Father, I swear to you—"

"Get out," Lindrian said. "I want to talk to your sister in private."

"Father, I love you!" the youth persisted.

"What's the matter?" said the dying man. "Are you afraid I'll disinherit you and give everything to her? I will if you don't make yourself scarce. Now, scat!"

Fendolac threw up his hands and withdrew, closing the door behind him.

"That was unjust," Shamur said, seating herself on a low-backed green velvet chair. "That young man has his faults, but he does care for you. Now he may live out his days wondering if his father ever truly cared for him."

"Well, pray forgive me for wounding his tender sensibilities," Lindrian said, "but dying in pain makes a person irritable. I'll dry his tears later. " He waved a tremulous, liver-spotted hand, dismissing the matter. "Right now, I need to talk to my aunt."

Shamur was surprised. Indeed, though he was a man at the end of his life and she, still strong and hale, she *was* his aunt and not his eldest daughter as the rest of the world believed. Neither of them had explicitly acknowledged that fact for a number of years, not even when they were certain no one else could overhear.

"About what, nephew?" she asked.

"I fear I've done you a great wrong."

Shamur shook her head. "Has my situation weighed on your conscience for all these years? Please, you mustn't fret any longer. The switch was your father's idea, and in any case, it was *my* choice to replace your poor daughter as Thamalon's betrothed. I wish it hadn't been necessary, but I couldn't permit the impoverishment of my family when a wedding and twenty chests of Uskevren gold could avert it."

"I'm not talking about the substitution," Lindrian said, "although I suspect your marriage made you far more unhappy than you've ever confided. It's, well, it's that I've kept a secret from you. For the past twenty-four years, I've known the identity of the foe who worked behind the scenes to destroy our family's every venture, then finally murdered my little girl."

"Are you serious?" she asked. She'd never stopped praying that someday she'd discover who had relentlessly attacked her family, slain her beloved grand-niece, and so forced her into her current dreary existence, but after so many years, she'd essentially abandoned hope of ever seeing the murderer punished. "Who was it?"

"Thamalon."

"I beg your pardon?"

"Thamalon Uskevren, the very husband to whom, may Sune Firehair forgive me, we sold you."

Shamur frowned. "Lindrian, your illness is filling your head with fancies. You think you know this, but you don't."

"Yes, I do."

She sighed. "All right, if you say so."

"Don't patronize me! It's my body failing, not my mind."

"But what you're saying doesn't make sense," she said. "Why would he drive our House to the brink of ruin, then rescue us? Why seek my grand-niece's hand, try to kill her, then ultimately go ahead and marry her, as he imagined he was doing?"

"Because his plans changed from one day to the next. I'll tell you the tale as I pieced it together once I discerned the atrocity at its center. As you recall, the other merchant-noble Houses had driven the Uskevren out of Selgaunt half a century ago for conspiring with pirates. By trading elsewhere, Thamalon acquired a new fortune, then dared to return to the city. For all his wealth, he wasn't received in the parlors of the Old Chauncel. The other nobles still held his father's crimes against him. To gain acceptance, he needed to marry into an honorable family."

"So he courted your daughter," Shamur said. "I've always assumed that was the reason, and while it might not inspire a troubadour to rhapsodize on the theme of love eternal, it isn't dishonorable. It certainly doesn't implicate him in any crimes."

"But you see, if we Karns had been prospering, Father and I would likely have spurned Thamalon like the rest." The old man pressed his hand to his chest as if his heart was paining him, but then, rather strangely, immediately snatched it away. "We certainly wouldn't have allowed him to marry my child, and he knew that. Accordingly, his agents poisoned our flocks and the soil in our cotton fields, collapsed the tunnels in our mines, burned our saw-mill, and hired brigands to raid our logging camps. This depleted our coffers and set a pack of creditors snapping at our heels. All so we would have no choice but to welcome an

Uskevren into the family if we wished to save our House."

Shamur shook his head. "Thamalon wouldn't have done that."

"Have you never known him to be ruthless?"

She hesitated. "Only to his enemies. Besides, this tale still doesn't hang together. You still haven't explained why, if he wanted your daughter for his wife, he nonetheless tried to kill her."

"Because he believed"—the dying man coughed long and hard, and when he resumed speaking, his voice was a painful rasp—"a better opportunity had come along. Do you remember Rosenna Foxmantle?"

"Yes."

"I imagine everyone does. That teasing smile and lilting laugh! I've never known a more captivating woman, and that year you came home to Selgaunt, every nobleman in the city was infatuated with her, Thamalon included."

"At the same time he was wooing your daughter?"

He gave her a cynical grin. "Now I suppose you're going to tell me that you've never known him to take an interest in another woman."

"No," she said flatly, "I won't tell you that."

"I'm glad we at least agree on that much. It wasn't just Rosenna's beauty that made the men love her. It was her vivacity. Her flirtatiousness. Her wildness. As it turned out, she was wild enough to dally with a charming pariah. I infer from what followed that she and Thamalon even spoke of marriage. An elopement, no doubt. They must have hoped that once they were wed, her kin would see little choice but to accept the situation."

"At which point," said Shamur, following the logic of the story despite herself, "Thamalon would acquire the status he craved and the woman he truly coveted as well. Moreover, he wouldn't need to expend any of his hard-won wealth to forestall the ruin of the Karns."

The old man nodded. "Precisely. Indeed, if he wished, once we were bankrupt he could purchase our holdings at bargain prices and own them outright."

"I still don't credit a word of this," she said, "but go on."

"The problem, of course, was that Thamalon and Shamur —*my* Shamur—were already betrothed. He couldn't just set her aside without risking challenges, a lawsuit, and, for all he knew, assassination. Moreover, such dishonorable behavior might have precluded his ever being accepted among the Old Chauncel at large, Foxmantle bride or no."

"Therefore, the only solution was to murder his fiancée."

"Which he proceeded to do, unaware, like everyone else outside the family, that another Karn, who looked exactly like my daughter and even bore the same name, had slipped back into Selgaunt and was living in secret in Argent Hall. He couldn't anticipate that an impostor would step forward to take the dead girl's place, proceed with the wedding, and so save our House from destitution.

"Nor did he have any notion that Rosenna would cast him aside if invited to wed the Overmaster's son, but that was what she did. Afterward, with no other prospects in the offing, Thamalon opted to go back to his original plan and marry a Karn."

Shamur frowned, considering. She didn't want to believe the story, yet it made a ghastly kind of sense, and in some respects it reflected the character of the Thamalon she knew, a man both calculating and lickerish, his appetites unflagging even now, in the autumn of his life. Still . . . "You haven't told me how you learned all this."

"By chance. Four years after your wedding, I took a turn serving as a Probiter. During that time, the Scepters arrested a ne'er-do-well named Clovis for bludgeoning a fellow scoundrel who had accused him of cheating at dice.

"There was no doubt of Clovis's guilt, and he had a long history of wrongdoing. Thus, he had little hope of escaping harsh punishment this time around, at least until he happened to spot me walking to court in my judge's robe.

"Clovis recognized me and bribed a jailer to bring me a message. It said that if I would arrange his release, he'd help me learn who poisoned my daughter."

Shamur frowned. "We made certain that the world at large never learned of the poisoning."

Lindrian nodded. "Thus it was clear that the wretch must actually know something. I interviewed him privately, agreed to his bargain, and he told me what he knew. It turned out he had no idea who had wished my daughter dead. He did, however, know who'd sold the whoreson the poison to do the job."

"Who?" Shamur asked.

"An apothecary called Audra Sweetdreams, who ran, and for all I know still does run, a shop in Lampblack Alley. She was Clovis's friend, or as near as such a scoundrel had to a friend. One night, giddy with some narcotic powder of her own devising, she'd boasted that a rich nobleman had paid her handsomely to help him poison Lindrian Karn's daughter, although for some reason, perhaps simply the irrationality of an addled mind, she'd refused to divulge the identity of her patron.

"The following day, I asked some of the Scepters about the woman. They'd never quite managed to catch her committing a crime, but were quite certain she consorted with thieves and other miscreants, providing them with illicit drugs, potions, and probably even poison on occasion."

"I assume you interrogated her as well," Shamur said.

"Of course. I had her arrested on a bogus charge then, when we spoke in private, I offered her much the same trade I'd already made with Clovis. If she gave me the name of the aristocrat to whom she'd sold the poison, she'd go free. If she withheld it, it wouldn't matter that she was innocent of the offense of which she was currently accused. I was a lord of the Old Chauncel and a Probiter, she, a commoner of dubious reputation, and I would have no trouble arranging her conviction and a savage punishment to follow.

"Well, as you already know, she eventually gave up Thamalon. She even told me how he administered the poison. You recall, we always wondered about that."

"Yes," Shamur said.

"It was quite ingenious, in a horrible way. She'd concocted

a clear, tasteless liquid harmless to males but deadly to females. Thamalon rubbed it on his lips, then applied it to my daughter's mouth with a kiss."

"That's monstrous," Shamur said. "Did you actually let this medusa go?"

"Yes. You would have done the same, had you given your word. Besides, she was only a tool. What I cared about was finding the fiend who instigated my daughter's death."

"Yet when you finally identified him, you did nothing!" she exploded. "Why didn't you tell me at the time?"

The old man lowered his eyes. "I feared the consequences. Our finances still hadn't fully recovered from the disasters Thamalon had inflicted upon us, and by that time our commercial ventures were thoroughly entwined with his own. If something disrupted that partnership, the House of Karn might yet fall into ruin. I reckoned vengeance wouldn't bring my daughter back, and I had the welfare of my other children to consider. And I was thinking of you."

"Me?"

"Yes. By that time, you were the mistress of a great House and the mother of a three year-old son you adored. I didn't want to tear your life apart."

"Then why in Mask's name are you doing it now?"

"Because it seems to me now that I was wrong. You have a right to know, and this was my final chance to tell you."

She struggled to compose herself. "Thank you. You . . . you have told me, and I'll need to sit alone and ponder what to do about it. For now, may we talk of other matters? What would you like me to do to help Fendolac and his siblings in the days ahead?"

He answered, but she barely heard him, for her mind was in turmoil. The gods knew, she didn't love Thamalon, far from it. Still, he was her husband of nearly thirty years, the father of her children, and never had she imagined him capable of such malevolence. Yet Lindrian, his illness notwithstanding, seemed entirely lucid, nor could she conceive of any reason for him to lie.

Somehow she had to discover the truth, and if Thamalon

truly had murdered the innocent lass who'd adored him, if he'd engineered the chain of events that had trapped Shamur in a loveless union and a life she loathed, then she already knew he'd have to pay.

CHAPTER 4

Shamur waited with masked impatience for Glynnis, her personal maid, to help her out of her mourning clothes and into her silk nightgown, and even to see her tucked away in the warmth of her canopy bed. At last the officious, chattering lass, who had apparently decided Lady Uskevren needed special coddling in the wake of her "father's" death, extinguished the enchanted sconce by touching the raised oval plate at its base, bade her mistress a final good-night, and retired from the suite, softly closing the door behind her.

Shamur gave Glynnis another few seconds to descend farther down the stairs, making absolutely sure she wouldn't hear her mistress stirring. Then she silently threw back the covers, rose, and pulled on the embroidered white cotton dress, hooded maroon wool cloak, and flimsy, frivolous shoes she'd surreptitiously pilfered from the room of Larajin, the clumsiest of the servants and, Shamur suspected, one of Thamalon's lemans as well. Like the other maids, Larajin generally wore livery, so this outfit was presumably a special one reserved for outings and festivals. Still, it was plainly the inexpensive clothing of a commoner, and ought to disguise a noblewoman, mysteriously prowling the benighted streets afoot and unescorted, very well. With luck, Shamur would have it back in the bottom of Larajin's trunk before the girl ever noticed it was missing.

She had two other items to take on her errand: a truncheon of seasoned ash she'd borrowed from the salle and a blue leather pouch of the platinum coins called suns. She tucked both in the fringed, striped sash Larajin used for a belt, placing them in the small of her back where the cloak was sure to hide them.

Lindrian had died an hour after sharing his secret. The old man's obsequies had taken up the next three days, until his kin finally interred him in the Karn ancestral vault. Ever since then, Shamur had been trying to slip away, but in the daylight hours, with servants swarming everywhere, pestering her with their sympathy and their need for instruction, with friends and relatives popping up every few seconds to offer condolences, it had proven impossible. Not since the first years of her marriage had she felt so stifled and confined.

At last it was night, and she fancied she could escape Stormweather Towers just as the adolescent Shamur had been accustomed to sneak out of Argent Hall. On how many nights had she yearned to attempt this very thing, only holding back because the stakes were too high. She would joyfully have risked her own well-being, but not that of her kin, nor in later years, of her children.

She opened the casement, and a cold winter breeze stung her face. Plump snowflakes drifted down from the clouds. A coach passed on the street five stories below, the bells affixed to the horses' harness chimed in time with their trotting.

Leaning out the window, Shamur peered about. The

conical tower housing her apartments rose from the back of the Uskevren mansion. On this side the house had no enclosing, protective wall like the one around the courtyard in the front. Rather, the westernmost face of Stormweather Towers was itself a fortification. Though entablatures, grotesquely carved rainspouts, stained-glass oculi, and other ornamentation abounded higher up, for the bottom two stories, the wall was forbiddingly smooth, with only a sparse scatter of lancet windows too narrow to offer any hope of entry. At the top of the mansion, crenellated battlements wound their way among the profusion of gables and turrets jutting from the roof.

At the moment, no sentry was in view, and Shamur supposed she'd better get moving before one appeared. Despite the hindrance of her cloak and skirt, she agilely climbed out the window, then pushed the casement shut, making sure it didn't latch. That accomplished, she started down the wall.

Larajin's shoes were too loose, and their soles were too slick for safety. If not for the cold, Shamur would have kicked them off and descended barefoot, although so far, with cornices, traceries, finials, and other decorations providing hand- and footholds, she was managing easily enough.

She thought of how awkward it would be to encounter Thazienne now, sneaking out of the mansion in this same fashion, and just for a moment, despite her bleak mood, she smiled.

In two minutes she reached the point where all the carved stone gingerbread abruptly gave way to an expanse of sheer, vertical granite. Larajin's ridiculous slippers were still flopping and sliding around on her feet, and to make things even more interesting, her hands were going numb. Shamur supposed that, having failed to find the maid's gloves, she should have worn a pair of her own. But she didn't own any that weren't sewn with pearls, made of the finest, softest calfskin, or manifestly costly in some other way, and she hadn't realized the cold would seep into her fingers so quickly.

She considered simply jumping, for in her youth, in

more desperate situations, she'd dropped farther and survived. Yet on one of those occasions, she'd sprained her ankle. She couldn't afford such an injury tonight, and besides, if she couldn't climb down the wall now, how could she be sure she could climb back up when her errand was through?

So she lowered herself once more, holding her body well away from the wall as Errendar Spillwine, the veteran house-breaker who'd taught her to climb, had always insisted. Her foot groped at the section of wall beneath her. At first, it felt absolutely flat, but according to Errendar, flatness was only a geometer's fancy. No surface, whether found in nature or fashioned by man, was ever entirely smooth. A climber could always find a hold if he knew how to look.

And perhaps the dear old reprobate had been correct, for eventually her toe caught in a slight depression, where the masons had failed to make the mortar flush with the blocks above and below. Considered as a foothold, it was precarious, but if her skill hadn't deserted her, it should do. She tested it, making sure it wasn't brittle, then trusted her weight to it.

The next toehold down was more dubious still, a shallow hollow where time and weather had worn a bit of one of the stone blocks away. The one beyond that should have been easier going, since it was the sill of one of the lancet windows, but evidently the day's sun had failed to warm the narrow recess, and the ledge still wore a veneer of ice.

In short, the climb was as difficult as Shamur had expected. She needed all her strength and skill to negotiate such inadequate perches. But she never lost her grip, nor did she ever come to a spot from which it was impossible to descend farther, and in a few minutes she alit on solid ground.

She felt a pang of satisfaction, but knew better than to stand about congratulating herself. A guard could still wander out onto the alure and spot her lurking at the base of the wall. She darted across the strip of frozen flowerbeds and pungent evergreens that ran along the rear of the mansion, vaulted the low wrought-iron fence, and scurried away down the street. She kept her hands inside her mantle and rubbed them together until they were warm.

Selgaunt was a city that never truly slumbered. Some merchant nobles, hoping to gain an advantage over their competitors, ran their manufactories round the clock, and there were nearly always merrymakers carousing, be they aristocrats dripping lace and jewels or ragged apprentices with scarcely a copper among them. Yet Shamur soon discerned that tonight the streets were largely empty, and the night was unusually quiet. Apparently the cold and snow had driven folk indoors.

At the first opportunity, she headed south, and as she neared the city wall, the houses and shops grew humbler, and on a few narrow side streets, downright shabby. Some of the men abroad in the night moved furtively, like mice sneaking through the domain of a cat, or wolves shadowing unwitting prey. Others strode with high heads and scornful eyes, displaying the arrogance of the seasoned bravo.

Shamur decided it would be wise to traverse this particular precinct circumspectly. She wished Larajin's cloak were black or charcoal gray, like the garments she herself had worn when committing her youthful indiscretions, but maroon would do, and at least the mantle was long and full enough to mask any trace of the white gown beneath. She swept every wisp of her pale, shining hair back into her cowl, then proceeded on her way. She didn't move on tiptoe, crouch, or dart from one bit of cover to the next. She didn't want anyone who might happen to spot her to realize she was trying to be stealthy. Still, keeping to the shadows, she blended into the darkness like a ghost. When a patrol of Scepters, the city guards, impressively martial in their black, silver-trimmed leather armor and green weathercloaks, came marching down the street, they passed within eight feet of her and never knew.

The snow was falling heavier, and the frigid breeze off Selgaunt Bay was moaning louder by the time Shamur reached Lampblack Alley. The cramped passage was as dark as its name suggested, for unlike the residents of more affluent neighborhoods, none of the inhabitants had seen fit to leave a light burning outside his door for the convenience of callers and passersby. Still, she could see that several yards down, just where the alley doglegged to the left, hung a signboard daubed with an alembic, mortar, and pestle.

Shamur strode toward the shop, and after a few paces, began to catch the telltale odor of an alchemist or apothecary's establishment: a complex amalgam of scents, some sweet, some foul, and all mixed with the tang of smoke and burning.

Light shone through the shutters, and voices murmured behind the four-paneled door as well. Pleased that it apparently wouldn't be necessary to rouse Audra Sweetdreams from her bed, Shamur tapped with the tarnished brass lion's mask door knocker.

The voices fell silent, and the light went out. Shamur smiled wryly, for she suspected she knew what was going on. She'd lived through the same moment herself a time or two. The people inside were hastily concealing the evidence of some criminal enterprise, or perhaps even preparing to flee out another exit.

"It's not the Scepters," Shamur called. "It's no one who means you any harm. I need your help, and I'm willing to pay for it."

When no one answered, she stooped to inspect the lock, and saw that it was nothing much. With her long-lost set of thief's tools, she could have opened it in a trice, and perhaps she could manage with a hairpin even now. But it might be quicker simply to kick in the door.

A scraping sound prompted her to straighten up, whereupon she saw that dim light shone within the shop again, and a small panel above the lion's mask had opened. A pair of dark eyes peered out of the spy hole. "What kind of help do you want?" asked a husky contralto voice.

"The answers to a few questions," Shamur said. "Are you Audra Sweetdreams?"

"I might be. You mentioned payment."

Shamur reached behind her back, unfastened her pouch,

extracted a coin, and held the white round up for the apothecary to see.

The panel bumped shut, and Shamur heard whispering, though as before, she couldn't make out the words. After a minute, the lock clicked and the door creaked open. "Come in," Audra Sweetdreams said.

The apothecary was a short, round-faced dumpling of a woman who, Shamur now saw, had needed to climb up on a stool to peek through the spy hole. She appeared to be in her fifties, and might have looked harmless, like some child's doting grandmother, if not for the slyness in her dimpled smile. She wore a slovenly brown gown covered with stains and burn marks.

In the corner lounged a dull-eyed fellow clad in a grimy scarlet doublet with the points undone. His skull was oddly shaped, pointed like an egg, and as if proud of this peculiarity, he'd shaved his head. He looked Shamur up and down, leered in approval, and casually saluted with the half-eaten chicken leg in his hand.

The shop itself was a chaos of crates and kegs. Bundles of dried, aromatic herbs and desiccated lizards dangled from the rafters. Animal teeth, bits of bone, dead beetles, and mushrooms caps lay scattered about the bases of a series of ceramic jars. On the same shelf reposed half a dozen empty green bottles, formed by a glassblower into slender whorled shapes of surprising beauty. Shamur surmised that Audra must use the vials for expensive compounds concocted for aristocratic patrons.

Compounds like poison and patrons like Thamalon, perhaps.

"What do you want to know?" Audra asked.

"First off," Shamur replied, "I want to know if you've ever concocted a venom lethal to women but harmless to men."

Audra's eyes widened in astonishment, or at least a simulation of it. "Mistress, this is a reputable establishment. How can you imagine I would ever deal in poisons? Well, to rid a home of rats and other vermin, but never for any sinister purpose."

Shamur tossed the platinum sun onto a stone table laden with retorts and an oven like those employed by potters. The coin shone in the light of enchanted bronze burners capable of producing a steady, adjustable jet of flame, which the apothecary evidently used like simple candles when not mixing remedies and elixirs. The noblewoman then brought out her blue leather purse, showing how fat it was. The money inside clinked.

"It's all platinum," Shamur said, "and all yours, if you help me. But don't waste my time. Do you brew such a poison or not?"

The plump woman hesitated. "I know it exists. I might be able to make it."

"I need to know if you ever have made it."

Audra grimaced. "Please understand, I don't know you, Mistress, nor do I know how you found me. I just might find my hand on the chopping block if I speak the wrong word in the wrong ear."

Shamur's mouth tightened. "Do I look like an informer?"

Audra shrugged. "I haven't yet decided what you look like."

"I assure you, I don't care about anything you've done recently, any affair in which the Scepters might still be interested. I want to find out about something that happened nearly thirty years ago, to Shamur Karn, daughter of Lindrian. No harm will come to you—"

Something smashed into the back of Shamur's head, and even as she fell forward, she realized what it must have been. She'd kept a wary eye on the shaven-headed lout in the corner, but unfortunately, Audra had another confederate in the room. Someone who'd hidden before Shamur ever came in, sneaked up behind her while the apothecary held her attention, and clubbed her.

At first she hadn't felt anything except a kind of shock, but as she sprawled on the floor, the pouch tumbling from her grasp, pain roared through her skull. It was so fierce that she wasn't sure she could move, but she knew she'd better try. She couldn't withstand a second such blow. If Larajin's thick wool cowl hadn't cushioned the first, she would no doubt be unconscious already.

A man bent over her, a sap in his hand. Her vision was blurry, but she could make out a braided black beard and the stained, uneven teeth exposed by a malicious grin. She wrenched herself onto her back, drew her legs up, and drove her feet into her attacker's gut.

Blackbeard grunted and stumbled backward. Shamur rolled under a table and into the next makeshift aisle haphazardly snaking its way through Audra's heaps of possessions.

She knew the maneuver had only bought her a moment. She scrambled to her feet, nearly fell again when a wave of pain and dizziness assailed her, and fumbled the truncheon out of her sash.

Meanwhile, Audra was saying, "Did you truly think a stranger could sashay in here and cozen me into confessing my complicity in a murder attempt? I think not! I don't know what your game is, but you already know too much to suit me. I'm going to have the lads beat your head in and claim your money that way."

Blackbeard scrambled around a pile of boxes into the end of the aisle. He hesitated when he spotted Shamur's weapon, then took in her useless two-handed grip on one end of it. She was holding it as if it were a greatsword, not a baton less than two feet long. Her apparent ineptitude must have given him confidence, because he bellowed and charged.

She waited until he was nearly on top of her, then shifted to the "short grip" Errendar had taught her: single-handed with most of the length of the club extending back along her forearm. Blackbeard swung his leather bludgeon in a vicious arc. Shamur swayed backward, evading the stroke, then rammed the stub of baton protruding from the top of her hand into her opponent's solar plexus.

Or rather, she tried, but the lingering effects of that savage blow to the head were still making her clumsy. She only managed to hit Blackbeard in the ribs, hard enough to hurt but not to stop him.

Now was the time for a two-handed grip, albeit not the preposterous one she'd employed before. She whipped the long section of her baton into her left hand then, gripping it at both ends, rammed it up at Blackbeard's throat.

And missed again. Snarling, she smashed the stick down at the bridge of her opponent's nose. Finally she hit the target, crushing bone and cartilage with a *crack!* She pulled the truncheon back and drove it forward, breaking several of Blackbeard's crooked teeth.

He reeled backward, and she followed to finish him off. Then two brawny arms whipped around her from behind, one pinioning her arms and the other choking her. She realized that with her brains rattled, she'd forgotten all about the man with the shaved scalp.

For a panicky second, her mind was blank, then she remembered the counter to a choke hold. She twisted her head into the crook of Baldhead's elbow, relieving the pressure on her throat. Then she stamped, raking her heel down her assailant's shin and smashing it down on his foot, and drove the long end of the baton backward into his belly.

The assault served to loosen his grip, and she wrenched herself free. Pivoting, putting all her weight behind it, she threw an elbow, her vulnerable forearm armored by the truncheon nestled against it. The stick crashed into Baldhead's temple, snapping his head back. His eyes rolled up, and his knees buckled.

Shamur heard footsteps pounding up behind her. She whirled just in time to keep her first attacker, his braided beard soaked with blood from his ruined nose and mouth, from smashing his sap down on the back of her head a second time.

Blackbeard feinted with the leather bludgeon, then lashed out with a kick to the stomach. Gripping the baton two-handed to make a horizontal bar, Shamur blocked the attack by jamming her weapon into the wounded man's shin. Then she smashed the stick up under his chin.

She'd hurt him again, but clearly, he wasn't done, because

he took another swing with the sap. She stopped its descent as she'd stopped the kick, then used another elbow strike. He still wouldn't fall down, so she hooked the truncheon behind his neck and grabbed the long end with her left hand. Squeezing his throat behind her crossed arms, she choked him until he collapsed.

Shamur pivoted toward Audra. The apothecary stood gawking at the carnage, her eyes filled with a horror that afforded the victor a moment of dark amusement.

"There was no need for this," Shamur panted. "I told you I wasn't going to make any troub—"

Audra bolted. Shamur cursed and scrambled after her.

Her short legs notwithstanding, Audra made it to one of the cluttered shelves on the wall just ahead of her pursuer. She grabbed a corked beaker of some gray, bubbling fluid and swung it back behind her head to throw it.

Shamur dived and tackled the fat woman, slamming her backward into the shelves. Tangled together, the combatants fell to the floor. Shards of leathery orange eggshell, an old brown book, and the preserved head of a huge black bat, the fangs of which had been scraped and filed, showered down around them.

Shamur heaved herself on top of Audra, dealt the apothecary a backhand blow, then wrested the beaker from her grasp. Tugging at the stopper, she said, "How would you like a little drink?"

Audra thrashed, but Shamur had her well pinned. "No!" the pudgy woman cried. "Please!"

"Then tell me what I want to know."

Audra swallowed. "All right. I did make the poison intended for Shamur Karn, and why it didn't kill her I can't say, unless my client never gave it to her."

"Who was he?"

"Thamalon Uskevren, the same noble who eventually married her."

Shamur's jaw tightened. She'd known Lindrian had no reason to lie, yet she'd still hoped that somehow, he would turn out to be mistaken. Now, however, no reasonable person could doubt that Thamalon truly had murdered Lindrian's innocent daughter.

And this vile creature had furnished the means! Suddenly shivering and light-headed with rage, the noblewoman said, "I have two things to tell you. The first is that Thamalon did administer your venom. The second is that I am Shamur Uskevren."

Audra gaped, and then renewed her efforts to escape. Perhaps she expected Shamur to go ahead and pour the contents of the beaker down her gullet, and if so, she was perceptive, because for an instant the other woman wished to do precisely that. Then, however, her fury gave way to a revulsion that simply made her want to distance herself from her captive as quickly as possible. For Lindrian had been right. Wicked though she was, Audra had only been a tool. True vengeance must be sought elsewhere.

"If you or your idiot accomplices tell anyone I was here," Shamur said, "then I swear to you, I will kill you."

She rose, retrieved her fallen pouch, and withdrew into a freezing night no colder than her heart.

Audra was pressing a bag full of snow to her split lip and bruised cheek when another caller rapped on the door. That cursed Uskevren harridan had only been gone an hour, but the apothecary wasn't surprised that her client in the moon mask had turned up so soon. He was plainly a wizard, so it stood to reason he had ways of knowing things that ordinary people lacked.

Black-bearded Pedvel was swilling brandy to dull the pain of his broken nose, shattered teeth, and bruised throat, while Sawys perched on a stool alternately massaging his mashed foot and bald, battered head. Audra looked at them, silently bidding one of them get up and answer the knock, but they just stared sullenly back at her. After a moment she sighed, rose, and, her bruised limbs aching, hobbled to the door herself.

When she opened the spy hole, she saw that the newcomer was indeed her anonymous employer, accompanied as usual by his familiar spirit, a walking shadow whose shape shifted and flowed from second to second. She unlocked the door and admitted them.

The wizard looked at her compress. "Nothing but snow to ease your pain?" he asked, a hint of amusement in his prim tenor voice. "That doesn't inspire much confidence in your nostrums and panaceas."

"Go to the Abyss," Audra said.

"His allegiance lies elsewhere," said the familiar, his fanged maw smirking. "But that was a pretty good guess."

The wizard shot the spirit a pale-eyed glance that, despite the mask concealing his expression, successfully conveyed annoyance. Then, returning his attention to Audra, he asked, "We agreed that you were to capture the woman and detain her for several hours, during which time you'd let slip what she came to hear, and that afterward she'd 'escape.' Clearly, that didn't happen. What did?"

"It looks as if the genteel Lady Uskevren beat them half to death," the familiar said, sniggering.

"She took us by surprise," Pedvel growled, his voice roughened and slurred by his injuries. "Why didn't you tell us she knew how to fight?"

"Perhaps because I didn't anticipate that two strong young men would find it difficult to subdue one slender, middle-aged woman," the spellcaster said, "even if she had survived a previous scuffle or two."

"Why did we have to fight at all?" Sawys asked. "She was willing to pay for what she wanted."

"Because if the intelligence had come too easily, she might have scented a ruse," the wizard explained. "Whereas, believing she risked her life for it, she'll trust it. That's human nature."

"Well, why didn't you at least warn me that harpy was the very woman I'm supposed to have poisoned?" Audra demanded. "After I confessed to it, and she revealed herself, I thought she was going to kill me on the spot."

"Had I informed you, would you have consented to help me stage this little piece of make-believe?" the masked man asked. "Besides, I reckoned that if you knew her identity in advance, you might have difficulty pretending to be surprised should she disclose it. You're scarcely accomplished thespians, you know."

"Maybe not," Audra said, "but I got the job done. Even when the plan had come apart, when your Lady Uskevren was sitting on me threatening to pour essence of slithering tracker down my throat, I kept my head." Regained it, actually, but there was no point telling him that for a few moments there, astonished by the other woman's ferocity, she'd panicked. "I told her it was her husband who'd wished her dead and made her believe it too. Now I want my money."

"Of course," the masked man said, producing a kidskin purse from beneath his mantle.

Audra took the bag and untied the lacing securing the mouth. Inside were platinum suns, golden fivestars, and a number of sapphires and pearls. She grinned, and Pedvel and Sawys got up and limped over to inspect the booty.

"Satisfactory?" the wizard asked.

"Yes," said Audra, liking the man a good deal more than she had a moment ago.

"Good," the wizard said. "We're quits, then. But now we have a new piece of business to transact."

"Have you got another job for us?" Pedvel asked, leering over Audra's shoulder at the gleaming treasure in her hands.

"Unfortunately not," said the mage. "I've thought it over, and I'm afraid I don't trust you to depart Selgaunt as you promised. You just don't seem like very reliable people, and should you linger, spreading your newfound wealth around, regaling your whores and drinking companions with the tale of how you acquired it, word could get back to the Uskevren. And that would ruin everything."

Audra frowned. "We gave you our word and we'll keep it."

"That's very reassuring," said the masked man, "but even

so, I see no reason why I should allow you the chance to change your minds. You see, a fellow like me only has to deal gently with people like you if they're likely to be of further use or have powerful friends to avenge them, and sadly, you fall in neither category."

Audra abruptly grasped that the sorcerer was saying he meant to murder them. Which meant they'd better dispatch him first, this instant, before he could start casting spells. "Get him!" she screamed. She threw a handful of jewels and specie at the wizard's face, then lunged at him.

The makeshift missiles clattered on the sickle-shaped mask but seemingly without startling him or penetrating the eye holes as she'd hoped. He stepped nimbly backward, taking himself out of reach of her clutching hands, and brushed her on the shoulder with his staff.

Magenta light danced and crackled on the wood. Wracked by an agonizing power, her muscles twitched and shuddered. Paralyzed by her spasms, she fell to the floor.

From there, she saw that her confederates had finally begun to attack. Though favoring his injured foot, Sawys did his best to charge the mage while holding a three-legged stool above his head. The wizard retreated once more, giving himself time to recite a rhymed couplet, produce the severed gray tip of a squid's tentacle from one of the hidden pockets in his cloak, and swing it in a small circle.

Inky tentacles erupted from the floorboards all around Sawys's feet. They flailed at him, coiled around his limbs, and dragged him down. He shrieked briefly, then fell silent. His bones cracked and crunched as the tentacles squeezed him.

Perhaps profiting from his comrade's unfortunate example, Pedvel fought more warily, popping up from behind a pile of boxes or other cover to hurl a burner or flask, then ducking down again, making it difficult for his adversary to target him. The magician murmured and brandished a scrap of tortoiseshell, and after that Pedvel's missiles rebounded harmlessly from an invisible shield. Pacing deliberately, the ferule of his staff bumping softly on the floor, the masked man advanced with the obvious intention of cornering his opponent.

But it looked like it might take him a minute, a minute during which Audra could escape into the night. Her muscles were still jumping, but not as badly as before. She thought she could move, and when she tried, she found she was right.

She crawled on hands and knees, staying so low that the mage shouldn't be able to see her. After what seemed an eternity, she came in sight of the door. She sprang to her feet and ran for it.

Darkness fell across the exit like a curtain, with two yellow eyes and a grinning maw in the center of it: the wizard's familiar, barring the way.

Audra dodged toward the window, but the spirit swayed to the side and cut her off. She pivoted back toward the door, and he was there. He let her lurch left and right a few more times, always interposing himself between her and freedom, then, evidently tiring of the game, widened his body so it covered both means of egress at once.

Behind her, magic hissed and chilled the air. Red light flickered. Pedvel screamed.

"I'll let you in on a joke," the familiar said. "I'm no more solid than fog. You could have fled right through me."

For an instant, Audra failed to comprehend what he was saying. Then she flung herself at the door.

The spirit's shadowy substance felt vile in a way she couldn't describe, but he hadn't lied. She was reaching clear through him, opening the lock, and then she heard the wizard murmuring.

Just as she yanked open the door, daggers, arrows, or something else equally pointed and lethal slammed into her back. Suddenly choking on warm, coppery fluid, she fell, and, peeling himself off the wall, the familiar crouched over her to watch her die. The last thing she saw was his murky grin.

CHAPTER 5

Shamur pulled on the cabinet door and was not surprised to find it locked, Thamalon being the prudent soul he was. She picked up one of the long pins she'd bent into something vaguely resembling a proper thief's tool and set to work.

Since her interlude with Audra Sweetdreams the night before, Shamur had been hard-pressed to contain her fury whenever she encountered her husband. Her mind boiled with fancies of bloody retribution, and her hand fairly twitched with the impulse to drive a blade into his flesh. Yet at the same time, some small part of her, a part that recalled the sweetness she had occasionally discovered in his arms and the way he'd gobbled and made faces to amuse their infant children, still sought to avoid the confrontation to come. She despised that weak, equivocating portion of her nature, and to silence it, she'd crept to Thamalon's receiving room to search for more evidence of his guilt, for all that she'd proved it beyond a doubt already.

It had been obliging of him, she sardonically reflected, to absent himself from home tonight. He'd claimed he had to make sure that one of his merchantmen was loaded and ready to sail with the morning tide, but she suspected he was visiting one of his doxies. Perhaps wide-eyed little Larajin had begun to bore him.

The parlor smelled of lemon oil, a testament to the diligence of the servants. Since Shamur had only bothered to light a single sconce, it was rather dark, and certain of the shapes around her, like the white bearskin rug from the Great Glacier and the harp that Thamalon vowed he would learn to play someday, looked strange and subtly unreal swimming in the gloom.

All was silent, inside the room and beyond. Shamur knew that elsewhere in the mansion, a handful of guards and lackeys were performing various tasks while the rest of the household slumbered, but she couldn't hear them up here on the second floor.

Then something did make a noise. Just as the cabinet yielded to her efforts, the latch securing the door to the passage clicked. The brass handle turned.

Shamur fleetingly considered hiding, but wasn't sure she could manage it in the split second remaining, not with the sconce burning, anyway. So she simply closed the cabinet, scooped up her makeshift lockpicks, and concealed them beneath the blue sussapine sleeve drooping over her hand. An instant later Erevis stepped through the door.

The gaunt major-domo had evidently come inside rather recently, for he still wore a dark gray cloak which, though woven of good-quality broadcloth, hung about his gangly form like a winding-sheet. The garments beneath the mantle, at least what Shamur could see of them, were equally unattractive: subfusc, devoid of ornament, and generally funereal.

Erevis was not a demonstrative man. Indeed, Shamur

believed he prided himself on his composure. Still, his deep-set, melancholy eyes widened slightly in surprise when he beheld her. For though the matriarch of Stormweather Towers presumably had the right to visit her husband's apartments, she rarely chose to exercise that prerogative even when Thamalon was there.

"Good evening, my lady," the butler said.

"Erevis," she replied. "You've been out of doors, I see. A night on the town?" Not that she cared where the chief steward had been, but she'd rather ask questions than give him an opening to do the same.

"No, my lady," he said. "I couldn't sleep, so I decided to walk the house and grounds, just to make sure that everything is in order and the night staff are performing their duties."

"Commendable," Shamur said, "but I hope now that you've verified that all is as it should be, you'll be able to rest. Sleep well." Her tone, though cordial enough, made it clear that he was dismissed.

He hesitated, then said, "Thank you, my lady. Good night." He turned toward the door, she started to relax, and then, in his graceless way, he lurched back around. "Is there something I could help you with?"

Shamur felt a pang of annoyance, though, with the ease of long practice, she kept any trace of it from showing. She should have known she wouldn't be able to rid herself of Erevis so easily. Though he'd always served her well, he was ultimately Thamalon's man, not hers, and, knowing something of the cool relations between his lord and lady, he was reluctant to leave her here alone. Mask only knew what he thought she was up to, but if she wanted him to go away, and to refrain from informing Thamalon of her visit later on, she'd have to disarm his suspicions with a persuasive excuse for her presence.

"I'm fine, thank you," she said. "I'm looking for something, that's all."

Erevis nodded. "I thought as much, my lady. Lord Uskevren has an abundance of drawers, shelves, chests, cabinets, and armoires, here in this suite and elsewhere in the mansion, and if it isn't presumptuous of me to say so, I probably have a better sense of what he keeps where than you do. If you'll permit me to assist you, I may be able to shorten your search."

"That's kind of you," she said, "but I can manage."

"Will you at least tell me what it is? Perhaps I've seen it lying about."

She heaved a sigh. "Moon above, you're stubborn. And you must think I'm acting very strangely."

"No, my lady. Such a notion never entered my mind."

She smiled. "You're tactful as well. All right, since you leave me little alternative, I'm going to tell you what I'm looking for, and then you'll comprehend why I need to search by myself. I wouldn't confide in most people, but I know I can depend on your discretion."

"Of course, my lady."

"Many years ago, when we first were married, Thamalon gave me a love token. A tenday ago, we argued rather vehemently, and I threw the gift back in his face."

"Ah," Erevis said.

Shamur was a bit bemused that the butler didn't seem surprised by the thought of his reserved, dignified mistress flinging objects angrily about like a fishwife in a pantomime. Perhaps all the servants imagined that Lord and Lady Uskevren were given to furious rows whenever closeted together.

"Well," she continued, "now I'd like the object back. Sometimes . . . sometimes Thamalon and I have trouble expressing our fonder feelings to one another, but if he sees his present in my hand, he'll understand that I want to mend our quarrel."

Erevis frowned. "Yes, my lady, but I still don't quite grasp why you can't tell me what the token is."

"It's a . . . sort of toy intended for private moments," she said, "and if you discovered precisely what, then you'd know rather more about my personal inclinations than I would prefer."

"Oh," he said, and then his dark, deep-set eyes flew wide open. "*Oh!* Yes, of *course* I don't want to know . . . uh, that is, I mean to say, I understand the difficulty. I understand, and with your permission, I'll withdraw."

"Good night, Erevis," she said.

She managed to hold in a grin until he closed the door behind him, but for all her finely honed skill at dissembling, it was hard, for she'd never seen the sober major-domo so flustered. She was confident he'd never speak of their embarrassing conversation to anyone, *especially* Thamalon.

But her mirth couldn't endure for long, not considering the nature of her errand. By the time she reopened the cabinet, she was frowning once again.

She searched the parlor and wardrobe without result. That left the bedchamber, one of the few rooms where Thamalon's enthusiasm for things elven had been allowed to influence the décor; a colorful tapestry, the weaver's panoramic, and, Shamur suspected, entirely fanciful depiction of life on the elf island of Evermeet, adorned one of the walls. A casement opened onto a small balcony, and an ornately carved walnut bed even larger than Shamur's own took up fully a quarter of the inlaid floor. A long sword and target hung beside the headboard, so that if danger ever threatened in the dead of night, Thamalon could arm himself the instant he awoke.

Always ready for anything, Shamur thought. *But, husband, you won't be ready for me.* She continued her search, and found what she was seeking shortly thereafter.

Thamalon kept a small chest beneath the bed, a shabby, battered leather box he'd carried about in those desperate, starveling days when he'd struggled to rebuild the Uskevren fortune. These days, he used it primarily as a repository for date-nut bread, almond cookies, a silver flask of brandy, a book or two, and other items he might suddenly crave when already comfortably ensconced beneath his silk sheets, furs, and eiderdowns.

Or at least Shamur assumed that was the box's primary purpose, for unlike many of the drawers and cabinets, it wasn't locked. Indeed, infrequent guest in this chamber though she had been, over the years she'd watched him root around in it half a hundred times. Had Errendar not schooled her to overlook no possibility when conducting a search, she might not even have bothered to check inside it.

When she did, the flask was there at the very bottom of the chest, green, delicate, whorled, and unmistakably one of Audra Sweetdreams's bottles. An inch of clear fluid sat in the bottom.

For a moment Shamur didn't know what she felt, and then the rage came, black, cold, and overwhelming. She'd imagined she hated Thamalon before, but it was nothing compared to the loathing that gripped her now. The monster had kept the poison—the poison with which, he believed, he had once tried to murder her—under the very bed where the two of them had lain together and quite possibly conceived their children. Had its proximity amused him? Had he laughed every time he'd opened the chest and given her the chance to spy the emerald glass glinting at the bottom? Had it excited him to know that if he wished, he could caress or kiss the venom onto her lips as she slept?

She forswore any further hesitation or second thoughts. Thamalon was going to die, and before the month was out. All she needed was a plan.

She pondered for a few moments, until her idly roving eyes fell on the tapestry of Evermeet again. Then a notion came to her, and her lips stretched into a feral grin.

CHAPTER 6

The receiving room was lavishly furnished in accordance with the taste of a bygone generation, when the colors in style were teal and ivory and it had been fashionable to inset clear, faceted crystals on every available surface. Few of them sparkled, however, for much of the chamber was shrouded in gloom. Marance had only bothered to light two white beeswax tapers, which burned in latten candelabra on the marble mantelpiece. Ossian Talendar, who had come to see if there was anything his "dead" uncle required, supposed that if the wizard spent a great deal of time in his current state, he actually didn't require even that meager bit of illumination. For Marance sat motionless in a high-backed, claw-and-ball-footed chair, his rather horrible pearly eyes staring at nothing. For the moment he looked genuinely deceased, albeit only recently so, and his appearance prompted Ossian to wonder for the hundredth time whether he ought to be elated or frightened that his father Nuldrevyn, patriarch of the entire Talendar family, had appointed him the mage's aide-de-camp.

Actually, he felt both emotions together, though the fear had been only a thread of disquiet at first. Certainly, it was uncanny that his father had discovered a kinsman slain nearly three decades before wandering the inner precincts of Old High Hall, the Talendar castle, on the night of the Feast of the Moon a month and half ago. But Ossian, who fancied himself an adventurer, had watched certain priests converse with the shades of the dead and even command corpses and skeletons to rise and shamble about. He'd survived a skirmish with one of the ghouls that had plagued Selgaunt a year ago. He wouldn't have been much inclined to cower in dread even if Nuldrevyn hadn't assured him that Marance had returned to help the family, not afflict it.

In fact, when his father had introduced them, Ossian had felt a trifle disappointed, for on first acquaintance, there was nothing spectral or monstrous about Marance unless one counted the eyes, which, however freakish, were merely the ones he'd been born with. Actually, he was such a soft-spoken, bookish fellow that it was hard to believe he was even the celebrated family hero who'd performed extraordinary feats of magic and waged savage war on the Talendar's foes, let alone a visitor from the netherworld.

In the weeks that followed, however, Ossian noticed certain peculiarities of Marance's behavior. When dining with a companion, Marance only consumed a bite or two, and, as far as Ossian could tell, when alone, the wizard never bothered to eat or drink at all. He didn't seem to sleep, either, although sometimes, as now, he appeared to enter a trance. Occasionally he even neglected to breathe.

Ossian didn't know why these petty irregularities unsettled him so. It wasn't as if his uncle had a naked skull for a head or was a rotten, stinking cadaver covered in grave mold. Yet at odd moments the younger man almost felt that he would prefer such disfigurements. At least then he would never feel that the spellcaster was posing as something he wasn't.

Still, Ossian believed that Marance had been candid about the reason for his return, and surely that was all that truly mattered, since the mage proposed to win an extraordinary victory for himself and his living kindred. Ossian ought to be delighted to assist, for both the thrill of the exploit itself and the ascendancy over his siblings and cousins he would achieve through its successful resolution.

Outside in the passage, a cat screeched. Startled from his musings, Ossian strode to the door to see what was happening.

Old High Hall was the biggest merchant-noble residence in Selgaunt, as befitted a family that considered itself the foremost in the land. Indeed, the castle was too big for even the horde of Talendar and retainers that presently dwelled there, and in consequence, Nuldrevyn had ordered certain precincts of the house closed up. Wishing to keep Marance's resurrection a secret for fear that someone would find it troubling or gossip about it to outsiders, the Talendar lord had put his brother in a suite in one of the disused sections.

Even though none of the servants had been entrusted with the secret of his presence, Marance's new apartments were somewhat clean, because Ossian had taken a broom and feather duster to them himself. The corridor outside, however, was dirty and musty-smelling. Cobwebs full of insect husks hung in dusty tatters, and footprints mottled the film of dust on the floor.

For a moment, Ossian couldn't see anything amiss. Then a tabby cat hurtled around a corner, shot past the toes of the nobleman's pointed red boots, and, its claws scrabbling on the floor, vanished through the door to one of the vacant suites.

Ossian peered about for the source of the animal's distress. He had a good idea what he was looking for, but even so, never saw the feline's tormentor approach. Shrieking, an amber-eyed shadow exploded from the general gloom directly into his face.

Ossian nearly squawked and recoiled, but he'd decided early on that it would be a bad idea to show any fear around Marance's familiar, and he mastered himself in time. He merely blinked, then took a casual step backward, distancing himself from Bileworm in an unhurried and dignified fashion.

"I always imagined the baatezu as possessed of a terrible majesty," Ossian said. "Your infantile japes come as a considerable disappointment."

"Some of the great lords are that way," Bileworm said, seeming to take no offense. "But I'm not a fiend or abishai at all, really, just a specimen of one of the vassal races following in their train. If you see that puss again, keep your distance. It used to like being picked up and stroked, but I doubt it will welcome such attentions ever again. Is Master still in his trance?"

"Yes."

"Then you'll never have a better chance to slide your dagger into his heart, undead abomination that he is. It will likely save you a great deal of sorrow in the end."

Ossian laughed. "Aren't you afraid I'll tell him you suggested that?"

Bileworm leered, the fanged, V-shaped grin just barely visible amid the shifting shadow-stuff that comprised his face. "He already knows what manner of servant I am." His form elongating, he slid past Ossian into the parlor.

Once inside, the spirit hurled himself into an armchair, then immediately sprang to his feet again. Bobbing up and down, he stalked along the wall, inspecting murky portraits of Ossian's ancestors, most of them possessed of the tall, thin frame and clever face that ran in the family and which Ossian himself had inherited. Many of the subjects had chosen to be painted wearing the family colors of crimson and black, and with the Talendar badge, a perched raven with a drop of blood falling from its beak, showing somewhere about their persons.

"Now here's a monster," said Bileworm, regarding a limned head sporting a wide-brimmed velvet hat. "You can read the cruelty in those beady little eyes. I'll wager he doted on the thumbscrew and the rack, and charged the servants with offenses they hadn't committed when he ran short of victims who truly deserved to be punished."

"That's Hobart Talendar," Ossian said dryly, "commonly remembered as Hobart the Kind. During his term of office as Hulorn—merchant mayor of the city—he outraged many of his fellow aristocrats by seizing the food they were hoarding. He distributed it to the poor to alleviate a famine."

"So he did," said a mild tenor voice. Ossian turned to see Marance shifting himself in his chair. "A shrewder man would have taxed the other nobles for the privilege of keeping the food, don't you think? I'm glad our endeavors will benefit the House of Talendar to a far greater extent than old Hobart's penchant for philanthropy."

"You sound as if there's been some progress," Ossian said.

"There has indeed," Marance said. He picked up his black staff off the floor, not for any particular purpose, apparently, but simply because he felt like having it in his pallid hands. "Go and fetch Nuldrevyn, nephew. It's time we told him what we've been up to."

"It's very late," Ossian said uncertainly, "and Father just rode back from Ordulin a little while ago."

Marance smiled his prim, close-lipped little smile. "You don't understand. You probably think you do, but you're too young. You can't comprehend how it feels to wait for vengeance for as long as Nuldrevyn and I have. I assure you, he'll be ecstatic to hear what I have to tell him, even if you have to roust him out of bed. Now please, go get him."

Ossian obeyed.

Wrapped in his lynx robe, his feet in the shabby slippers his wife was forever threatening to throw away, Nuldrevyn

Talendar nonetheless shivered at the chill in the dusty air. He supposed it was his own fault for not finding a way to heat this disused section of the house without alerting the servants to the fact that someone had taken up residence herein. Not that Marance had ever complained. He seemed to crave warmth no more than the food and drink that Ossian carried in to him.

Nuldrevyn blundered into a dangling shred of filthy cobweb which his old eyes had failed to spot in the gloom. He grimaced, wiped the sticky gossamer off his face, and trudged on down the corridor after his youngest son.

It had been a shock to encounter the resurrected Marance. Nuldrevyn's anxiety wasn't allayed by his younger brother's bland explanation that he'd just returned from the Nine Hells, one of the realms of the damned, nor by the leering shadow slinking at the wizard's side. Still, the House of Talendar had successfully trafficked with the powers of darkness before, and when Marance had promised that he'd returned to serve the family, not harm it, Nuldrevyn had opted to welcome him.

Afterward, eager but apprehensive as well, the Talendar lord had expected immediate and spectacular consequences. Thunderbolts, rains of fire, and hosts of the conjured minions that had ever been Marance's specialty as a wizard. Instead, his brother had simply cast one divination after another, and occasionally wandered the benighted city in a Man in the Moon mask, until Nuldrevyn had begun to wonder if the wizard was ever going to do anything. Perhaps he'd simply rattle around his musty apartments forever, like a harmless phantom.

But it seemed that during Nuldrevyn's sojourn in the capital, things had finally started to happen. Now he simply had to hope that Marance's scheme, whatever it was, was a sound one.

Nuldrevyn was hobbling by the time he reached the door to Marance's suite. In his youth, the Talendar lord had virtually lived in the saddle, but nowadays, a lengthy journey on horseback was a strain that inevitably left him stiff and sore.

He'd be damned if he'd travel in a coach or a litter, though. He might be old, but he wasn't a cripple yet.

Noticing his distress, Ossian took his arm and helped him to a chair. Ossian was a good lad, and with his long shanks and wry face, the very image of a Talendar. Indeed, he looked very much as his father had looked in his youth, before that mop of curly, gingery hair had turned white and fallen out. Nuldrevyn had already decided that Ossian would succeed him as head of the family, though of course he hadn't told him so. You couldn't tell young people such things, or they'd lose their edge.

Marance rose to welcome his brother. Then, just as Nuldrevyn's backside was settling on the cushion, a dark, thin, sinuous shape shot out from under the chair and up in front of his knees. The Talendar patriarch screamed and recoiled.

"Father!" Ossian said, clutching his shoulder. "Father, listen! It isn't a snake, it's that wretched imp!"

Marance strode forward and rammed the iron ferule of his staff through the black tendril. Purple light flared and crackled from the rod. The dark shape splashed to the floor where it lay convulsing, its shape fluctuating wildly from one instant to the next. Gradually, the stench of some foul substance charring filled the air, until finally Bileworm stopped writhing. Marance lifted the staff away.

"Is he dead?" Nuldrevyn croaked.

"No," Marance said. "He's too useful to kill, even for so heinous an offense. But I have punished him severely, and now I offer my apologies for his misconduct."

"How did he know I have a horror of snakes?" Nuldrevyn demanded. "Did you tell him?"

"Of course not," said Marance. A few wisps of magenta light were still oozing about on the polished ebon surface of his staff. "He simply has a talent for discovering such things, and he has dwelled in Old High Hall for a while now."

"You mean, he's been prowling about the castle spying?" Nuldrevyn asked.

Marance shrugged.

After a moment of silence, Nuldrevyn realized he'd received all the satisfaction he was likely to get, and, grimacing, resolved to put the matter aside. "Ossian said you want to see me."

"I do indeed," Marance said, smiling. "We have cause for celebration." He moved to the sideboard, where Nuldrevyn himself had placed a small wrought-iron wine rack stocked with a selection of his brother's favorite vintages. In his previous existence, Marance had fancied himself something of a connoisseur, and consumed such treasures with relish. But most of these bottles remained untouched, their surfaces cloudy with dust.

Now, however, Marance leaned his staff against the wall, selected a port, dexterously uncorked it, and decanted it into three silver goblets. He handed the extra ones to Nuldrevyn and Ossian, then lifted his own on high. "A toast," he said, "to the destruction of Thamalon Uskevren and his House, which, I'm pleased to report, is finally at hand."

They drank. "I'll gladly toast the ruination of the horse at anchor," Nuldrevyn said, alluding to the rival House's escutcheon, "as long as we can accomplish it without bringing misfortune on ourselves."

Still a shapeless smear on the floor, Bileworm began to creep and hump his way toward a dark corner as if he truly were a snake, and a sorely injured one at that.

"Ah, brother," said Marance, shaking his head, "you've grown so cautious. You were bolder in our youth. Do you remember the adventures we shared? Those midnight raids when we attacked Thamalon's caravans, burned his warehouses and ships, slaughtered his retainers, and yearned for a chance at the upstart himself?"

"Yes," Nuldrevyn replied, "and I remember how it all came out, too. My dear brother dead, and Thamalon reestablished among the Old Chauncel despite everything we tried to do." He frowned. "Understand me. I want the wretch and his issue dead. How could I not? But times have changed. The Old Owl has powerful friends and a seat on the city council. We can't afford to wage open war on him, lest we provoke other Houses into taking up arms against us. You'll have to act discreetly."

"I know that," Marance said. "You'd already made it abundantly clear, and I assure you, no one who matters will ever know that it was we Talendar who ushered Lord Uskevren into the grave. Tell me, do you remember the tales of the first Shamur Karn?"

Nuldrevyn cocked his head. "What does that have to do with anything?"

"I'll explain in due course," the wizard said, setting his goblet down on an inlaid walnut table. The cup was still full. "Do you remember?"

"Of course," Nuldrevyn said. "She was before our time, but people still tell the stories and sing the ballads. She was an aristocratic lass who craved excitement, put on a red-striped mask, and became the boldest thief Selgaunt has ever seen by preying on her fellow nobles. Finally one of her victims identified her, and she had to disappear."

Over in the corner, Bileworm began the process of rearranging his substance into humanoid form. He let out a hiss of pain.

"That's right," Marance said, drifting back to the sideboard to retrieve his staff. "As it turns out, that lass and the Shamur who married Thamalon are one and the same."

Nuldrevyn laughed. "That's mad!"

"Not at all," the wizard said.

"But if it were true, Lady Uskevren would be one hundred years old."

"There are magical ways of cheating time," Marance replied, "elixirs of longevity and such."

"Perhaps such things do exist," Nuldrevyn conceded, "but you yourself watched the Shamur of today grow from the cradle to maidenhood, don't you remember?"

"Yes," said Marance, "just as I recall how all the old men used to tease her about her uncanny resemblance to her notorious great-aunt. I assume you remember me putting a curse on her."

"Yes," said Nuldrevyn, "what a pity it didn't work. Had

she died, you would have completed the ruin of the Karns and delayed Thamalon's return to respectability with a single stroke."

"It did work," Marance said, "we just couldn't tell it at the time. Demure little Shamur died, but what we couldn't know was that her namesake had secretly returned to Selgaunt and taken up residence in Argent Hall. Or at any rate, the Karns knew how to contact her, and to save her family, she assumed the dead girl's identity and proceeded to marry Thamalon."

"I see," said Nuldrevyn. "Shamur the madcap rogue, the reckless, laughing rapscallion, the mistress of the sword, became the starched, straitlaced grande dame we know today. A woman whose one eccentricity is her abhorrence of weapons."

Marance's pale lips quirked upward. "She's quite an actor, isn't she?"

Nuldrevyn started to jeer, then hesitated. Marance had never been given to flights of fancy, and if he actually credited this bizarre idea, he must have a reason. "How do you know all this?" the Talendar patriarch asked.

In the corner, Bileworm extruded his wedge-shaped head from his squirming mass.

"It was divination put me on the trail," Marance said. "Casting the runes, peering at the stars, picking through the entrails of a beggar I killed, and all that sort of thing. The dark powers can tell you most anything, provided you know what to ask, though they hate to say anything straight out. The auspices kept pointing to Shamur as important to my schemes, and to a certain opera the Hulorn ordered performed a little over a year ago."

Nuldrevyn frowned. "That thing by Guerren Bloodquill? I was present that night. Some magic woven into the music made strange things happen. It turned one fellow into a limbless thing like a snake." He shivered at the memory. "Fortunately, Shamur and that daughter of hers stopped the performance before too many people got hurt."

"And how did they do that?" Marance asked.

Nuldrevyn hesitated. "To be honest, I don't remember."

"Of course not," said the wizard, "for the music put the entire audience into a stupor. But *I* know, because last week I sneaked into the Hulorn's amphitheater and cast a spell to evoke a vision of the past. To rescue you and your fellows, Shamur had to wield a sword like a master of arms, climb like a squirrel, and blend into the shadows like one of Bileworm's people."

"Just one of my many talents," the familiar groaned.

Marance gave the spirit a sour glance. "If I were you, I'd strive to be inconspicuous for a while."

"Shamur fighting," Nuldrevyn said. "That's . . . interesting. Incredible, actually. But it still doesn't prove she's the same woman as the thief in the red-striped mask. There could be another explanation."

"You're a hard fellow to convince," Marance said. "Since you remember hearing of the rogue's exploits, perhaps you recall what happened on the night her true identity was discovered."

"She was rifling old Gundar's strong room when the dwarf himself, his guards, and his household mage burst in on her," Nuldrevyn said. "In the struggle that followed, she lost her mask."

"Correct," Marance said, "and once I suspected that the thief and Lady Uskevren might be one and the same, I decided to conjure up a phantasma of that occasion as well. It was a long shot, but I hoped I might observe something that would confirm my hypothesis, and I did. I saw Gundar's spellcaster sear the rogue's left shoulder with a lance of heat from a wand. Happily, the woman who stopped Bloodquill's opera tore her garments in the process, and while watching my previous vision, I'd noticed she had an old burn scar on the very same spot."

"Incredible," Nuldrevyn repeated, though he realized, that, in fact, he now believed it. "Do you think Thamalon was aware of the substitution?"

"The auguries say no, and it stands to reason. Would the Karns risk telling him his original fiancée was dead, thus giving him the chance to back out of the betrothal?"

"And you think he still doesn't know?"

"Again, it's what my divinations indicate, and that too makes sense. If she didn't confide in him at the start, it would certainly be awkward to do so later."

"Gods above," muttered Nuldrevyn. "But how does it lead us to the destruction of the House of Uskevren?"

"Directly," Marance said. "Shamur is our weapon."

"How so? Are you planning to reveal the truth to the Old Owl and throw his household into turmoil? Expose Shamur's identity to the city at large in the hope that, even after all these years, the families she robbed will insist on her arrest?"

Marance chuckled. "Heavens, no. We don't want to make the Uskevren quarrel, fret, and waste their time in court. We want to exterminate them, and Shamur will begin the process for us by killing Thamalon."

"Why should she do that?" Nuldrevyn asked.

"Do you imagine she assumed her grand-niece's identity gladly? For the last three decades she's been acting a role that requires her to abstain from the escapades she loved. She must resent her husband, don't you think, this man who holds her captive in the prison of her dull, proper life and doesn't even know who she truly is, even if her predicament isn't actually his fault."

His human shape reconstituted, Bileworm rose to his feet. "You should never let fairness stand in the way of a good hate," he said, then sniggered.

"Shamur may detest Thamalon," Nuldrevyn admitted. "Gossip whispers as much. But if she hasn't seen fit to murder him in the last thirty years, why would she do so now?"

"Because I've nudged her along," Marance said. "I convinced her that her husband is indeed responsible for her unhappiness, because he poisoned her grand-niece and so made the substitution necessary. First, with a little help from Bileworm"—the living shadow made an extravagant bow—"the dying Lindrian Karn himself accused Thamalon. Then the apothecary who allegedly sold the Owl the deadly draught confessed to the transaction. And earlier tonight, Shamur found a flask of venom among her husband's effects. I had a ward on the bottle, so, when in my trance, I could discern whether she'd touched it."

"How did you get the poison into the house?" Ossian asked.

"I intercepted one of the Uskevren servants wandering the city on his night off, cast an enchantment on him, and induced him to convey the flask into Stormweather Towers for me," the wizard said. "Child's play, really. The important thing is that my divinations indicated that Shamur would require three 'proofs' of Thamalon's guilt before she acted. Now she's got them."

Nuldrevyn shook his head. "When you promised to destroy the Uskevren, I never expected a strategy as convoluted as this."

"How many times have people tried to kill Thamalon over the years?" Marance replied. "In our youth, you and I rode against him with all the armed might of the Talendar at our backs. In later years, his other foes sent bravos and assassins to waylay him, and commissioned spellcasters to assail him with their sendings. And all of it to no avail, because our quarry is too canny."

"Yet you think your scheme will succeed where all others failed," Nuldrevyn said.

"Yes," said the wizard. "We can be reasonably certain that Shamur will try to kill Thamalon, because she slew her share of men in her youth, when she reckoned she had cause. And the Owl, shrewd as he is, will never anticipate his wife of thirty years abruptly making an attempt on his life. She's one of the very few people who can slip inside his guard."

Nuldrevyn nodded. "Perhaps it is worth a try."

Marance smiled. "I appreciate your confidence. After Thamalon is slain, I'll pick off the rest of the family. Given what we know of the children, it ought to be easy enough, although I would like some helpers who know which end of a sword to grip."

"Why don't you just whistle up some hobgoblins or something, the way you used to?" Nuldrevyn said, lifting his cup to swallow the last of his wine.

"I probably will, before I'm through," Marance replied, "and I trust I'll manage something more interesting than hobgoblins. But human agents have a number of advantages over summoned creatures. They tend to be more intelligent and less conspicuous, they don't disappear after a set interval, and a rival mage can't dispel them."

"Very well," said Nuldrevyn, "but you can't use Talendar guards."

The last few words of the sentence sounded peculiar in his own ears, and after a moment, he realized why. Bileworm had spoken them in unison with him. The old man scowled at the mockery.

"I know," Marance said. "Even if the warriors didn't wear their uniforms, somebody might recognize one of them, and then our House would be held accountable for their actions. That's why I asked you to provide me a lieutenant who knows his way around the underworld." He gave an avuncular smile to Ossian, who, among his other responsibilities, was indeed his father's liaison to Selgaunt's criminal community.

"All right," said Ossian, a shade hesitantly, "I can hire a crew of ruffians for you. I suppose."

"Don't worry," Marance said, "I won't kill them when I'm done with them. Nobody will miss that apothecary and her friends, but I understand how desirable it is for we Talendar to maintain our secret alliance with the major outlaw fraternities of the city. Besides, I won't have any reason to slay my helpers. By the time I'm ready to dismiss them, there won't be anyone left for them to warn."

Ossian grinned. "Thank you, uncle. I appreciate your restraint."

"I still wonder if this scheme is going to work," Nuldrevyn grumbled, still irked over Bileworm's impudence. "Thamalon knows how to handle himself in a fight. If Shamur gives him a chance to defend himself, he could easily kill her instead of the other way around."

"If so," said Marance, "then we'll still be one dead Uskev-ren to the good. Don't worry, brother. While I do have confidence in my strategy, I know that events may not fall out precisely as desired, and I've planned for every contingency. One way or another, I'm going to clip the Old Owl's wings."

CHAPTER 7

Shamur gave Thamalon time to draw his long sword and come on guard, but not an instant longer. She immediately sprang into distance, feinted a head cut, and then, when her husband's blade came up to parry, attempted a strike to the chest.

Thamalon reacted to the true attack in time. Retreating, he swept his sword to his left to close the line. The two blades rang together, and Shamur waited to counterparry his riposte, but instead of attacking in his turn, he simply took a second step backward.

"For the love of Sune," he said, his black brows drawn down in a fierce scowl, his cheek bloody from the shallow gash she'd cut there, "at least explain what this is all about."

"I told you," she said. "I know what you did."

She advanced and attacked again, beating his

blade aside, then lunging and driving her point at his throat.

He hopped back, and the attack fell short. Shouting, her skirts whispering on the fallen snow, she ran at him, striving to plunge her point across those last few inches. He pivoted and brushed her weapon out of line. Now her blade was passé, beyond his body and poorly positioned for either offense or defense. Her safest option was to dash past her opponent and spin around to face him.

So that was what she attempted, meanwhile watching for his riposte so she could counter. Unfortunately, she was so intent on his sword that she lost sight of what his other hand was doing.

Suddenly his unlit horn lantern was hurtling down at her skull. She saw she had no hope of dodging it, so she threw up her unarmed hand and caught the blow on her forearm. One of the milky oval windows shattered, and the pewter frame around it buckled. The impact numbed her limb and knocked her off balance.

From the corner of her eye, she glimpsed him sprinting after her, the lantern raised for a second blow. Frantically, her boots slipping in the snow, she wrenched herself around and thrust her broadsword at his face, an attack out of distance but one that at least served to bring him up short.

Shamur scowled. Skilled combatant that he was, Thamalon had nearly had her then. It didn't matter how furious she was, she mustn't attack so recklessly, as if there was nothing more at stake than a touch in a friendly fencing bout. This duel was life and death. More warily now, sizing up her adversary, looking for openings, waiting for an advantageous moment to attack, she moved in on him again.

"Just tell me!" Thamalon said. A snowflake drifted down to light on his shoulder. The frigid wind moaned.

"And then you'll lie and deny it, and I won't believe you," Shamur said. "Why don't we save ourselves some time, and simply fight?"

She slashed at his torso, and he used the battered lantern like a buckler to block the cut. Her blade lodged in it somehow, and when she jerked it back, it tore the makeshift shield from his grasp and weighted her own weapon down, rendering it useless. Seeing his opportunity, he charged her, his long sword lifted high to brain her with the heavy round steel pommel. She retreated hastily and flailed with her own sword to shake free the lantern. It landed with a clank on the ground. She extended her point, and Thamalon had to wrench himself to one side to avoid impaling himself.

That desperate attempt to check his momentum sent him reeling. He was virtually defenseless, but Shamur couldn't take advantage of it. Her scramble backward had deprived her of her own balance, and in the instant it took her to recover, he did so as well.

But she knew there would be other openings, and, smiling, she advanced on him again.

"Tell me," he said. The blood had run down to the ermine collar of his winter cloak, staining the white fur red.

Shamur beat his blade to the side, then thrust at his shoulder. Hopping back a step, his black boots with their gold and silver spurs crunching in the hindering, treacherous snow, he deflected her blade with a lateral parry. She waited an instant for his riposte, then, when it didn't come, lunged closer and renewed her attack, trying to hook around the long sword that still theoretically closed the line.

That was what Thamalon had been waiting for. With flawless timing, he waited until she was entirely committed to her action and he widened the parry. The two blades scraping together, he shoved Shamur's broadsword so far to his left that it had no hope of piercing its target. Worse, she was passé again, virtually unable to make another attack until she cocked her arm back as far as it would go or withdrew from such close quarters. Trying to take advantage of the situation, he grabbed for her wrist with his unarmed hand.

It was a mistake. He might be as good a fencer as she, but she very much suspected she was the better brawler, a skill she'd honed in disreputable taverns, thieves' dens, and alleys from Sembia to the Moonsea. She whipped her sword arm far to the side, easily avoiding his attempt to seize it, and smashed the heel of her empty hand into her husband's jaw.

Thamalon's head snapped back and he stumbled. Shamur recovered from her lunge and swept the broadsword in a savage cut at his torso.

By the time he saw the blow coming, it was too late to parry, but he managed to jump back. Her attack, which should have sheared through ribs and into the lung beneath, merely grazed him, ripping his lambskin jacket, doublet, shirt, and scoring the flesh beneath.

Snarling, she instantly attacked again. He retreated out of distance. She started to rush after him, then stopped, reminding herself again that, vengeful as she was, she couldn't let it make her rash. Thamalon would take advantage of any mistake.

So, taking her time, catching her breath, she stalked closer, then began to advance and retreat, advance and retreat, with the mincing, cadenced, subtle steps of a fencer attempting to hoodwink his opponent's perception of the distance. He hitched back and forth in time with her.

"I drew first blood, old man," she sneered. Perhaps she could rattle him with taunts and insults, although actually, she doubted it. As far as she knew, none of his other foes had ever succeeded with such a ploy.

"Second," said Thamalon, calmly as she'd expected, "depending on how you're counting."

"I don't count the scratch on the cheek," she said. "You hadn't drawn a weapon. That was just to rouse you from your usual senescent daze."

"Well," he replied, "if I'm all that senile, and you can kill me any time you like, then what harm would it do for you to explain to me what this is all abou—"

As he spoke, she stepped forward, but then did not retreat again. Lulled by and still following the rhythm she'd established and now abandoned, Thamalon advanced into distance. She instantly cut at his head.

It was the perfect moment for it, because even the greatest warrior who ever lived couldn't retreat at the same instant he was stepping forward. But Thamalon whipped the long sword just in time to stop her weapon from splitting his head. The impact rang like a bell, and notched both of their blades.

He riposted with a cut at her leg. She counterparried, feinted an attack to his flank, then tried for his head again. He skipped back out of distance, his point extended to hold her back.

He continued to fight in much the same manner, constantly giving ground. Many swordsmen habitually relied on the edge, sometimes carrying blades that scarcely even possessed a point. But the tip of Thamalon's weapon was sharp as a needle, and he knew as well as Shamur how to use it. As she advanced, he constantly threatened her wrist. Knowing that a combatant is most vulnerable at the moment he attacks, he clearly wanted her to try to penetrate deep into the distance with killing strokes at his torso and head. Since his sword wouldn't have as far to travel, he planned to catch her with a stop thrust to the forearm before her blade could touch him.

It was a patient, defensive mode of fighting such as might be expected of such a careful, calculating man. Shamur's natural inclination was to fight far more aggressively, yet she comprehended Thamalon's style of swordplay very well. She'd often employed it in her youth, when robbing her fellow merchant-nobles in the street. Not wishing to kill them or their bodyguards either, she'd waited for the chance to inflict wounds that incapacitated but would neither slay nor cripple. Or better still, to capture her opponent's blade and spin it out of his grasp.

Given her understanding of Thamalon's strategy, she doubted it would serve him well in the long run. He couldn't retreat forever, not with the tangle of bare oaks, maples, and brush surrounding the clearing. Every time he fetched up against it, it halted him as effectively as a wall, and provided her with an excellent chance to attack. Besides, if one didn't count the half century that the rest of the world had somehow experienced without her, he was more than ten years her senior, and already bleeding as well. Therefore, let him play his waiting game. She was willing to wager that his stamina would flag before hers.

His constant retreating did give him the chance to talk, however. "Tell me," he said, just a hint of exertion, of shortness of breath, in his voice. *Tell me, tell me,* over and over again.

Finally the incessant repetition wrung an answer out of her. "The poisoning," she said, "almost thirty years ago."

"What poisoning?"

"You can't stop lying, can you, no matter how futile it is. It isn't in your nature."

She made what appeared to be a rather clumsy cut at his shoulder, one that left her arm extended and exposed when it fell short.

As she'd intended, Thamalon instantly thrust at her wrist. She knocked his attack out of line with a semicircular parry, then, keeping pressure on his sword to hold it in its ineffectual position, charged him.

He ran backward, came off the blade, and smashed her weapon away an instant before it could shear into his throat. She tried a second cut as she ran by him, but he parried that one, too. She whirled back around to face him.

"I'm not lying," Thamalon said, his white hair clotted with sweat, and his left profile smeared with red. "I beg you to tell me what you mean."

"Only weeks before your wedding," she gritted, "you poisoned your fiancée, a gentle, innocent girl who adored you." Her fist clenched on the hilt of her broadsword too tightly to manipulate it properly, and she loosened her grip again.

"Someone poisoned you?" he asked, feigning bewilderment almost convincingly. Perhaps it helped that he truly was baffled as to how she'd discovered his secret. "Why wasn't I told at the time? And how can you think it was me?"

"I know it was you," she said, trying to bind his blade. He spun his point to avoid the contact, then thrust at her biceps. She snapped her broadsword back across her body to parry, then extended in her turn, and Thamalon took yet another retreat.

She sprang forward, lunged, and thrust at his leading foot. Once again, he took the bait. He snatched his foot back half a step, and his point flashed out to pierce the back of her hand. She whirled her arm and blade higher, avoiding his counterattack, shifted forward, and cut at his chest. He yanked the long sword back and parried. For a few heartbeats they attacked and defended, grunting with effort, their blades clashing fast as a castle bell sounding an alarm. Finally, Thamalon broke off the exchange by retreating, and the two duelists began to circle one another.

"What makes you think I poisoned you?" he asked. Shamur could tell he was making an effort to control his breathing.

"Not me," she said, hoping to surprise and befuddle him, "my kinswoman, also named Shamur. As a matter of fact, your venom killed her." The instant she finished speaking, she attacked with a cut to the chest.

She obviously hadn't disrupted his concentration as she'd hoped, for he immediately sidestepped to avoid her blade while simultaneously thrusting at her sword arm. But she saw him begin to pivot on his leading foot, and adjusted her aim accordingly. He yanked his hand back just in time to keep her from severing it at the wrist. She renewed the attack, they battled fiercely for a few more seconds, and then he scrambled backward with another shallow cut along his forearm.

Shamur wasn't even sure just which of her attacks had slipped past his guard, but she supposed it didn't matter.

"Second blood," she said.

"What makes you believe I murdered the other Shamur?" Thamalon panted.

Shamur was momentarily surprised he had nothing to say about what must be the perplexing question of her true identity. Then she realized that for the moment at least, it didn't matter to him. Whoever she might be in reality, he realized he wouldn't induce her to break off the fight by inquiring. But he hoped he could do it by convincing her he was innocent of the poisoning, and so the cool, shrewd soul that he was, that was the issue he intended to pursue.

"Lindrian told me on his death bed," she replied. "Now will you stop pretending?"

"I'm not pretending," he insisted. "Tell me exactly what Lindrian said."

A bit at a time, she did, and about accosting Audra Sweetdreams and finding the green flask as well, the explanation broken up by fierce passages of arms whenever he permitted her to close the distance. By the time she finished, the light was failing, and the sky a somber blue rapidly darkening to black.

"Sick men sometimes lose their wits," Thamalon panted. His unarmed hand rose to fumble with the golden clasp of his cloak.

"Lindrian was rational," Shamur replied, looking for the right moment to attack.

"Well, then, people can be induced to lie, by magic or otherwise."

He pulled the cloak from his shoulders and dangled it by its bloodstained collar.

"Lindrian had been bedridden for months," she said. "How likely is it that someone got to him in the very heart of Argent Hall?"

"I imagine it could be done."

Shamur frowned momentarily, for Thamalon was correct. Some intruder could have penetrated Argent Hall. It was conceivable that she herself could have managed a comparable feat in her youth. But even so, she knew very well her nephew hadn't misled her, because she'd verified his assertions in Audra Sweetdreams's shop and Thamalon's own bedchamber.

"I see you're changing your tactics," she said. "I promise, the cape won't save you. I understand that manner of fighting, too."

"You've known me for thirty years," he said, circling. He flicked the cloak at her, but she discerned that the action was a harmless display intended to distract her attention from his sword, and she ignored it. "Do you honestly believe I would have murdered a sweet young girl?"

"I've known you to be hard as diamond to get what you wanted," she said.

"Well, I never wanted to marry Rosenna Foxmantle," Thamalon said. He flicked the cape again, more forcefully, making the cloth snap like a whip. "The woman was little better than a harlot."

"And you know about harlots, don't you?" Shamur cut over his blade into the open line, then extended her arm and lunged.

He stepped back and over, shifting his left foot in front of his right and his cape hand ahead of his sword hand. The heavy wool mantle swept in a circle intended to brush Shamur's thrust to the side.

It was the defense she'd been hoping for. She let Thamalon feel the cape collide with her weapon, then instantly whipped the blade down and up into line again, freeing it of the folds of cloth that he'd hoped would hamper it. When he stepped through, putting the whole weight of his body behind a low-line stab at her thigh, she met the attack with a thrust in opposition. Her sword pressed his away and cut the inside of his leg just above the knee. It was yet another superficial wound, and she cried out in frustration.

Their exchange had brought them into close quarters, and he shoved her backward. At once, he tossed the cape, trying to drop it over her head and blind her, but she wasn't so off balance that she couldn't bat it away with her blade.

"First the lantern, then the cloak," she said. "You just can't hold onto a shield, can you?"

She advanced and he retreated, unfortunately not limping as far as she could tell. Above the trees, the first stars of the evening had begun to shine.

"Why would I have proposed to you . . . your counterpart . . . *whoever* if I weren't in love with her?" Thamalon asked. The bloodstain on his lambskin jacket looked black in the gathering gloom. "Not for money, plainly. You Karns didn't have any."

"For position," Shamur said. "Our marriage was the key to your acceptance by the Old Chauncel."

To her surprise, Thamalon snorted. "Perhaps you truly aren't the girl I courted so many years ago, for you certainly don't seem to understand the way things work in Selgaunt. Admittedly, our wedding helped reestablish the House of Uskevren, but it wasn't essential. Ultimately, and despite all their flowery paeans to honor and culture, most merchant nobles respect two things: money, and the strength to defend it. Once the Old Chauncel decided I had plenty of both, they would have opened their doors to me eventually."

She hesitated, for once again, he'd made a seemingly cogent point, though not, of course, sufficient to convince her. "I guess you simply weren't willing to wait."

She took three leisurely steps to accustom her retreating foe to that pace, then suddenly closed the distance with a fast one. She feinted a head cut, then a side cut, then came back to attack his head in truth. Thamalon blocked her out with a high parry, then spun his long sword in the beginning of a cheek cut. She raised her broadsword to counter, and his blade streaked down at her leg.

She hopped back and lashed her weapon down in a sweeping low-line parry. The swords rang together, then something jabbed her thigh. But it was only a little sting, and when she glanced down, she saw to her relief that he hadn't wounded her any more grievously than she had thus far managed to hurt him. Her second parry hadn't quite stopped his attack, but it had robbed it of most of its force. She slashed at his sword arm, and he hopped back.

"Suppose I did try to kill my fiancée," Thamalon said. His back foot slipped in the snow, but he recovered his balance before she could take advantage of it. "Do you honestly think I'd leave the murder weapon in an unlocked box in my bed chamber forever after, where you could so easily discover it? We have vaults in the cellar for hiding our secrets!"

She scowled. For a second, her weary sword arm quivered, till she willed the tremor away. "Ordinarily, I would agree that such carelessness is unlike you," she admitted, "except for one thing. Until I visited Audra Sweetdreams, I had no way of knowing what the bottle was."

"Well, do you think I'd leave it where our young children could stumble onto it and take a curious sip?"

"Oh," she sneered, gliding forward, "I'm to believe you care about the children now."

He retreated before her, realized he'd almost backed himself up against the trees, and pivoted to alter course. She chose that moment to attack, and pressed him hard until he succeeded in breaking away.

"Use your head," he rasped, his chest heaving. "If you were a shady dealer in illicit potions, would you dispense them in costly and highly recognizable glassware? For that matter, how likely is it that this Audra of yours gave me such a flask, and here she is still using exactly the same kind three decades later? I tell you, Shamur, someone induced her to lie, then planted the bottle in my room."

"I see," Shamur said. "Lindrian was a liar, and so is Audra. Everyone lies but you."

"They did lie. Some schemer has perpetrated an elaborate ruse to provoke you into doing precisely what you're doing now."

"Why, when the world at large has no idea that the genteel Lady Uskevren knows how to kill?"

"Curse it, woman, whatever you choose to believe, consider this. If you slay me, someone is bound to find out."

Shamur laughed. "What do I care? After you're dead, I'll ride for Cormyr, and Selgaunt will never see me again. There's nothing here I'll miss." She grimaced. "Well, the children, but I've made my peace with that."

"All right," he growled, "if you won't see reason, let's finish it. You've made my life a misery for thirty years, and the Stalker take my soul to hunt through the sky if I let you rob me of what's left of it!" He sprang forward, his long sword streaking at her head.

Retreating, Shamur parried, cut at his chest, and instantly his blade smashed hers aside. She realized then that he hadn't expected his first action to reach its target. He'd been trying to draw a fast, direct stab from her, which, since he'd been expecting it, he'd easily deflected. Now his point flashed at her heart.

Leaping backward, she parried. His point dipped, evading her sweeping blade, and rose to threaten her torso anew. He bellowed a war cry and lunged. She took another retreat, spun her broadsword in a circular parry, and closed him out a split second before his weapon could pierce her breast.

She cut at his eyes, and the long sword swept up, forming a horizontal bar that hoisted her blade above his head. Holding her weapon trapped at the juncture of his blade and his guard, he stepped in close and pivoted his point down for a jab at her abdomen. Sucking in her belly, she flung herself around him. Her sword scraped free, and she thrust at the expanse of exposed ribs under his upraised arm. Not one fencer in a hundred could have whirled and parried that attack in time, but he did, then came at her again.

She almost felt as if she were dueling a new opponent, for his current mode of fighting, a relentless onslaught of strong, lethal attacks, was utterly different from the defensive style of evasions and counterattacks he'd employed before. She thought that if he'd battled this way from the beginning, he might even have defeated her, but he'd waited too long to start. He was tired now, and after a few more fierce exchanges, it seemed to her that his actions were finally starting to slow. Only a bit, but so evenly matched were they that a bit was all she needed.

She stepped just a hair into the distance, inviting attack, and he obliged her with a feint at her knee, then jabbed a cut at her chest. She stepped forward and swept her blade from right to left. The captain of her father's household guard, the veteran soldier who'd given an importunate, boisterous little girl her first instruction in swordplay, had taught her it was foolish to try such an action. If her opponent thwarted her attempt to defend, her own advance would likely carry her onto his blade. But Shamur didn't fail. She'd sensed exactly where and how Thamalon's true attack would come, and she bashed his sword aside and cut with her own.

Thanks to her advance, she was dangerously close, and he scrambled backward. Feinting and disengaging repeatedly, she pursued him.

He kept retreating, the long sword whirling and leaping from side to side and up and down as he searched for her blade. But perhaps she'd unconsciously assimilated his favorite patterns, the ones he fell into when pressed so hard he had not an instant to think, for she anticipated and avoided every parry. Each spring of her long legs brought her point a little closer to his flesh, and she thought that here at last was the phrase that would end with her broadsword buried in his vitals.

Then the heel of his back foot caught on something hidden beneath a drift of snow. He stumbled, his sword arm flailing too wide to have any hope of deflecting her attack. She truly had him now, and he knew it; she could read the knowledge in his stricken expression. There was no panic there, but frustration and a final flare of defiance.

Screaming, she cut at his neck.

And then pulled the broadsword up over his head a split second before it could strike home.

She hadn't known she was going to spare him, and it took her a moment to understand why. Though his arguments hadn't persuaded her, they'd carried a certain weight, and more telling still had been the fact that up until the very end, when he'd despaired of ever convincing her, he hadn't once attempted a mortal blow. He'd always cut and thrust at her limbs, never her torso or head. His reluctance to take her life even to protect his own suggested more powerfully than words that perhaps he wasn't the fiend she'd thought him after all.

How strange to discover that somewhere down deep in her mind, she'd been working toward such a conclusion, without even knowing it until now.

Thamalon recovered his balance, came back on guard,

but made no threatening actions. "I take it you've had a change of heart," he said.

"Shut up!" she snarled, for her anger had by no means dissipated. The resentment that had smoldered in her heart for thirty years, and which the tale of the poisoning had fanned into full-blown hatred, still burned inside her, but now it was muddled with doubt and other painful feelings she couldn't even identify.

"Forgive me," Thamalon said gently, "I wasn't trying to mock you. Why don't we put our swords up?"

"You might as well," said a mild tenor voice.

CHAPTER 8

Shamur whirled. At the perimeter of the snowy glade, figures wavered into view, evidently emerging from some sort of glamour that had rendered them invisible before. Most were men armed with crossbows and blades of various sorts. Judging from their bearing, they knew how to use such weapons, but she didn't think they were warriors, or at least, not the sort of warriors whom any honorable lord would recruit for his retinue. Their paucity of body armor, tawdry finery, slouching postures, smirks, and sneers all suggested the bully and the bravo. They'd stationed themselves around the edge of the clearing so as to surround the Uskevren, whose final passage of arms had carried them back to the center of the open space.

Standing safely behind a pair of the ruffians was a man about as tall as Thamalon, his features concealed behind an ambiguously smiling crescent-shaped Man in the Moon mask. His robe and cloak were dark, and he held a black, knobbed staff in his pallid hand. Behind him, indistinct in the failing twilight, its shape subtly altering as it shifted from one foot to the other, was some sort of animate shadow. Shamur inferred that the pair were a wizard and his familiar.

"I imagine this is the fellow who attempted to gull you," Thamalon said calmly.

"I deserve most of the credit," said the shadow, and Shamur jumped, because the spirit had spoken in an exact imitation of Lindrian's labored, quavering voice.

"I did gull her," said the mage, ignoring his spectral attendant, "she just didn't follow through." He turned his head toward Shamur. The gloaming turned the mask's eye holes into pits of shadow. She used his regard as an excuse to take a leery step backward. "It's too bad you didn't opt to murder him in his sleep, Lady Uskevren. Then he wouldn't have had the opportunity to talk you out of it."

"I must compliment you on your skill at chicanery," Thamalon said. "Ordinarily, Shamur is nobody's fool."

"I suspect she enjoys thinking the worst of you," the wizard said, "and that helped."

"Tricking us is one thing," Shamur said. "But how did you and your men get out here in the woods?"

"We tracked you," the shadow said, "veiled in Master's spells of concealment."

"You see, my lady," said the wizard, "I made quite extensive plans for your husband's destruction. In addition to manipulating you, I put a watch on Stormweather Towers, and when you two rode out alone, we followed. And thank goodness for that, because this way, everything works out. While you failed to kill Thamalon, you did lure him far away from his retainers, and I daresay that my associates and I won't have a great deal of difficulty disposing of the both of you ourselves."

"Your bravos could have shot us down as we dueled," Shamur said.

"You mustn't get your hopes up because of that," the magician said. "I'm afraid that you too must die. It was just that I don't believe in revealing myself to an enemy unnecessarily, even when I hold every advantage. Besides, it would have gratified my sense of irony had Thamalon, who has survived the attentions of so many ill-wishers, perished at the hands of his own wife."

"Who are you?" Thamalon asked.

"Lord Uskevren," the wizard said in mock distress, "you wound me. How could you forget—"

As the mage spoke, Shamur took a second subtle step backward, positioning herself beside the broken lantern. Nimbly as a juggler, she suddenly tossed her broadsword from her right hand to her left and kicked the lamp up into the air. She grabbed it, pivoted, and hurled it at a crossbowman on the opposite side of the clearing from the mage.

By the time the missile smashed the bravo in the face, she was sprinting after it, and Thamalon, who had, Mask be thanked, reacted instantly, was pounding along beside her. But the crossbows! She zigzagged to throw off the shooters' aim, then dived to the ground when she heard the ragged, snapping chorus of the weapons discharging their bolts. Unscathed, she leaped back up, and another quarrel, loosed by a bravo who'd taken his time, thrummed past her temple, yanking at strands of her long, pale hair as it passed.

She glanced at Thamalon and saw that, miraculously, he hadn't been hit, either. Evidently, surprise and the darkness had spoiled their enemies' aim. He gave her a nod, and they raced on.

Though his brow was gashed and his nose, pulped, the rogue Shamur had struck with the lantern was still on his feet, and she was running straight at his leveled crossbow. She watched his trigger finger, praying that despite the darkness, she'd see it move. Then it did twitch, the weapon clacked and twanged, and she threw herself to the side.

The quarrel grazed her arm. Snarling at the sudden sting, she charged the rogue, her sword extended to complete the ruin of his face.

Eyes wide with alarm, he dropped the crossbow, scurried backward, and fumbled for the hilt of his falchion. Shamur would have reached him before he ever managed to draw it, except that two more bravos dashed in, one from either side, to intercept her and Thamalon. They too had abandoned their deadly but slow-loading crossbows in favor of their blades.

Shamur knew without looking that other bullies were also running toward her. If she and Thamalon couldn't break through these first three before the rest arrived, they'd be overwhelmed. She attacked ferociously, and her husband did the same.

The first opponent to engage her was a wiry, black-bearded man with a gold ring in his lower lip and a short sword in either hand. She feinted a cut at his knee and whirled her broadsword at his head. He parried and held her weapon with the blade in his left hand, then stepped in and stabbed at her belly with the one in his right.

Striking the flat of the short sword with her unarmed fist, she knocked the attack out of line, observing as she did that her opponent's hands and throat were tattooed with rows of overlapping scales. She chopped his throat with the edge of her stiffened hand, then shoved him away.

By that time, the man with the bloody face had his falchion in hand. She advanced on him, and he gave ground, evidently well aware that he only had to hold the Uskevren here for a few heartbeats until his comrades could dash up and take them from behind.

She cut at his leading leg, and he parried. She tried to dart around him, but he jumped in front of her and nearly landed a whistling slash at her face. All the while, she could hear his friends' footsteps thudding closer.

Then Thamalon sprang from the darkness. He'd evidently bested the ruffian who'd engaged him, and now he rushed at Shamur's opponent from the side. The bravo tried to turn and defend himself, but was a split second too slow. Thamalon's bloody long sword plunged into his neck.

The dead man started to fall, the Uskevren lord yanked

his weapon free, and he and Shamur ran out of the clearing and toward the trees, into what had now become a black and freezing winter night.

Garris Quinn, a fleshy, sallow rogue with a pair of kid gloves tucked foppishly through the band of his copotain hat, watched flabbergasted as the nobles disappeared into the woods with several of the men under his command in hot pursuit. His slack-jawed expression turned sheepish and wary when he turned to look at Master. "I guess they took the lads by surprise," he said.

"I guess they did," said Bileworm, leering. Actually, he thought, Garris had no reason to be afraid. No matter how vexed Master was, he wouldn't waste time chastising this lout and his underlings for their incompetence. Not while Shamur and Thamalon were running loose.

And the familiar was right, for Master merely sighed and said, "Two of your fellows will stay near me to serve as my bodyguards. Someone must also return to the men we left with the horses and warn them to be on the lookout. Everyone else will help flush and kill our quarry. In an *organized* fashion, if you please."

Garris scurried off to see that the wizard's orders were carried out. "Organized or not," Bileworm said, "in the woods, in the night, our friends have at least a slim chance of escaping."

"That's why I intend to arrange for reinforcements," Master said, "reinforcements who see well in the dark, and will materialize ahead of Thamalon and Shamur and cut them off."

The wizard thrust the ferule of his staff into the frozen ground as easily as if it had been soft sand. Then, having freed both hands, he produced a tiny leather bag and a stub of candle from one of the hidden pockets in his cloak, held them high, and whispered an incantation.

Another voice, seeming to come from everywhere and

nowhere, hissed a response, and power crackled through the air. A blue flame flared upward from the candle wick, and violet light pulsed from the mouth of the sack. An instant later, bursts of soft purple radiance flickered off in the distance among the trees.

Her heart pounding and the breath burning in her lungs, Shamur ran. In the clearing, dueling, her skirts hadn't especially troubled her, but now they seemed to snag on every fallen branch or patch of brush.

Even so, with her longer legs, she was keeping pace with Thamalon, and moving far more quietly as well. To her thief's ears, his every stride seemed excruciatingly loud, and she feared they'd never shake their pursuers off their trail.

Somewhere behind them, a voice cried out in pain. Shamur suspected that one of the bravos had tripped or run into a low-hanging branch as he plunged headlong through the darkness. A mishap, she knew, that could just as easily have befallen her or Thamalon, with fatal consequences.

At her back, other voices babbled, the sound receding as she fled. Perhaps the rogue who'd hurt himself had been at the head of the pack, and his accident had delayed everyone else. At any rate, she didn't hear them thumping along at her heels anymore, and thanks to the tangle of branches overhead, patches of the ground beneath were free of snow, which ought to prevent the bullies from following her or Thamalon's tracks. The two nobles changed direction one more time, and then she gestured to a hollow in the ground behind the broad trunk of an ancient oak. They crouched down in the depression to catch their breath.

As soon as she stopped moving, the cold bit into her body, and she wistfully thought of her cloak left back in the glade. She felt as if she'd left most of her strength back there as well, squandered in the protracted duel.

Bloody from the wounds she'd given him, panting and shivering at the same time, Thamalon didn't seem to be in any better shape than she was, but he gave her a smile. "When I said I wished we could spend more time together," he whispered, "this wasn't precisely what I had in mind."

She grinned. "Shall we try for the horses?"

He shook his head. "Our friend in the mask will be expecting us to do that."

"You're right. Well, now that we've shaken them off our tails, they'll have to spread out to hunt us. We could hunt them as well."

"I certainly wouldn't mind seeing Master Moon's blood on my blade, or that of his agents, either, but still, that strategy seems a little chancy."

She grimaced. "I suppose so. They have magic on their side, and if just one of them got off a shout, he could bring the whole band down on our heads. Besides, you don't know how to creep up on someone silently."

"I'll have you know," he said indignantly, "that I'm a first-rate stalker. I mastered the art hunting small game around Storl Oak when I was a boy."

"If you say so," Shamur said. "I suppose our best course is simply to put more distance between our pursuers and ourselves. Perhaps eventually work our way out of the woods and back to Rauthauvyr's Road."

"Agreed." He looked up at the stars floating above the canopy of bare branches, taking his bearings. "Let's head northeast."

"All right." They took a last cautious look about, then rose to their feet. At that moment, points of purple light winked at various points in the forest.

"Oh, joy," Shamur said, "the wizard has decided to use his spells on us."

"Be careful," Thamalon replied. "Mystra only knows what sort of effect he's conjured."

Go teach your grandmother to turn a spindle, she thought sourly. She'd been contending with hostile spellcasters before he was born.

They skulked through the trees, and she had to concede that Thamalon could move fairly quietly when he wasn't running flat out. Her teeth began to chatter, and she clenched her jaw to stop the noise.

Soon she heard the wizard's henchmen moving around her, bawling to one another, cursing, and crashing through the brush. Shamur smiled, for she wanted the bravos to make a commotion. That way, she'd know where they were.

Unfortunately, something else was moving as stealthily as she was. So stealthily, in fact, that she had no warning of its presence until she and Thamalon crept right up to a lightning-blasted beech with a blackened crevice running down its trunk. Then she caught a foul stench, and heard a scratching sound. An ochre, six-legged rat the size of a dog exploded from the crack.

Shamur swung her sword at the ugly thing, but it dodged the blade and rushed at her ankle, its huge, stained incisors poised to take her foot off. She kicked it away, and it squealed and scuttled at her again.

She sidestepped, thrust, and this time caught it behind the shoulder, her point plunging all the way through its body to pin it to the ground. Convulsing, it screamed until Thamalon struck its head off.

"It's an osquip," he said, "and not native to these woods."

"I know," she said, "the magician summoned it, and thanks to its screeching, everyone knows where we are. Run!"

They dashed on, and a stitch started throbbing in her side. Another osquip scuttled out from under a bush right in front of her, and she had to leap over it to avoid a collision. She whirled, swinging her broadsword, her aim a matter of pure instinct, and split the beast's muzzle precisely between its beady eyes, dispatching it.

Thamalon cursed. Shamur turned to see one of the ruffians emerge from the trees to their left. The rogue's eyes widened as he beheld the fugitives. He was going to shout and pinpoint their location yet again, and there was no way she could get to him in time.

Thamalon dropped the long sword, reached into his sleeve, whipped out a throwing knife, and hurled it, all in one smooth blur of motion. The rogue made a choking sound and collapsed with the weapon buried in his breast.

"I . . . didn't know you could throw knives," Shamur wheezed, her side still aching fiercely.

"I suppose you don't approve of spouses keeping secrets from one another," he replied, his labored breathing all but masking the sarcasm in his tone. He picked up his sword and lurched into motion. Biting back a groan, she stumbled after him.

Violet light pulsed among the trees, and then again a minute later. Shamur had hoped their principal adversary was a wizard of modest talents, who could cast such a summoning only once, but plainly, that wasn't the case. Evidently he could augment his forces repeatedly, until he had sufficient minions to comb every inch of the benighted woods and overwhelm anyone they found there. The odds against her and Thamalon were even longer than she'd first imagined.

She hoped they'd traveled far enough from the spot where the osquip had squealed that they could stop running and resume skulking. The relentless, driving pace had become agonizing. She started to slow down, and then a bubble of purple phosphorescence appeared, swelled, and vanished directly in front of her. It left in its place a hulking lizard man, its scaly tail lashing and its forked tongue flickering from its jaws. The reptilian creature had a club studded with sharp bits of stone in one clawed hand and a crude wicker shield in the other.

As one, Shamur and Thamalon rushed it, hoping to dispatch it before it could take any sort of action. But the lizard man hopped sideways, interposing the noblewoman's body between her husband and itself, and caught her first attack on its shield. Hissing, it struck back, and she ducked the blow.

Thamalon darted around the lizard man and cut at its back. Pivoting, its tail sweeping past Shamur's feet, the creature roared and blocked the blow with its shield. As it struck at Thamalon, who avoided the blow by jumping back,

Shamur cut at its midsection, plunging the broadsword deep into its flesh.

The lizard man collapsed into a drift of dry, brown oak leaves, but Shamur could take no pleasure in the victory, for she knew that its bellowing and the crash of blades on the wicker shield had revealed their whereabouts yet again. She could hear the hunters calling to one another as they moved in from every side.

She suspected that she and Thamalon would never escape. They might as well make a stand here, while they still had a bit of strength left, and see how many of their attackers they could slay before they were cut down in their turn. But that would be tantamount to giving up, and so she started to run instead.

Thamalon grabbed her by the arm. "This way," he said, pointing with the gory tip of his long sword to indicate a slightly different direction. She didn't see why he thought his choice was any better, but it didn't seem to be any worse, either, and there was scarcely time for discussion. So she nodded and let him lead the way.

Another osquip, this one eight-legged, scuttled from the shadows. Thamalon cut at it, missed, his blade jarring on the frozen earth, and the huge rat darted at his leg. He snatched his foot back, and then Shamur hacked her broadsword down into the creature's spine. The osquip fell and lay screeching like a damned soul.

As Shamur lifted her broadsword to administer the coup de grace, a crossbow bolt streaked out of the night, narrowly missed Thamalon, and crunched into the bole of an oak. There was no point in silencing the osquip if other foes were already close enough to snipe at them, so she and Thamalon simply fled, leaving the beast to writhe and shriek on the ground.

"Just . . . a little . . . farther," Thamalon gasped

Shamur couldn't imagine how he could find the breath to run and try to encourage her at the same time. She also had no idea what he was talking about, but after twenty more stumbling, excruciating strides, she found out.

Suddenly, she and Thamalon plunged from the trees into a large clearing. Perhaps ancient enchantments prevented the surrounding woods from encroaching on the space, for at its center rose the dark shape of a small ruined fortress. Shamur realized that her husband had been heading in the castle's direction all along, so they could take refuge inside if it turned out to be necessary.

Sadly, it was necessary. Their enemies were closing in, and they were too spent to run much farther. The fortress was a better redoubt than she could have expected to find, even though its crumbling sandstone ramparts could do no more than delay the defenders' inevitable annihilation, and that only if the fugitives could reach the interior alive.

Thamalon led her toward a gate in the castle's north wall. Crossbows clacked. The quarrels thrummed through the dark but missed their marks.

Suddenly a pair of lizard men seemed to pounce from nowhere; exhausted as she was, dashing at breakneck speed, Shamur hadn't noticed their approach. The one that attacked her bore no weapons, but it raked at her chest with claws sharp as any dagger. She recoiled, and the creature's talons merely shredded her gown and tore away the silver and sapphire brooch Tamlin had given her on her birthday.

The lizard man lunged at her again, clawed hands raised, fanged jaws gaping, but not before she came on guard. Exploiting the superior reach the broadsword afforded her, she thrust at the reptile's throat, then instantly stepped back and prepared to parry, perceiving even as she did so that she wouldn't actually need to defend. Blood spurted from the lizard man's throat. It clutched at the wound, then sprawled at her feet.

She pivoted and saw that Thamalon had just dispatched the other lizard man. His foe had carried a battle-axe and a sturdy, leather-covered target, and the nobleman hesitated over the shield as if wondering whether he could afford the time to pull it from the creature's arm and take it for himself. Then two rogues emerged from the trees, and Thamalon cursed, whirled, and ran up the motte on which the ruin sat. Shamur followed.

The fortress gate had once been comprised of two leaves. The one on the left had fallen from its hinges, and the nobles had to run over it to get inside. Their footsteps boomed on the planks.

Shamur and Thamalon flung themselves behind the leaf that was still standing, shielded at last, if only for the moment, from flying quarrels. Panting, soaked in perspiration despite the chill night air, leaning heavily on the gate, the blonde woman peered about the snowy courtyard.

As she'd already inferred from viewing its exterior, the fortress had no donjon. Instead, rows of humbler structures, several with collapsed roofs, stood along the walls, where they'd no doubt served as a barracks, kitchen, dining hall, stable, storerooms, smithy, shrine, and every other facility such an outpost required. A wagon with the front wheels missing sat up on a trestle in the far corner of the yard.

There seemed to be no superior defensive position farther inside. They might as well fight here, at the gate. At least that way, she wouldn't have to stagger any farther.

Thamalon peered out at the clearing. "They're coming," he wheezed, "and I need you to hold them." He turned and trotted away.

"What are you doing?" she demanded. "There's nowhere better to go, and I need you here!"

If he heard, he evidently grudged the time to reply, for he just kept going, and then she heard footsteps crunching in the snow beyond the entrance. She peeked around the gate.

She didn't see as many foes as she'd expected. Perhaps some of the bravos and conjured creatures were still making their way through the woods. Moreover, the bullies were hanging back at the verge of the clearing, seemingly happy to let the wizard's inhuman minions risk their lives to take the common quarry.

Still, a sufficiency of the conjured servitors were hurrying across the snow to do precisely that. A couple had already reached the base of the mound.

Shamur's throat was parched. Wishing for a drink of water, some scrap of relief to ease her plight if only for an instant, she forced herself to stand without support and lifted her broadsword from where it trailed on the ground. The notched, wet blade was heavy in her hand.

An osquip swarmed through the gate, and she killed it. In the moment it took to free the broadsword from the carcass, a lizard man leaped through the opening. She parried the first thrust of its spear, and had her riposte deflected in its turn. Shifting back and forth, they traded attacks until she finally dispatched it with a cut to the head.

As it fell, she realized she was now standing unshielded in the castle entrance. She dodged to the side, and a pair of crossbow bolts whizzed through the space where she'd just been standing.

"Thamalon!" she croaked. No one answered.

Then she smelled an acrid odor, and an instant later, a dark horror scuttled through the gate. Its shape superficially resembled that of a centaur, with a human's head, arms, and torso set atop a hard-shelled, eight-legged body. A segmented tail, ten feet long and culminating in a curved stinger, lashed about behind it.

Shamur cut at the spot where a human would have a navel, just above the point where skin gave way to chitin. Its blank yellow eyes flaring, the manscorpion lashed a clawed hand down to block the blow, sacrificing one of its three fingers to stop what would otherwise have been a mortal stroke.

The creature hissed and threatened her with its unmaimed hand. It was attempting to distract her, she suspected, from the true attack, and sure enough, an instant later, its tail whipped up over its body, lashing its stinger down at her head.

She scrambled backward, and the stinger scored the earth. The manscorpion scuttled forward, taking some of the ground she'd given up and clearing the narrow entrance for a second such creature to hurry through.

Shamur felt a surge of despair. Exhausted as she was, how could she fight both of them by herself? Where was Thamalon? Then one manscorpion scuttled right, the other to the left, maneuvering to catch their quarry between them, and she had no more time for doubt or questions.

She darted to the left, outflanking the wounded tlincalli, as she recalled the name, and putting it between herself and its companion. Bellowing, she charged, and the manscorpion's sting whipped at her in a horizontal arc. Without breaking stride, she blocked the attack with her broadsword, vaulted onto the creature's back, then leaped at the second abomination.

Still circling to engage its prey, the unwounded tlincalli had doubtless assumed it could not be attacked until it completed the maneuver. Now, suddenly, death was flying at it through the air. Crying out in alarm, it raised its hands to fend Shamur off, but it was an instant too slow. Knowing that no fighter can use his strength to best effect when his feet aren't planted, she hacked with all her might. Her broadsword bit deep into the tlincalli's hairless brow.

The manscorpion fell and so did she, slamming down on her side. As she struggled to yank her sword free, the remaining tlincalli's tail hurtled down at her. She wrenched herself to the side, and the curved stinger smashed into the earth and splashed her with drops of venom. She grabbed the tail just beneath the deadly hook to keep it from striking at her a second time, whereupon the manscorpion whipped the member back, dragging her bumping across the snowy ground toward its ready claws. It was this pulling, rather than her own all-but-depleted strength, that actually drew her blade from the dead tlincalli's skull.

Bending at the waist, its four front legs bowing, the manscorpion stooped to rake her with its unwounded hand. Grunting, she evaded the attack, gashing the creature's forearm in the process, then drove her point up at its belly.

Her aim was too low, hitting chitin instead of skin, but the broadsword crunched through its armor. The manscorpion convulsed and toppled, and she had to scramble backward to keep it from smashing down on top of her.

Rising, she studied the writhing tlincalli, making sure it truly was incapacitated, and then, gasping, staggered toward the gate. She had to resume her station there before the rest of her enemies swarmed through the gap. If several of them attacked her at once, they'd surely drag her down.

She almost didn't make it in time, for just as she reached the entrance, a pair of lizard men skulked through. She charged and somehow managed to slay them both before they turned their chert-tipped spears in her direction.

After that, she had nothing to do but gasp for breath and wait for the next onslaught, which, she suspected, was likely to finish her. She simply had nothing left.

At least she'd perish with a sword in her hand. Better that, she'd often thought, than dying withered, decrepit, and sick, like poor old Lindrian. There was still no sign of Thamalon, and she supposed that, his courage failing, he'd hidden himself in one of the derelict buildings in the pathetic hope that his enemies wouldn't be able to find him. It gave her a bitter satisfaction to think that, even if he wasn't a murderer, her repugnance for him was justified after all.

Standing at the foot of the motte, Marance, who had enhanced his night vision with an enchantment, watched in disgust as Shamur killed two more of his lizard men, then ducked back behind the cover of the remaining leaf of the double gate.

"Unbelievable," he said. "She must be exhausted, yet none of our henchmen or conjured minions can dispose of her."

Bileworm leered. "Perhaps you should march up to the gate and fight it out with her yourself."

Marance sighed. "As I've told you on many occasions, jackanapes, I'm the warlord, overseeing the entire battle-field, not simply one of the spearmen. I'm too important to stand in the shield wall unless I absolutely have to."

"Then I suppose you'll have to wait for one of the troops to kill her. Or toss some magic at her when she shows herself again."

"I could," Marance agreed, but even a well-placed and exceptionally potent thunderbolt would only kill Shamur, not her husband, who hadn't been seen since he'd dashed inside the gate, and it was Thamalon's death that the wizard chiefly craved. If he was going to cast a spell, then let it be one that would destroy the both of them.

"We have sentries watching all four faces of the castle?" he asked.

"Yes," Bileworm replied.

"Make a circuit," Marance said. "Make certain they're at their posts. Meanwhile, I will indeed attempt 'a little magic.' "

Actually, it would be one of the most powerful spells in his repertoire, which was why he hadn't used it hitherto. Sorceries drew their power primarily from the fundamental forces and structure of the cosmos, but also drained a measure of the caster's vitality. Ordinary wizards restored their strength with rest and nourishment, but, suspended between life and death as he was, Marance had discovered that such commonplace measures would not replenish him. Perhaps his liege lord had arranged it thus to insure that he wouldn't attempt to remain in the realm of the living forever, but must return in due time to the iron city of Dis.

Petty spells, like the ones that had summoned the osquips, lizard men, and tlincallis, leeched away such an infinitesimal fraction of his strength that he cast them freely. Greater magic, however, required enough to make him pause and consider. He saw little reason to hold back when the man he wished to chastise most of all was at his mercy.

He took out his bag and candle, held them high, and whispered the charm. The candle spat blue flame ten feet into the air, and then the ground began to shake.

The first tremor nearly jolted Shamur off her aching, unsteady legs. Clutching the gate to steady herself, she peeked out at the clearing.

Violet light pulsed on the snow at the foot of the motte, and then, with a sustained, grinding roar, twisting and thrashing as it emerged from its confinement, a black, vaguely manlike shape outlined in purple fire heaved itself up from beneath the shroud of white. Pale eyes glittered in its crude lump of a head. The sustained quaking ceased with its birthing, but its lurching strides were themselves sufficient to shake the ground as it started up the slope.

Shamur had once seen an earth elemental conjured, and she reckoned this creature was something similar. But this was much bigger, so huge that the sandstone battlements only came up to its breast. So immense that she had no hope of fighting it.

She started to scramble backward, and then, too vast to pass through the gate, without hesitation it simply walked through the wall. The bulwark exploded into rubble, filling the night with hurtling, plummeting scraps of rock.

One advantage of conjuring a servant tall as a tower, Marance reflected, was that he could watch it do its work even when it was standing inside an enclosure. The corrupted elemental lifted its fists above its head, then slammed them down, over and over again. Surely, it was smashing Thamalon and Shamur into jelly.

A creature created for rage and mindless destruction, the giant then proceeded to tear down the entire fortress, and the crash and rumble of stone thundered through the night. The rogues stared in awe. Bound by Marance's command to seek and slay the Uskevren, osquips, lizard men, and tlincallis advanced helplessly into the heart of the demolition, no doubt to be crushed by falling debris. With a modicum of effort, the wizard could have freed them of the compulsion, but given their ephemeral status, it scarcely seemed worthwhile. Like his band of scoundrels, he preferred to stand at his ease and watch the spectacle.

When the destruction was complete, Marance pulled his staff from the ground and murmured a spell of dismissal. The elemental crumbled like a clod of mud dissolving in a rainstorm.

Marance turned to Bileworm and said, "You quiz the sentries. I'm going to take a look at the wreckage."

Lengthening his legs to take longer paces, the familiar hurried away. The wizard headed for the motte, then glanced back at his two bodyguards, who, thus prompted, reluctantly trailed along behind him.

When he reached the crest of the mound, Marance saw that the devastation was, if anything, even more all-encompassing than it had looked from a distance. Absolutely nothing remained but a field of crushed stone and the heap of earth left by the departure of the elemental.

Bileworm loped out of the dark. "According to the watchers, the Uskevren never came out," he said. "Not over the top of a wall, and not through any sort of postern, either."

"They're buried somewhere beneath all this, then," said Marance, and with that utter certainty came a blaze of exultation tempered with just a hint of anticlimax. He'd craved his revenge for so long, and now, abruptly, the truly important part of it was over. "Farewell, Thamalon. We're quits now, or will be, once I kill your children." He started back down the motte, and his attendants followed.

"How long will the slaughter take, do you think?" Bileworm asked.

"A day or two at most," Marance said, "for Nuldrevyn and Ossian both agree that the sons, Thamalon the Second and Talbot, are wastrels and fools. The daughter, Thazienne, might have more brains and gumption, but she's ill. I daresay the two of us can sit back and watch while our friends here"— he nodded at the bodyguards—"do the bulk of the work."

While the surviving osquips, tlincallis, and lizard men vanished, their summonings running out of power, Garris assembled the bravos for the trek back to the horses. Just as he declared them ready to depart, Marance noticed a small object gleaming in the moonlight atop a patch of trampled, blood-spattered snow. He idly stooped to inspect it, observed it was Shamur's brooch, and picked it up.

"A trophy?" Bileworm asked.

"If you like," the wizard replied. "A little memento to set on a shelf back home."

CHAPTER 9

Tamlin had just succeeded in luring the giggling Nenda and Vinda, the buxom twins who served ale, wine, and liquor at the Laughing Game-cock, into the closet, when someone rudely took hold of his shoulder and shook him. He turned, opened his eyes, and the closet turned into his own spacious featherbed, just as, judging from the sunlight streaming through the casement, night had changed to morning.

Tamlin's head pounded, and his mouth was dry as dust. Squinting against the glare, he scowled at the freckle-faced, pug-nosed fellow who'd awakened him. "I could have you flogged for this," he said, and then regretted it, a little.

If Escevar resented this reminder that, although Tamlin's closest friend, he was also a mere servant, no one could have told it from his unwavering smile. "You told me to wake you," he said.

"Impossible," Tamlin said, "for you jolted me out of a beautiful dream into a hideous nightmare. Weeping Ilmater, my head!"

"I have the remedy," Escevar said, his auburn curls shining in the light from the window. "Hair of the dog." He gestured to the nightstand, and the uncorked wine bottle and silver goblet sitting atop it.

"You torturer!" Tamlin exclaimed. "Why didn't you point it out before?"

Disdaining the cup, he fumbled the bottle into his unsteady hand and guzzled from the neck. Usk's Fine Old, the spiced clarry his father made, slid down his throat to ease his hangover. It amused him to think how disgusted the old man would be to see him gulp it so. The bottle was half empty when he finally took it away from his lips.

"Better?" Escevar asked.

"Marginally," Tamlin said. In truth, he felt quite a bit better, but wasn't quite ready to relinquish the martyr's role. "Why in Sune's name did I want you to wake me?"

"You and I, Gellie Malveen, and some others are going hawking, and we're likely to be late if you don't hurry."

"I'm not going to be late. I'm not going at all. Gellie's an ass to plan an outing before noon." He made a show of settling back down on the bed.

"As you wish, Deuce. Sleep well." Escevar turned toward the door.

"No, wait." Tamlin forced himself to throw back his covers and sit up on the side of the bed. Though a fire still crackled in the hearth, the parquet floor was cold against the soles of his feet. "We were going to take Brom along, weren't we? And collect Fendolac along the way?"

"Your memory is improving," said the redhead.

Brom Selwick seemed a nice enough fellow, albeit possessed of a tedious zeal which reminded Tamlin unpleasantly of Father and the old man's faithful butler Erevis. Unfortunately, thanks to his déclassé upbringing, the wizard lacked the graces of a gentleman, and while that might be tolerable in a groom or scullion, it was inappropriate in a highly placed retainer whose position required him to mingle on familiar terms with the nobility. Tamlin had thought it might be amusing to teach Brom how to behave, and had intended this morning's excursion to contribute to his education.

While Fendolac, of course, had just lost his father. Tamlin had hoped a little sport would distract him from his grief.

"Then I suppose the excursion is an act of charity," the noble said, taking another swig from the bottle, "and I'm stuck. Not that Father will appreciate my sacrifice. He'll keep on calling me indolent and worthless, same as ever." He grinned. "Anyway, I'd better get dressed."

"I'll ring for your valet," Escevar said.

"No, please. I can't stand to see another face or listen to another voice just yet. You help me."

Tamlin kept nipping at the clarry while he and Escevar retired to his wardrobe. They rummaged through trunks and armoires to create a suitable outfit that the nobleman had never worn before, at least in the sense that he'd never before combined this particular cambric shirt with that branched velvet doublet, or that scarlet riding cape with these crimson lugged boots. By the time the bottle was empty, there was only one element still lacking.

Tamlin had never shared his siblings' passion for weapons and fencing. He liked to think that was his mother coming out in him. Still, no gentleman was properly dressed without a sword. It needn't be a functional sword, however, and for the stylish young nobles of Selgaunt, who had guards to protect them and tended to favor whimsy over practicality, it often wasn't. Moved by that same frivolous spirit, Tamlin selected an object d'art; a long, slender blade, spun from rosy glass, in a scabbard. The delicate ornament had been specially enchanted to a resilience sufficient to withstand casual bumps and jostles.

He attached the crystal trinket to his favorite gold sword belt, and then he and Escevar walked to the kitchen, where squat Brilla, who presided there, bustled about to provide them with fragrant, fresh-baked manchet bread, marmalade, and ale. Tamlin had once overheard the maids Dolly and Larajin complain of Brilla's harshness, and to this day, he couldn't understand it. The woman was always sweet as a sugar-sop to him.

With food in his belly, he felt better still, and as he and Escevar made their way to the courtyard, he was actually smiling in anticipation of the day ahead.

When he stepped outside into the bracing cold, he found that all was in readiness. The grooms had the horses saddled, and a pair of greyhounds roamed excitedly about the cobbles. Master Cletus, the falconer, had two hooded hawks waiting on their conical wooden blocks, while a third already perched on Brom's gauntleted wrist. It was a tiercel, ordinarily a hawk for ladies and boys, but as much bird, Tamlin had thought, as the wizard should try to manage his first time out. Judging from the leery way Brom was handling the bird, his arm extended to keep its beak and talons as far as possible from his face, Tamlin had been correct. Meanwhile, aloof from all the commotion, Vox lounged in a doorway.

Vox was Tamlin's personal bodyguard, and few who saw him doubted his fitness for the task. A hulking, swarthy, middle-aged mute with a shaggy black beard and long hair tied in a braid, he wore studded leather armor. A bastard sword rode sheathed on his back, a short sword and dirk hung at his waist, and he'd tucked another dagger into each of his high boots where squares of bronze were riveted to stop an enemy's blade.

When the greyhounds spotted Tamlin, they dashed up to fawn on him. He crooned to them and petted them for a moment, then advanced to greet his human retainers. The dogs romped along at his heels.

"Good morning!" Tamlin said. "It's a meeting of the masters, I see, master falconer and master magician, too. It looks like you're all ready to go, Brom."

"Uh, yes," the skinny young wizard replied. "Master Cletus insisted that I start becoming accustomed to the bird, and vice versa. But in truth, I wonder if this outing is wise. We might be needed here."

Tamlin grinned. "You just want to stay indoors, where it's warm." He'd noticed Brom's aversion to the cold on the very day that Father brought him into the household. "But I promise you, once the birds start flying, you'll forget all about the chill. Falconry is the grandest game on earth, or at least the grandest you can play without a pretty girl."

"It's not the cold," Brom said. "Are you aware that Lord and Lady Uskevren didn't come home last night?"

"I wasn't, and now that I am, I say, so what?"

"Master Cale is quite concerned."

Tamlin snorted. "He would be. Any excuse to be glum and grim! But the fact of the matter is, Father is frequently gone overnight, and sometimes Mother is too when she visits her friends."

"I understand that," said Brom, his cheeks ruddy above his patchy beard, "but according to Erevis, when Lady Uskevren is going to sleep elsewhere, she always informs him in advance, and if you'll excuse my commenting on their personal habits, it's extremely unusual for your mother and father to spend a night away from home in one another's company."

"Well, maybe the old goat is finally starting to appreciate her. Look, wizard, as I understand it, Father was busy with those dreary emissaries from the other side of the sea all morning, and in consequence, he and Mother didn't depart until mid-afternoon. They probably couldn't make it back before dark, and it was truly cold last night, and snowing as well. Rather than ride all the way home through the worst of it, they likely stopped at an inn, or one of the family tallhouses closer to the bridge."

"That does sound plausible," Brom admitted. The tiercel shifted its feet, jingling the bell attached to its ankle, and he flinched just a little. "But I had a bad feeling when they rode out without an escort, and without any of us knowing precisely where they were headed, or why."

"You're every bit as bad as Erevis, fretting over 'feelings'! I guarantee you, nothing happened to my parents, and even if it had, Father can take care of himself. Believe me, I know. I spent my boyhood stupefied with boredom at the umpteenth retelling of his exploits, his doomed but valiant defense of the first Stormweather Towers, his daring trading expeditions into Cormyr and the Dales, his defiant return to Selgaunt, and all the rest of it."

"So you're not worried at all?"

"Why should I be? That's why my family employs retainers, to worry for us and sort our problems out. Retainers like you, but you won't do any sorting today. Today you're going to learn hawking!"

Brom smiled wryly. "Very well, sir—"

"Deuce, please."

"Deuce, then. I hear and obey."

The wizard had to give the tiercel back to Cletus while he clambered onto his mount. Meanwhile, Escevar collected the saker he was fond of, and Tamlin took Honeylass, his bronze gyrfalcon, onto his wrist.

"I think we'll ride by the river," he said, stroking the hawk's feathers. "Perhaps you can take a crane."

When everyone was in the saddle, the hawking party headed out the gate into the busy street, the greyhounds loping at the head of the procession. Tamlin, Escevar, and Brom rode palfreys, while Vox, bringing up the rear, sat astride a massive black destrier strong enough to bear his weight.

Tamlin soon noticed that Brom managed a horse almost as awkwardly as he did a hawk. He started giving the magician pointers, alternating between expounding on equestrianism and discussing the art of seduction with Escevar, who was jogging along on his other side. So much talking quickly dried his throat, but fortunately, the grooms had performed their duties well. They'd hung a wineskin from his pommel, and no doubt tucked a flask of brandy or aqua vitae in his saddlebag as well.

Tamlin was just tugging the leather stopper out of the wineskin, the action made a trifle more difficult by Honeylass's weight on his wrist, when a barrier of glistening ice, its edges momentarily flickering with blue and violet light, sprang up to bar the way. It materialized just in front of the greyhounds, who yelped and recoiled, while the horses whinnied and shied. Brom's mount reared, and the spellcaster nearly fell off. The tiercel on his arm screamed and spread its wings.

"Watch out!" Escevar shouted.

Dropping the wineskin, Tamlin wheeled his dappled gelding around and perceived that he and his companions had ridden into an ambuscade, with the barricade of ice conjured to hold them in the killing box. Men with crossbows were leaning out of upper-story windows, while others with naked blades scrambled from doorways and the mouths of alleys. The other innocent folk unfortunate enough to be trapped on this particular stretch of street at this particular time scurried to get out of the waylayers' path.

Though Tamlin had no particular love of fighting, either for sport or in deadly earnest, every nobleman was schooled in the martial arts, and his training now took over. Guiding his steed with his knees, he dropped the wineskin and reached for his sword, remembering only as he grasped the hilt that it was a blunt, fragile ornament of glass. He wouldn't even be able to wield it unless he freed it from the loops that secured it to his belt, and then it would almost certainly break into pieces on the first swing. Useless!

A crossbow bolt whizzed past his head.

As a ragged child who seldom had a penny in his pocket, Brom Selwick had loved the puppeteers, storytellers, and itinerant players who provided free entertainment in the plazas and markets of Selgaunt. And in the tales of high adventure and bloodcurdling terror the young Brom had relished most, wizards, whether good or evil, had all been of a certain type. Keen of eye, aquiline of countenance, and luxuriant of beard, the mages uniformly possessed an imperious manner, even as they fairly reeked of awesome powers and secret knowledge.

Brom knew full well that he did not measure up to

this popular stereotype. Most people saw him as bookish, awkward, and diffident, and he had to admit that in many situations, it was all true. But if casual acquaintances inferred from his mild demeanor that he was useless in a fight, in that they were very much mistaken.

Upon completing his apprenticeship in the mystic arts, Brom had taken service as a ship's mage, and as he sailed about the Sea of Fallen Stars, honed his battle sorcery in numerous clashes with corsairs from the Pirate Isles and later the savage sea creatures called sahuagin, when they waged their war upon mankind. He most certainly could acquit himself well in combat.

Ordinarily, that was. When he didn't have a wild killer bird screeching and flapping on his wrist, and a frightened mare shifting and heaving beneath him more treacherously than, it seemed to him now, any storm-tossed cog ever had.

The horse tried to lurch into a gallop, though Mystra only knew where it thought there was to escape to. Nearly thrown from the saddle, Brom heaved on the reins with all his strength and forced the animal to stand. The wretched tiercel screeched again, and clutched his wrist so tightly that it hurt despite his thick falconer's glove.

Brom surveyed the battlefield and spied swordsmen and their ilk charging up the snowy street, crossbowmen in windows, and, perched high above the action atop a roof, a masked figure in dark blue clothing with a vague, murky shape crouched at his side. No doubt it was the wizard who'd produced the wall of ice, attended by some sort of familiar.

Brom decided he must trust Vox and Escevar to fend off the attackers on the ground, for only his magic could reach the others. And since the masked wizard didn't appear to be conjuring at the moment, the crossbowmen posed the more immediate threat.

Wishing he'd brought his staff—it had no magical attributes, but he always felt more wizardly when he had it in his hands—Brom shouted a word of power and thrust out his fist, springing his fingers open as his arm became fully extended. Though the tiercel's weight hampered him, the gesture nonetheless adhered to the proper form. Shafts of scarlet light leaped from his fingertips, and, their trajectories diverging, struck five of the crossbowmen. Two of the bullies fell from their windows and slammed down on the ground. The others were thrown backward out of sight.

Brom needed the materials tucked away in his pockets to work most of the rest of his spells, and he couldn't take them out, juggle the hawk, and control the agitated palfrey at the same time. He abruptly remembered Master Cletus explaining that if he unhooded the tiercel and flipped his arm, the bird would fly. He hastily released it to go wherever it wanted, and then one of the surviving crossbowmen shot his mare in the head.

The animal dropped. Brom frantically kicked free of the stirrups, and, thanks more to luck than athleticism, a quality of which he had little, flung himself clear of the falling carcass.

Even though the greater portion of his body lacked grace, his hands were deft enough. Even as he floundered in the cold, much-trodden snow, he snatched a wisp of cobweb from a pocket, recited an incantation, and used the gossamer to trace a mystic symbol on the air.

A thick swatch of meshed gray cables materialized across the row of windows from which attackers were still shooting. Suddenly trapped amid the sticky strands, the crossbowmen struggled vainly to extricate themselves, then called to the mage on the roof for help.

Ah yes, thought Brom, his teeth bared in a fierce grin that would have amazed any acquaintance who had never seen him in the heat of battle, our friend on the roof. He glanced about, making sure he was in no immediate danger from any of the enemy swordsmen, then began sending the masked wizard a little token of his regard. He snatched out a tiny ball composed of sulfur and guano, murmured a couplet, and tossed the orb into the air. The ball hurtled up at the spell-caster in blue, and as it did so, swelled in size and burst into crackling yellow flame, so it resembled a missile of blazing naphtha hurled from a catapult.

Brom expected that the other mage would die in the impending blast, but the detonation never happened. Evidently the masked man had warded himself with some manner of defensive enchantment, for the burning missile winked out of existence a yard or so before it struck its target. Brom couldn't be sure at such a distance, but he thought he saw the shadow creature leer at him.

It seemed to Tamlin that with the crossbowmen out of commission, the enemy was having a harder time of it. Then Tamlin saw his bodyguard. His black braid streaming out behind him, revealing the ugly scar on his neck, Vox rode among the bravos like an avenging fury. His bastard sword flashed up and down, up and down, and it seemed that every time it descended, a foeman perished. His huge mount was scarcely less formidable, kicking, biting, and trampling the fallen beneath its hooves.

Escevar lacked the advantage of a trained war-horse, but he was a skilled rider, and evidently his chestnut palfrey was game, for its master seemed to have no difficulty guiding it amongst the bravos. Whooping as if the fight were nothing more than some sort of roughhousing game, the redhead hacked and slashed with a will, and while he was scarcely the warrior Vox was, something, his sheer audacity perhaps, had thus far kept him safe from harm.

After a futile attempt at slaying the masked wizard, Brom too had turned his attention to neutralizing the attackers on the ground, blinding some with a handful of sparkling golden powder and choking others with a vile-smelling greenish vapor. Tamlin suspected that if one of the bravos could only close with Brom, he could put an end to the unarmed mage and his troublesome spells in a trice, but so far, none of them had managed it.

Meanwhile, the scion of the House of Uskevren sheltered helplessly between his friends and the barrier of ice with his ridiculous pink crystal bodkin at his side. It made him feel vaguely ashamed, and he scowled and reminded himself that after all, these people were paid to protect him.

Bubbles of purple light appeared among the combatants, swelled, and burst, leaving in their place gaunt, mottled green things that would have been half again as tall as a man had they stood fully erect. Their limbs were long and graceless, and masses of iron-gray tendrils writhed atop their heads. Their black eyes were round and sunken, their noses, grotesquely long, and their wide mouths were lined with yellow fangs.

The enemy swordsmen instinctively shied away from the trolls. Vox, Escevar, and Brom maneuvered frantically to engage these new and far more formidable foes. But four creatures had materialized, and the Uskevren retainers only managed to intercept three of them. Despite its clumsy, ill-made appearance, the remaining troll shambled toward Tamlin fast as a man could run, its clawed, four-fingered hands dragging through the snow.

Tamlin's dappled gelding went wild with fear, and as he fought to control the animal, he felt on the brink of panic himself. With the ice barrier behind him and the troll in front, there was nowhere to run. Even if by some miracle he could dodge around the creature—and he was all but certain that one of those long, thin arms would whip out and pluck him from the saddle if he tried—he doubted any unarmed man could ride unscathed through the band of bravos behind it. Finally, he realized there was one place to go, even if it would only buy him a few seconds.

He snatched off Honeylass's leather hood and sent her toward the troll's head. The gyrfalcon had never been trained to attack such monstrosities, and, winging to the left, she sensibly veered off at once. Even so, the troll apparently considered the hawk a threat, or perhaps the conjured creature was simply startled. At any rate, it stopped charging long enough to swat Honeylass from the air, then took another moment to shake the bird's carcass off its long, curved claws.

Meanwhile, Tamlin spurred the gelding toward the

open entrance to someone's shop. He ducked beneath the lintel of the doorway, and the horse knocked over a rack of men's hats, which fell to the floor with a crash. Soft caps, high-crowned copotains, and other examples of masculine headwear tumbled about, some of them to be immediately trampled by the gelding's stamping feet.

Tamlin tried to straighten up, bumped his head on the ceiling, cursed, and stooped once more. His scalp smarting, he peered about the shop. As he'd feared, there didn't seem to be another exit, certainly not one he could take a horse through, and if he attempted to flee on foot, he suspected the nimble, long-legged troll would run him down.

The hatter, a stout, black-bearded man with orange dye stains on his fingertips, evidently knew why Tamlin had ridden into the shop, for he gaped up at the aristocrat with horror in his eyes. "Get out of here!" he wailed.

"A weapon!" Tamlin replied. All shopkeepers kept weapons on the premises to fend off thieves, didn't they? Torm's fist, he hoped so!

"Get out!" the merchant repeated.

"The troll will burst in here in a matter of seconds," Tamlin replied. "One of us will have to fight it. Unless you want to do it, give me a weapon!"

The hatter threw up his hands and raced for the counter at the back of the shop. Deciding he'd be better off on foot than trying to maneuver his terrified horse through the clutter of hat racks and tables, Tamlin dismounted and followed the other man.

The hatter reached around under the counter, produced a cudgel, and thrust the weapon at Tamlin, who regarded it with a feeling not far from despair. A blunt little stick like this might rattle the brains of a common rogue, but it would be virtually useless against a troll. But the club was still, he reflected, marginally better than the glass sword; at least people wouldn't laugh so hard when they saw it in his cold, dead hand. He reached for it, the horse screamed, and the troll made a horrible, wet slobbering sound as it hurtled through the door.

Tamlin whirled to face his pursuer, and it was only then that he glimpsed the rusty single-bitted axe leaning in a shadowy corner. It wasn't a battle-axe but a tool for hewing wood to fuel the stove in the center of the room, which was probably why the panicky dolt of a hatter hadn't thought of it, but it would serve Tamlin better than a cudgel if he could only get to it in time.

He dashed for it, hoping the troll would stop to slaughter his horse, but no such luck. Crouched as it was, the creature had no difficulty maneuvering under the comparatively low ceiling, and it charged straight at him, yellow foam flying from its jaws, the claws at the end of one long arm stretched out to rend him.

Tamlin thrust out his own arm and knocked over a rack of beaver and ermine hats. It fell in the troll's path, and, as he'd prayed, the creature stumbled over it, affording him the final second he needed to grab the axe.

That was the good aspect of his situation. The bad was that the troll had him in a corner. He fought better with a sword, the gentleman's arm, than an axe, and the implement in his hands wasn't even a proper weapon.

He tried to control his breathing, tried to be calm, tried to remember the combat training that he'd often attended so grudgingly, tried it all in that last instant and then the troll was on him.

The creature raked at him with both hands simultaneously. He swayed back, and the filthy claws at the end of the long green fingers missed him by an inch. The rending motion rocked the troll forward, and, following through, it brought its mouth down to bite. Its maw gaped wide enough to engulf his entire head, and its breath was so foul that his stomach turned.

Tamlin thrust upward with the axe as if it were a spear. The steel head cracked against the troll's jaw, breaking fangs and jolting the creature back. The noble immediately chopped a gash in its breast, then cut at its knee and nearly severed its leg. The moss-green horror fell backward, and as it did, Tamlin seized the opportunity to spring past it and extricate himself from the corner.

Though the wounds Tamlin had inflicted would have incapacitated any human being, the troll was scarcely that, and the aristocrat knew his stalker wasn't finished. Sure enough, still quick despite the injury to its leg, the black-eyed thing spun around and flung itself at him with claws outstretched.

Tamlin scrambled backward and kept retreating as the troll crawled after him, its claws splintering the floorboards.

Tamlin reckoned that if he wanted to survive this encounter, he'd better finish the brute off fast. He stopped retreating, giving the troll another chance to grab at him, then met the creature's arm with a stroke of the axe. The bit crunched into the troll's wrist and sheared off its four-fingered hand.

Instantly he rushed in to attack the troll's body and head, while the creature reared up, supported by its remaining hand. It bit at him, and he dodged. It clubbed at him with its raw, bloody stump, and he parried with the axe, meanwhile shifting into position to chop its good arm.

The axe cut into the stringy muscle just above its elbow, whereupon, suddenly unable to support itself, the troll crashed facedown on the floor. Bellowing with rage, Tamlin hewed at the creature's head and spine.

The troll heaved itself over onto its side, where it tried to fend off the axe with its handless arm, kick Tamlin with its three-toed feet, and thrash and flop itself into position to bite his leg. He avoided its flailing legs and gnashing fangs and kept on hewing until something grabbed hold of his ankle.

He let out a startled gasp and looked down to see the troll's severed hand clutching his leg. In the instant he was thus distracted, the troll finally landed a kick to the side of his head, flinging him backward and into another display rack. The collision knocked it over, and he sprawled to the floor amid an assortment of felt tricornes.

For a second, the world seemed silent and empty of significance. He realized dimly that the kick had stunned him, that he might even be in danger of passing out, and he struggled to break through the daze. By the time he managed it, he felt a crawling on his thigh.

The troll's hand had clambered up his leg. Though still a little addled, he realized that it might have found it difficult to plunge its claws through his thick leather boots, but would have no trouble with the velvet breeches higher up.

Somehow, Tamlin had kept hold of the axe. He used the butt of the haft to knock the severed hand off his thigh and followed up with a chop. The hand hopped backward, avoiding the stroke, and then a shadow fell over him.

He looked up. The troll had gotten back on its feet and was now bending over him, its fanged, reeking jaws hurtling down to tear his face off. He whirled the axe up to meet them.

The bloody bit thudded deep into the creature's head. The troll lurched sideways and collapsed. Tamlin studied it for a second, making sure it truly had stopped moving, then wrenched himself around to see what the severed hand was doing. It was inert as well.

Tamlin floundered to his feet, gave the troll a few more axe strokes for good measure, then turned to the hatter, who was cowering behind the counter.

"Burn this thing," the noble panted. "Otherwise, it will come back to life."

A soft slurping sound came from the troll's mangled body as its hand began to regenerate.

"*Me* burn it!" the hatter replied. "What about you?"

Tamlin realized it was a good question. He could tell from the noise that the battle still raged outside, and it would be perfectly reasonable for him to chop an exit in the rear wall and avoid the rest of it. He doubted anyone would blame him. As he'd already observed to himself, when necessary, retainers were supposed to sacrifice themselves to cover their lord's retreat. Still, now that he finally had a weapon, he found he couldn't quite bring himself to decamp.

"I have to go help Escevar," he said.

He noticed that the gelding was still present. He'd always heard that horses were rather stupid beasts, and perhaps the palfrey had lacked the wit to find its way back out the exit, or perhaps it had been as afraid of the commotion outside the shop as of the troll within. Whatever the reason, Tamlin was glad the steed was still available for his use. He crossed the room, grabbed the balky animal by the halter, and dragged it toward the exit.

"Who's going to pay for all this damage?" the hatter called after him.

Scrambling backward, wishing fervently that he hadn't squandered his ball of flame on the wizard atop the roof, Brom snatched two small vials and a tiny speaking trumpet fashioned from the tip of a ram's horn out of his pockets. He anointed the horn with the contents of the vials, swirled it through an intricate mystic pass, lifted it to its lips, and shouted.

The blast of sound that erupted from the trumpet's bell was far louder than any voice augmented by mere mechanical means. It jabbed painfully into Brom's ears, and the troll that was scuttling after him, and at which he had aimed the magical noise, fared worse. The creature clutched at its ears, swayed, and collapsed.

Mystra grant the ugly thing would stay down for a minute or two before rising to menace him anew. Wheezing, mentally reviewing which of the spells he'd prepared had already been cast and which were still available, Brom surveyed the battlefield.

One troll, its upper body crisscrossed by long cuts presumably delivered by Vox's bastard sword, lay crumpled in the snow, and the black-bearded bodyguard was furiously battling another.

His chest and thigh bloody, Escevar strove to defend himself from half a dozen bravos. Evidently some of the ruffians had overcome their wariness of the trolls and advanced up the street to reinforce them.

Tamlin was nowhere to be seen.

Moving in a leisurely way, the masked wizard raised his arms to commence another spell.

Brom suspected that if he and his companions didn't escape this trap before the enemy wizard completed his next conjuration, they were going to die. Which meant he had to create a way out. It took priority over everything, even locating Lord Uskevren's missing heir or assisting the hard-pressed Escevar.

He turned his back on the battle to face the wall of gleaming, translucent ice. He was half deaf from the shouting magic, and now he was glad, for with the clamor of the battle muted, he would find it that much easier to concentrate.

It had become apparent early on that the man in blue was an accomplished wizard, and nothing he'd created would be easily dispelled. But, Brom told himself, if he performed the abjuration perfectly, it could be done. Refusing to hurry, he stood tall, recited the incantation with impeccable clarity and cadence, and swung his arms apart with perfect timing.

The ice vanished.

"Run! This way!" Brom called.

Vox drove his troll back with a two-handed sweep of his sword, then wheeled his destrier and rode for the open path. Escevar looked as if he understood and was likewise trying to break free, but the bravos kept him hemmed in.

Intending to cast a spell to help his fellow retainer, Brom reached into his mantle for a small iron bar. Before he could fish it out, Tamlin led his horse out of a shop entrance, looked wildly about, and swung himself into the saddle. Shouting a war cry, the young aristocrat charged his friend's assailants and scattered them with strokes from a gory axe. Tamlin, Escevar, and Vox raced on out of the broken killing box toward safety.

Leaving Brom afoot and alone.

As the enemy advanced on him, he wondered if any of his companions had even realized he was still alive, his horse was dead, and they were abandoning him to die. With his most potent magic already spent, he couldn't fend off all these attackers alone. He preferred to believe that none of them had known, although Vox and Escevar might well have felt that their first duty was to escort their master safely away, while Tamlin, Brom suspected, was rather too fond of himself to risk his skin for a retainer whom he'd only known a short time.

A grinning troll slunk toward him, claws poised to rip. Bubbles of violet light swelled as the masked wizard summoned new minions, though Brom couldn't believe that the conjuror truly thought he needed them. Then, though with his abused ears, he couldn't hear it, through the soles of his buskins he felt the rhythmic shocks of something pounding up behind him.

Brom spun around. Tamlin was racing toward him, evidently guiding his mount with his knees, for he had one hand outstretched and the woodcutter's axe grasped in the other. The dappled gelding's flanks were bloody from his spurs, and its hooves threw up puffs of snow.

The nobleman wheeled the horse, slowing of necessity, but not stopping. Brom scrambled forward, clutched at Tamlin's hand and the tooled red leather saddle, and tried to hoist himself up onto the moving animal. His right hand fumbled and slipped away from the pommel, and he felt himself begin to fall. Grunting with the strain, Tamlin held him in place until he achieved a firm grip. The gelding ran back up the street with the wizard half draped across its neck and half dangling beside its shoulder.

Brom looked back. Their enemies were sprinting after them, and the troll in the lead was nearly close enough to reach out and grab the palfrey's streaming tail. Certain the pursuers were going to catch up, the wizard wondered if he could possibly cast a spell from his present precarious position, and whether he should drop back into the street and let the gelding race on unencumbered by his awkward and unbalanced weight. Then Tamlin dug in the spurs, shouted encouragement, and somehow the horse found the strength to gallop even faster than before, leaving their foes behind.

They rounded a corner and almost collided with Vox and Escevar hurtling back in the other direction. "I've got him!" Tamlin cried. "Follow me!" The retainers turned their steeds around.

They kept galloping until, Brom judged, there was no danger of their adversaries catching up with them, at which point Tamlin called for a stop in a spacious plaza. At the other end of the square, urchins were flinging snowballs at one another and any passersby unwary enough to wander into range.

Brom gratefully abandoned his uncomfortable perch and peered up at his companions. Though a troll's claws had twice shredded his armor and lightly scored the flesh beneath, Vox was as stolid as ever. The more seriously wounded Escevar, however, was pale and shaky, in marked contrast to his exuberance earlier on. Ruddy-faced and breathing heavily, Tamlin was clearly having difficulty calming down, although whether he was seething with anger or fear, Brom couldn't tell. Probably a mixture of the two.

"I didn't mean to abandon you," said Tamlin to the wizard. "I just lost track of you in all the chaos. I rode back as soon as I realized you weren't with us."

Or else you did intend to forsake me, but had a change of heart, thought Brom, but even if that was true, he wasn't inclined to hold it against Tamlin. In the end, the aristocrat had risked his own life to rescue him, and that was all that mattered. "Thank you," the wizard said.

Vox tapped his massive chest with his forefinger.

"I know," Tamlin said, "I should have told you to go. But I was excited, and I figured every second counted. Are you all right, Escevar?"

The redhead gave him a jerky nod.

"We'll get you to a healer as soon as the horses have had a moment to rest," Tamlin said, and then a quaver of agitation entered his voice. "Ilmater's tears, it just came home to me that Honeylass is dead! The other birds are lost. And the poor greyhounds! I forgot all about them until this second. Did anyone see what happened to the dogs?"

"No," said Brom. "As you said, all was confusion. I'm afraid it's likely they're slain or run away for good."

"Curse it!" With trembling hands, Tamlin extricated his glass blade from the loops on his golden sword belt. The ornament had miraculously emerged unscathed from the battle, but now its owner lashed it against the wall of a vendor's kiosk, shattering it into tiny fragments.

"Did that make you feel better?" Brom asked.

Tamlin smiled. "A little."

"Then we'd better think about what just happened," the spellcaster said. "Obviously, that ambuscade was no haphazard affair with robbers assaulting the first gentleman who happened along. That was a carefully planned attempt to assassinate the heir to the House of Uskevren, and I daresay it's no coincidence that it happened the morning after your parents vanished."

Tamlin grimaced. "I hate to admit it, but you're probably right. Damn my father for disappearing! It's his province to deal with this sort of unpleasantness, not mine. But since he's gone, I suppose we'd better get back to Stormweather Towers and confer with the others."

CHAPTER 10

It was Larajin who'd come to the library to inform Talbot of the conclave, and she opted to walk along with him to the great hall as well. Ordinarily, he would have taken pleasure in her company, for he and the willowy maid with the rust-colored hair and striking hazel eyes had been friends for as long as he could remember. At present, however, he was frustrated at his lack of progress in the researches that he had prayed would provide a cure for his affliction, and, their futility notwithstanding, equally vexed at being summoned away.

"Why is Tamlin, of all people, calling a family meeting?" he grumbled. "What does he want to talk about, brandy and lace?"

"I don't know," Larajin said, the silver bells on her golden turban chiming as she moved. The turban was a part of her maidservant's livery, devised to warn her masters, who might desire privacy, of her approach. "But it was Master Cale who bade me pass the word to you, and he said the matter is urgent."

"Ordinarily, that would be good enough for me," Talbot conceded. "But—"

One of the household pets, a fawn-colored mastiff, wandered out of a doorway just ahead. It gave the humans an incurious glance, turned, started to amble away from them, then suddenly spun back around. Crouching, the fur standing up on its back, the dog bared its teeth and growled.

Talbot winced. He understood what was happening, for he'd experienced it on various occasions since the calamity that had befallen him just over a year ago. For the most part, animals responded to him the same as they had before, but periodically, they sensed the wolf-thing that lurked inside him and wrested control of his body at every full moon. He suspected it was more likely to happen at moments like this, when he was angry.

"Brownie!" Larajin said. "What's gotten into you?" Heedless of the mastiff's menacing demeanor, she advanced and slapped her thigh. "Heel!"

Brownie slunk to her side, and Talbot wasn't altogether surprised. Larajin had always had a way with animals, and for some reason, over the past several months or so, the rapport had deepened to the point that she rarely experienced any difficulty inducing any of the various beasts inhabiting Stormweather Towers to do her bidding.

"I'll take him back in here and calm him down," said the maid, taking hold of the mastiff's leather collar. "You go on." She led the now-docile animal back through the doorway. Talbot trudged on to the conclave alone, his mood even more sour than before.

The feast hall was a large chamber adorned with marble-sheathed pillars and lamps of brown iridescent glass. In fact, Talbot reflected as he entered, it was so spacious that it was ridiculous for a mere six people to use it for a meeting. They would have been just as comfortable, possibly more so, in a smaller room, and then the servants wouldn't have been inconvenienced when they had to trek from one end of the mansion to the other. As it was, the help would have to avoid both the centrally located feast hall and the galleries overlooking it, lest they overhear a confidential discussion. Talbot supposed that it had never occurred to his preening peacock of a brother to preside over a conference anywhere except in the grandest setting available.

Talbot saw that all the others had arrived before him. Jander Orvist, the captain of the household guard, gave him a terse nod. Jander was a lean, middle-aged man with a thin, humorless trap of a mouth, fierce silvery eyes, and a pronounced gray widow's peak. No matter how innocent or festive the occasion, Talbot had never known the grizzled warrior to wear anything but the blue tunic of the Uskevren's soldiery, nor seen him without a long sword ready to hand.

Clad in a décolleté emerald caffa gown her mother hated, Tazi sat glowering, impatient for the meeting to commence and probably to end, until she gave her younger brother a welcoming smile. Erevis in his ill-fitting doublet looked somber as ever. His polished oak staff leaning against the arm of his chair, Brom seemed equally grave, but then, eager to impress, he tended to appear that way even when performing the most trivial duty.

It was Tamlin, who had of course usurped Father's seat at the head of the long inlaid table, who gave Talbot his first intimation that he ought to take this meeting seriously. Not simply because he was frowning. Tamlin *occasionally* adopted a serious manner, and it was usually over something utterly trivial. But today the heir had a bruise coming up on the left side of his face, and although he was dressed as gorgeously as ever, in a sky-blue outfit that made Talbot unpleasantly conscious of his own uncombed hair, lack of a doublet, and stale, half open shirt, he had, as was rare of late, added a businesslike long sword and poniard to his ensemble. The hilts were excessively ornate, made of gold adorned with sapphires, but to Talbot's knowledgeable eye, the weapons looked as if they'd serve well in a melee even so. Even more curiously, an axe, a simple laborer's tool, lay on the table before him.

"You took your time getting here," said Tamlin, a little petulantly.

"Sorry," Talbot grunted, flinging himself into the empty seat beside Tazi. "What's going on?"

"Mother and Father are missing," Tamlin said, milking the announcement for all the drama it was worth, "and not two hours ago, someone tried to assassinate me."

"What?" Talbot exclaimed, while Tazi's sea-green eyes widened. In contrast, the retainers didn't look surprised, merely concerned. Plainly, they'd heard the news already.

"Tell it all from the beginning," Jander suggested. "That way, we'll have it clear in our heads."

"I—" said Brom and Erevis in unison, then the gangling wizard waved his hand, deferring to the steward.

"I can tell about Lord and Lady Uskevren's departure," said Erevis, who proceeded to do so. Talbot knew his parents had ridden out, but this was the first he'd heard of the retainers' misgivings.

"We could dispatch search parties," Tazi said when the bald major-domo finished.

"We will," Erevis replied, "but first, let's try to discern exactly what's going on. Master Tamlin, please, tell us about the ambuscade."

Tamlin nodded and gave them the tale. Talbot assumed it was factual in its essence, though embellished to make the teller seem more of a hero. For could his self-centered popinjay of a brother truly have slain a troll single-handed, or, when already free of the trap, ridden back into dire peril to rescue a retainer? To say the least, it was unlikely. At one point, Talbot elbowed Tazi, and the pair exchanged ironic, skeptical glances. Still, there were weightier matters to consider than their elder brother's mendacity, and their shared amusement lasted only an instant.

"It's far from certain that these two situations actually have anything to do with one another," observed Talbot at the story's conclusion. "Mother and Father left the mansion of their own volition, they haven't been gone that long, and there are any number of reasons why they might be slow in returning."

"With all due respect," said Brom, "as I mentioned before, Lady Uskevren's manner seemed odd."

"Still—" Talbot began.

Tazi lifted her hand. "There's something about Mother that none of the rest of you knows. A little over a year ago, when she and I went to hear the Hulorn's opera—"

"There was harmful magic woven into the music," said Tamlin, impatiently, "and you and Mother had to snatch away the conductor's baton or something to halt the performance and break the spell. We do know. We've heard the story."

Tazi glared at him. "You haven't heard all of it. Stopping the opera was more difficult than anyone knows, and in the course of it, Mother took up a sword and battled statues come to life, fighting as well as anyone in this room. She also scaled a wall, jumped off a roof into a tree, then climbed through the branches nimbly as a squirrel. Through it all, she was grinning and joking like a different person, an adventurer who relished risk and didn't care a rotten apple about decorum."

Tamlin snorted. "That's absurd. Mother doesn't like weapons. I doubt she ever handled any implement more formidable than an embroidery needle in her entire life."

"I swear to you, it happened," the black-haired girl retorted, her level tone so convincing that Talbot realized that, although her assertion was indeed "absurd," he believed her. Apparently everyone else did as well, for the hall fell silent for a moment as they tried to assimilate what they'd heard.

Erevis gazed at Tazi. "You might have told someone before today," he said, a hint of reproach in his voice.

To Talbot's surprise, his sister, who never accepted blame or rebuke from anyone, flushed and lowered her eyes. "She asked me to keep her secret."

But why would you, Talbot silently wondered, when you

and she were always at one another's throats? Then he realized that his mother had probably been in a position to reveal some secret of Thazienne's as well.

As if he'd arrived at a similar inference, Jander scowled and said, "There have always been too cursed many secrets in this household. I don't know what most of them are, but I sense they exist, and I always feared one of them would rear up and bite us on the arse someday."

"If this one has," Tamlin said. "I'm not certain it did. How is it Mother knew how to fight, and what has it got to do with what's happening now?"

Tazi grimaced. "I don't know," she admitted. "She never would explain herself. But I suspect there's a connection."

"Perhaps," said Erevis, frowning, "but I for one don't understand it, just as we have absolutely no clue as to what's become of Lord and Lady Uskevren. Perhaps we should focus on the situation we know more about: the attempted assassination. Let's think about who might have been behind it."

"My guess is that the masked wizard was leading the attack," said Tamlin. "But that doesn't mean he was the instigator. He could have been acting for someone else."

"I agree," said Erevis. "The question is, who? The Foehammer knows, the Uskevren have made their share of enemies over the years. But there are five rival Houses that wished the family ill long before you three were even born, and all remain inimical to this day."

Tazi ran her fingers through her hair, a sign that she was pondering. "Soargyl, Talendar, Baerodreemer, Ithivisk, and Malveen."

Tamlin frowned. "Gellie Malveen is a friend of mine."

Tazi gazed at him with withering scorn. "Let's hope that our fears are groundless, and no one has murdered Father. If an idiot like you is now head of the family, we're doomed."

Tamlin flushed. "If I am in charge—"

"Please!" said Erevis, and Tamlin fell silent. The heir had never been fond of the butler the way his siblings were, but perhaps he'd come to respect him after the events of last winter, when undead marauders had attacked the mansion, and, to everyone's amazement, Erevis had demonstrated that he knew how to fight.

As, apparently, did Mother. Talbot sighed, for Jander was right. Every member of the family, except, he supposed, his feckless brother, harbored secrets, and in consequence their lives were complicated and strange. Not for the first time, he imagined how pleasant it would be to abdicate his position here and become a simple player. But he knew he never could, not when he might one day need his House's resources to rid himself of the beast within.

"I believe that what Mistress Thazienne was trying to say," Erevis continued, "was that while young Gellie may indeed be your friend, it's always been the way of Selgaunt for nobles to trade and socialize one day and attempt to destroy one another the next. Moreover, however your crony feels, it's unlikely that his opinion would soften the animus of the elders of his House."

"Think about it," Tazi said. "Your precious Gellie knew you meant to ride from Stormweather Towers to Argent Hall this morning. He and the other Malveen would have known where to set the trap."

"It doesn't matter," Tamlin retorted. "There are plenty of other ways that an enemy might have learned of my plans."

"Yes," Erevis said, "in point of fact, there are. We haven't shortened our list of suspects at all, and therefore, Masters Tamlin and Brom, I ask you: Did you observe *anything* that might enable us to do so?"

The heir and the magician frowned, thinking, then finally shook their heads.

"Wonderful," said Tazi, in a tone that left no doubt that she thought there must have been a clue right in front of their eyes, had the two men only had the wit to notice. She turned to Brom. "Can't you use magic to discover who attacked you, and to find out what's become of Father and Mother while you're at it?"

Brom's thin face colored. "I'm afraid I'm not much of a hand at divination. No wizard can learn every spell in existence, and I've concentrated on other areas."

"Of course you have," said Tazi sardonically. "Moon above, I wish that old Cordrivval was still with us." Brom's predecessor Cordrivval Imleth, who had perished not so long ago in the Uskevren's service, had been an accomplished diviner.

"Don't belittle Master Selwick," Tamlin snapped. "He saved my life today."

"Don't worry," said Tazi, "I won't hold that against him."

Her brother scowled. "As I started to remark before, if something has happened to Mother and Father, and I am the head of this House, then I shall demand to be treated with respect. The insolent just might find themselves out on the street."

Talbot pushed his seat back from the table and started to rise. "How would you like a bruise on the other side of your face?" he asked his brother. "That way, the two halves will match."

"Stop it!" Brom bellowed, and at that startling roar, emerging from such an unassuming fellow, the siblings jerked around to stare at him. The wizard paled and swallowed. "Uh, that is to say, I beg your pardon. I didn't mean to raise my voice, but your squabbling isn't helping."

Tazi's mouth tightened. "No, it isn't, and I don't mean to make things difficult. It's just . . . the last time I saw Mother, we quarreled as usual. Now, I wish we hadn't."

"I understand," said Tamlin, "I'm just as worried about her as you are. And about Father too, I suppose."

"Well, we agree on that, anyway," said Talbot, settling back down on his chair.

"Good," said Erevis. "Now, we don't know very much, but based on what we do know, we can assume that unknown enemies have launched a campaign to destroy the House of Uskevren. They tried to assassinate you, Master Tamlin, and may have kidnapped or even killed your parents. We can expect further attempts on the lives of all three of you siblings.

"Here's what I propose we do about it," the steward

continued. "We'll look for Lord and Lady Uskevren. We'll mobilize our network of spies to see what they can discover. And we'll get you three children out of town forthwith, where you'll remain until this matter is resolved."

Tamlin nodded. "That sounds sensible enough."

Talbot agreed. It did sound sensible, but rather to his surprise, something about the suggestion stuck in his craw. "I have a performance tonight," he said.

Tamlin snorted. "Really, brother, I daresay Mistress Quickly will manage without you somehow."

"I'm sure she could," Talbot said, then paused, groping for the proper words, waving his hand before him as if he thought he could pluck them from the air. "It's just . . . our foes drove the Uskevren out of Selgaunt once before, and Father fought for years to regain our place here. I don't think we should let ourselves be driven forth again, not even for a little while. I don't want the other Houses to think us craven. That could incite all our rivals to attack us, and bring trouble down on our heads for years to come."

"At least you'd be alive to endure the trouble," Erevis said.

"Despite what you said, we're not children anymore," Talbot replied. "We can take care of ourselves." At least he hoped so.

"Do you know," said Jander to Erevis, "if they did stay in the city, and went about their usual affairs to prove they're not afraid, we could use them to bait a trap of our own. Guard them well but discreetly, overwhelm the assassins the next time they attack, wring some answers out of a captive, and get to the bottom of this."

Erevis shook his head. "I don't think Lord and Lady Uskevren would approve."

"Well, they're not here," said Tamlin unexpectedly, "and perhaps the troll's kick scrambled my brains, but reluctant as I am to say it, I think Talbot and Jander are making sense. We brothers shouldn't leave."

Tazi glared at him. "I don't like the implications of that last remark. I can handle myself as well as either of you."

"Ordinarily, that may be true," said Erevis, "but you're just emerging from a long convalescence." Tazi tried to speak, and the steward raised his hand to forestall her. "I know you're *nearly* well, but I still see you sway and stumble at odd moments. You can't afford to risk a murder attempt until that stops happening."

"I won't leave Selgaunt while Mother and Father are missing," Tazi said, "and you can't make me."

"Perhaps not," Erevis said, "but in that case, you should at least stay here in the mansion, where you'll be safe."

"I agree," Talbot said.

Tamlin nodded. "So do I."

"Damn it—" Tazi began, her green eyes blazing.

"As acting head of the family, I'm ordering you to do it," Tamlin said, cutting her off. "Just as I'm directing Captain Orvist to make sure you obey."

"So I'm your prisoner," Tazi spat. "Well, you can all burn in the Pit!" Then the defiance seemed to go out of her. "Oh, all right, I'll sit and rot in my cell."

"Thank you," Erevis said. "Now, let's discuss how we'll protect Master Talbot at the theater, and Master Tamlin when he goes to confer with the emissaries from across the sea."

"What?" Tamlin yelped. "I can't negotiate. I hate that kind of thing. Let's just stall the envoys and hope Father turns up."

"I already put them off once this morning," the major-domo replied, "when it became apparent that Lord Uskevren wasn't going to appear in time to keep the appointment. This alliance could be very beneficial to your family. Besides, if you want to create the appearance that the Uskevren aren't afraid to go about their business as usual, and if you are, as you've mentioned more than once, the acting head of the House—"

"Enough," Tamlin groaned, "I'll do it. But I'd far rather contend with another ambuscade."

Tazi gave him a sweet smile. "I hope you have the opportunity to do both."

CHAPTER 11

Its pale eyes shining, the earthen giant strode through the fortress wall as if it were made of paper, and a chip of flying stone stung Shamur's sword hand. She tried to dart around behind the elemental, where she hoped to remain undetected, but she was too slow. The dark, ungainly thing had spotted her already, and now it raised its fist to crush her.

Shamur poised herself to dodge the blow, race forward, cut at the creature's lead foot, and try to cripple it. Not that she truly thought her puny broadsword could hurt the elemental, but she'd rather die like a badger than a mouse.

Just as she shifted her weight forward, a hand gripped her forearm and pulled her back. She stumbled, momentarily off balance, and the giant's fist plummeted down.

She flung herself frantically aside, and the person who had taken hold of her must have done the same, because the elemental's blow missed them both. The impact shook the ground, threw up gouts of snow and soil, and jolted the humans off their feet.

As they scrambled up, she looked around to see Thamalon. Tugging at her again, he cried, "This way!"

He ran toward the north side of the courtyard, and, wondering what he could possibly have in mind, she followed. The shocks of their pursuer's footsteps made it a challenge merely to stay on their feet, and they had to keep glancing back to watch for its next attack.

The elemental raised its foot to stamp, and they scrambled out from underneath. Then Thamalon led Shamur into one of the buildings constructed along the base of the wall.

Glancing about, she found herself in a chapel, with a few rows of benches, and plaster statues of Torm, Tempus, and other deities perched on little wooden stands. Rocked by the giant's footsteps, some had already fallen off and shattered. Having seen the elemental stride through the castle ramparts, she knew, as Thamalon seemingly did not, that this place was no refuge. Not unless some god intended to manifest to protect his effigy from harm, and she rather suspected that wasn't going to happen.

But Shamur's husband kept rushing her toward the other end of the chamber, and after a moment, she saw the reason why. A short time ago, he'd evidently shifted the altar aside to uncover a square opening in the floor.

With a clattering crash, the elemental swept the roof of the chapel away as easily as a maid clearing cobwebs with a broom, leaving the chamber open to the sky. Leaning over the top of the wall, the creature reached for its quarry.

Shamur could see the top rung of a ladder affixed just below the rim of the shaft, but she and Thamalon had run out of time to use it. The nobleman took a last stride and jumped, and as the creature's hand plunged down at her, she did the same.

She fell for less than a second, then hit bottom, lost her

balance, and sprawled on an earthen floor. An instant later, the giant's hand smashed into the mouth of the shaft, and, too large to penetrate farther, lodged there, blocking out what little light had reached the bottom before. Clods of dirt pattered down.

Immediately there came a grinding, crunching noise, and more earth fell. Shamur realized the elemental was trying to force its arm down the shaft, and she thought it entirely possible that it would succeed. Even if its raw strength proved insufficient, it might have some sort of power over soil and stone.

Groping for her in the blackness, Thamalon's hand brushed the top of her head. "Did you hurt yourself falling?" he asked. "Are you still able to walk?"

"I am."

"Then come on." He hauled her to her feet, then pulled her into what must be some sort of narrow, low-ceilinged tunnel. By banging her shoulder on one, she discovered that splintery wooden supports stood at intervals along the way.

The lightless passage shook, the supports groaned, and chunks of dirt rained down. Crashing and pounding sounded through the earth. Evidently the giant had abandoned its efforts to force its hand down the shaft and was tramping around overhead demolishing the rest of the castle. Shamur couldn't guess whether the creature was hoping she and Thamalon would come up elsewhere in the ruin, expressing its pique that they'd eluded it, or deliberately trying to collapse the tunnel.

In any case, she feared that the ceiling might indeed be on the verge of falling. Just ahead of her in the darkness, one of the support timbers gave a sharp crack. Dirt showered down all around her, and then something much, much harder crashed down on top of her head. The sharp, unexpected pain slammed her down on her knees. She felt consciousness guttering out and struggled desperately to hold on, but still, everything slipped away.

❧ ❧ ❧ ❧ ❧

Shamur cried out in frustration and fear, and her eyes flew open. Peering about, she saw she was lying in a dilapidated lean-to, likely some hunter or charcoal burner's shelter. A fire smoked and crackled in the center of the floor, and the russet cloak she'd dropped back in the clearing covered her like a blanket. Outside the hut, daylight shone on a tangle of leafless, snow-silvered trees, proof that she was still in the woods.

Wrapped in his own cape with its bloodstained ermine collar, utterly filthy, Thamalon sat cross-legged on the other side of the fire, watching her. His long sword lay naked beside him, while her own weapon was nowhere in sight. She supposed she'd lost it when she'd been knocked unconscious.

"You called out," he said, his tone cool, his face impassive. "You're awake."

"Yes," she said, her throat so dry that her voice was a painful rasp. She swallowed. "I was dreaming about our escape. You must have realized I'd gotten hurt, and carried me out of the tunnel."

"Yes."

"How did you know the passage existed?"

"First things first. Do you still want to kill me?"

Her eyes widened in surprise. She sat up, though it made her head throb cruelly. "Ilmater's bonds, of course not! I know now that you didn't poison my grand-niece. That shadow that spoke with Lindrian's voice . . . I don't understand it, but somehow, when I talked to him, I was actually talking to it. Moreover, the fact that the phantom's master could even conceive of such a ruse implies that *he's* the one who truly committed the murder."

"Or rather, that he has ties to those who did," Thamalon said, his voice little warmer than before. "He seems too young to have slain anyone thirty years ago. How are you?"

"Sore—especially my head—stiff, cold, grimy, thirsty, and hungry," she said. "But essentially all right."

"I can do a little something about the hunger," he said,

handing her a bundle of paper, which, when she unfolded it, proved to contain a square of date-nut bread. Trust him not to venture into the woods without a snack tucked into the pigskin pouch on his belt, or a flint, steel, and tinderbox, for that matter.

She took a bite of the pastry. "I still want to hear how you knew about the tunnel," she said through the first mouthful.

His green eyes widened, and she realized that never in their three decades together had he ever seen her gobble a morsel with such unladylike voracity. But of course it was far too late to worry about such things now.

"I've built my share of strongholds over the years," Thamalon said. "Trading outposts and Stormweather Towers itself. I wanted to make them secure, so I undertook a study of fortifications, during which I happened to learn that these old castles Rauthauvyr raised often had a secret tunnel leading out. I didn't know exactly where it would be located, so I had to leave you to guard my back while I went to look for it."

"And since they didn't know it existed, our enemies must think the giant killed us, and our bodies lay buried somewhere in the wreckage of the fort."

"Since they stopped hunting us and went home, it would appear so."

"Good. We should try to figure out who the wizard is."

"Not so fast," said Thamalon. "I've had faceless enemies before. This one will keep for a few more minutes. What I want to know now, and without another second of delay, is, who are *you*? I've thought of one possibility, but it seems preposterous."

Shamur hesitated. She'd guarded the secret for so long it was hard to divulge it even now. Finally she said, "If you're thinking I'm the first Shamur, the robber in the tales and ballads, you're right."

"Explain," he said. "All of it."

And so she did, beginning with the bored, hoydenish adolescent she'd been more than eighty years ago, a girl who had started sneaking out of Argent Hall to taste the boisterous life of the streets, and eventually become a thief for the excitement.

Thamalon grimaced. "So that's where Thazienne gets it."

Shamur blinked in surprise. "You know about her thieving?"

"Not everyone manages to deceive me," he said sourly. "The way you two quarrel, I'm surprised you know. But go on with your tale."

"Well, you know that after I was unmasked, I had to flee Selgaunt. Later, I fell in with a band of treasure hunters who were looting ruins south of the Moonsea. We broke into the wrong crypt, a chamber given over to magical devices the like of which I've never encountered before or since, where a guardian spirit appeared to battle us." She could see the entity even as she spoke, a clawed, towering, shadowy thing, quick and savage as a leopard, and as terrible in its way as the masked wizard's elemental.

"Naturally," she continued, "the wizards and priests among us threw spells at the spirit. Somehow, their sorceries brought the devices in the vault to life, and they started shooting bolts of magical energy around. One of them struck an amulet I was wearing. I knew the pendant bore an enchantment, but had never discovered the purpose.

"The pearl in the amulet exploded, and instantly, or so it seemed to me, everything was different. Quiet. The spirit was gone. Much of the ceiling had fallen in, crushing the arcane apparatuses. My comrades lay dead, and looked as if they had been so for many years.

"When I returned to civilization, I found out that in fact, they had. Somehow, fifty years had passed for the rest of the world, but not for me.

"I reckoned that after so much time, it would be safe to return to Selgaunt, at least if I was discreet. You know what I found when I arrived. My family on the brink of ruin, their only hope an alliance by marriage with the House of Uskevren. So when the betrothed girl was murdered, they prevailed on me to impersonate her and wed you in her place."

"How did they talk you into such a travesty?" asked Thamalon.

Shamur shrugged. "After my displacement in time, they were the only people in the world I cared for, or even knew. Moreover, it was uncanny how my grand-niece had looked exactly like me, and even owned my name. I'd never truly believed in fate, but it gave me the strange, fey sense that it was my destiny to take her place."

"Indeed," he said, "and while you were engaged in your philosophical ruminations, did it ever occur to you that you were dealing unjustly if not downright cruelly with me? Tricking me into a union with a stranger I didn't love, and who most certainly didn't care for me."

Shamur felt an unexpected twinge of shame. "To be honest," she said, "no. I didn't consider your rights or your feelings at all. As I said, we Karns were desperate. I suppose I should apologize."

He laughed. "Oh, please do. After all, you've only been causing me hurt for thirty years, culminating in an attempt to kill me. A little show of contrition will make everything right."

She sighed. "Thamalon—"

"Enough," he said. "I wanted to know how my life took the path it did, and you've told me. I don't need to hear professions of remorse. We have a problem to solve. Let's focus on that."

"Fine," she rapped. "Then, who was Master Moon, do you think?"

Thamalon shook his head. "I don't know. I have a nagging feeling I've heard his voice before, but I don't know where or when. You should have waited to make your move until he revealed his identity."

"I moved at a moment when he was busy enjoying the sound of his own voice, and his henchmen were distracted by it as well. If I'd waited, we might not have gotten a second chance."

"I suppose."

"Anyway, I have no idea who he is, either," she said. "Nor could I identify any of the hired bravos, which is what they almost certainly were. In my youth, I was acquainted with half the bullies and cutpurses in the city, but now. . . ." She shrugged.

"Then we're stymied," he said.

"Perhaps not. I can think of two people who might lead us to the wizard. One is Audra Sweetdreams, the other, the first rogue with whom I crossed swords as we broke free of the clearing. We might be able to find him, for I got a good look at his face, and also noticed he has fish-scale tattoos."

Thamalon's green eyes narrowed. "Some of the watermen carry such marks. Of course, there's no shortage of watermen."

"True," she agreed. "Still, it will be easier to search among them than to comb the whole city at random. Now, here's my thought. At the moment, we possess one advantage. Master Moon thinks I'm dead. He won't take any extraordinarily precautions to keep me from tracking him down, and I can take him by surprise when I do. So I'll make inquiries, and you'll go home and protect the children. If the wizard wanted to kill both of us, he's likely to strike at them as well, to annihilate the House of Uskevren for good."

"The 'inquiries' could be dangerous."

"I can take care of myself. Moreover, Master Moon did something to me that no one else has ever done. He made me his dupe. I mean to show him just how deeply I resent that."

"I know just how you feel," Thamalon said sardonically, "and I agree to your scheme with one amendment. I'm coming with you."

"No. I'm used to doing such things alone."

"Nonsense. You already told me you've had dealings with other thieves and traveled with a troop of adventurers. Are you worried I'll slow you down? You should have noticed by now that, 'old man,' though I may be, I can take care of *my*self as well."

"I am aware of that," she admitted. "But I don't understand why you would want to accompany me, now that you know that all of our life together has been a lie."

"I may detest you, woman, but at the moment, what does it matter? We have an enemy to ferret out, it's a risky task, and you'll be better off with someone watching your back. Besides, if you want Master Moon to believe you dead, the ruse will be more convincing if neither of us surfaces. Whereas if I turn up alive, it will suggest the possibility that you might have survived as well."

"But what about the children?"

"They've got Jander, Brom, and the guards to protect them. They should be safe for the time being, and in the long run, we'll ward them best by eliminating this threat as expeditiously as possible."

She threw up her hands. "Very well. We'll hunt together."

"Then if you're able, we should get moving. Our foes left our capes lying back in the glade, but they stole our horses, and it's a long walk back to town."

CHAPTER 12

At the point where the city wall ended and the docks began, Shamur and Thamalon stood and regarded the expanse of water where the River Arkhen, or the Elzimmer, as the townsfolk generally called it, flowed into Selgaunt Bay. It was evening, with a frigid wind moaning in from the sea, and so, as it did every night, the "floating city" of the watermen had come back into existence. By day, countless boats ferried passengers and cargo about the harbor and along the river, or ventured out to sea in search of fish. At dusk, those who lived and worked aboard these vessels brought them together to form a great tangle that sometimes extended all the way to the north shore. It then became possible to step, climb, or jump from one deck to the next.

Shamur and Thamalon hadn't needed to hike

all the way back into Selgaunt. Shortly after reaching Rauthauvyr's Road, they'd encountered a wagon full of travelers willing to give them a ride, and more than willing to trade them plain homespun garments for their own rich nobles' attire, which, though torn, blood-spattered, and filthy, could nonetheless be sold to a second-hand clothing dealer for a handsome price.

Thus rendered inconspicuous, Shamur enjoyed the comfort and freedom of a mannish outfit of blacks and grays the likes of which she hadn't worn in thirty years. The couple parted company with their benefactors in Overwater. In that wayfarers' haven, they sold Thamalon's gold and silver spurs to augment their store of ready cash, procured a healing salve for their sundry cuts and scrapes along with a bottle of black dye, and then went to a bathhouse. After they scrubbed the grime off, Shamur chopped her long tresses short, and both she and Thamalon colored their hair. Now thoroughly disguised, or so they hoped, they headed for a marketplace to equip themselves for the task ahead. Thamalon bought a new throwing knife and a gray steel buckler. Shamur purchased another broadsword, a dagger, and, once the shifty little merchant operating in the shabbiest corner of the market had been persuaded to trust her, a leather wallet lined with thief's tools.

Still later, back on the south side of the river, the aristocrats' first stop had been a futile one at Lampblack Alley, where they'd found Audra Sweetdreams and her two ruffians lying slain on the floor of her shop.

It had all taken more time than Shamur would have preferred, and she'd been impatient to reach the docks and begin the search for the tattooed bully. Still, the floating city exerted a kind of fascination. Colored lanterns shone aboard scores of sloops, skiffs, barges, and houseboats as if in imitation of the stars appearing overhead. Mouthwatering cooking odors wafted ashore from the boats, as did laughter and a lively tune performed on songhorn and hand drum. Despite herself, the noblewoman paused to take in the spectacle.

Thamalon said, "It is a bit of a marvel, isn't it?"

Surprised to hear her own thought echoed, Shamur turned to regard him, and saw that he'd finally left off glowering at her. He wore a simple, unadorned brown cloak, jerkin, trews, and low boots. It occurred to her that with his hair dark as his eyebrows, he must look rather as he had in those grim days before she ever met him, when the House of Uskevren was deemed ruined for all time in everyone's reckoning but his own.

"Yes," she replied. "I've always liked looking at it, and regretted that living where we do, as we do, I don't often see it anymore."

His mouth tightened. "Of course, you think I'm to blame for that, and for depriving you of all your other pleasures."

"No!" she said. Sweet Sune, it had been like this for a long, wearisome time now, a sad consequence of their estrangement. Even when one of them intended no derogation or reproach, the other was touchy and quick to take offense. "That isn't what I meant."

"If you say so. Come on." They walked out on the northernmost dock, and, the planks creaking beneath their feet and the smell of saltwater in their nostrils, approached the first of the boats tied up there. It was a barca with slanted eyes painted on each of its interchangeable ends and a square little cabin, where the skipper no doubt slept in foul weather, set in the center of the deck.

"Ahoy," called Thamalon, indicating that he wished to speak to someone onboard. He would have shouted "walking" had he merely wished to move across the barca on his way to some other craft, and then, their notions of courtesy satisfied, none of the watermen would have paid him or Shamur any mind, or at least, not if the nobles could pass for watermen themselves.

But they couldn't, for the society of the waves and currents was an insular one with its own patois, mores, and traditions, interdependent with the world ashore, yet separate in many respects. People claimed that some watermen lived and died without ever setting foot on solid ground, and although Shamur suspected that was an exaggeration, she was certain no landsman could prowl the floating city without attracting many a speculative eye.

A husky woman wrapped in an oilcloth mantle emerged from the barca's cabin. "Good evening," said Thamalon.

"Evening," she replied. "What do you want?"

"We're looking for someone," Shamur said. "We don't know his name, but he's thin, has a black beard, and is about as tall as my friend here. Wears a gold ring in his lower lip, has fish scales tattooed on his hands and throat, and carries a brace of short swords. Do you know him?"

The bargewoman's eyes narrowed. "What do you want him for?"

"There was a boating accident," Thamalon said. It was the story he and Shamur had agreed upon. "My master's daughter would have drowned if this fellow hadn't happened to be passing by on another vessel and fished her out of the drink. Lord Baerent wants to reward him, and if you help us find him, there are a few fivestars in it for you as well."

The bargewoman shook her head. "I don't know the man."

"Well, thank you anyway," Thamalon sighed. "We'll walk on through, then."

The nobles asked their questions on all the vessels tied up at the dock, then moved on to those farther offshore. As they made their way through the floating city, Thamalon was affable when addressing the watermen and taciturn otherwise.

Shamur hadn't much minded his sullenness all afternoon, but now, perhaps because he'd finally relaxed for just a moment, it grated on her. At last, as they walked from the bow to the stern of an old trawler, with nets and setlines hanging on every side, she said, "I truly don't blame you for separating me from the things I loved. I realize it was my choice to don the mask I wore."

"Yes, it was," he answered, "but I believe you blame me nonetheless. Why else would you grow so cold?"

"You had your doxies to console you," she said, then

winced at the venom in her voice. "I'm sorry. I didn't begin this conversation to find an excuse for a quarrel. Perhaps, unjust as it was, I did resent you to some extent, simply because I was so unhappy."

"Unhappy in your life of luxury and privilege."

"It wasn't what I wanted!"

"Apparently not." They reached the rear of the vessel, and he called down to the sleek, narrow passenger skiff moored underneath, to the family of rowers taking their ease on the seats. "Ahoy!"

The nobles inquired about for another hour, still meeting with no success. Shamur became increasingly convinced that they must already have spoken to someone who knew their quarry, but that suspicious individual had been loath to give up a fellow waterman to a pair of outsiders.

Eventually, as they crossed the deck of a barge that had yet to unload its cargo of bins of iron ore, Thamalon said, "I could wish that you'd played your role with greater skill."

Shamur eyed him quizzically. "I did my best."

"And I must admit, you hoodwinked everyone, but still, when I think about it now, your impersonation was less than impeccable. At first, you did seem like the sweet, gladsome girl I loved. You had to until after the wedding, I suppose. But soon enough, you petrified into the stiff, imperious creature you are now, as your grand-niece never would have done."

She shrugged. "I suppose I felt that if I couldn't be the rogue anymore, I might as well be the most dignified noble-woman Selgaunt has ever seen. It certainly kept me from slipping up and revealing any hint of the old Shamur."

"To my mind, it's almost as if you were punishing yourself for abandoning the life you cherished by making sure you'd be as lonely and divorced from your true nature as possible."

She frowned, not liking his conjecture but unable to dismiss it out of hand. She was still mulling it over when he grabbed her by the shoulder.

"Look!" he said, pointing.

She peered ahead and saw two figures talking on the

deck of a gaily painted galley, the kind that pleasure seekers chartered for an outing on the bay. Beneath the mast, illuminated by the glow of a yellow lantern, huddled a tattooed boy and the man she and Thamalon were seeking. She surmised that one of the watermen to whom they'd spoken had indeed been acquainted with the bravo, and had dispatched the youth to warn him.

"Let's go," she murmured, and at that moment, the bully peered out across the expanse of gently bobbing decks that separated them, spotted them, and bolted, vanishing over the opposite side of the galley.

Shamur's eyes took in the lay of the land, or whatever you called it when you were out on an aggregation of boats.

"Circle that way," she said, pointing. "Cut him off if he makes for the docks." Should the rogue succeed in reaching the shore, he could lose himself in the teeming streets beyond.

Evidently Thamalon understood her concern, for he set off as she'd bade him without question, leaving her with her longer legs to pursue their prey directly. Springing into motion, her cape streaming out behind her and her scabbard bumping at her hip, she began the chase.

She discovered at once how tricky it was to scramble or leap headlong from one deck to the next, particularly when the two surfaces were at different heights above the water, just as she realized that, although she knew how to swim, a slip and a fall into the frigid bay could easily kill her. She knew she mustn't slow down, else the man with the ring in his lip would elude her.

She leaped over a six-foot expanse of open water, caught hold of the pleasure galley's rail, and started to scramble aboard. Her own momentum nearly carried her onto the point of the boat hook that the lad whom she'd spotted moments before was tentatively poking at her face.

She clung to her perch with one hand and grabbed the tool with the other, ripped it from her assailant's grasp, and tossed it into the water.

"Scat!" she roared, and the boy flinched back, giving

her room to vault onto the deck and race to the other side. To her relief, the bully was still visible in full flight several boats away. Leaping to the next vessel in line, she continued the pursuit.

It soon became apparent that the lad with the boat hook wasn't the only waterman who wanted to hinder her. When she bounded onto an old hulk that some entrepreneur had converted into a floating tavern, where fish filets were grilling on wrought-iron braziers, several of the patrons surged forward to attack her. She snatched out her broadsword, dropped the man in the lead with a cut to the thigh, sent another reeling with a gashed arm, and the rest faltered. She ran at them, slashing wildly, and they gave way, though that wasn't the end of the harassment. Topers who hadn't been bold enough to attempt to lay hands on her pelted her with crockery, tankards, and even hunks of bread.

Thereafter, she ran with her sword in hand, and no one attacked her face to face. Some of the watermen tried their best to hinder her in other ways.

As she dashed from the bow to the stern of a skipjack, silently cursing the clutter on the deck, the boom suddenly spun around. It would have swept her into the water had she not instantly dropped flat.

Onboard another barge, she heard a creak, looked around, and spotted the arm of a crane pivoting to drop a net full of crates on her head. She put on a burst of speed, and the boxes crashed down behind her. The crane operator cursed.

Frequently she suffered a stinging bombardment of belaying pins, fishing tackle, and any other missiles the watermen found ready to hand.

Shamur wondered whether they'd be so keen to protect her quarry if they realized he was a hired killer. She supposed she'd never know, for she couldn't spare the time or the breath to tell them.

Perhaps she wouldn't even if she could, for as she ran, leaped, and dodged, testing her instincts and agility, risking calamity with every stride, she felt the old exhilaration.

Perhaps she was mad, but this was the kind of perilous sport she needed to be happy. Delighting in the play of her muscles, at each obstacle overcome, at the kiss of the icy air on her face, she grinned fiercely.

She bounded onto a ketch amidships. The only person on deck was a small, bald, wizened man wrapped in a voluminous black robe. He was perched in the stern, well away from her and not blocking the direction she needed to go, and she assumed that he at least had no intention of interfering with her. Then, from the corner of her eye, she glimpsed him sweeping his hands and mystic passes as he chanted rhyming words of power.

The spellcaster tossed sparkling powder into the air, and beams of multi-colored light sizzled from his fingers in a fan-shaped burst. Shamur wrenched herself behind the cover of the mainmast, but a shaft of scarlet radiance grazed her shoulder even so. She felt dizzy and weak for a moment, and then the sensation passed.

She darted from her place of concealment, intent on distancing herself from the warlock as rapidly as possible, but he was already jabbering and twirling his arms again. Magic moaned and crackled through the air.

Suddenly, she had no idea why she'd been in such a rush to get away. The wizard seemed such a nice fellow, she ought to stay and make friends, see if she could oblige him in some way—

"No!" she shouted, and the enchantment lost its grip on her mind.

Shamur decided she couldn't just run and give him the chance to hurl yet another spell at her retreating form. She noticed a bucket—a bait bucket, judging from the fishy smell—sitting near the foot of the mainmast, snatched it up, and threw it.

The missile bashed the bald man on the temple, and, dazed, he collapsed to his knees. Grinning, she headed for the other side of the ketch, and then something struck her calf, stuck there, and yanked her off her feet.

As she slammed down on the deck, she saw that it was

a long, sticky tongue that had caught her, and at the other end was a goggle-eyed frog as big as a man. The spellcaster's pet or familiar, she supposed. Despite its size, with its natural ability to change color to match its surroundings, she hadn't noticed it crouching in the gloom, and now its tongue dragged her closer, its huge mouth gaping to swallow her whole.

She wrenched herself around into position to cut at the creature's tongue. One swing gashed it deeply and a second hacked it in two to lash about, showering blood.

The frog croaked, hopped into distance, and tried to bite her. Gripping her sword with both hands, she thrust at the creature's throat. The blade plunged in almost to the hilt, and the amphibian collapsed.

Shamur scrambled to her feet, took hold of the weapon, and tried to pull it from the carcass. But even when she tugged with all her might, the broadsword wouldn't slide free.

She knew she had no more time to fool with it, not with the bravo racing farther away every second. Grimacing, she abandoned the weapon, drew her dagger, and ran on.

She finally caught up with the tattooed man at the very edge of the floating city, where the clustered vessels gave way to open water. Naturally, the crafts farther in were unable to move until their assembly dissolved at dawn, but those here at the verge could depart at will, and, standing aboard a small sloop, using a boat hook to push off from the vessel next to it, the bravo was endeavoring to do so.

Another waterman, the rightful master of the vessel, presumably, lay motionless on the deck. Shamur assumed that he at least hadn't been interested in helping her quarry escape, and so the bravo had found it necessary to subdue him in order to commandeer the sloop. And thank Mask for that, because if something hadn't delayed the wretch, she never would have caught up with him in time.

One final leap across the black water landed her on the sloop, which rocked as it took her weight. The tattooed man pivoted to face her, his neck bruised where she'd struck him the night before. His eyes widened in surprise, and he smiled.

"Where's your friend?" he rasped. Apparently the blow to the throat had roughened his voice as well.

"On his way."

"But too late to help you," he said, and Shamur realized he was right. The sloop was still drifting away from its neighbor, and the gap was now too wide for Thamalon to jump. "And you, baggage, have lost your sword."

She expected him to reach for his short swords, but he whipped out a dagger with a curved blade instead.

Shamur doubted it was chivalry prompting him to opt for a shorter blade like her own. He was probably proud of his skill with a dagger, proud enough to rely on it whenever practical. Whereas, though she had some experience with all the white arms, as bladed weapons were called, she was most confident with the sword. She knew the basics of knife fighting, but no more.

Well, she told herself, that would just make it more interesting, as would the fact that while he would have no compunction about killing her, she must take care not to give him a mortal wound. Otherwise, she wouldn't be able to interrogate him afterward.

She assumed a stance similar to the one she employed when fighting with a sword, her weapon hand in the lead. Smiling, knees slightly bent the bravo minced toward her with his empty hand leading, and poised to guard his abdomen, his dagger hand cocked back. He sucked in his midsection to make it less of a target.

Shamur retreated, using her longer reach to threaten him and slow his advance, meanwhile studying his technique. She knew she couldn't keep evading him for long, not in the cramped arena of the deck, but she hoped that if she figured out his style before he closed, she could turn that understanding to good advantage.

The bravo glided forward with stylized steps reminiscent of an allemande, sometimes tossing his weapon from one hand to the other. Once he twirled, momentarily giving her his back, then snapped back around with a cut that would likely have taken her in the throat, had she accepted the invitation to attack.

He did indeed appear to be a master of the dagger, tricky and sufficiently confident of his skill to be flamboyant. Shamur reckoned that she might be in even more trouble than she'd thought.

In the few seconds she'd spent studying him, he'd nearly backed her up into the very end of the bow. Unwilling to let herself be cornered, she sidestepped, and that was the instant the bravo attacked in earnest.

His hand streaked at her, and she made a cut intended to intercept it. But his thrust stopped short, her counterattack missed, and she saw at that same instant that his fist was empty. Somehow, without her seeing it, he'd transferred his dagger to his other hand, and now she glimpsed it plunging toward her abdomen.

She twisted, wrenching herself aside, and the thrust missed by a hair. With her left hand, she grabbed for his wrist, seeking to immobilize his weapon, but in one graceful blur of motion, he spun his arm away and danced back safely out of distance.

Shamur pursued him back toward the stern. She stepped and thrust, stepped and thrust, accustoming him to the pace at which she was advancing, then sprang forward with a sudden burst of acceleration which she hoped would catch him by surprise.

It didn't. He instantly dropped to one knee, and her dagger and outstretched arm flew over his head. Meanwhile, his blade drove up at her stomach.

With her own impetus driving her toward his point, she had no time to parry, but could only attempt to dodge. Once again, she was fortunate, for the dagger missed her flesh, though it snagged in her cloak and yanked her off balance before it ripped free. She grabbed one of the lines to steady herself, heard his noisy breathing coming up behind her, and spun back around to face him.

The dagger leaped back and forth between his hands.

She sensed that he wanted her to attack at that instant when the blade was in flight, and refused to respond to the invitation. After a few seconds, he suddenly abandoned the ploy and lunged to stab her in the chest.

She attempted an evasive movement of her own, pivoting on her front leg to avoid his point while thrusting at his throat. His initial attack missed, but he blocked with his left arm and took her weapon out of line as well. To her surprise, he sprang closer, seizing her with his unweaponed hand and lifting his knife arm high.

With his black-bearded features only inches from her own, blocking out everything else, she couldn't see his right hand performing its next manipulation, but she didn't have to. She understood very well what it must be doing. Spinning the knife, reversing his grip so he could drive the point into her spine.

Her own weapon was passé and out of position for an instantaneous stab at his back, nor did she think she could break free of his hold in the split second remaining. So she butted him in the face.

His nose broke with a crack, his body jerked, and, thanks be to Mask, his dagger didn't slam down into her flesh. She instantly followed up with a second head butt, a stomp to the foot, and a knee to the groin.

His grip slackened. Shoving him back, she tore herself free, gave him a snap kick to the knee, and, seeing that he was staggering, too hurt and dazed for the moment to wield his dagger, stepped in and slammed the pommel of her own weapon against his forehead.

The bravo fell, and she grinned in satisfaction. Many would say she'd been lucky to defeat such an opponent, but she preferred to think that while he had been the better dagger fighter, she was the stronger combatant in general, and that was what had yielded her the victory.

"Ho!"

Shamur turned. Thamalon was standing aboard a catboat at the edge of the floating city. He had his buckler in his left hand and his throwing knife in his right, and although the watermen who inhabited the craft were regarding him sourly, they weren't making any hostile moves.

"By the time the ruffian reached this part of the cluster," Thamalon said, "it was obvious he didn't intend to make for the docks. So I followed after you."

"Good," she replied. "Bide there a moment."

Shamur scrutinized the bravo. Whimpering, he seemed to be conscious, but incapacitated nonetheless. She dropped his dagger and short swords over the side, and, keeping a wary eye on him, found a sweep and rowed the sloop up to the catboat. The two hulls banged together, and one of the watermen cursed.

"Sorry," she told him, then turned to Thamalon. "Climb aboard. We might as well chat with our friend here privately, without any other misguided boaters attempting to interfere with us."

"Good idea." Thamalon stepped onto the sloop, and she pushed off with the oar.

Once she was sure they were drifting away, Shamur glanced around to catch Thamalon staring at her with a strange expression on her face, and for some reason, his regard made her feel self-conscious. "What?" she demanded.

The nobleman blinked. "Nothing." He stooped to examine the waterman from whom the bravo had attempted to steal the sloop. "This fellow should be all right. It looks as if our friend just knocked him out."

"He's lucky the bastard didn't stick a knife in him," said Shamur. "Perhaps he had qualms about killing a fellow boater. Anyway, let's talk to him." She nudged the captive with the toe of her boot. "We know you're awake. Let's chat."

The captive warily opened his eyes. "What do you want with me?" he croaked. "You talk like I'm some sort of ruffian, but I haven't done anything wrong."

"You bolted as soon as you heard that two strangers were seeking you, ostensibly to give you a reward," Thamalon said. "Is that the act of an innocent man? To me, it seems more like the jumpiness of a blackguard who took part in the assassination of two nobles less than twenty-four hours ago."

The bravo swallowed. "I don't know what you're talking about."

"You're lying," Shamur said, "and there's no chance of you convincing us otherwise. It was dark when you saw us last, and we've changed our appearances since, but look at my face. Look closely."

The bully did as she'd bade him, then blanched and cringed. "You people are dead!"

"No," said Shamur, "just very annoyed. We can vent our spleen on you, or you can tell us who hired you and your fellow toughs."

"I don't know. I was just a member of a crew," the waterman said, "just doing as I was told. I never heard the wizard's name, nor saw him without the moon mask."

"Then tell us how you wound up working for him," she said.

He hesitated. "I can't. If I turn nose, the others will kill me."

"Do you think we won't?" she replied. "Husband, I believe this fool needs to be convinced that we're in earnest." She hefted her dagger. "What shall we take, a thumb?"

"An eye," said Thamalon with a lightness that served well to reinforce the bluff. "It always gets a man's attention when you pop an eye."

"Very well."

They flung themselves onto the bravo, who screamed and flailed wildly, but who, spent and battered as he was, could do little to keep them from pinning him to the deck.

"Try to avoid any further struggling," Thamalon advised the rogue. "If you thrash about, the blade could plunge too far down, all the way into your brain."

"No!" the bravo shrieked. "Get off me! I'll tell! I'll tell!"

"Drat," said Shamur, "I never get to have any fun. All right, then, spill it."

"The thing is, I belong to the Quippers," the ruffian said.

The nobles exchanged glances. Named for a species of savage freshwater fish that, traveling in schools, posed a threat to even the largest animal, the Quippers were a notorious outlaw fraternity operating chiefly on the waterfront, where their crimes often involved smuggling, theft, and extortion. The gang had been in existence for a long while; Shamur had had dealings with them in her youth, and in recent years Thamalon had occasionally tried to suppress them and so eliminate a threat to honest merchants.

"Then was the murder scheme a reprisal against me?" Thamalon asked.

"No," the bravo said. "We were hired, just as you first supposed, but I swear, I don't know by whom."

"Then we'll have to ask some of your cohorts," Shamur said. "Where do the Quippers have their stronghold these days?"

"In the Scab," the ruffian said.

Thamalon frowned. "That's unfortunate, but never mind. Let's discuss your future. You've already said yourself that your cronies will kill you for informing on them, and I personally will make sure that the Scepters start hunting you tomorrow. If you want to live, I'd advise you to flee Selgaunt this very night."

"How?" the bravo rasped. "The way your woman beat me, I can hardly walk."

"I'm sure you'll manage," Shamur said. "Meanwhile, you're a waterman, so make yourself useful. Bring this boat back around to link up with the others."

Groaning and grunting the while, the bravo obeyed. When the sloop floated next to the catboat once again, Thamalon waved his hand, bidding the man with the ring in his lip begone. Perhaps fearing that his captors would change their minds, the ruffian limped quickly away.

"I hope he doesn't run and warn his gang," Shamur said.

"I doubt he will," Thamalon replied. "He meant it when he whined that they routinely kill informers. In any event, we couldn't very well maintain the pretense that we're dead and turn him over to the Scepters, also. Nor could we drag a prisoner around with us. So unless you had the stomach to kill him in cold blood . . ."

"No," she said. "Anyway, I assume our next stop is the Scab."

He looked at her, and once again, she noticed that same odd quality in his gaze. "I hope you don't mean tonight. At the risk of you curling up your lip and calling me 'old man' again, I have to say that after what we've been through, I've had enough cold weather and exertion for a while. I'd rather repair to one of those shabby little inns along the harbor, and tackle the rest of the Quippers tomorrow."

She smiled. "I must confess, I'm not quite as young as I once was, either, and I daresay that's not such a bad idea."

CHAPTER 13

Bileworm had spent much of his existence in proximity to colossal fortresses built of iron, basalt, and sorcery, but even he had to admit that the playhouse called the Wide Realms presented a pleasing spectacle, if only in a tawdry, terrestrial sort of way. The entrance to the theater, a ring-shaped structure with a tiring house and stage at the rear and a pair of multi-level galleries curving out and around to meet at the gate in the front, shone like a jewel in fields of magical light, as did the gaudy pennants flying and banners hanging from the thatched roof. The humbler patrons had all packed inside prior to the start of the performance, but a few aristocrats were still arriving, pulling up in their carriages, on horseback, or strolling behind torch-bearing linkboys in scarlet capes. Music, the declamations of the actors, and, periodically, applause, cheers, laughter, catcalls, and booing, drifted up through the open space in the center of the building.

Of course, Bileworm hadn't come to admire the view but to scout the disposition of the enemy, and having accomplished his task, he supposed he'd better return to Master and report. He turned and skulked along the rooftops, a shadow moving virtually invisibly against the night sky, until, lengthening and then shortening his leg, he stepped lightly down into the alley where the wizard and his mortal henchmen waited.

Garris Quinn, clad tonight in a plum-colored hat with an upturned brim and yellow plume, a loose, thigh-length mandilion overcoat in the same colors, and baggy galligaskin breeches, glanced around, discovered Bileworm leering at his elbow, yelped, and recoiled.

Not the least bit startled by his aide's outburst, or at least not betraying it if he was, Master casually turned toward his familiar. "What have you learned?" the masked wizard asked.

"They're guarding the lad," Bileworm said, "just as you expected. They have warriors hiding in four buildings adjacent to the Wide Realms, six to ten in each detachment. I imagine other guards are waiting inside the playhouse."

"Thank you for giving us the benefit of your tactical expertise," said Master, a hint of impatience perceptible in his tone. He'd been out of sorts since Thamalon Uskevren's eldest boy had escaped him earlier that day.

"Then it's a trap," Garris said uneasily.

Master sighed. "I'm surrounded by strategists, it seems. Naturally it's a trap. Did you think that with young Talbot's parents missing, and his brother already assaulted, his retainers would let him wander off to do his acting unprotected? But we're going to trap the trappers."

Garris nodded. "All right. Do we attack?" The bravos massed behind him stirred.

"Not yet," said Master. "Since I want to neutralize all the warriors outside without giving any of them a chance to warn their compatriots inside, Bileworm and I will attend to that particular chore by ourselves while you fellows wait here."

The spirit sniggered. "I thought you promised I could take it easy from now on."

"All you have to do is lead me to the guards," Master replied, "so it shouldn't tax your stamina unduly. Specifically, I want you to guide me to the aspects of the watch posts opposite the Wide Realms. Presumably, the soldiers are all peering out at the playhouse, and if we approach their positions from behind, they shouldn't see us coming."

Bileworm grinned. "Consider it done." He escorted Master to the improvised sentry station on the east side of the theater, a candlemaker's shop. The familiar assumed the warriors had paid the proprietor, his family, and any apprentices to clear out for the evening.

Unfortunately, the establishment had no back door. "You could climb in through a window," Bileworm whispered.

"I might make noise," Master replied, his voice equally low. "Let's try a little magic."

The wizard removed a pinch of sesame from one of the pockets in his dark blue mantle, swept his hand in an intricate mystical pass, and whispered a sibilant tercet. The air in the vicinity rippled for a moment, like hot desert air birthing a mirage, then a round hole appeared in the wall of the shop.

Master slipped inside. Bileworm followed and found himself in a storeroom, with tubs of beeswax and tallow sitting about. Voices murmured through the doorway leading to the front of the shop.

The wizard took out a blowpipe, tiptoed to the opening, raised the weapon to his lips, and puffed explosively. Bileworm watched several armed men fall unconscious; the unlucky ones who'd been standing thumped down to the floor. After a moment, two of them started to snore.

"I concocted this dust when I was young, and used up most of it before my death," Master remarked. "I was pleasantly surprised to return thirty years later and find the rest still in its jar. I guess no one else in the family knew what it was."

"Are we going to kill these mortals?" Bileworm asked.

Master sighed. "I wish you'd grow up a little. We have riper fruit to pick. Come on, we'll go back out through the hole."

As they made their exit, Bileworm reflected that Master simply lacked panache. Yes, they had no need to murder the slumbering warriors. Yes, it would require a few moments that might be spent more efficiently elsewhere. Yes, the method he had in mind would cause a stir when they'd already resolved to be stealthy. But still, with all the combustibles on hand, the candlemaker's shop could be made to burn magnificently, and the heat would almost certainly wake the soldiers up in time to perish in agony in the flames.

Deploring a squandered opportunity, the spirit led Master to the other watch posts. The warriors stationed to the south and west succumbed as easily as the first detachment, but matters fell out a bit differently at the last stop on their circuit, a fragrant perfumery, the shelves behind the counter lined with porcelain and crystal bottles. After the blowpipe discharged its contents, one warrior remained on his feet, a lean, middle-aged man with a stern, humorless mouth, pale, narrow eyes, and a grizzled widow's peak. Judging from the markings on the blue surcoat he wore over his mail, he was probably Jander Orvist, captain of the Uskevren household guard.

Though surely startled by the sudden collapse of his men, Jander nonetheless reacted quickly. He drew his long sword and charged the wizard. Giving ground, Master plucked a packet of folded paper from his mantle, brandished it, and spoke a word of power.

Jander was only a stride away from being close enough to attack when the spell took hold. A smear of slick white slime materialized beneath his boots. Slipping, he cut at the wizard anyway, a stroke that would have landed had not Master parried it with his staff. Purple radiance sizzled from the black wood, down the blade of the long sword, and into Jander's body, playing about his armored limbs as he fell.

Twitching and shuddering, Jander tried to flounder back to his feet, made it as far as his knees, and, realizing he could go no farther, drew in a ragged breath to shout. Master rattled off a brief incantation and spun his arm in an intricate gesture that ended with him planting his hand on the fallen captain's shoulder.

Magenta light and a kind of ragged darkness flickered about the point of contact. His mouth drawn in a rictus of agony, Jander convulsed and then collapsed, his sinewy warrior's body now withered to little more than skin and bones.

Bileworm leered. "He should have skipped off to dreamland with his men."

"He couldn't," Master replied, "his spirit was too strong." Evidently having run out of dust to charge it, he set the blowpipe down atop the counter. "Let's fetch Garris and the others."

Brom had been to the theater before, but had generally found himself in the cheap seats far back from the stage, or even squashed in the press of groundlings standing in the open area in front of it. It was still a novel experience to sit up close with plenty of elbow room in a box overlooking the stage, and he wished he had the leisure to enjoy it.

But he didn't. Like the warriors in mufti stationed about the playhouse, he had to watch for the first signs of an attempt on Master Talbot's life.

He would have found it easier had all the members of the audience been content to sit or stand and watch the performance. Unfortunately, however, the Wide Realms was a raucous carnival of diversions, of which the tragedy unfolding onstage sometimes seemed the least compelling. People were chattering to their friends, munching pears and sausages, passing wineskins and jugs of ale and applejack around, playing cards, throwing dice, tossing a knife in a game of mumblety-peg, and conducting assignations with their sweethearts or bawds. It all combined to make a shifting, churning confusion, in which even the most blatant sign of hostile intent might go unnoticed for a few moments. Brom worried that for all their vigilance, he and his comrades would fail to spot it in time.

Yet when trouble erupted, it did so in the one place where no one could have missed it, on the stage itself.

A shaggy white wig on his head and long, snowy whiskers gummed to his chin, leaning heavily on his gnarled staff, Talbot railed at his absent son for betraying him. Some of the groundlings yelled to tell him that no, the prince was faithful, the evil counselor had lied, but of course the deluded old monarch Talbot was portraying mustn't hear them, or else it would ruin the story.

The part of King Imre was a departure for Tal, who was usually cast in secondary roles that showed off his theatrical fencing more than his acting ability, and he was enjoying the challenge, though not as much as he might have if he weren't waiting for someone to try to murder him. In the wings, Mistress Quickly and some of the other players watched his performance with encouraging smiles.

Behind them sat an iron cage, a prop, but also Tal's prison on nights of the full moon. He thought briefly how odd, even sad, it was that he'd never felt able to tell his own family of his transformations, yet had nonetheless confided in the members of the troupe. Perhaps it was because, while he didn't necessarily love them any more than he did his parents, Tazi, or even Tamlin, he supposed, he trusted his fellow players not to judge him.

A chorus of shouts jarred him from his momentary reverie. For a second, he thought the groundlings were still trying to enlighten old Imre about his heir, then realized they were crying, "Look up! Look up!"

Nothing in the scene should have provoked such an outburst. He turned, lifted his head, and beheld a pair of black spiders, each as big as a donkey, leaping down from the balcony stage above.

The only other actor on stage was Lommy, playing the role of Imre's court fool. His fantastic yellow motley and clown makeup concealed the fact that he wasn't human but a tasloi, with the greenish skin, thin black fur, golden eyes, and apish frame of his kind. When he spotted the spiders, he fled.

Talbot was relieved to see his unarmed friend take himself out of harm's way. He was confident that neither of the spiders would chase after the tasloi, because these were clearly summoned creatures like the ones Tamlin had encountered, charged with the task of killing one specific victim.

Since Tal was that victim, he reached for the long sword hanging at his side. Brom had cast a glamour on it to keep anyone from seeing it, but it became visible as it scraped clear of the scabbard. The noble wore a brigandine as well, the armor concealed beneath Imre's crimson robes.

The spiders scuttled toward him, and he willed himself to be calm. Certain members of the audience were screaming, some sincerely, others in the giddy manner of folk relishing an imaginary peril. Apparently, unfazed by the fact that the sick, doddering old king had inexplicably turned into a swordsman, or that giant arachnids invading the royal palace would seem to have nothing to do with the rest of the plot, these latter assumed the spiders were part of the show.

Fortunately, the hideous creatures didn't work in concert as men might have done. They came at him separately, and one closed the distance before the other. Hoping to dispatch it before its comrade entered the fray, Talbot lunged at it at once.

His blade sank deep into the spider's mask, bursting two of its clustered, globular eyes, but the creature kept scuttling forward, drops of oily amber venom glistening at the ends of its fangs.

Talbot scrambled out of the spider's path, ripped the long

sword free, and, knowing he could have at most a second or two left before the other arachnid pounced at him, cut at the place where the wounded creature's head joined its thorax.

The blow half severed the head. The spider continued to turn in his direction, and he feared he still hadn't killed it. Then it crumpled.

Tal heard footsteps drumming up behind, spun around, and cut. His sword sheared off one of the second spider's chitinous front legs. The arachnid lurched off balance for a moment, then scuttled toward him scarcely less nimbly than before.

Shouting a battle cry, Talbot lunged to meet it, and his point slammed deep into the center of the spider's pulsing mouth. It still kept coming, ramming into him, knocking him down, and crouching on top of him. Heedless of the fact that it was driving his blade even deeper inside its body, the creature dipped its head and bit him.

Talbot went rigid with terror, but only felt a pressure, not the agony he'd expected. The steel plates riveted on the brigandine kept the poisonous fangs from penetrating his flesh on the first try, and the spider never got a second. Rather, it convulsed and slumped on top of him.

Tal clambered out from beneath the carcass and yanked the long sword free. Some members of the audience were still cheering and whooping, but more were now screaming in earnest. The noble peered about, trying to make out the totality of what was going on, and why none of his retainers had yet rushed to his aid. He was still struggling to sort out the chaos before him when he heard the door at the rear of the stage bang open, and something scratching and scrambling in the balconies above. He pivoted and came on guard.

Galvanized by the appearance of the spiders, Brom sprang from his chair, spun the head of his staff in a mystic pass, and began to recite an incantation that would launch darts of destructive force at the creatures. Then something, perhaps a sight half-glimpsed from the corner of his eye, perhaps simply an intuition honed in scores of battles, warned him that he was in danger. Abandoning his conjuration, he threw himself flat.

Crossbow bolts whizzed over his head and cracked into the walls. An instant later, a blast of cold swept over him, so bitter that he cried out, and his body clenched. Had it struck him squarely, it might have stopped his heart or frozen him solid, but the paling at the front of the box shielded him from the worst of it.

Shivering, wishing his foe had chosen to strike at him with any force other than cold, Brom fumbled a flake of turtle shell from one of his pockets, rattled off an incantation that would protect him from any more quarrels, then peeked over the rime-encrusted paling.

From that vantage point, he could see that the wizard in the crescent-shaped mask, a number of bravos, and more conjured servitors, giant spiders and the pot-bellied, long-armed creatures called ettercaps, had burst in through the front entrance. All the wizard's minions were trying to work their way toward the stage and Talbot. Due to the press of the panicking crowd, the ruffians were finding it hard going, but the summoned creatures, clambering along the palings at the front of the middle and upper galleries, were covering the distance more rapidly. The Uskevren guards had taken out their crossbows and swords and were doing their best to slay the attackers, and a few other courageous members of the audience had elected to engage them as well, but the defenders were too few to hold back the tide. Brom wondered what had happened to the soldiers stationed outside the playhouse. Why hadn't they intercepted the masked wizard and his accomplices before the villains ever made it past the gate, and why weren't they charging in after them now?

Brom really had no time to puzzle over their absence, nor to hurl his magic against any of the spiders, ettercaps, or bravos, either, because the masked wizard had cast an enchantment of flight and risen above the crowd. His dark blue mantle fluttering about him, purple fire dancing on the black staff he held above his head, he was soaring directly toward Brom.

"I suspected I'd see you again," the masked man said.

Assuming that the other wizard had once again armored himself against lesser spells, Brom hastily attempted one of the greater. Snatching out a handful of clear glass marbles, he raised them high and rattled off the proper incantation. The orbs exploded into powder, veils of shimmering ruby light coiled through the air, and then a corona of brighter radiance blazed around the masked man's head.

Brom peered intently, trying to judge the effect. If the charm had worked, it had robbed the other wizard of the ability to cast spells by stripping away most of his intellect, and the change would likely manifest itself immediately, in a wail of anguish, perhaps, or a general appearance of confusion.

But the masked man simply kept gliding closer as gracefully as before. "You're good," he said in his mild, dry voice, "but I fancy I was better even before my death, and I've learned all manner of tricks in the years since. Allow me to demonstrate."

Green and purple lightning crackled down the length of his staff.

Crouched on the roof of the Soargyl family's box, Thazienne had been feeling smug till the trouble began. Her brothers, Erevis, and Brom had been idiots to think they could hold her prisoner and hog all the excitement of unknown enemies, attempted assassinations, and the ensuing battles for themselves. It had been simplicity itself to slip out the casement in her bedchamber and climb down the wall. Afterward, she'd hurried to the Kit, the inn where she kept a room, weapons, and an outfit of dark, oiled, close-fitting leather, suited up for action, and then headed to the Wide Realms. The playhouse wall was considerably easier to scale than that of Stormweather Towers, and once she reached the roof, she had only to avoid rustling the snowy thatch while she found a perch on one of the solid rafters underneath. Tazi hunkered down, watched, and waited.

It only took Talbot a few seconds to kill the first two spiders, but by then, all manner of interesting things were happening. Three more arachnids were making their way onto the stage, as were a pair of swordsmen. A veritable horde of bravos and conjured creatures had pushed in through the front gate. The wizard in the moon mask was flying through the air, heading straight toward the Uskevren family box where Brom was stationed.

Thazienne's first impulse was to rush down onto the stage and fight alongside her hulking brother, but aspects of the situation unfolding below nagged at her. For one thing, as she could see from her elevated position, none of the soldiers positioned outside the playhouse was rushing toward it, which meant that Tal and his supporters were severely outnumbered. For another, since the enemy had evidently found a point of entry at the back of the tiring house, why had the majority of them come in through the gate at the opposite end of the playhouse, placing themselves considerably farther away from their quarry than necessary?

She could conceive of one explanation. The wizard in blue was a commander who planned for contingencies and did his best to control his opponents' actions. The spiders and ruffians already onstage were no feint but a deadly serious threat. But suppose Talbot somehow disposed of them all before their fellows reached the stage. Then, with the bulk of his retainers having mysteriously failed to appear, and an overwhelming force charging toward him, he would see no option but to flee in the only logical direction: back toward that door at the rear of the theater. Where, Tazi suspected, an ambuscade awaited him.

If she was mistaken, if no one was lurking there, she would have wasted valuable time that she could have spent helping Tal fend off the attackers who had already reached him. If she was right, then someone had to clear away the trap and provide him a means of egress, or he'd never make it out of the playhouse alive.

Running lightly, trusting her thief's agility to keep her feet on the sturdy beams beneath the flimsy thatch, she dashed to the rear of the Wide Realms and peered downward. As she'd anticipated, there was an open door there, and clustered around it, half a dozen ettercaps. Four clung higher up on the wall like ticks attached to the hide of some unfortunate host; the pair directly above the exit appeared to be clutching a net. The other two crouched on the ground on either side of the door, ready to attack Talbot the instant he plunged through.

Other than observing captured specimens in carnivals and menageries, Tazi had no firsthand experience with ettercaps, but it was her understanding that the brutes were adept at laying snares and catching unwary woodsmen unawares. That was probably why the masked wizard had selected them for this duty, but she was going to show them what sneaking and attacking by surprise were truly all about. She silently swung her legs over the edge of the roof, then hesitated.

What if everyone was right? What if she actually wasn't well yet, nor ready for a fight to the death against superior numbers?

Scowling, she thrust the timorous thought away. She *was* recovered, curse it, and even if she wasn't, it didn't matter, not with Talbot's life in jeopardy. She started down the wall.

In some ways, it was the most challenging climb she'd ever attempted. She had to find her hand- and footholds in the dark, then transfer her weight in utter silence, lest the ettercaps hear her coming. Yet she also had to descend quickly, for if she took too much time, she might well engage the foe too late to do Talbot any good.

She held her body well away from the wall. Took care that no matter how she exerted herself, her breathing didn't become audible. Meanwhile she could feel her heart pounding, and half feared that the ettercaps would hear it beating.

Or else one of them would simply happen to glance upward, and all her efforts at stealth would be in vain.

None of them did. Compelled by the masked wizard's power, they kept watching the door with a single-minded intensity, and at last Tazi reached a point just above the ettercap hanging highest on the wall.

The creature was suspended head down. A pity, that, for she would have preferred to kick it in its vaguely equine skull, right between the long, pointed ears with the tufts of bristles on the ends. But the base of its spine was in easy reach, and she stamped on it with all her might.

Bone crunched; the ettercap screamed and fell from its perch. One of its fellows skittered around to orient on Tazi. Twisting, she kicked at that one, too, and the reinforced toe of her boot caught it in its red-eyed face, snapping the two tusks that protruded over its lower lip and jolting its head back. The brute tumbled to the ground.

Now that Thazienne no longer had the advantage of surprise, it would be foolish to continue trying to fight and hang on a vertical surface at the same time. She sprang away from the wall, landed well beyond the two ettercaps crouched on the ground, dropped, and rolled through a frigid snow drift.

The net flew through the air. She rolled again, and it clattered down beside her. As she scrambled up, the two ettercaps who'd thrown it hopped down from their perches, and then, screeching and chittering, all four of the uninjured ones shambled toward her.

She knew she mustn't let them encircle her. She whipped out her long sword, dodged to the left, then sprang at her closest opponent.

The ettercap raked at her with the filthy claws at the ends of its elongated fingers. She ducked beneath the attack. The poison glands in its upper lip swelling, the creature lunged to bite her, and she met the threat with a cut that bisected its throat.

As the ettercap toppled, she spun away from it, meanwhile whirling her blade in a sweeping parry that, though executed blindly, knocked away the taloned hand of the conjured being that had sought to attack her from behind. Perhaps she'd startled it or stung its fingers, for it faltered. She feinted a head cut to addle it still further, then drove her blade into its chest.

The creature dropped. Pulling her weapon free, she peered about and saw that the two remaining ettercaps had succeeded in placing themselves on opposite sides of her and were warily moving in. They thought that when she turned to defend herself from one, the other would be able to rend her or sink its venomous canines into her from behind.

Their tactics might well prevail, if she permitted them to close in on her, press her, and generally control the tempo of the exchange. To forestall that, she bellowed and sprinted at the one crouched between her and the wall.

Its crimson eyes goggling in surprise at her precipitous action, the ettercap nonetheless managed to throw up one of its long, wiry arms to fend off her blade, but she dipped her point beneath the block and plunged it into the brute's belly.

As she yanked the sword free, she heard the remaining ettercap charging up right behind her, and realized she didn't even have time to whirl around to face it. Reversing her weapon and gripping the hilt with both hands, she thrust it backward under her arm, ducking simultaneously.

Just as she'd hoped, the ettercap's raking hands, aimed high, lashed harmlessly over her head. Meanwhile, the long sword slammed into flesh.

She sidestepped clear, turned, raised her weapon for another stroke or parry, then saw it wasn't necessary. The ettercap she'd just stabbed was collapsing, and the other five were sprawled motionless on the ground.

Tazi felt a swell of exultation as intense as any she'd ever known. She hadn't been a fool to trust in her skills and prowess. She was finally her old self again.

But she knew she had no time to stand and revel in the knowledge. She dashed for the door.

A different sort of arachnid, black with brown stripes, leaped from one of the window stages, its bony-ridged legs extended like lances to stab its prey. Talbot leaped aside, and the sword spider crashed down beside him. He drove his blade into its thorax, and it shuddered, listed to one side, and fell.

As usual, while he'd been busy eliminating one threat, others were moving in on him. From the corner of his eye, he spotted a bravo skulking up on his flank. The tough was phenomenally ugly, as if, in punishment for some crime, he'd been magically transformed into something inhuman, and the spell to restore him had only barely done the job. Tal whirled to face him, and his King Imre wig picked that moment to slip down over his eyes.

Knowing that the ruffian would seize the instant of his blindness to attack, Tal parried by sheer instinct. His blade rang on that of his opponent's, blocking his cut to the flank. The wig fell down to the floor, and Tal hacked at his adversary's sword hand, half severing it. Keening, the ugly man dropped to his knees.

One of the round-bellied ettercaps charged Talbot, its thin arms with their long-fingered hands outstretched, only to plummet abruptly from sight when a trapdoor opened beneath its feet. An instant later, a flying chariot drawn by pink dragons dropped from on high, nearly braining a ruffian who had been in the process of aiming a crossbow at Tal. The startled bravo jumped, his finger pulled on the trigger, and the bolt flew wild.

Talbot grinned. Evidently, Lommy and his brother Otter, who generally operated the Wide Realms's array of mechanical tricks and effects, had made their way to the controls beneath the stage and in the hut above and were trying to use them to help Talbot. Other members of the troupe were striving to do the same by flinging missiles and abuse from the relative safety of the wings.

Uskevren warriors were still fighting doggedly here

and there about the theater, and Brom was still keeping the masked wizard busy. Their duel stained the walls with flashes of colored light, even as it filled the air with cracklings, hissings, thrummings, waves of heat and cold, and foul odors.

Meanwhile, Tal was battling as well as he ever had in his life; Master Ferrick, his teacher, would have been proud. Yet he suspected that none of it, not his own skill nor the valor and ingenuity of his supporters, would matter in the end. The enemy's superior numbers would soon carry the day, for, strong as he was, even he couldn't keep fighting this furiously for much longer, with never an instant's respite to catch his breath. Already he was panting, and could feel fatigue building in his muscles.

If only he could bolt through the door at the rear of the stage! It looked to be his only hope of survival, and he wouldn't be abandoning his allies, because all his would-be slayers would pursue him. But those same enemies were pressing him so hard that it was impossible to break away.

Retreating before another ettercap's advance, he heard a rattling overhead, looked up, and saw a falling star. The tasloi operating the hoists and windlasses had doubtless dropped the piece of stage dressing in hopes of hitting one of his assailants, but unfortunately, his timing was off.

Tal tried to dodge, but was too slow. Though only made of painted plywood, the star still struck him square and hard and dashed him to the floor.

He tried to drag himself out from underneath it, but his limbs barely stirred. Through blurry eyes, he watched his foes, human and otherwise, rushing in at him, and understood in a murky way that he was stunned, helpless, and in consequence about to die.

Then a primal, indomitable other roared up from the depths of his mind. He flung the star off and leaped to his feet. The moon wasn't full, he wasn't sprouting fur or fangs, but for this one moment, the wolf had nonetheless emerged to preserve the life the two of them shared.

The nearest bravos quailed before his feral grimace, or

perhaps the growl rumbling in his throat. The summoned creatures kept coming. Tal decapitated a green spider, gutted an ettercap, and stormed into the midst of his foes.

Somewhere deep inside himself, the rational, human Talbot cried out in protest, for in its berserk fury, the wolf was taking the wrong tack. If he rushed in among them, he might wreak havoc for a moment, but then his foes would assail him from all sides and overwhelm him. Alas, his bestial alter ego refused to heed him.

Talbot drove his long sword through the torso of a one-eyed tough armed with a battle-axe, killed a spider at the instant it shimmered from a translucent, ghostly condition into solidity, then, suddenly, he glimpsed another blade flashing alongside his own.

Startled, he glanced to see who his new ally was. Tazi, clad in a suit of dark leather he'd never seen her wear before, had darted out of nowhere to help him, and somehow, her unexpected appearance banished the wolf. He was himself once more.

His sister's sudden assault had likewise caught the enemy by surprise. Together with the wolf's devastating onslaught, it served to scatter them and drive them back.

It was the opportunity Talbot had been waiting for. "Come on!" he gasped, and he and Thazienne dashed for the exit at the back of the stage.

As the enemy lunged after them, a painted backdrop depicting a castle by the sea crashed down between the hunted and the hunters, delaying the latter for a precious moment. Tal heard his fellow players cheer.

The Uskevren's box had been reduced to a sad condition. Portions of the paneling and seats had been variously charred, shattered, warped, and covered in frost. Brom was sure he didn't look in any better shape. He was bruised, bloody, and blistered, and his good mocado doublet, purchased shortly after Lord Uskevren hired him and the first truly genteel article of clothing he'd ever owned, hung in tatters about his lanky frame.

Meanwhile, his masked opponent with the strange, pale eyes hovered unscathed in the air beyond the paling, looking exactly as he had at the start of their combat.

Sadly, Brom's situation was every bit as dire as it appeared. His adversary hadn't misspoken; he *was* the stronger wizard. Until now, Brom had managed to hold his own, but he knew he'd been lucky, and at this point, he'd expended most of his genuinely potent spells already. His rival's next assault was likely to finish him off.

Brom supposed he wouldn't have been human if he hadn't been tempted to turn tail. He imagined that if he fled the box, he'd probably survive, for after all, he wasn't the victim the other wizard actually wanted to kill. The masked man—*dead* man, if what he'd said before was true—had only engaged him for tactical reasons, to pin him down and keep him from magically preventing Master Talbot's murder.

But Brom vowed he wouldn't run. Lord Uskevren had trusted him to serve and defend his House, and he intended to do his duty.

He extracted a grubby cotton glove from his mantle, and then, although he hadn't dared to pay much attention to the fracas onstage since he started fighting himself, something about the situation below snagged his attention.

Mistress Thazienne had appeared to support her brother, and together, they flung his assailants back, turned, and fled for an exit. A backdrop smashed down behind them.

If only the masked wizard didn't realize they were escaping! But no. Perhaps he'd noticed where Brom was peering, or maybe it was simply the prompting of instinct, but in any case, he turned his head and looked, also.

"Well," he said to his fellow spellcaster, "it would appear that we don't need to continue our contest." He floated upward, seemingly intending to soar over the tiring house and intercept the Uskevren when they came out the other side.

Brom would have liked nothing better than to let the

other mage depart. But he knew Talbot and Thazienne needed a longer lead on their most formidable enemy to have any real hope of survival, and so he chanted and snapped the glove as if he were cracking a whip.

A huge, white, ghostly hand appeared in front of the masked wizard, hurtled at him, and shoved him backward through the air. For a moment, the spellcaster floundered helplessly against its luminous palm, then used his power of flight to distance himself from it. That gave him the space and freedom of movement to shout a word of power and swing his staff in an arc. The knob at the end slammed into the product of Brom's magic, and the hand vanished in an explosion of magenta fire.

The masked man turned toward Brom. "That was pointless. The Uskevren cadets are dashing headlong into a trap. Even if you slew me, it wouldn't save them. But if you insist on fighting to the bitter end, so be it." Snatching a packet from one of his pockets, he began to conjure.

Brom frantically did the same. If he could finish first, somehow slip a bit of countermagic past his enemy's wards, and disrupt the enchantment that held him aloft, the pale-eyed man would plummet—

He didn't finish first. Purple and emerald fire leaped from the other wizard's staff and engulfed him. For an instant, Brom had the terrifying impression that his flesh was attenuating, deforming, flying apart into particles finer than dust, and then he knew nothing more.

Talbot and Tazi plunged through the exit onto the snowy ground behind the playhouse, where the bodies of several more ettercaps lay motionless. The Wide Realms possessed an enchantment that held inclement weather at bay, and now Tal gasped at the bitter chill in the night air.

He and his sister sprinted toward a holding area where the palfreys and carriages of folk currently inside the theater awaited their owners' pleasure. Evidently the hostlers understood that something was amiss inside the walls, for they gaped at the newcomers. Or perhaps they were actually gawking in horror at the spiders, ettercaps, and ruffians charging over the open ground behind them. For though Tal hadn't looked back to check, he was confident his pursuers had yet to abandon the chase.

"Run!" he shouted to the hostlers, coachmen, footmen, and other servants loitering about.

True, the bravos and conjured creatures weren't actually hunting these innocents, but that was no guarantee that the hostile force wouldn't attack them if they were still lingering when it arrived.

The attendants scattered. Talbot untied his brown gelding, scrambled onto its back, and Tazi leaped onto the snow-white mare Brom had ridden.

Now that Tal was actually astride a mount, he risked a glance back at the playhouse. Sure enough, here came several spiders and ettercaps scuttling after him, and one or two toughs as well. Meanwhile, a spark of purple fire rose above the tiring house like a star of evil omen. Tal assumed it was the masked wizard, likewise taking up the pursuit.

The young noble shivered, and then he and Tazi spurred their steeds. They galloped for Stormweather Towers and left their foes behind.

CHAPTER 14

Had Nuldrevyn not already known it was morning, he could never have divined it from looking into Marance's suite. With the heavy, musty-spelling draperies still covering the windows, the hearth cold, and only a pair of candles burning, the parlor was as gloomy and chilly as ever.

The Talendar patriarch supposed he should have been glad of that, for he'd wanted his resurrected brother to dwell here discreetly, without doing anything to reveal his presence. Now he wished the chamber seemed a bit more like the abode of a living man and rather less like a tomb.

Marance himself sat before a chess table, the edges of the board set with the dusty, colorless crystals that adorned so many articles in the room. Fingering one of the ebony rooks, he was evidently playing a game against himself, albeit with the distracted air of a man who was devoting most of his thought to weightier matters. Meanwhile, occupying one of the divans, the loathsome Bileworm was a writhing, contorting mass, constantly shifting from one twisted, crippled-looking shape to another for some purpose Nuldrevyn couldn't comprehend, unless it was merely the familiar's amusement.

After a moment, both occupants of the suite sensed the presence of the visitors standing at the doorway. Marance turned, and, rising, gave his brother and nephew a smile. Bileworm rearranged his tangled substance into something more nearly resembling the shadow of a human being.

"Come in, kinsmen," Marance said. "Sit down."

Nuldrevyn kept a wary eye on Bileworm as he settled onto his chair, making sure the spirit wouldn't attempt another prank. As if divining his erstwhile victim's thoughts, the familiar gave him a leer.

"Can I pour you some wine?" Marance asked.

"Thank you, no," Nuldrevyn said. "Brother, we need to talk."

The wizard arched an eyebrow. "That sounds ominous."

"I don't mean it to," Nuldrevyn replied. "It's just that I'm concerned about what happened yesterday."

"Because my prey eluded me?" Marance strolled back to the chess table and retrieved his staff. "Then in all candor, I have to say that if I were you, I could find it in my heart to be patient. After I died, you had thirty years to exterminate the Uskevren, and you never succeeded in killing a single one of them. I've only been back in the world of the living for a few weeks, and already I've accounted for Thamalon and Shamur. And I would have bagged the youngsters yesterday, except for the Uskevren family mage. He was a better spellcaster than I expected, but he's out of the picture now."

"I don't think Father is upset that you haven't killed Thamalon the Second and the others yet," said Ossian, a bit diffidently. "Rather, he has concerns about your methods."

"Indeed," Marance said. "Then speak on, Nuldrevyn. I never close my ears to sound advice."

"I wasn't happy with that attack you conducted in broad daylight on a public street," Nuldrevyn said, "but it wasn't entirely reckless, so I held my tongue."

Bileworm opened his mouth, stuck out a waggling length of shadow stuff three feet long, and grabbed it with both hands.

"Stop that," Marance rapped, and the spirit obeyed. "As usual, brother, I apologize for my idiot servant's impudence. You were saying?"

"I feel that the attack inside the theater *was* too reckless," Nuldrevyn continued doggedly. "Your bravos and spiders hurt a number of innocent people."

Marance shrugged. "Since no one knows to hold the House of Talendar accountable, what difference does it make?"

"None, perhaps," Nuldrevyn said, "but my concern is that if matters had fallen out just a little differently, someone *could* have linked our family to the assault."

The mage frowned. "I don't see how."

"One of your henchmen could have been captured and interrogated," Nuldrevyn said.

"It wouldn't have mattered," Marance said. "They didn't know who I was. They didn't even know who Ossian was, correct?" He turned to the younger man for confirmation.

"That's true," Ossian admitted.

Smiling his gentle little smile, Marance pivoted back toward Nuldrevyn. "You see? The lad knows what he's about, and thanks to his circumspection, no one could possibly follow the thread that leads from the bullies to us."

"Perhaps," Nuldrevyn said, "but when you entered that theater, you were venturing into a crowd. What if someone had stabbed you in the back, or snatched off your mask?"

Marance shook his head. "Now you're being silly. I know how to handle myself, and even if I didn't, I was flying through the air well out of people's reach for nearly the entire time."

"Well, what if someone had gotten a good look at those white eyes of yours?"

"It wouldn't have mattered," Marance replied. "Your hypothetical observer still wouldn't have recognized me, nor would anyone to whom he spoke. I've been dead thirty years, Nuldrevyn. No one remembers me anymore. Even Thamalon, my slayer, couldn't place me."

"Maybe not," the old man said, "but I still think it would be wise for you to lay low."

"Lay low?" Marance repeated.

"Just for a little while," Ossian said quickly, "until the uproar over the attack on the playhouse dies down, and people stop looking for the man responsible."

"Such a delay is unnecessary," Marance said, "and I'm afraid it's unacceptable as well. I've waited a long time for my revenge. I don't intend to wait any longer."

"You've already killed Thamalon and Shamur," said Nuldrevyn. "Surely that was the main thing."

"Yes," said Marance, "but it wasn't the whole thing, nor will it be until the House of Uskevren is extinct."

"I promise," said Ossian, "we'll rid ourselves of Tamlin and his sibs eventually.

"I wonder if you could," Marance replied. "So far, they haven't turned out to be the dimwitted weaklings I was led to expect, and in any case, lad, you aren't hearing me. The Uskevren have to die by *my* hand, *now*, before my liege calls me back to the Iron City."

Nuldrevyn grimaced. "It's just that Ossian and I are worried—"

"To perdition with your worries," Marance said. "Don't you think you owe me this bit of satisfaction?"

Nuldrevyn hesitated. "I don't know what you mean."

"That's because I've never reproached you with it," Marance said. "But I told you that after Thamalon cut open my belly, it took me a long, excruciating time to succumb to my wound, a period during which I waited in vain for my brother to ride back to look for me. Had you done so, you might well have been able to save my life."

Nuldrevyn gaped at his brother in horror. "After Thamalon and his men broke our company, all was confusion.

I didn't see what happened to you, and assumed you were either dead or fleeing for your life like the rest of us survivors. Surely you know that if I'd had any inkling you needed me, I would have dared any peril to reach you!"

"If so," Marance replied, "then you should be equally keen to help me now. Are you?"

As Nuldrevyn gazed into the wizard's peculiar eyes, he felt a frisson of unease. He told himself it was nonsense. Dead and damned though he might be, Marance remained his brother and would never hurt him. Still, though it shamed him, he found himself reluctant to put his faith to the test.

"Of course I want to help you," the old man said. "Destroy Thamalon's get and we'll all dance on their graves. I just needed to make sure you intend to be careful."

"Absolutely," Marance said. "Even if I didn't wish to shield you, I would still have excellent reason to watch my step. What do you think would happen if someone here in the mortal realm killed me a second time?"

"I don't know," Nuldrevyn replied. "I wasn't even sure you could be killed. Wouldn't you simply go back to being a grandee in the netherworld? Or rise to attack the Uskevren once more?"

"Alas, no," the wizard said. "I have it on good authority that I'd turn back into a larva frying in a fire pit, and I daresay my rivals at court, baatezu lords who resent the fact that a human has risen to their level, would make very sure that I never escaped the flames or my uncouth shape again."

The wizard smiled. "But rest assured, neither you nor I are going to find ourselves embarrassed in that way or any other. My next ploy will carry our little campaign of vengeance to a successful conclusion. For while I was meditating, it suddenly came to me that I possess the means to destroy all three of Thamalon's cubs with a single stroke." He reached inside his mantle and produced a silver and sapphire brooch. "It's wonderful how the dark powers guide our hands, don't you think, even when we imagine we're doing something as inconsequential as picking up a souvenir."

CHAPTER 15

Shamur was cutting at the air, testing the heft and balance of yet another new broadsword, when she overheard a bushy-bearded butcher in a bloody apron regaling several associates with a booming account of attempts on her children's lives. Suddenly alarmed, she hastily paid the asking price for the weapon—the vendor was plainly surprised that she hadn't bothered to haggle—then strode across the marketplace to the newsmonger. Thamalon tramped along behind her.

"Mammoth spiders and scorpions crawling everywhere," the butcher said, milking the story for all it was worth, "so thick that the walls were black with them! A dozen evil necromancers conjuring showers of hail and vitriol from the air! The battle completely demolished the playhouse! Should you visit the site this morning, you won't see a building at all, just a field strewn with wreckage."

"Excuse me," Shamur said.

"My brother-in-law was there," the bearded man continued, not heeding her. "He witnessed every—"

"Excuse me," she repeated, more forcefully.

He rounded on her. "What?"

"I realize you're trying to tell this tale in your own fashion, but I beg you to clarify one point straightaway. Were any of the Uskevren sibs or their retainers killed?"

The butcher sneered. "I understand they lost their wizard and the captain of their household guard during the fight, but the sprouts all got away." For an instant, Shamur felt lightheaded with relief. "Isn't that always the way? Feuding nobles tear Selgaunt apart and endanger the lives of us commoners, but somehow the arrogant bastards themselves survive to plague us another day."

"And meanwhile, where's the Hulorn?" asked a goodwife with a wicker basket slung over her arm. "Reciting poetry? Swooning over a painting? Not keeping the peace, that's for sure!"

"We'd be better off without an aristocracy," said a tanner, his trade apparent from the stink that clung to him. "There are other ways to run things. The philosopher Rutilinus said . . ."

Shamur and Thamalon moved away.

"Torm's fist," the nobleman said, "we knew the children were in a certain amount of danger, but I certainly didn't expect two attacks in less than twenty-four hours. Deadly serious attacks, by the sound of it, even allowing for the exaggeration that inflates any tale as it makes the rounds."

"Our side must have believed itself prepared for the second assault," she said, "yet poor Captain Orvist and Master Selwick were slain anyway. That's . . . troubling."

"To say the least." Thamalon looked fretful and irresolute as she had seldom seen him, and for some reason, the sight tied a knot of complex emotion in her breast.

"You love the children, don't you?" she said.

He snorted. "You sound surprised."

"You always seem so disappointed in them."

"I am. Each of them has a great deal of growing up to do before he or she would be fit to lead our House, or even support it in any meaningful way, and it's disgusting that they aren't even trying! But that doesn't mean I don't care about them, or that I'm ready to give up on them."

Shamur shook her head. "I didn't realize. In recent years, after we Karns recouped our fortune, and the children were nearly grown, that was one of the reasons I continued my masquerade."

"I don't follow."

"I was afraid to give you the opportunity to annul our marriage, illegitimatize Tamlin, Thazienne, and Talbot, remarry, and sire an heir more to your liking."

He scowled. "It's clear why I was never able to understand you, woman, but it's becoming painfully obvious that you never understood me, either, and since *I* wasn't trying to conceal my true nature, that's a puzzle. But I suppose we have more immediate questions to ponder. We know now that the children are in graver peril than we supposed. Should we stop prowling the city incognito and go home, so we can look after them?"

Shamur frowned as she mulled it over. Finally she said, "They still have guards, Erevis, and the walls of a fortified mansion to protect them. Moreover, judging from our friend the butcher's admittedly garbled account, they did a fair job of fighting on their own behalf."

Thamalon snorted. "That must have been a fluke."

Shamur felt a reflexive surge of anger. They'd quarreled so often over Tamlin and Talbot, he belittling them, or so it had seemed to her, and she defending them. "That's unkind and unfair."

To her surprise, he hesitated, then said, "Yes, I suppose it is. Whatever their flaws, Tazi and Tal at least know how to swing a sword. Tamlin, too, perhaps. But be that as it may, you were observing that even with Jander and Brom gone, the children still enjoy a fair amount of protection."

"Yes, and I hope they have the sense to be careful from

now on. So perhaps in the long run, we'll serve them best by holding to our present course and tracking down Master Moon. Whereas if we emerge from hiding, he might well go to ground for a month or a year, then strike again when we relax our guard."

"You have a point," Thamalon said. "I guess it's on to the Scab, then."

Shamur attached the scabbard of her new sword to her belt, and the two nobles headed south, away from the waterfront and into the warehouse district. A frigid breeze chilled their faces and plucked at the folds of their cloaks. Snowflakes began to fall from the leaden clouds overhead.

"Are the children truly as feckless as you make them out?" she asked after a time.

"Of course they are," he said. "If you weren't always so keen to disagree with me, you'd perceive it, too."

"Do you think the estrangement between us is somehow to blame?"

"I don't know," Thamalon replied. She sensed that he felt as uncomfortable contemplating the possibility as she did. "I tried to be a good parent. So did you. Who could do more?"

"I wonder if I tried hard enough," she said. They halted at an intersection to let an ox cart laden with garden statuary go by. "How could I have, when my children don't really even know me?"

"Don't think that," he said. "Yes, you wore a mask for them as you did for everyone else. But the love and care you gave them were genuine, were they not? That was your true self, shining through."

"I hope so. Still, my situation must have influenced the way I treated them. It surely poisoned the bond I shared with Thazienne. From early on, when we first realized what a young hellion she was, I tried to mold her into the kind of staid, proper noblewoman that I myself hated being, and looking back, I don't even know why. Was I jealous of her for fencing, wrestling, and enjoying the life of the streets when I could no longer do those things myself? Am I that petty and spiteful?"

"Judging from my own experience," said Thamalon, "yes." He grimaced. "No, never mind, I shouldn't have said that. Your coldness toward me has no bearing on your performance as a mother. Actually, I believe you always meant well in your dealings with all the children, Tazi included. What's more, you were right to think she needs some reining in. Eventually, her penchant for theft is likely to land her in serious trouble."

"You may be right," she said, picking her way around a mound of filthy slush. "After all, that's what happened to me." They walked a few more paces. "I've been thinking about what you said before. You were right. I couldn't emulate my grand-niece's warm, gentle nature for very long. Once we were married, I had to change, in order to push you away."

Thamalon laughed an ugly little laugh. "You don't have to keep reiterating that you found me repulsive. I've already gotten the message."

"That's *not* what I meant." They strode past a furniture maker's factory whining and banging with the sounds of lathes, saws, and hammers. Shamur had to raise her voice a bit to make herself heard over the racket. "You didn't repel me. You were sweet and loving, and that was the problem. I realized the affection wasn't actually for me but for a dead girl, that your fondness would turn to rage and loathing if you ever discovered I was an impostor, and somehow that made our closeness too strange, difficult, and even painful to bear."

"I'm sure that had you revealed your true identity in the first year or two," he said, "I would have reacted as you say. Later on, I would still have been dismayed, but by that time you were an integral part of my life and the mother of our children. Perhaps, once I recovered from the shock, it wouldn't actually have mattered. Since you never found it in your heart to trust me, we'll never know."

Shamur didn't know what to say to that. She was relieved when they rounded a corner and the Scab came into view, recalling them to the task at hand.

Like much of Selgaunt, the Scab was built largely of brownstone. Some people claimed that the sandstone blocks that had gone to construct it possessed an odd, rusty tint that made them precisely the color of clotted blood. Others maintained that the walls in the rookery were the same hue as those found elsewhere, but that fanciful minds perceived them differently because of the area's sinister reputation. For while the city had other dangerous neighborhoods, the Scab was generally regarded as the worst. A maze of narrow, twisting alleys and decaying tenements, it was home to the poorest of the poor and every variety of vice and depravity. Shamur had heard that the Scepters never entered the rookery except in force, and even then with the greatest reluctance, which she supposed made it a desirable haven for the Quippers.

"Not an especially charming sight, is it?" Thamalon said.

"Not to my eye," she agreed. "Watch yourself in there. We mustn't look nervous or otherwise out of place."

"Don't worry about me," he replied. "Unlike my father, I never made common cause with pirates or bandits. But in the bad old days, when my fortunes were at low ebb, and scoundrels of all stripes assumed one lone, friendless trader would prove an easy mark, it helped me to learn to treat with them on their own level. Shall we?"

He gestured toward the arched entrance to the Scab. Once, the gate had probably been imposing, but now it was covered with lewd graffiti and looked as if it might collapse at any moment.

When they passed through, the first thing Shamur noticed was the mingled stench of various types of waste. Like the residents of other precincts, the inhabitants of the Scab tossed their refuse into the street, the difference being that no night-carter dared enter the rookery to collect it. The smell was sickening even with the muck half frozen. She hated to think how foul it was in the summer.

She and Thamalon began working their way from one tavern to the next, for despite the evidence of poverty abundant on every side, the Scab had more than its share of such establishments, squalid little ordinaries operating in dank, low cellars, cramped rooms devoid of seating, or even out in the open wherever some entrepreneur chose to set a keg on a pair of trestles. The nobles eavesdropped on the conversations of the rough men swilling stale beer and raw spirit, and joined in when it seemed feasible. Shamur was relieved to see that, as he'd promised, her husband's impersonation of a blackguard was reasonably convincing.

She enjoyed the game of fishing for information, knowing that if they misspoke, they'd likely face a room full of naked blades. But when they were simply traversing the streets, the sordid life of the Scab depressed her. Primarily, it was the children. She saw infants gaunt with starvation. Toddlers scavenging through the mounds of trash. Gangs of ragged, hard-eyed youths ranging the streets in search of the weak and unwary, not robbing for sport as she once had, but simply to survive. Little girls selling their bodies. Even a filthy, drunken surgeon of sorts who mutilated youngsters to prepare them for a life of begging.

At this last spectacle, Thamalon gave a wordless growl of disgust. "I've always heard it was bad in here, but I never dreamed it was this bad. There must be a way to clean up this cesspit, or tear it down and build something better. To put the needy inhabitants to work, and send the villains packing."

"The thought does you credit," she replied. "Someday soon, you can explore the subject with the city council, assuming, of course, that we make it out of here alive."

"Yes," he said, "assuming that." They descended a short flight of stairs to yet another wretched cellar taproom, the sole difference being that the proprietor of this one had apparently gone to the trouble to give it a name and a sign, clumsily daubing a pair of crossed blades on the door.

Snitch liked spying in the Crossed Daggers. The tavern was no warmer or more comfortable than a number of other filthy little taverns scattered through the Scab, nor was the conversation of the inebriated louts who drank there any more diverting. But the host, prompted by what Snitch regarded as preposterous optimism, kept a bottle of good brandy under the bar, just in case a discerning and prosperous customer ever wandered in by mistake. A galltrit like Snitch, a gray, bat-winged gremlin the size of a human hand, had no trouble sneaking up and raiding the supply, then slipping back to his hidey-hole undetected. Licking his chops with his long tongue, relishing the aftertaste of the liquor, he was just about to resume his post, a shadowy depression in the dilapidated wall, when the man in brown and the woman in black and gray walked in.

At first glance, they looked like just another pair of bravos, cleaner and less brutish than some, perhaps, but nothing out of the ordinary save for the fact that Snitch had never seen them before. Still, Avos the Fisher had captured and trained him to be his watchdog when he was only a pup. He'd been spying long enough to develop an instinct for it, and that sensibility told him to observe the newcomers closely. His crimson eyes narrowed, and his big, pointed ears perked up.

For a few minutes, the strangers sipped their ale quietly, seemingly keeping to themselves, but Snitch, a professional eavesdropper himself, sensed that they were attending to the conversations of the other patrons. As time passed, he judged from the subtle way they shifted closer that they were particularly interested in the remarks of a scrofulous tough with symbols of strength and good fortune tattooed on his cheeks and brow. The drunk was boring the taverner with a slurred account of his various exploits as a hired sword.

The willowy woman sauntered up beside him, rested her hand lightly on his, and, when he lurched around to face her, gave him a smile.

"Moon above," she purred, "I've been through a scrape or two in my time, but nothing as dicey as you describe. You just might be the toughest warrior I've ever met, and I insist that you do me the honor of letting me buy you a drink."

Snitch noticed the woman's companion looking on with a hint of ironic amusement in his green eyes, but the drunk took her flattery at face value. "Sure, darling," he said, leering, "you bet."

He tried to throw his arm around her and yank her close, but she evaded the fumbling attempt so deftly that, inebriated as he was, he might not realize she'd even moved, let alone avoided the embrace on purpose.

"I imagine you get hired for all the serious fighting that goes on around here," the woman said. "Did the Quippers use you on that crew they put together a day or two ago?"

Snitch bared his needlelike fangs. Since no one outside the gang was supposed to know about that particular job, his master would be more than interested to know that strangers were asking questions about it. The galltrit waited until none of the humans was looking in his direction, then spread his membranous wings, sprang from his perch, and flew out the door.

❧ ❧ ❧ ❧ ❧

Shamur and Thamalon trudged down yet another twisted alley in search of the next tavern. The cold wind whistled down the narrow passage. The snow began to fall a little harder.

"Another miss," Thamalon grumbled, "and I daresay the oaf with the tattoos would have confided in you if he'd known anything. Your imitation of a lickerish trollop was quite convincing."

"You'd know, wouldn't you?" she snapped.

"Ah," he said, "I see we're back to decrying my venery."

She felt a pang of guilt. "I'm sorry. I don't know why I do that, either. Plainly, you don't deserve it. Everyone in our circle takes lovers, and no one regards it as shameful, or indeed, anything but natural. Even the cuckolds and forsaken wives don't care. Why should they, when they're dallying with paramours of their own?"

"You never did," he said, "at least as far as I know."

"No."

"Another way of spiting yourself, belike."

"I don't know," she said. "Perhaps I simply realized that if my masquerade made it awkward to be intimate with you, I'd likely have the same problem with any other man."

"I'll tell you a secret," he said. "When we first married, I didn't want the same kind of half-hearted union as our peers. I intended to forsake all other women and devote myself to you alone. But later, when you rebuffed me . . ." He shrugged.

"Of course," she said glumly. "Why shouldn't you seek the beds of other women, when I appeared so averse to having you in my own?" She sighed. "Tazi asked me that very question once. Of course, I refused to discuss the matter like a human being. I went all cold and haughty, the way I usually do with her."

He grunted. "I can't say I'm sorry. I see no reason to burden the children with every sad detail of our travesty of a marriage, although I suppose they must realize—" He stopped abruptly to stare down the alleyway.

Shamur did the same. Bullies armed with slings, cudgels, and blades were slinking out of doorways and up cellar steps.

"Well," she said, "it would appear that once again, some busybody has seen fit to alert someone else that two outsiders are poking their noses in where they don't belong."

"I'd rather not fight if we can avoid it," Thamalon said. "They have us outnumbered, and with those slings, they could bring us down before we ever came into sword range."

"I agree," she said. "Let's try to get out of here."

They turned and strolled back in the direction from which they'd come, resisting the urge to look behind them or run headlong, lest they provoke the bravos into charging. Meanwhile, Shamur listened intently, trying to judge whether the toughs were quickening their pace to close the distance.

Suddenly she heard a thrumming, and a split second

later, a sling bullet whizzed past her ear. She and Thamalon broke into a sprint, zigzagging to throw off the aim of the slingers, and the bullies shouted and pounded after them.

A lead pellet cracked down into the frozen earth behind her. Her foot skidded on a patch of ice, but, her arms flailing, she managed to stay on her feet. Then another contingent of sneering bravos stepped into view ahead of her and Thamalon.

Now trapped between two groups of enemies, the Uskevren peered wildly about. Finally Shamur spotted a gap between two tenements. The crumbling brownstones had slumped toward one another, bringing their upper stories into contact, but a space remained at ground level.

"This way!" she shouted, and she and Thamalon scrambled toward the murky tunnel. Sling bullets hurtled all around them, but miraculously, none found its mark. She darted into the gap, and he followed. The corridor was so cramped it would have been impossible to run side by side.

It would take a good marksman to sling a missile down such a passage, but it could be done. Shamur feared she and Thamalon had a few seconds at most to find an exit before another barrage of pellets hurtled at their backs. She had all but given up hope of doing so when a gap in the wall to the right swam out of the gloom.

She plunged around the corner and found herself at the terminus of another alley. As she and Thamalon ran down it, the thudding footsteps of their pursuers echoing behind them, Shamur realized she had no idea where the passage was taking them, for both she and her husband were strangers to the Scab. They would have to flee blindly, uncertain which of the labyrinthine paths led out of the rookery and which looped back around to their points of origin. Whereas the enemy doubtless knew the slum intimately, down to every shortcut, twist, and turn. She suspected the bullies might not have much trouble keeping track of their quarry, getting ahead of them, or herding them wherever they wanted them to go.

Sure enough, the nobles sprinted around a bend and

found several ruffians waiting. Instantly, the enemy whirled their slings. Shamur and Thamalon wheeled and retreated. They heard other foes rushing up from that direction, and scrambled down another branching passage.

It went on like that for a long, wearisome time, until both nobles were panting and drenched in perspiration. Whenever Shamur thought she'd spotted a route to safety, toughs would appear to cut them off, and they had to flee back deeper into the Scab. She was grateful that at least the ordinary inhabitants of the rookery didn't seem interested in aiding the Quippers, but they were evidently too leery of the gang to try to help their intended victims, either. Whenever the hunted or hunters approached, the poor darted into their homes, slammed and barred the doors behind them, and peeked out between the nailed boards or rickety, crooked shutters on their windows.

At last the Uskevren staggered into a malodorous little courtyard, where beady-eyed rats rustled through piles of festering trash. Three other alleyways led away from this spot, and, by now thoroughly disoriented, Shamur had no notion which one to take. Since for the moment, none of the Quippers seemed to be right on their heels, she paused to take her bearings and catch her breath.

Thamalon slumped against a soot-stained wall. "We did better fleeing through the woods," he wheezed. "The daylight and these closed-in spaces are killing us. We may have to try to fight, and the odds be damned."

"Perhaps," she said, shivering and drawing her cloak about her. Now that she'd stopped running, the wind was doing its best to freeze her sweaty tunic. "If we have to make a stand, let's do it somewhere they can only come at us from one direction, and only one or two at a time. But I consider that the option of last resort."

"Agreed. And wife, whatever happens, I want you to know one thing."

"What's that?"

"I blame you for our predicament. If you recall, I suggested we go home."

For a moment, she bristled, then realized he'd made a joke. "Don't be a spoilsport," she said, grinning. "Home is dull compared to this."

She still hadn't managed to figure out what direction they should take, but she could hear hunters calling to one another, stalking closer, and knew they shouldn't remain in the courtyard any longer.

"How about this way?" she said, pointing to an alley at random.

"It looks as good as any," he replied. "Let's move."

In fact, when they crept to the other end of the crooked passage and peeked around the corner, she decided their selection might be quite good indeed, for it had brought them back almost to the point at which they'd entered the Scab. The graffiti-blemished arch was about sixty feet to their right, and no one appeared to be guarding it.

"It looks too good to be true," Thamalon whispered.

"I know what you mean," she replied, "but in my experience, people don't always hunt you in the most effective way possible. Perhaps the Quippers really didn't leave any sentries here."

"Or perhaps not enough of them," he said, "and so far, this is as close as we've come to escaping this maze. Let's try to make a run for it."

They charged out into the narrow street and dashed toward the gate. Four bravos scrambled from their places of concealment to cut them off.

To the Pit with it, Shamur thought. She'd overcome worse odds in her day. Grinning fiercely, she drew her sword and ran on. Beside her, Thamalon did the same.

Something hummed, and she heard the distinctive smack of a sling bullet slamming into flesh and bone. Thamalon made a choking sound and fell.

She lurched to a halt, spun around, and saw the half dozen toughs rushing up the street behind her. Another sling bullet whizzed past her as she crouched beside her husband.

The back of his head was bloody, and he was clearly dazed. "Get up!" she said, tugging on his arm.

"Can't," he croaked. "You run. Maybe you can still get away."

Perhaps she could, particularly, it suddenly occurred to her, if she took to the rooftops. Certainly it would be prudent to make the attempt. But she couldn't find it in her heart to leave him lying helpless in the street when, for all she knew, the bullies meant to slay him out of hand.

"We're both going to get away," she said. "I'm going to kill every one of these bastards, and then we'll stroll on out of here."

She leaped to her feet, screamed, and charged the larger of the two groups of toughs. They clearly hadn't expected that, and for an instant, they froze. One of the slingers was still trying to fumble his short sword out of its scabbard when she cut him down.

Pivoting, she dropped a second ruffian with a thrust to the throat, and took a third out of action with a slash to the sword arm. The remaining ones fell back.

She could hear the four who'd been lurking near the gate pounding up behind her. She had only seconds to kill the men in front of her so she could whirl and fight the others. She advanced, the broadsword low, inviting attack in the high line. A scar-faced man in a red doublet took the bait and slashed at her face. She parried and drove her point into his chest.

At that same instant, another ruffian attacked. Since she was still yanking her weapon from his comrade's body, she had to slap his dagger out of line with her unweaponed hand. Then the broadsword pulled free, but the bravo had lunged in too close for her to readily use the blade. She smashed the pommel against his temple, and he dropped.

One left! She pivoted to engage him, and then her time ran out.

Pain blazed in the center of her back. Certain that someone had stabbed her, she snarled and tried to pivot around to maim him in turn, but lost her balance and fell. The surviving toughs surrounded her, striking and kicking, until she no longer had any strength to resist.

CHAPTER 16

Wyla found Magnus and Chade loafing in their usual hidey-hole in the loft, at the far end of the warehouse from her own cluttered little office. She often wondered that they didn't find a new haven in which to hunker down and shirk, someplace she hadn't yet discovered, but perhaps they were too lazy even to bother with that.

"Come on, sluggards," the thickset woman with the graying ponytail said. "There's work to be done."

"I guess," said Magnus, a stooped, middle-aged man with jug-handle ears. To her surprise, he didn't sound sheepish or put-upon, but instead, somber and worried as if he and his fellow laborer had been having an uncharacteristically serious conversation.

"Is something the matter?" she asked.

"You must have heard about the trouble," said Chade. A swarthy, rather handsome young man with a mellifluous baritone voice, he was as usual rather too well dressed for his job of lugging bales and boxes about. "The Uskevren heir and cadets were attacked yesterday. Captain Orvist and Master Selwick died in the fighting. What's more, it's rumored that Lord Uskevren himself hasn't been seen for a couple of days."

"Certainly I've heard about it," Wyla said. "What I don't understand is what it has to do with you two gentlemen of leisure stacking crates onto wagons."

"I know how things used to be," Magnus said. "Back when Lord Uskevren first came back to town. Enemy Houses attacked his caravans, shops, manufactories, and *warehouses* to try and ruin his family a second time."

"Those days are over," Wyla said. "Besides, if any rogues showed up here to make trouble, don't you think the three of us could show them off?"

She fingered the well-worn hilt of the long sword hanging at her side. She'd owned the blade since her youth, when she'd served the House of Uskevren as a warrior. Eventually a lamed leg had ended her martial career, whereupon Lord Thamalon, who'd realized her talents from the beginning, had made her one of his factors. She had little use for the weapon these days, and sometimes its weight made her bad leg ache, but she would have felt undressed without it.

"We'd damn well try to drive them off," said Chade, "and failing that, I suppose *we* could run away. But I'm not worried about us so much as Lord Uskevren himself. Do you think he's all right?"

"Absolutely," Wyla said, "and since I rode with him through the hardest and most dangerous of times, and saw firsthand what a cunning and doughty warrior he is, I'm in a position to know."

"I hope so," said Chade. "He's a good man to work for, not like some. Remember how he invited us all to Stormweather Towers for that feast, and helped when Fossandor's mother was going to lose her cottage?"

"I do," said Wyla, "and I tell you again, whatever it is that's happening, he and his family will be fine. Unless all his workers shirk their tasks, and his trading empire collapses."

Magnus rolled his eyes. "All right, we get the point."

He and Chade clambered to their feet, stepped from behind the rampart of crates upon which they relied to conceal themselves from her view, and started down the ladder to the warehouse floor. Wyla followed. As with wearing her sword, negotiating the ladder was hard on her leg. With her muscular arms, it was actually easier to hoist herself up and down on the lift. She refused to resort to such a shift, however, lest it make her feel like a cripple in truth.

Magnus and Chade sauntered outside to wheel a wagon into position for loading, slamming the door behind them. Wyla limped back toward her office, through a shadowy, cavernous space packed with wood carvings, rolled carpets, kegs of nails, stoneware, cheap pine coffins, unassembled looms, and countless other items the House of Uskevren bought, manufactured, and sold.

A mild tenor voice said, "I'm sorry, but you're wrong."

Wyla spun around. A stranger dressed in a crescent-shaped Man in the Moon mask and a dark blue mantle stepped from behind a shelf laden with scythes, sickles, hoes, and plows. A creature of oozing darkness, its precise shape difficult to make out in the dimness, flowed out in his wake.

"You're the wizard who led the attacks on Lord Thamalon's children," Wyla breathed.

"I am indeed," the masked man said, "and as I was observing, as a result of my efforts, I'm afraid the House of Uskevren is actually rather far from being 'all right.' I killed Thamalon and Shamur already, and with your help, I'm about to dispose of their children as well."

Wyla didn't understand what the spellcaster meant, nor did she especially care. She was too busy trying to figure out how she might possibly survive this encounter, for plainly, whatever else was afoot, the masked man must surely mean her harm.

It would be useless to scream. With its rows of shelving and stacks of goods piled everywhere, the warehouse swallowed sound. And, given her lameness, it would be equally futile to turn and run. The wizard would undoubtedly have sufficient time to cast a spell on her before she scrambled out of sight, and for all she knew, his shadowy companion might pounce on her from behind.

She had only one option, then. Try to get in close, hurt the masked man, and keep on hurting him until he was dead. Her old master-at-arms had taught her that was how you kept a hostile wizard from working any magic.

She'd have a better chance if she could somehow catch him by surprise. To that end, she said, "Just tell me what you want from me, and I'll do it. I don't want to die."

"Would that I could trust you," the wizard replied. "But I remember how devoted you were to Thamalon in the old days, I rather doubt you've—"

She whipped out her sword and charged him.

Reacting instantly, the wizard skipped nimbly backward, snatched a small length of iron from one of his pockets, brandished it, and rattled off a rhyme.

Purple fire flared from the end of his polished staff, bathing her in stinging though tepid flame. Her muscles clenched painfully, depriving her of the ability to move. Off balance, she fell facedown on the floor.

Struggling to jump back up, all Wyla's rigid body could do was shudder. He took hold of her, and, grunting, rolled her over onto her back. Gazing helplessly up at him, she noticed the strange pale eyes peering from their holes in his blandly smiling mask.

"That ploy might almost have worked," he said, "except that two nights ago, Shamur Uskevren made a move and caught me flatfooted when I was in mid-sentence. I've been more careful since. Good-bye, Wyla." He took hold of a portion of his mantle, folded it to make a double thickness, then pressed it down on her face.

Bileworm watched avidly as Master smothered the woman. By his standards, it wasn't an especially long or excruciating death, but he could certainly imagine Wyla's terror and frustration as, deprived of all capacity to resist, she suffocated, and that gave him something to savor.

After a minute, Master took the folds of cloth away and held his hand above her mouth, making sure her breathing had ceased.

"Well, thank goodness that's done," he said. "I thought those two loafers in the loft were never going to leave."

"Shall I?" Bileworm asked.

"Of course."

The spirit spiraled upward, stretching his substance thin, then swooped down and slid through the tiny space between Wyla's upper and lower teeth. Once he was completely inside her, and had aligned his own ethereal limbs with the coarse matter of the corpse's, sensation came. The floor, hard and cold against his back. His hand clenched painfully tight on the sword hilt. A slight rawness on his face, where the weave of Master's mantle had chafed Wyla's skin.

He reached inside himself for the lame warrior's memories. For an instant, he glimpsed a chaotic jumble of images and sensations, loves and hates, joys, sorrows, and regrets. Then it burst like a bubble and left nothingness behind.

He frowned, prompting Master to ask, "What's the matter?"

"We have a problem," Bileworm said, climbing to his feet, surprised by the sharpness of the twinge in the calf of the bad leg. "I own the body, but her mind is gone."

"Don't worry. It shouldn't matter."

Bileworm hesitated. "Are you sure?"

"Of course. No one will doubt you're the person you appear to be. Why should they? Nor will our dupes, worried as they surely are, bother you with personal questions to which you have no answers. Their only concern will be the tidings you bring."

CHAPTER 17

Shamur watched with admiration as Thamalon, seemingly recovered from the ill effects of his head wound, approached the dais and throne at the far end of the cavernous chamber. With his chin held high and his easy smile, he looked more like an honored envoy at the court of some friendly monarch than a prisoner in a den of robbers and murderers.

Meanwhile, the chieftain of the Quippers, a blond, square-jawed hulk as huge as Talbot or Vox, evidently liked to affect the appearance of a simple fisherman, for he sported the sandals, slop-hose, and open, sleeveless tunic that such folk often wore in clement weather. The creature on his knee, however, rather spoiled the illusion, for it was a gray, red-eyed galltrit. Such gremlins lived in filth and, like leeches, subsisted on the blood of others. No common waterman would treat such a nasty beast like a pet. Shamur suspected no one would, unless his own disposition and habits were equally foul.

Arriving at the foot of the dais, Thamalon inclined his head, respectfully but by no means servilely. "Good morning, or is it afternoon by now? Either way, you must be Avos the Fisher. My name is Balan, and my companion is Evaine. We work for the House of Karn."

It was a bold lie, but not, Shamur thought, an idiotic one. Though Thamalon had opposed the Quippers off and on for a number of years, it had always been through the medium of the Scepters and other agents, never face to face. It was quite possible that none of the rogues assembled in this room had ever seen him up close, or her either. Or at least, not unless the knave in question was one of the those who had accompanied Master Moon into the woods.

Even if some of them had, the Uskevren still might go unrecognized. They'd changed their appearances since the previous encounter, and, by venturing unescorted into the Scab, had behaved in a manner that no one would expect of an aristocrat. Moreover, all the scoundrels gathered here presumably "knew" that Shamur and Thamalon were dead, and that false certainty might serve to disguise them best of all.

She held her breath as she waited to see if he was going to get away with the deception.

By the time the ruffians in the street had finished subduing and disarming her, she'd realized she hadn't been stabbed or cut in the back after all, just clubbed very painfully, and thereafter, all the toughs had contented themselves with battering her with the flats of their blades, their boots, or other blunt implements. Evidently they wanted to take her and Thamalon alive for questioning.

The bravos tended in the most cursory fashion to their wounded comrades, rifled the pockets of the slain ones, then roughly hauled the nobles to their feet and marched them away, one scoundrel running on ahead to carry the news of their apprehension. At first the Quippers virtually had to carry Thamalon, but to Shamur's relief, he revived by the time they reached their destination.

On the outside, that terminus was yet another grimy, crumbling brownstone tenement. Inside, she saw that the Quippers had transformed the bottom two floors of the building into what might almost be deemed a parody of a spacious, lordly hall, tearing out the ceiling and most of the interior walls to create a single open space. The renovation had left scars and grit behind. Rats scuttled in the shadows. Trash and litter rotted wherever anyone had cared to drop it.

Yet atop the rubble and decay lay a veneer of luxury, like sweet frosting on a toadstool. Costly furniture, disintegrating rapidly from the hard and careless use it was receiving, stood haphazardly about the floor, along with kegs of ale and racks of wine. Paintings and tapestries hung crookedly on the walls. Some had been used for target practice, and the hilts of throwing knives jutted from their surfaces. Others had been scrawled upon in the expression of a coarse and ribald wit. Shamur surmised that all these once-fine articles constituted booty stolen from the docks. A miscellany of nautical implements, including oars, harpoons, nets, and a collection of painted figureheads, added yet another note of bizarreness to the décor.

The hall was likewise full of surly-looking toughs and their hard-eyed doxies, many of whom had peered curiously as the Uskevren's captors shoved them toward Avos the Fisher's seat.

Now the huge rogue sneered down at Thamalon. "What did you think you were playing at," he rumbled, in a voice as deep as Shamur had ever heard issue from a human throat, "poking around in my domain?"

Shamur felt a frisson of excitement. Avos hadn't challenged Thamalon's assertion that the two of them were mere agents of the House of Karn. Evidently he believed it. The nobles were still in deadly peril, of course, but perhaps not quite as much as if the Quippers had known who they really were. It was just conceivable that they might be able to talk their way out of this predicament.

Thamalon smiled up at Avos. "In retrospect, it doesn't seem like such a good idea. But our master commanded us to come to the Scab and ferret out information. We hoped we could obtain it and depart without attracting unwanted attention. Plainly, we were overly optimistic."

Avos snorted. "Aye, cully, you were. There was a time when you might have slipped in and out unnoticed, but not anymore. These days, *I* rule the Scab, and I know it every time a roach crawls or a louse bites. Now, what were you trying to find out?"

Thamalon shrugged. "If your spies"—at this the galltrit preened and leered, baring its pointed fangs, and Avos scratched it behind the ear—"overheard us, you presumably know already. We're inquiring into the murders of Shamur Uskevren, who was born a Karn, and her husband."

Some of the watchers muttered to one another. Avos shot them a glare, and they subsided. "Why, I didn't even know they had been murdered," the big man said, in a tone of mock innocence that made it plain he didn't care whether Thamalon believed him or not. "What makes you think the Quippers had anything to do with it?"

"Lord Karn is certain you did," Thamalon replied. "As I understand it, one member of your band, a fellow with fish-scale tattoos and a gold ring in his lip, related the tale to the wrong streetwalker, who subsequently sold it to my employer."

"That pinhead!" one of the onlookers exclaimed.

"Quiet!" Avos snarled, then gave Thamalon a malevolent smile. "I can't imagine how you'd ever be able to repeat anything I say, but I suppose I should deny everything just as a matter of principle."

"That would be prudent, though futile," Thamalon said. "The assassination of two of the most prominent nobles in the city is a grave matter. Should your involvement become common knowledge, Selgaunt might rouse itself and do whatever's necessary to eradicate the Quippers. Fortunately for you, however, Lord Karn understands you fellows were acting for someone else, a peer from a rival House, most likely, and that's the man he particularly wants to chastise. So I propose a bargain on his behalf. Give up the person who hired you, and the House of Karn will keep your secret and leave you in peace. We'll even pay you."

Avos's piggy pale blue eyes narrowed. "Why didn't you seek me out right off if you wanted to make a deal like that?"

"Because we didn't actually *want* to," Thamalon said. "The Karns would have preferred to learn their enemy's identity without having to spare you the retribution you deserve, let alone compensate you. But my partner and I are realists. Our current situation being what it is, we'd much rather reach an accommodation with you than have you kill us."

Avos grinned. "But that's what I ought to do. It would send a message to everybody else who might want to come sniffing around my little fiefdom."

"It's not a message that will deter Lord Karn. He has plenty of other agents."

"Maybe so, cully, but we're not afraid of any of them. Lots of high-and-mighty merchant nobles have tried before to wipe out the Quippers, and we're still here."

"But I imagine life is pleasanter when you're spared the necessity of defending yourselves against such a siege."

"That's doesn't mean we'd turn traitor or informer to keep it from happening."

"Of course not," Thamalon said dryly. "I'm sure you're a steadfast band of brothers. Loyal as paladins in a romance, but only, and this is the key point, to one another. I suspect that any outsider who opts to trust you takes his chances. Am I right?"

"No, you're not right," the big man growled, "not always. But . . . I didn't altogether like the way this particular job went down. Oh, Uskevren and his lady dying, that was grand. That was fine as cakes and wine. But too many of the lads have been killed or hurt, lads I need to attend to *my* business, and nobody bothered to warn me what we were getting into. I don't appreciate that. So, Balan, swear by your god that Lord

Karn will abide by any agreement you make, and then tell me how much gold you're offering."

"No!" shouted one of the onlookers, a small man with a pointed black goatee, and lines of gold piping running up the legs of his breeches and the breast of his doublet. "You can't set these snoopers free. *She* killed some of our mates! That woman there!"

"Shut up, Donvan!" Avos roared, and the little man quailed. "If a female could kill them, we're better off without them."

Shamur could tell from his subordinates' expressions that some resented their leader's cold dismissal of the deaths of their comrades, but no one saw fit to voice another protest.

Her heart raced with exhilaration. Against all rational expectation, Thamalon had succeeded. His glib trader's tongue had won them their lives and even the information they had sought.

Or so it seemed until someone shouted, "Hold it!"

She turned and saw a plump, unhealthy-looking man in a costly but hideous mauve and chartreuse doublet, the same would-be coxcomb who had stood with Master Moon and the shadow creature at the edge of the clearing, scurrying forward. Evidently he'd entered the brownstone unnoticed a moment or two before.

"What do *you* want, Garris?" Avos asked, an edge of impatience in his voice.

"Look at them!" Garris cried. "Everybody look! Don't you recognize them? Avos, I know I said I watched them die, but somehow, these people are Lord and Lady Uskevren themselves!"

The room fell silent as everyone gawked at the nobles. Shamur looked at the armed men clustered all around her and decided it would be pointless to try to break for the door. Finally, Avos exclaimed, "Umberlee's kiss, it's true!"

His composure unruffled, Thamalon gave Garris a nod. "You have a keen eye, sir." He turned back toward the giant on the throne. "I see no reason why this revelation should spoil our negotiations. I'm still willing to pay for the name of the man who hired you, and now, of course, to ransom my wife and myself as well."

Avos laughed. "You've got brass, old man, I'll give you that. But I don't suppose you truly believe we'd ever turn you loose. You've always gone out of your way to persecute the Quippers, and now we're going to return the favor. Then later, after we've had our fun, I'll sell what's left of you to your secret enemy. You can find out who he is when you look him in the face, that is, if we let you keep your eyes. Grab them, mates!"

So be it, Shamur thought. Thamalon's gambit had failed, and now she must try the ploy she had conceived on the walk to the outlaws' lair. One of the toughs who were moving in to seize her was half a step in advance of the others. Rounding on him, her bruised limbs protesting, she shouted, "Bring a waste, cove!" Then she kicked him in the groin.

Someone tried to grab her from behind. "Shamur knows that cog," she growled.

She thrust her elbow back into his gut, stamped on his foot, and then, when his grip loosened, pivoted and smashed her forearm into his jaw. His front teeth broke, and he reeled backward.

She spun back around to face the rogues rushing up behind her. "Come on!" she screamed. "You capons! You cousins! Shamur will bash out your crashing-cheats! She'll curb out your glaziers and eat them like grapes!"

Since she knew she had no chance of fighting her way free, her resistance was in one sense a sham. But she had to buy herself sufficient time to let them hear her rant. For all she knew, they might have intended to stuff a gag in her mouth before commencing whatever torture they had in mind.

Now, plainly, they had heard her. They were hanging back and staring, some with more comprehension than others. "She speaks Cant," Donvan said.

Cant was the secret patois of the most professional of thieves, useful both for confounding eavesdroppers and as a means of mutual recognition. Shamur had mastered it in her youth, and still remembered most of it though she hadn't had occasion to use it since her displacement in time.

"You're damn right, copesmate," she said. "Of course, Shamur talks Cant. She pledged to Mask when she was only a rumpscuttle lass, before any of you flicks and ferrets were even born. She's practiced the figging law, nipping purses with a cuttle-bung. She's been a charm and a cony-catcher, a foin, a padder, and a prigger of prancers, a warp and a stall. Later, she married that gentry cove there." She jerked her chin at Thamalon, currently standing battered and helpless in the grip of two of his captors. "But slipping on his fambling-cheat didn't change what Shamur was inside."

"You've led a colorful life," Avos drawled, "but so what? Did you think we'd spare you just because you were once a fellow rogue? Not likely!"

"I was more than a rogue," Shamur replied. "I was a Quipper."

The bravos and doxies babbled to one another. Avos said, "Nonsense."

"It was more than thirty years ago," she replied, "before your time or that of anyone in this hall." And since she was lying, thank the gods for that! "But I can still give the sign: Sharp eyes, sharp blade. Still tread, still tongue." In her mind, she blessed the lovesick, drunken Quipper who had once whispered the gang's secret protocols in her adolescent ear.

Some of the blackguards were visibly impressed by her recitation. Avos simply scowled and said, "I still don't believe you were ever one of us, but if you were, you're now a traitor for slaying some of your own brothers, and we have even better reason to hurt you."

"I slew them in self-defense," Shamur said, "as our rule permits. But we don't even need to debate that, and I'll tell you why. We say, once a Quipper, always a Quipper, do we not? Even death can't break the bond; the shades of our predecessors are waiting to welcome us into the chapter of the brotherhood they've established in Hell."

Avos grinned. "Then if you're telling the truth, you'll be seeing them soon."

"Not necessarily," Shamur replied, "because it is likewise our tradition that any of our members accused of wrongdoing has the right to demand a trial by combat against the chieftain of the gang, and go free if he prevails."

The big man laughed. "You want to fight me?"

"Yes," she said.

"Do it, captain!" someone shouted. "We haven't watched you scrap in a while."

Shamur could see enthusiasm for the idea running through the crowd like a fever. In all likelihood, a number of the rogues simply craved the spectacle of a bloody duel. Some seemed to think it a splendid joke that the slender captive would think to challenge their enormous and no doubt formidable leader. While others, perhaps, wanted to see Avos annoyed and inconvenienced, because they still resented his indifference to the slaying of their fellows, or disliked his bullying ways in general.

"Don't be stupid," Avos said to his followers. "The wench is lying. How many female Quippers have there ever been? Damn few!"

"She knows Cant and the Quipper signs," said Garris, and then flinched when Avos scowled at him.

"Who cares if she was a Quipper or not?" cried another ruffian. "Let's have a little sport!"

"Yes," Donvan said ironically, "why not? After all, Avos, if you can't defeat a female, we're better off without you."

The blond hulk snorted. "All right, mates, if that's how everybody wants it, I suppose it doesn't matter if Lady Uskevren here"—his sneering tone turned the title into a mockery—"dies quickly. It's her man I truly want to pick apart, just as he's the package our associate will really want to buy. But I can't promise you much of a show. Not only is the prisoner a woman, she's well past her prime."

"I wouldn't be surprised if the Quippers I've already killed thought that very same thing," Shamur replied. "Give me back my broadsword, and I'll do my best to make our contest as interesting as possible."

Avos sneered. "If you truly were a Quipper, you should

remember that in a duel like this, he who was challenged has the choice of weapons."

In fact, Shamur hadn't known, and now she felt a twinge of apprehension. "Oh, of course," she said lightly. "What did you have in mind?"

"I'll show you," he said.

Avos snapped his fingers, gave the galltrit a final caress, then set the creature gently on the arm of his chair. As he rose and stepped down from the dais, one of his underlings hurried up with two unusual sets of weapons, each composed of a short sword and a fishing gaff, a sturdy, four-foot shaft of wood with a barbed steel hook at the end.

Shamur had never heard of anyone fighting with such a tool. She wondered if Avos had invented this particular mode of combat, and was its sole master. That would certainly tilt the odds in his favor whenever any of his fellow Quippers dared to challenge him.

"Look them over," Avos said, "then choose the ones you like."

She took him at his word, hefting the weapons to check their weight and balance and finding little to choose between them. She settled on the gaff that was a hair lighter and the short sword with the narrower, sharper point. "These will do," she said.

"Good," he said. "Now, just so we're clear: Your husband doesn't claim to be a Quipper, and even if a god reaches down and smites me, which is about the only way I can see you winning, Thamalon stays with us."

"Fair enough," she said. "Let's do this."

"After you, milady." He waved her toward a circle sloppily painted on the concrete floor. Judging from the rusty stains inside it, it had served as a dueling arena on a number of previous occasions.

Shamur and Avos took their places at opposite ends of the ring. The other ruffians crowded around its border. Garris, assuming the director's role, declared, "The fight will continue until one duelist yields or is unable to continue. Fighters, come on guard." Shamur copied her opponent's stance, slightly crouched, with the gaff in the lead hand. "And . . . begin!"

The two combatants circled, sizing one another up, looking for openings. Shamur was likewise trying to figure out how one fought with this particular set of weapons. The essential principle seemed clear enough: Use the long gaff to snare an opponent, either by hooking one of his limbs or snagging his flesh with the barbed point, then yank him close and thrust the short sword into his vitals. With his superior reach and strength, Avos could no doubt execute all the variations on the basic maneuver very well.

Still, she could envision an effective counter. Parry her enemy's gaff with her own, then hold the parry to keep his weapon at bay while *she* closed the distance, bringing them both well into short sword range before he was expecting it. Caught by surprise at such close quarters, Avos would have a hard time defending against a low thrust to the belly.

The Quipper chieftain stepped forward just far enough to flick his gaff's hook behind her shoulder. Beginning the sequence of actions she'd devised, she parried, but her weapon never made contact with that of her opponent.

Instantly, with a quickness phenomenal in so huge a man, Avos dropped into a squat. He slipped the gaff around the calf of her lead leg and yanked it toward him. Shamur kicked frantically to free herself, and by sheer good luck more than anything else, her leg came out of the hook. The point caught in her leather boot for a second, then tore free.

Now she was reeling and in imminent danger of toppling backward. Avos surged up out of his squat and rushed her, his short sword leveled at her breast. Some of his comrades cheered in anticipation of the death thrust.

As well they might, for, utterly bereft of balance as she was, Shamur could neither parry, dodge, nor attempt a counterattack. She reckoned that all she could do was finish falling, and so she endeavored to do so as quickly as possible, *hurling* herself down to the cold, hard concrete floor.

As she'd hoped, Avos blundered right over the top of her. She tried to hook his ankle with her gaff before he could wheel back around to face her, but she missed.

She grinned as she scrambled back to her feet. Sometimes, for some perverse reason, it struck her funny when she cheated death by a hair, and this was one of those occasions.

"Very good," she said to Avos, "you nearly had me. But I think I'm starting to get the hang of this game. Feint, deceive, then attack, just like in ordinary fencing."

He sneered. "Got it figured out already, have you?" Advancing, he swung his gaff like a war club, whipping the head in a backhanded strike at her face.

She stepped back out of distance and kept on retreating around the circle, counterattacking and riposting vigorously enough to keep him from pressing her as hard as he might have otherwise, but essentially remaining on the defensive while she waited for him to use the same high feint, drop, and hook to the leg he'd tried before. She reckoned it was only a matter of time. The combination had almost won him the fight. Eventually he was bound to try it again. She just had to stay alive until he did.

Actually, that wasn't turning out to be an enormous problem. He was discovering the same thing she had learned while chasing Thamalon about the clearing. It was difficult to hurt an opponent who constantly gave ground. Indeed, she began to enjoy thwarting him, and grinned at the frustration in his ruddy, sweaty face and porcine eyes.

At last he threatened her shoulder, and her instincts told her he was attempting the compound attack she wanted him to make. She parried anyway, to convince him the trick was working and to protect herself in case she was mistaken, and he dropped to one knee. His gaff swept at her leg.

Having anticipated the attack, she hopped to one side and easily avoided it. Before he could come back to any sort of guard, she lashed her own gaff at his head.

She meant to set the barb in his flesh, but, perhaps because of her unfamiliarity with this peculiar weapon, that didn't happen. Still, clanking against his skull, the steel hook split open his scalp.

The spectators roared. Shamur aimed her short sword and lunged. Avos blindly swept his gaff up in a blow that, though it failed to connect solidly, brushed her back and gave him time to lurch to his feet.

Blood streamed from the scalp wound, trickling down the ruffian's face. Shamur relished the sight of it, and his shocked expression even more so.

"I told you I was getting the hang of it," she said.

Avos shouted and rushed her. She retreated, waiting for the right opportunity, and, thirty seconds later, bashed him again.

Thamalon supposed he should have been too concerned about the fundamental question of their survival to dwell on lesser matters, but once again, as at other moments during the past two days, he found himself marveling at Shamur's deportment in the face of danger.

The Uskevren lord had done plenty of fighting during his long and turbulent life. He liked to think he had seen it through with reasonable fortitude. But while he had certainly savored his victories, and taken pleasure in fencing and jousting for sport, he had never enjoyed the actual experience of mortal combat. That chilling awareness that if his opponent proved the better warrior, or perchance merely the luckier one, his life was quite possibly going to end.

Shamur, on the other hand, clearly did delight in it. Though she must be sore from the beating she'd taken, her pleasure was manifest in her smile and the gleam in her eyes, a show of vivacity such as he had seldom seen from her in over a quarter century of marriage. Ilmater's tears, now and again she even laughed, generally immediately after a close call that would have left many people white and sick with shock.

When he'd first learned her secret, and she'd told him she needed this sort of stimulation to be happy, he had, in his consternation and anger, assumed she was talking nonsense. Now, however, he could see that her assertion might well be true, and sensed just how profoundly she had denied her own nature when she assumed her grand-niece's identity.

Perhaps her love of risk was part of what made her such a superb fighter, for that she surely was. Avos was younger, stronger, had the superior reach, and possessed the substantial advantage of having trained with the odd set of weapons, yet Shamur was beating him. Thamalon was glad that, assuming the Quippers honored their pledge, she at least was likely to leave this wretched place alive.

Or so he thought until he chanced to glimpse a flicker of motion from the corner of his eye.

He turned his head to spy the galltrit flying upward toward the high ceiling. The stealthy little creature carried what appeared to be a toy crossbow in its diminutive hands.

Thamalon suspected the quarrel was poisoned. In all likelihood, no spectator would notice the tiny missile striking its target, yet the venom would be potent enough to hamper Shamur and allow the hard-pressed Avos to overcome her, win the duel by a cheat, and still maintain the respect of his underlings.

Thamalon would have liked to point out the gremlin's obvious intent to the other Quippers, but there was no time. The rogues were focused on the duel, and by the time he managed to divert one's attention, the galltrit would already have taken its shot and fluttered away. Nor would it be efficacious to shout and warn Shamur. The way the crowd was yelling, she likely wouldn't hear him, and even if she did, the distraction might provide Avos with just the chance he needed to land a telling blow.

Fortunately, Thamalon's guards were as interested in the duel as everyone else, too interested to watch him especially closely. Exploding into motion, he shoved one away, snatched the poniard from the other's sheath, pushed him away as well, turned, and hurled the dagger.

The poniard wasn't well balanced for throwing, but it flew true anyway, and pierced the galltrit's breast. The bat-winged imp gave a thin, quavering cry and fell, thudding down in the combat circle.

By that time several ruffians were moving in on Thamalon with blades in their hands and murder in their eyes. Suspecting they had at best only a murky idea of what had just occurred, the noble pointed frantically at the gray, diminutive corpse.

"Look at the gremlin!" he roared in his most imperious tone. "Look at that little crossbow. The cursed thing was going to cheat on behalf of its master, and if I'm to be harmed for killing it to keep the fight fair, then by Tyr Grimjaws, you stinking Quippers have no honor at all!"

The ruffians hesitated, then black-bearded Donvan said, "His lordship's got a point, and besides, we want to sell him, not kill him. Put up your weapons and watch the rest of the show."

The galltrit's body thumped down inside the dueling circle. As soon as Shamur caught sight of the little crossbow in the creature's hand, she understood what it had been up to. She grinned at Avos. "Did you signal the gremlin somehow, or did it simply know to intervene whenever you were losing a challenge?"

An ugly muttering started through the crowd. Some of the Quippers had no doubt watched Avos slaughter their friends inside this ring. Now they had reason to doubt that he'd beaten them fairly.

For a moment, Avos looked stricken. Aghast. Then his square, ruddy face grew redder still, and pure rage blazed in his pale blue eyes. He bellowed and charged, swinging the gaff at Shamur's face.

She parried, and the force of his blow sent a shock down her arm. Instantly, contemptuous of any attempt she might have made to riposte, he stepped through with his back foot and drove his short sword at her chest.

She parried with her blade and attempted a thrust of her

own, but he was still surging forward, spoiling her aim, and instead of piercing his bowels, her point simply grazed along his ribs.

Seemingly unfazed by this new wound, Avos slammed into her and sent her staggering. He tried to hook her leg and she barely managed to bat his gaff away with her own. Instantly he sprang forward and lashed the weapon at her head.

Recovering her balance, she swayed back, and the gaff missed her nose by half an inch. Whirling the weapon over his head, he rushed her yet again.

She smiled, for she understood what he was doing. Since his tricks hadn't worked, he was playing the big man's game, trying to overwhelm her with sheer might and relentless aggression. It was a strategy that had won many a fight for many a strapping fellow like himself, but it was incompatible with a strong defense. If a fighter possessed the skill to withstand his onslaught for long enough—and Shamur reckoned that she did—Avos would inevitably leave himself wide open for a riposte or stop cut.

She gave ground, parrying, gritting her teeth at the appalling power in the strokes that stung her fingers and once or twice nearly bashed her weapons from her hands. Until finally Avos blundered forward with a poorly aimed attack, so poorly aimed, in fact, that she was confident he would be unable to correct and strike her if she simply sidestepped. As he plunged past her, she swept her gaff low, hooked his ankle, and pulled.

Avos crashed face down on the floor. His foot flailed free of the hook, and he tried to scramble up. Shamur swung the gaff high and slammed it down on top of his head, splitting his scalp anew. Losing his grip on his weapons, he slumped. Dropping the gaff, she sprang on top of him, wrenched him onto his back, and poised her short sword at his throat.

The spectators howled. Avos gazed up at her with astonishment and fear in his eyes. "I yield," he said.

Shamur chuckled. "I figured you probably would."

"So you can back off now. You're free to go."

"Those were the terms before the galltrit tried to cheat for you. I think it's appropriate that we amend them. Lord Uskevren and I are both leaving."

Avos scowled. "No." She was surprised that he'd stick at releasing Thamalon with her blade at his neck, but perhaps he felt impelled to try to salvage a bit of his pride, or at least a scrap of his underlings' respect. "He stays."

Shamur raised her sword to threaten his eyes. "Tell your friends to let him go right now, or by Mask, mine is the last face you will ever see. Nor will I stop cutting after that."

"You hurt me, the other Quippers will hurt him."

"But you'll still be hurt. Don't play that game with me, Avos, you won't like the way it turns out. You should realize by now that I'm not the sort of woman who shrinks at the sight of blood, not even her husband's."

"All right," Avos growled, "let the nobleman go."

Shamur held her breath, for she was by no means certain that the rogues would let such a lucrative prize slip through their fingers merely to save their defeated and discredited chieftain. But perhaps some of them still held Avos in some esteem. Others surely didn't, but maybe they also felt that Shamur had fought valiantly enough to earn her husband's liberation as well as her own. Or perhaps no one wanted to be the first to advocate allowing Avos's mutilation, for fear that nobody else would agree with him. Whatever the reason, after a moment, Thamalon's guards stepped away from him, and none of the other toughs objected.

"Good," Shamur said. "Now, someone fetch the weapons, money, and jewels you took from us."

Donvan collected the articles and handed them over to Thamalon.

"Now get out of here," Avos said.

"Call me a cynic," Shamur replied, "but I can't help wondering whether you'd still consent to our departure if my blade were no longer tickling you. So here's how it will be. You're going to walk us out of the Scab, with our sword points at your back every step of the way. Now stand up very slowly."

Thamalon sauntered to her side. "Nicely done," he said.

She smiled. "It would all have been for naught if you hadn't killed the galltrit."

"I believe we still require a name."

"You're right. I nearly forgot." She prodded Avos in the kidney with her sword. "Enlighten us."

"I don't know who the wizard in the moon mask is," the ruffian answered grudgingly, "but the nobleman who paid me to supply men to aid the spellcaster is Ossian Talendar."

CHAPTER 18

Thazienne plucked her towel from its peg and wiped the perspiration from her face. Beside her, Talbot poured water from a jug and, throwing back his head, glugged it down. A stray drop escaped the corner of his mouth and trickled down his unshaven chin.

Though stiff and sore from their exertions the night before, the two of them had nonetheless felt a common urge to go to the mansion's training hall this morning. Perhaps they'd wanted to work the kinks out, or hone their skills for battles yet to come. Tazi suspected that Tal at least had hoped some hard fencing would distract him from his guilt.

However, judging from his somber expression, it didn't seem to have worked, and when he spoke, he proved that it hadn't. "I still don't understand why it happened."

Tazi sighed. "Yes, you do, you just don't want to let it go."

"How can I? I feel badly enough about Jander, but Master Selwick was alive when we fled out the back of the tiring house. I never would have abandoned him if I'd known the other wizard would hold off chasing us long enough to kill him!"

"The enemy wizard was flying, and I saw a couple of our men bounce crossbow bolts off him to no effect. Even if we had lingered, we couldn't have saved Brom."

"Still—"

"Enough!" she cried. "Haven't you ever listened to Father's stories? Battles are unpredictable, and people die in them. That's just the way it is."

"Well, none of our friends died in mine," Tamlin said.

Startled, Thazienne pivoted to see her foppish brother standing in the doorway. He was as exquisitely dressed as usual in a red and purple ensemble, but to her surprise, he was still carrying the woodcutter's axe from yesterday, now slung across his back. Evidently he'd prevailed upon one of the servants to fashion some sort of scabbard for it.

Tal glowered at him. "What's that remark supposed to mean?"

"Just that when I was attacked, I wasn't expecting trouble," Tamlin replied. "I only had three comrades to stand beside me, not a company of guards, and none of us were slain. I led everyone to safety. It's a pity my brother the master swordsman can't say the same."

"That's it," Talbot said. He advanced on Tamlin with mayhem in his eyes.

Tazi had occasionally thought she'd enjoy nothing more than to see Talbot catch their supercilious brother apart from his hulking bodyguard and drub the snottiness out of him. Now, however, the prospect simply made her feel impatient.

"Stop it!" she shouted. The two males turned to look at her. "Remember what Master Selwick said. It doesn't help to fight among ourselves."

Tamlin grimaced. "You're right. Brother, I apologize. I know you're not to blame for Brom's death. It's just that I feel badly about it. If he hadn't conjured away the barrier of ice, I'd most likely be dead myself, and Escevar and Vox with me."

"I suppose that by keeping the masked mage off our backs, he saved Tazi and me as well," Talbot said. "Now the only way to repay him is to avenge him."

"And the same quite possibly holds true for Mother and Father," Tazi said.

For a moment, they all stood silent, and then Talbot made a visible effort to throw off the somber mood that had overtaken them all. "What are you doing here?" he said to Tamlin. "Don't tell me you want to train."

"The gods forbid," said Tamlin. "Actually, I was searching for the two of you. Cale says someone is demanding to speak to us, a factor from one of the warehouses."

"If it's some business thing," Tazi said, "surely you can handle it by yourself."

"For that matter, Erevis ought to be able to attend to it by himself," Tamlin replied. "But he says the woman wants us, all three of us, and such being the case, I see no reason why I should go endure the boredom by myself. It's time you two idlers understood the sort of misery I've been subjected to since Father disappeared."

"Oh, all right," Talbot groaned. "Let's get it over with."

As they tramped through the great house, Tazi said, "Dare I ask why you're still dragging around the axe?"

"It brought me luck once," Tamlin replied. "I intend to keep it by me until this affair is over."

Tazi sighed. "Say no more." Her older brother's superstitious streak was yet another of his irritating foibles.

Tamlin led his sibs to the great hall, where Erevis stood tall and stiff, and a stocky woman with her graying hair pulled back in a long ponytail paced restlessly about. It was Wyla, not merely one of Father's workers but a valued retainer who had served him since his youth, often been a guest at Stormweather Towers, and given Tazi and Tal some of their earliest fencing lessons. Surely Erevis had told Tamlin who was calling, but the younger man hadn't relayed the name to his siblings because he had never noticed or didn't recall who Wyla was. Weeping Ilmater, he truly was an imbecile, and Tazi gave him an irritated scowl.

Then, however, she saw how Wyla was moving, and her annoyance gave way to concern. She hurried toward the older woman. "What's wrong with you?" she asked.

Wyla's left hand twitched upward from her side, almost as if she had an urge to fend Tazi off, or shield herself in some way, although of course, the noblewoman knew she must simply have startled her. "What do you mean?" the factor asked.

"Your limp," said Thazienne. "It's much worse than usual."

"Oh." Wyla gave her an odd little smile. "Lately, my leg aches badly when it's cold. I suppose I'm getting old."

"Well, for Sune's sake, sit down." Tazi pulled out one of the chairs at the long, inlaid table, and the factor lowered herself into it. "Didn't Erevis invite you to take a seat?"

"Of course not, Mistress," the steward said sardonically. "You know I make it a rule to show visitors as little hospitality as humanly possible. That was why I didn't bother to fetch any refreshments, either." He gestured toward a pair of trays, one laden with a silver pitcher of mulled red wine and matching goblets, the other with bread, cheese, sliced apples, and grapes.

As Tazi might have expected, that was all the invitation Tamlin needed to pour himself a drink. "So, how may we help you?" he said to Wyla.

The factor hesitated, then said, "Master Cale, I beg your pardon, but what I have to say is for the young lords' and lady's ears alone."

Erevis blinked in surprise. Talbot said, "Wyla, though I have no idea what you mean to tell us, I'm certain you can do so in front of Erevis."

"Please, indulge me," Wyla replied.

Tamlin shrugged. "Whatever it takes to move this along.

We can always call Erevis back in a minute, or relay what we want him to know later on."

"I suppose," said Tal reluctantly. He turned to Erevis. "If you wouldn't mind . . ."

"Of course not," said the major-domo, "and I'll make certain none of the other servants overhears your deliberations, either." He turned and marched out in his herky-jerky way, the light of the brown iridescent lamps gleaming on his bald pate.

The Uskevren sat down.

"All right," said Thazienne, "tell us."

"I saw Lord and Lady Uskevren this morning," Wyla said. "They sneaked into the warehouse and sent me here to talk to you. They even saw fit to give me a token to prove it, though I hope you've known me long enough to make that superfluous." She set a silver and sapphire brooch on the tabletop.

Overcome with relief, Tazi slumped and closed her eyes. Though she would rather have died than admit it to anyone else, until this moment, she'd been all but certain her parents were dead.

"I gave that brooch to Mother," Tamlin said.

"We remember," said Tal. He peered quizzically at Wyla. "But why didn't Mother and Father come home and talk to us themselves?"

"They didn't explain everything to me," Wyla said. "I gather they were in a hurry to get away from the warehouse before anyone else spotted them. But as I understand it, the same enemy who attacked you tried to kill them as well, and for the time being, they want the villain to believe the attempt succeeded. That way, when the time comes, they can strike at him by surprise."

"I suppose that makes a certain amount of sense," Tazi said. "But why keep their survival a secret from members of our own household?"

"Because they suspect that one or more of your retainers are spies. How else did the enemy know when your parents would leave the city unescorted, or what route you, Master

Tamlin, would take as you rode out to go hawking, or that you, Master Talbot, had warriors stationed in buildings adjacent to the Wide Realms?"

Tazi frowned. As Tamlin, dunce though he was, had observed during the conclave the day before, there were various ways in which a foe could discover what the Uskevren were up to, but a spy was certainly one plausible explanation.

"I suppose we might have a traitor in our midst," she said, "but Wyla, you must know it couldn't possibly be Erevis. We trust him as implicitly as we do you."

Wyla shook her head. "I simply know Lord Uskevren insisted that only you three were to know he and your mother are still alive, just as he stressed that he wants you to inform absolutely no one else."

"That makes sense to me," said Tamlin. "I've never been as enamored of Cale as my brother and sister. Last winter that walking skeleton revealed a side of himself we'd never suspected. Perhaps he harbors other secrets."

Thazienne flushed with anger. "He showed us that 'side' in the course of saving my life."

"I agree with you," Talbot told her. "Erevis is unquestionably loyal. Still, perhaps he confides in someone else who isn't. Perhaps it would be wise to obey Father's instructions to the letter. The gods know, *I* have no idea what to do next. At any rate, I'm sure we haven't heard everything yet. Our sire wouldn't bother to communicate simply to reassure us that he and Mother are alive, not in the middle of a crisis when security is an issue. He's too canny and calculating for that."

"You're right," Wyla said. "He also told me to tell you—"

A hiss sounded from overhead.

Startled, they all looked up. Jester, a brindled cat and one of the household pets, glared down through the marble balustrade that bordered the west gallery with pure malevolence in her yellow eyes.

"What's the matter with her?" asked Tamlin, peering up at the agitated feline. "It's as if she senses a threat."

Wyla's left arm twitched upward. Perhaps, Tazi thought,

she had a recurring twinge in her chest, felt an urge to press her hand against the sore spot, but was too proud to let anyone else see she was in pain. That would be like her.

"No!" Talbot rapped. "I mean, Jester's been acting strangely for the last day or so. Going into heat, probably. I'll get a servant to remove her." He rose and strode to the door. "Ho, somebody! We need a little help!"

When Jester had been carried off yowling, writhing, and scratching, Tamlin said, "Now, what else did Father say?"

"Do you know a tavern called the Drum and Mirror?" Wyla asked.

"I do," Tazi said.

"Good," Wyla said. "Your parents want you to meet them there at midnight. I gather they mean to explain how you're to help them put an end to the current threat. As you've no doubt surmised, they want you to come alone, and without telling anyone your destination."

Tamlin frowned. "I don't much like the thought of going anywhere without Vox and Escevar."

"If you insist on keeping Erevis in the dark," Tazi snapped, "then you can damn well dispense with your little retinue as well."

"I suppose," her elder brother grumbled.

"Good," said Talbot, "but I must say, this seems odd. I never would have expected Father to summon us out into the night unescorted when he knows someone wants to kill us." He smiled crookedly. "After all, he thinks we're a trio of helpless idiots."

"Speak for yourself," Tazi said.

"I only know what he told me," Wyla said.

"I'm sure he reasoned that if no one knows we're going," said Tamlin, "no one can ambush us, and he's right, so we'll go. Anything to put an end to this unpleasantness and get things back to normal."

"All right, I agree," said Talbot. He grinned. "Of course, if she still wants to be contrary, our sister may insist on staying home this time around."

Tazi threw a slice of bread at him.

As there was little of consequence left to say, Tamlin and Tal took their leave of Wyla shortly thereafter. The factor started to struggle up from her chair, and Tazi put her hand on the other woman's arm. "You're more than welcome to stay and rest for a while," she said. "You seem tired."

"No," said Wyla, lurching upright. "I must go. I have matters I must attend to."

Thazienne smiled. "Are you worried about what Magnus and Chade might be doing, or not doing, during your absence?"

For a split second, Wyla looked blank, then said, "Magnus and Chade, yes, exactly! Excuse me, Mistress, please." She turned and hurried away as quickly as her uneven gait would allow.

Tazi shook her head. Talbot was right, things did seem strange. Father's summons. Jester throwing a fit. And Wyla's manner as well. Why was she so ill at ease, and why, when the two of them were alone, had she called the noblewoman "Mistress" instead of "Tazi" as she normally would?

Abruptly feeling impatient with herself, Thazienne snorted her misgivings away. Father desired secrecy, the cat craved a mate, Wyla was ill as well as upset over the troubles that had overtaken her employer's House, and none of it was anything to fret over. The important thing was that Father and Mother were alive and well and evidently had conceived a strategy to unmask and defeat the unknown enemy.

Tazi stuffed a piece of apple in her mouth and filled a cup with warm, spiced wine.

CHAPTER 19

When Nuldrevyn and Ossian reached Marance's shadowy suite, the wizard was lounging on a velvet-cushioned farthingale chair. Bileworm was limping about the room in a fantastic, frenetic manner, lengthening, shortening, and altering the form of one leg from moment to moment.

Nuldrevyn viewed the wizard and his familiar with the usual mix of hope and anxiety. "Ossian says you want to see me," the old man said. "I trust it's important. You've called me away from a conference with the fellow who runs our most profitable marble quarry."

"Then I apologize," said Marance, rising, staff in hand, from his chair. "But I also promise you won't be sorry you came."

"From that," said Nuldrevyn, "I take it you're

finally ready to share the details of your new scheme."

"I am indeed," said Marance, his white eyes shining in the gloom. "Please, sit down and be comfortable." He waved his kinsmen to the cluster of chairs where they'd sat and palavered before.

Nuldrevyn kept an eye on Bileworm as he seated himself, making sure the spirit couldn't pop out and surprise him. The familiar leered at the nobleman, and just for an instant, stretched and twisted himself into a sinusoidal form suggestive of a snake. Nuldrevyn went rigid but managed to avoid flinching outright.

The old man scowled and returned his attention to Marance. "All right," he said, "tell us."

"Of course," the wizard said. "I hit on this plan by pondering what went amiss with the previous ones. How did the Uskevren cubs escape? By outfighting me? No. By running away. So this time, I intend to deny them the opportunity."

"Didn't you already try to do that," Nuldrevyn asked, "by placing a barrier of ice behind the heir, and stationing some of your conjured creatures at the door in the rear of the Wide Realms?"

Marance's lips quirked upward. "In point of fact, yes. But in the former case, I didn't reckon on Master Selwick being such an accomplished wizard, and in the latter, I didn't anticipate Thamalon's allegedly invalid daughter turning up and fighting like a lioness. This time, nothing will go wrong. I'm going to trap our prey in the center of the High Bridge. With our forces sweeping in from both sides to catch them by surprise, and other warriors sealing off each end of the bridge just in case the Uskevren should somehow get past the first lot, it's inconceivable that the youngsters will survive."

Nuldrevyn nodded, envisioning the snare. "It is an interesting idea," he conceded. "Once in a while, you hear of someone diving off the High Bridge and surviving, but never in winter with the river so icy cold. However, the scheme only works if you have a way of luring the Uskevren to the killing ground at the right time."

"That's already taken care of," said Marance.

"I deserve most of the credit," said Bileworm in a husky contralto voice. His body shortened and thickened until it became the silhouette of a stocky woman with a long ponytail, except that his wide, gray, fanged grin split the inky shadow-stuff of the face. "Master said it would be easy, but it wasn't. Since I failed to catch Wyla's memories, I didn't get the limp right, and my presence drove a cat wild. But still, I convinced everyone! I should be acting in the Wide Realms myself!"

"What Bileworm is trying to explain," Marance said dryly, "is that cloaked in the flesh of a trusted family friend, he persuaded the Uskevren to come alone to a tavern at the center of the bridge for what they believe will be a secret meeting with their missing parents at midnight."

"Not bad," Nuldrevyn said, "but what about the guard-houses on the bridge? There are some, you know."

"Only a couple," the wizard said. "I wish I still had some sleep dust left, but I fancy that even without it, I can quietly eliminate the sentries in advance."

"It's a good plan," said Ossian hesitantly, "but you alluded to 'warriors.' I hope you didn't mean the bravos I obtained for you, because most of them are wounded, slain, or have decided your service is too dangerous and decamped. I doubt I could find you another such group by tonight."

"You needn't bother trying," said Marance. "I don't want you to think I'm unappreciative of your efforts, nephew, because I'm not, but I am tired of trying to work with the scrapings of Selgaunt's gutters. If any of those clods had known how to aim a crossbow, or had possessed the modicum of nerve necessary to fight alongside conjured creatures that I had explained were magically constrained from harming them, our campaign would be farther advanced than it is."

"So you're simply going to rely on your summoned beasts?" Nuldrevyn asked.

"No," said Marance. "If you recall, I explained why that isn't a sound idea. Actually, I'll require a number of your household guards, and I'd like to enlist the aid of one of your wizards as well. A nice brace of destructive spells, blazing unexpectedly out of the dark from either side, may well slay the Uskevren before they even have a chance to reach for their swords."

Nuldrevyn's throat abrupt felt thick with anxiety, but he realized that this time, he had to stand up to his brother. "Marance, we discussed that, too. We agreed that using our own soldiers would constitute an unacceptable risk."

"Circumstances change," Marance replied. "Perspectives change. It's now clear to me that we must take the chance to assure our victory, and really, if we instruct our retainers not to flaunt the Talendar black and crimson, it's extremely unlikely that anyone will recognize them in the dead of night."

Nuldrevyn shook his head. "I'm not convinced of that."

"My poor brother. I recall when you would not only have endorsed this scheme, you would have demanded to stand in the vanguard and butcher an Uskevren or two with your own hand. Have the years diminished you so much?"

"I don't feel diminished," Nuldrevyn replied, "but as you observed, perspectives change. When we were young, I thought only of what could be won. Now, I understand what must be preserved."

Marance cocked his head. "I don't understand."

"If we exterminate the Uskevren," Nuldrevyn replied, "it will give us satisfaction. In the long run, it may also enrich our House. Yet suppose we fail or even succeed, but are unmasked in the process. What happens if everyone discovers that it's the Talendar who attempted to assassinate Thamalon's children, creating mayhem and terror in public places, and trafficking with—forgive me—the powers of darkness?"

"Then you brazen it out," Marance said, "and spread a few bribes around as needed."

"That might work," Nuldrevyn said, "and it might not. We have other enemies besides the Uskevren, foes who, confident that under the circumstances the Hulorn and the Scepters will look the other way, might seize on the incident as an excuse to make war on us. Do you want to see your name dishonored, your ancestral home burned, and your kinsmen slaughtered or driven into exile, just as it happened to Thamalon's people?"

"Brother, you're waxing hysterical. It's inconceivable that such a calamity will befall us."

"No, it isn't," Nuldrevyn said, "and we have to take cognizance of all the possibilities."

"And let them paralyze us?" the spellcaster asked.

"I just ask you to remember that there's more to life than vengeance," Nuldrevyn said. "There's the pride we feel in the honor, power, and wealth of our House. The joys and luxuries our position affords us. We have a new generation just coming up, Ossian and all the others like him, and I feel an obligation to pass the Talendar way of life on intact to them."

Marance shook his head. "Brother, I'll be candid with you. I don't know if it was the simple fact of death that changed me, or if my years in the underworld are responsible, but the truth is that I *don't* entirely remember what it is to take pride in the House of Talendar, or to fret about its future. Oh, I know in the abstract that I once cared about such matters, but only the cold ash of those feelings remains. In contrast, I still retain a considerable yen for revenge, and you must pardon me if I satisfy it without a second of unnecessary delay."

"But you already have," Ossian said. "The man who killed you is dead, as is his wife. I promise I won't rest until his offspring perish, also. So can't you be satisfied for just a little while, until we devise another plan? I understand that, thanks to Thamalon Uskevren, you passed through pain and horror, but you came out all right, didn't you? You still exist, you're a grandee in your Iron City—"

"The highest lord in Hell is still in Hell," Marance snapped. "Kindly refrain from commenting on what you can't understand. Nuldrevyn, I've heard your objections, and answered them as best I could. Beyond that, I can only pledge to be careful. Now, for sake of the love we bear one another, and the hatred we both hold for the House of Uskevren, I beg you to consent to my plan."

Nuldrevyn swallowed. "I'm sorry, but I cannot."

A trace of sadness came into Marance's face. "I'm sorry, too," he said. He rose from his chair, and though nothing in his manner so much as hinted at hostile intent, the Talendar lord abruptly sensed that Marance meant to direct some sort of magic against Ossian and himself.

Ossian had apparently come to the same conclusion, for he surged up out of his seat. By a lucky chance, he'd ventured out of the castle earlier today, and was still carrying a long sword. The gold-hilted weapon hissed as he yanked it from its scabbard.

For his part, Nuldrevyn lacked a sword, but since boyhood, had never been without a dagger ready to hand. He rose as hastily as his stiff joints would allow, and silently drew the knife from its well-oiled sheath.

Ossian lunged at Marance fast and hard, trying to dispatch him before he could cast a spell. The wizard parried the chest cut with his staff. Gray steel rang on black wood, and purple sparks crackled at the point of contact. The ginger-haired youth reeled backward, and Marance reached into his mantle to fish out the necessary ingredient for a spell.

That, Nuldrevyn thought, was all right, because to deal with the son, Marance had turned his back on the father. Perhaps the wizard thought the patriarch of the House of Talendar was too ancient and infirm to pose any sort of threat. If so, Nuldrevyn would show him just how wrong he was. One thrust to the spine should end this confrontation and send his wayward brother back to the Pit. He wouldn't enjoy doing it, but with Ossian imperiled he saw no other choice.

Nuldrevyn took a split second to aim his blade at a specific target, in this case, a point midway between Marance's shoulder blades. The old man started to step into distance, and a huge black snake reared up in front of him.

Even as Nuldrevyn cried out, recoiled, lost his balance,

and fell, he discerned it wasn't an actual serpent, just Bile-worm mimicking one, but the knowledge didn't help. No matter how he tried, he couldn't force himself to get back up, not with the spirit's murky, wedge-shaped head looming over him. All he could do was cower and watch the duel between his son and brother unfold.

Ossian had recovered his equilibrium and was pushing Marance back with a rapid series of feints, deceives, and attacks. The knobbed end of the wizard's staff sizzled with purple flame, and he held it extended to slow his adversary's advance. Meanwhile Marance chanted, swept his unweaponed hand in a mystic pass, and tossed a pinch of black dust into the air.

The air turned hot, then cold. For an instant, a bitter taste stung Nuldrevyn's tongue. Magenta fire blazed from the staff and engulfed the old man's son.

To Nuldrevyn's horror, Ossian dwindled in stature, so quickly that the eye could barely follow the process. One instant, he was taller than his foe. The next, small as a mouse.

"That doesn't look good at all," said Bileworm to Nuldrevyn. "Don't you want to go help the boy? You know I'm made of gossamer. I can't stop you." He flickered out a forked tongue into his prisoner's face, and Nuldrevyn sobbed and cringed.

Ossian dropped his pin-sized sword and bolted for the doorway. Marance discarded his staff—the purple flame went out as soon as it left his hand—whirled the cloak off his shoulders, and cast it like a net. The garment fell on top of the shrunken man.

Marance hurried up to the cape, kneeled, groped about for a moment, then located Ossian beneath it. He held the young aristocrat immobile with one hand, reached under the garment with the other, and extracted him.

"I regret it came to this," Marance said to the squirming mite in his fist. "I've grown truly fond of you."

He picked up the cloak, stuffed Ossian into one of the larger pockets on the inside, then squeezed the opening shut. Nuldrevyn could see the youth struggling inside the cloth for a little while, and then the motion stopped.

Nuldrevyn's best-loved son had died of asphyxia, and, paralyzed by his dread of snakes, he hadn't lifted a finger to save him. His eyes stinging with tears, the old man wished that same crippling fear would stop his heart.

"I'm sorry," Marance told him. He removed Ossian's corpse from the pocket and set it on the floor.

"You monster!" Nuldrevyn whispered.

"That's unfair," the mage said. "I wanted you and the lad for my allies, never my enemies, but you turned on me. Yet even so, I don't wish to kill you, that's what a devoted, forgiving brother I am. However, I will need to keep you from interfering in my plan."

Marance retrieved his staff, put on his cloak, and took a candle from one of the pockets. He held the taper aloft, recited words of power, and turned widdershins. A purple flame kindled itself on the wick, ghostly voices murmured, and a gigantic snake shimmered into existence on the floor.

Marance pointed to his brother, and the serpent obediently slithered in Nuldrevyn's direction. Its copper eyes, the candlelight rippling on its steel-gray scales, and the cold thickness of its sinuous coils were so overwhelmingly ghastly they made Bileworm's impersonation of a snake seem ludicrous by comparison. Weeping and whimpering, Nuldrevyn floundered helplessly away from the new and even more intimidating terror.

In a few seconds, he backed himself into a corner. Black tongue dancing, the snake raised its head high and stared down at him. Meanwhile, Bileworm flowed back into something approximating human form.

The ferule of his staff tapping on the floor, Marance walked closer to his brother. "As you may be aware," said the mage, "summoned creatures often vanish back to their points of origin after a relatively brief period of service. But you mustn't get your hopes up, because I made certain this one will linger long past midnight. While it's watching over you, you mustn't call for help or try to escape, else the beast will strike, and its bite is venomous in the extreme."

"Can't we just kill him?" Bileworm wheedled. "Don't I need to become him so I can direct his retainers to obey your commands?"

"They'll take orders from young Ossian just as well."

Bobbing up and down, swaying this way and that, Bileworm made a show of inspecting the diminutive corpse. "It's going to be a very tight fit," he said, "and I think the guards might notice a difference."

Marance sighed. "The body will revert to its former dimensions in a bit."

"Aha!" said the spirit. "Well, in that case, give me a halloo when it does." He strode closer to Nuldrevyn and, craning and stooping, peered at him avidly, drinking in his fear, grief, and shame.

CHAPTER 20

With more snow falling from the night sky and a
frigid wind whistling out of the north, the pitched
roof of the brownstone tallhouse was scarcely a
comfortable perch. But no matter how Shamur
shivered and clenched her jaw against the cold,
she reckoned she had no choice but to remain,
for this building was one of the few structures in
the immediate area lofty enough to afford a view
inside the enceinte of Old High Hall, the Talendar
castle. She was glad she and Thamalon had made
time to go to a shrine and pay a priest to heal the
bruises, scrapes, and swellings the Quippers had
given them, else the vigil would have been even
less pleasant than it was.

It was a vigil that Shamur hadn't required Thamalon to keep. Seeing no reason why both of them
needed to spy, she'd suggested he wait somewhere

warm. Perhaps he'd feared she'd think him soft or a shirker, for he'd insisted on sharing the chore with her, and, to her relief, had scaled the side of the tallhouse with considerable agility for a sexagenarian who had never taken instruction from a housebreaker like Errendar Spillwine.

Within the facade of the Talendar mansion, another window went dark. Soon, she thought, it would be time to move. Thanks be to Mask that the noble family hadn't opted to host a feast or ball tonight. Then the castle might have swarmed with boisterous revelers and bustling servants until dawn.

"I have something to tell you," said Thamalon, tightly bundled in his cloak.

"What's that?" she asked.

"When this affair is over, you can leave me without fear of reprisals against the House of Karn or the children. You can also come back and visit our brood whenever you like."

Shamur reckoned that she ought to be overjoyed, and in fact, she did feel a tingle of excitement, but it was muted and undercut by some other, less comfortable emotion. "Thank you. That's far kinder than I had any reason to expect."

He shrugged. "What should I do, drag you into court and complain to the Probiters that for the last thirty years, I've been married to the wrong woman, but up until now didn't know the truth? I'd be the laughingstock of Selgaunt. Besides, I suppose I owe you something for seeing me safely out of the Quippers' lair. I wasn't sure you'd be able to, or even that you meant to try."

"Don't tell me you were taken in by my agreeing to Avos's terms," she replied. "That was simply necessary to move things along. We're comrades in this venture, and I was always resolved that both of us would escape, or neither. That was why I aimed my short sword at his belly and never his heart. Even had I pierced his guts, he likely wouldn't have died at once. Thus, I still could have extorted your release by threatening him with further harm."

Thamalon chuckled. "Such a delicate little flower I married."

"There's something I ought to tell you. Two things, really. The first is that back in the days when I was a thief, Old High Hall was rumored to be impregnable to the kind of intrusion we intend, and I certainly never heard of any burglar surviving such an attempt. The second is that I haven't attempted to slip inside a fortress like this since I was an adolescent. I fear my skills are rusty."

"Nonsense. I've seen you fight and climb."

"But I'll need other abilities tonight, ones I have yet to test."

"Wife, I know where this is going. You're going to offer me another chance to stay safely behind, aren't you?"

"It's a sound idea. If something befalls me, you'll still be alive and free to search for Master Moon and protect the children."

"You said it yourself. We're partners. You watch my back, and I watch yours. In any case, I trust you."

She smiled. "All right, fool. On your own head be it."

They sat in silence on the cold, rough shingles for a while longer, while the snowflakes tumbled, the stars twinkled, and the lights in Old High Hall winked out one by one. Finally she judged the mansion was dark enough. She said as much to Thamalon, whereupon the two of them descended to the ground, then crept toward the enceinte.

In Shamur's youth, Old High Hall had been the sort of old-fashioned stronghold that Argent Hall remained today, with a perimeter wall high enough to balk an army. At some point during her long absence from Selgaunt, however, the Talendar had seen fit to tear down that enceinte and put up one that was only about twelve feet tall. She wished she could find that encouraging, but she knew better. The rival House had only become more wealthy over the past several decades, and it stood to reason that the measures they took to deter thieves had become more sophisticated and effective.

The Uskevren reached the base of the wall without being noticed, at least as far as Shamur could tell. The masons had made some effort to smooth the sandstone blocks and the mortared chinks between so as to make climbing difficult, but she was confident she'd find adequate finger- and toe-holds. What concerned her was the mechanical and magical traps that might be concealed in the stonework. She kept an eye out for such things as she ascended.

She made it to the top without incident, peeked over the wall, and saw a snowy garden on the other side. It didn't appear to possess any magical flowers like the Karns' famous silver roses, which flourished even in the dead of winter, but the servants had shoveled the paths anyway, perhaps so strollers could admire the statuary.

Since Shamur saw no sentries rushing in her direction, she turned her attention to the coping on the summit of the wall. Most climbers would unthinkingly, blindly grab hold of it as they ascended, making it an excellent location for poisoned spikes, sharp scraps of glass, or some other type of mantrap. She didn't see anything of the sort, nor magical sigils incised in the stone, but still, her instincts warned her not to trust the surface. Clinging to the facade of the wall one-handed, she extracted a slender steel probe from her kit and pressed it against the top.

In the twinkling of an eye, the patch of sandstone immediately beneath the metal rod reshaped itself into a pair of jagged jaws, which shot up, clashed together, and bit the probe in half. Startled, Shamur jerked backward and nearly lost her grip.

She recovered her balance, peered over the coping again, making sure no one had heard the magical trap activate and come to investigate. She studied the stone jaws. They hadn't tried to bite her a second time. In fact, they seemed to be softening and slumping ever so slightly, as if, having failed to seize a victim, the projections were melting back into the block from which they had erupted. Shamur warily prodded them with the stub of the probe, and even that failed to provoke another attack.

She grinned. If the jaws could strike only once, that made it easy. She discarded the remaining piece of the probe, which was a bit too short for the task she had in mind, drew her dagger and used it to trigger several traps on either side of the first one, enjoying the game of snatching the blade back before the jaws could catch it.

"What are you doing?" Thamalon whispered from below.

"Making a point of entry." She lay on her belly atop the hard, irregular bumps of the unsuccessful mantraps, anchored herself with one hand, and stretched down the other. "Come on, I'll help you up. Just don't let any part of your anatomy swing up over a section of the coping that's still level, or a trap's liable to snip it off."

"I understand." He gripped her hand, she heaved, and he clambered up. They dropped inside the enclosure.

At once they hunkered down motionless, while Shamur peered and listened for signs that someone else was in their immediate vicinity. It seemed that nobody was. She gave Thamalon a nod to indicate that so far, they were all right.

"It's a miracle nobody heard the traps going off," he whispered.

"It's a ways to the house," she replied, "and I doubt anyone wanders the grounds on a chilly night like tonight if he can avoid it. Still, there are guards somewhere, so let's be careful."

He inclined his head. She motioned for him to follow her, then skulked to the right.

Shamur used all her old tricks to approach the mansion. She instructed Thamalon to stay low, take advantage of every bit of cover, and look before he moved. She kept an eye out for tripwires and odd depressions or humps in the earth that might mark the site of a mantrap, for all that the snowdrifts made them difficult to spot. She stalked behind rather than in front of any light source, such as the glowing magical lamps which the Talendar had mounted here and there on posts, lest she reveal herself in silhouette or cast a shadow. And she crept to the leeward, so no watchdog could catch her scent.

For a while, she was on edge, but by the time she and Thamalon slipped by the first patrolling spearman, she had relaxed and begun to enjoy the challenge. Win or lose, live or die, the incursion was grand sport. Never had she felt more alive, more keenly aware of her surroundings or of her own body. She savored the beauty of the fat, almost luminous snowflakes and the bracing kiss of the cold breeze, even as she eased along with a sure grace that made silence all but effortless.

But she supposed that Thamalon, who had never been a burglar, might well be finding their venture nerve-wracking. She glanced back over her shoulder and was pleased when he gave her a nod that suggested that if he wasn't having fun, he was at least bearing up well under the strain.

She glided forward, then the world twisted itself into a nightmare.

One moment, she was calmly leading Thamalon past a marble statue of a lammasu, a winged lion with a human head, the flowerbeds encircling its plinth, and the ring of stone benches surrounding those. The next, everything shifted. Though Shamur didn't actually see them move, she was virtually certain that all the objects in view had changed position, and though she couldn't make out exactly how their appearances had altered, they now seemed ugly and vile.

On the night of Guerren Bloodquill's opera, Shamur had seen her surroundings abruptly alter in far more overt and astonishing ways. Statues had come to life, and space had folded, opening gateways to the far reaches of the world. But none of those transformations had affected her as this one did. She shuddered, and her stomach churned. Behind her, Thamalon let out a moan.

She struggled in vain to compose herself, and then a skeletal creature in a ragged shroud swooped out of the darkness, its fleshless fingers poised to snatch and claw. At that moment, it seemed the most terrifying threat she'd ever encountered, and, sobbing, she whipped out her broadsword and hacked at it. From the corner of her eye, she saw Thamalon pivot to confront a skull-headed assailant of his own.

Panic robbed her sword arm of much of its accustomed skill, and her first blow missed. The revenant whirled around her, scratching and gibbering, exuding a foul stink of decay, and when she turned to keep the dead thing in front of her, her own motion seemed to cause the landscape to shift even more violently, albeit undefinably, than before. A surge of vertigo made her reel.

The phantom picked that moment to pounce at her, and despite her dizziness, she did her best to cut at it. Her stroke swept into the undead creature's black, rotting cerements, and it vanished. The blow also spun Shamur off her feet.

As she peered frantically about, she found that her disorientation was all but complete. Spatial relationships made little sense. From moment to moment, she had difficulty determining which objects were adjacent to one another, which were near and which were far. Though she could have sworn she had blundered about in a complete circle, she never so much as glimpsed Thamalon or his attacker. She could hear him grunt and his boots creak, but couldn't figure out from which direction the sounds were originating.

Another spectral assailant floated toward her. She clambered to her feet and staggered to meet it. The revenant seemed to disappear. Then she discerned that the stone lammasu, which a moment ago had appeared to be on her right, now loomed on her left. Assuming she could trust that perception, in the course of just a few steps, she'd managed to spin herself completely around. Which in turn meant that the phantom was even now rushing at her back.

She whirled, cutting blindly. The broadsword struck the phantom's yellow skull and swept it into nonexistence.

Shamur noticed she was panting. She struggled to control her breathing and thus her overwhelming terror. She had to figure a way out of this trap now, this second, before yet another dead thing hurtled at her.

It didn't make sense that she was so profoundly afraid, gasping, shaking, her heart pounding. She'd encountered apparent distortions of space and time before, and though the revenants were foul and unsettling, she'd faced far more formidable adversaries in her time. She suspected that she and Thamalon had triggered some sort of magical field of disorientation, dizziness, and terror. It was possible that the phantoms weren't even real, just one illusory aspect of a trap intended to immobilize its victims until one of the patrolling warriors happened by.

She clung to that notion for a heartbeat or two, until another keening wraith dived at her, at that point logic gave way to raw, animal fear. By the time that, slashing wildly, she dispatched the thing, it was hard even to remember what she'd just been thinking, let alone put any faith in her conclusions.

How could the ghostly attackers be phantasmal when they looked and sounded so real? How could the warping of the landscape be a mere deception when she could see the world dancing and contorting around her? And even if it was all in her mind, that didn't mean there was any way to escape it. She was going to die here, the revenants would claw her apart, her heart would burst from fear, or—

At that moment, when sanity was slipping from her grasp, Thamalon reappeared in her tear-blurred field of vision. He hadn't had a chance or else in his distress hadn't remembered to remove his buckler from his belt, and she desperately, reflexively snatched at his unweaponed hand.

Their fingers met. He turned his head and saw her, and, plainly feeling the same frantic need for contact as herself, he yanked her to his side.

Clinging to Thamalon anchored her somehow. For the moment at least, terror loosened its grip. Suspecting this was the last lucid interval she was likely to get, she tried to reason her way out of the trap.

She couldn't trust her eyes, her ears, her nose, or her perception of direction, yet surely there was some aspect of reality the enchantment hadn't muddled. Despite her awkward, flailing swordplay, the revenants had never actually touched her, and perhaps that meant they couldn't. That would imply that the magically induced confusion didn't extend to her sense of touch.

She and Thamalon had been approaching the mansion from downwind. Perhaps if she kept the frigid, howling gusts in her face, and didn't permit any other cues to mislead her, she could lead her husband out of the area tainted by the spell.

Unfortunately, that would mean closing her eyes, and what if she was wrong, and the phantoms truly existed? She'd have no way to defend herself as they ripped her apart!

With a snarl, she thrust that crippling thought away. If she was wrong, she and Thamalon were dead anyway. "Walk with me," she said, squinting her eyes shut. "Don't let go of my hand."

Her lack of vision didn't end the fear, the nausea, or the sense that the world was writhing and jerking around her, nor did it keep her from hearing the wails or smelling the fetor of the revenants. She struggled to ignore all such distractions and focus only on the frigid caress of the wind. Thamalon jerked on her hand as he lurched about swinging his long sword at the apparitions.

Then he stopped and murmured, "Valkur's shield, you did it. You got us out."

Shamur opened her eyes to find the world returned to normal. She looked back toward the marble lammasu. No wraiths were streaking in pursuit of mortal prey.

She drew a long breath and let it out slowly, to calm her racing heart and purge the dregs of the terror from her system. "The Talendar must give interesting garden parties."

Thamalon grinned. "I imagine they only set the snare at times when no one is supposed to be in this part of the grounds."

"You think? And here I thought they prided themselves on their sense of humor. Are you ready to press on?"

"When you are." They sheathed their swords and sneaked toward the house.

Like Argent Hall, the Talendar mansion had once been a stark donjon, but as their wealth increased and their taste for luxury and ostentation grew apace, the occupants had modified and extended the building to a far greater extent than the Karns had ever imagined. Old High Hall had become a sprawling, rococo confection graced with a profusion of friezes, cornices, arches, and similar ornamentation. It was a truism in Selgaunt that the Talendar never tired of stripping away the old decorations and replacing them with something more fashionable or even avant-garde, and scaffolding currently extended along a portion of the west wing. The framework looked as if would provide an easy means of ascent to an upper-story window, but given the family's reputation for wariness, Shamur suspected that appearance was deceptive. A mantrap waited up there somewhere, or at least the two spearmen walking the alures on the roof were watching the scaffold with special care. Crouching at the edge of the open space surrounding the keep, she looked for a safer means of access.

After a few moments, she noticed a sort of secondary portal projecting from the body of the house, bordered by pilasters and capped with a block of carved stone more than half again as tall as the recessed door itself. Just above that coping were round stained-glass windows, that, if her memory of various dances and parties wasn't playing her false, ran along the wall of a clerestory overlooking one of several spacious halls.

She pointed to the entry, and Thamalon nodded. They waited until neither of the guards were looking in their direction, then darted up to the portal and crouched in its shadow.

Shamur quickly climbed to the top of the capstone, then, feeling vulnerable and exposed to the view of the sentries above her, examined the windows. She hoped they'd been designed to open. Otherwise she'd have to extract one from its frame, a time-consuming process that would greatly increase the likelihood of someone catching sight of her.

But fortunately, it wasn't going to come to that. A moment's scrutiny revealed the simplest of latches. She worked a thin strip of steel between the stile and post, popped the fastener, cracked open the window, and peeked inside at a shadowy gallery illuminated only by a single oil lamp burning at the far end. No one was in sight.

Shamur tied off a thin rope and dropped it to enable Thamalon to ascend to her as quickly and quietly as possible. When he joined her, she freed the line, coiled it, started through the window, and froze.

"What's wrong?" Thamalon whispered.

"Nightingale floor," she replied, "built to squeak when anyone treads on it. I *am* rusty. I nearly failed to notice in time."

He peered past her at the gloomy interior of the building. "It's a marvel you noticed at all."

She shrugged the compliment away. "You can generally tell by the kind of wood, and the pattern in which the planks were laid."

"Does this mean we can't go in this way?"

"Luckily, no, but you must step precisely where I do."

"Very well. Lead on."

She did, taking care to trust her weight only to those spots where she reckoned the floorboards made contact with the joists beneath. She and Thamalon reached the arched entrance without either making a sound.

After that, they crept through the keep, listening for the voices and footfalls of others, ducking for cover and avoiding being seen whenever possible, strolling casually and pretending they belonged in the mansion when observation was unavoidable. Had they waited another hour or so to break in, there would have been fewer people roaming about, but Errendar Spillwine had taught Shamur that shortly before midnight was an advantageous time to enter a wealthy house. Many of the occupants had either retired already or were preoccupied with preparing to do so, and unfamiliar persons walking the corridors were less likely to excite alarm would be the case later on.

Finally, lurking in the doorway to a playroom full of balls, dolls, toy men-at-arms, and hobbyhorses, the Uskevren spied what they had been searching for. A brown-haired young man with a wispy mustache and the characteristic slim frame and wry, intelligent face of the Talendar, some bastard son of a female servant, perhaps, judging from the fact that he wore an ill-fitting hand-me-down doublet cut in last year's style, ambled rather unsteadily down the corridor.

The youth was alone. Indeed, as far as Shamur could tell, no one else was even in the immediate vicinity. So she lunged from the doorway, seized the lad, poised her dagger at his throat, and hauled him into the playroom. Thamalon shut the door behind them.

As she'd expected, the youth smelled of wine, but she saw no confusion in his wide, bloodshot eyes. Perhaps fear had sobered him up.

"What do you want?" he croaked.

"Tell me about the plan to assassinate the Uskevren," she said.

"I don't know what you're talking about."

Shamur believed him. It made sense that few members of the household would be privy to a criminal conspiracy. "Then tell me where Ossian Talendar is."

"Gone."

She increased the pressure of the keen edge against his neck. "Don't lie, or I swear to Mask, I'll kill you."

"It's true! He left a couple hours ago and took some of the warriors and Lord Talendar's mage along with him! Some other wizard in a moon mask went along, too, somebody I never saw before."

Shamur and Thamalon exchanged glances.

"Where did they go?" Thamalon asked.

"I don't know," said the boy. "They didn't tell anybody. All I know is that the guards didn't wear their uniforms, or take any arms or armor they couldn't hide under weathercloaks."

Shamur frowned. Did Ossian and the masked wizard mean to attack Stormweather Towers itself? No, surely not, they must realize that even with Jander and Master Selwick dead, such an effort had little chance of success. Did they then have hopes of catching one or more of the Uskevren children away from home? That seemed equally unlikely. Tamlin, Thazienne, and Talbot knew they were being hunted, and thus ought to have sense enough to stay in after dark.

Perhaps the enemy meant to attack and burn one of Thamalon's warehouses or merchantmen at anchor, as in the days when the vendetta between the rival Houses was at its fiercest.

"Nuldrevyn must know what's afoot," said Thamalon. "Where is he?"

"I don't know that, either," said the youth.

"Nonsense," Thamalon rapped. "The lackeys and retainers in a great house always have some notion of where their master is and what he's up to. The lad's playing games with us, milady. Carve him up a bit to prove we're in earnest."

"No!" yelped the youth, squirming futilely in Shamur's grasp. "I'm telling the truth!"

"Then explain," Thamalon said.

"No one's seen Lord Talendar since this afternoon. Master Ossian fetched him away from a conference with a quarryman, then returned later to tell the fellow that something had come up, and his lordship couldn't give him any more time. We've all been kind of wondering where the old man's gotten to."

"You're sure he didn't depart with Ossian and the others?" Shamur asked.

"Yes," said the boy. "Somebody would have noticed."

"And no one saw the masked spellcaster arrive?" she persisted. "Suddenly he was simply here inside the castle?"

"That's right."

Shamur nodded. "Is there a part of the mansion where people don't generally go? Where Lord Talendar and Master Ossian could confer with a third party without anybody else knowing it? Where, perhaps, a guest could even take up residence without the rank-and-file members of the household getting wind of it?"

"I suppose. I mean, there's a section nobody's used for at least a generation."

Shamur looked at Thamalon. "Perhaps we'll find Nuldrevyn there, or failing that, some clue to Master Moon's identity or his current intentions. I admit it's by no means a certainty, but I don't have any other ideas."

"Nor do I," Thamalon said. "Tell us how to get there, boy."

The youth obeyed, whereupon the intruders gagged him with a long gown commandeered from a marionette, trussed him to a chair with a pair of jump ropes, and left him in the playroom.

The Uskevren reached the disused portion of the house without incident. Once they entered its precincts, and no longer had to worry about appearing suspicious, they drew their swords, and Thamalon readied his buckler. Ere long, Shamur grinned with excitement, for she could tell from the broken cobwebs and the scuff marks on the dusty floor that someone else had recently walked these frigid, gloomy corridors.

Then she glimpsed dim light spilling from one of the doorways ahead. She and Thamalon crept up to it and peered beyond the threshold. On the other side was the parlor of a suite, luxurious and stylish once with clear, faceted crystals decorating many of the articles inside. Now it was musty and dark. The only illumination shone from the stub of a single white candle in the latten holder on the marble mantelpiece. It looked as if someone might have initially have lit two or three, but the others had already burned out. That wan, wavering glow barely sufficed to reveal the enormous, coiled shape in the corner, and the motionless human figure behind it that might be either a prisoner or a corpse.

Shamur gave Thamalon an inquiring look. He flicked his long sword in the suggestion of a cut, indicating they should attack the snake, and she nodded in agreement. Though she had no way of knowing precisely what was transpiring here, it seemed likely that Master Moon had conjured up the reptile to guard or kill the man on the floor. Therefore, the Uskevren needed to kill the beast so they could interrogate the fellow if he was still alive, or search his body and the apartment if he wasn't.

Hoping to take the serpent by surprise, the Uskevren stepped forward. Meanwhile, Shamur wondered if their efforts to cat-foot into striking distance were unnecessary, for a learned comrade of hers had once told her that snakes were deaf. Then the huge, steel-gray creature demonstrated that, however deficient its hearing, it had some way of sensing enemies at its back, for it swiveled its wedge-shaped head and regarded them with malevolent coppery eyes.

The Uskevren charged, and the serpent struck, its head streaking forward like a bolt from a crossbow. Thamalon caught the attack on his buckler, the metal rang, and the force of the impact sent him reeling backward.

Shamur drove her point at the snake's flank. The broadsword glanced off the creature's scales as if they were fine plate armor. She had succeeded in attracting the serpent's attention, however. It twisted around, gave a screeching hiss, and struck. Lacking a shield, and dubious of her ability to parry such an attack with her blade, she sprang backward out of range.

Its long body uncoiling, the serpent slithered after her, striking repeatedly. She kept on dodging, riposting when possible, always failing to penetrate the scales, and did her inadequate best to keep the beast from backing her up against a wall. Every time she started to dart to the side, the reptile whipped its head around on that long, sinuous neck and cut her off.

The snake had almost succeeded in trapping her when Thamalon, his buckler pocked where the creature's fang had struck it and corroded where venom had spattered from the point of impact, cut at its spine from behind. He too failed to penetrate the scales, but he distracted the serpent, and Shamur lunged out into the center of the room.

The snake struck at Thamalon, who sidestepped, brushed the attack away with the buckler, and attempted to counter. Before he could complete the action, the serpent, employing a new tactic, lashed its tail around at his ankles and tumbled him off his feet.

The reptile's enormous gray head plunged at the stunned and supine man. Shamur frantically leaped forward and swung her broadsword with all her strength. The edge failed to gash the creature's snout, but it did bash it aside and so prevent its long, curved ivory fangs from piercing Thamalon's body.

She had assumed the snake would now turn its attention to her, but it persisted in trying to strike at the human on the floor, and so she hacked at it again. This time, her stroke landed but failed to deflect the enormous head. Her eyes widened in horror, and then Thamalon, who had evidently recovered his wits, rolled out from under the plummeting fangs.

Shamur managed to keep the snake occupied while her husband scrambled to his feet. Once more, they assailed the reptile together, narrowly dodging its strikes and thrashing tail, and again failing to do it any discernible harm. She knew it would be only a matter of time before the beast had a bit of luck and plunged its poisonous, swordlike teeth into one of them.

She also knew how to fight a foe with impervious armor. Strike at the parts the armor didn't cover. Unfortunately, in the snake's case, they were all on its head, which the creature carried so high it nearly brushed the ceiling. It was effectively out of reach except for those instants when the serpent struck, and then the reptile withdrew it so quickly that by the time its human foes completed a parry or evasive maneuver and were ready to riposte, the opportunity was gone.

If Shamur wanted to attack the head, she needed to abandon any attempt to fight defensively and meet it with a stop thrust as it hurtled down. She twirled her blade in a gesture she hoped would draw the snake's attention.

It did. The head plunged at her, and she lunged at it. Her point flashed between its fangs and punched through the roof of its pale, gaping mouth.

She knew she'd hurt it badly, probably fatally, but the head kept driving forward, the maw engulfing her arm. The snout smashed into her shoulder and knocked her down. Now the upper part of the serpent's body was flopping spastically on top of her legs, pinning her down, while its jaws gnashed with bruising force, trying to spear her imprisoned arm with one of the fangs.

Thamalon lunged and drove his long sword deep into one of the huge copper eyes. The snake thrashed wildly, then stopped moving.

"Are you all right?" Thamalon asked.

Shamur carefully extracted her arm and broadsword from the dead creature's mouth, then inspected the limb for punctures. "I think so," she said.

"That was an idiotic tactic," he grumbled. "It was pure good luck the brute didn't get its fangs into you."

She laughed. "You offer to Tymora, you ought to know that fortune smiles on the bold." She extricated herself from the scaly mass on top of her, then sprang to her feet. "Let's take a look at our friend in the corner."

When they moved close enough for a good look, she was surprised to see that the man on the floor was Nuldrevyn Talendar himself. Had the conspirators had a falling out? The aristocrat was still curled motionless in a ball, but she could see that he was breathing.

Thamalon kneeled beside his rival and touched him gently on the arm. Without opening his eyes, Nuldrevyn shrieked and began to thrash.

Shamur stared in astonishment. Never had she seen the arrogant patriarch of the House of Talendar in such a panicked state, nor would she have imagined he could ever be reduced to such a condition, except perhaps by prolonged torture.

Thamalon gripped Nuldrevyn's shoulders and said, "The snake is dead. We killed it. The snake is dead."

Nuldrevyn's struggles subsided into violent trembling, proving that Thamalon's surmise was correct. Even in his present circumstances, the Talendar lord wasn't afraid of the Uskevren, whom he had battled courageously for much of his life. He had never even opened his eyes to observe that they were there. It was an overwhelming and unreasoning dread of the serpent that had so unmanned him.

"The beast is no more," Thamalon persisted. "Look for yourself."

Nuldrevyn did so with much hesitation and anticipatory

flinching. To her disgust, Shamur felt a slight twinge of pity for him, even though she had little doubt that, his present situation notwithstanding, the Talendar lord had at the very least endorsed the scheme to murder her family and herself. At last he regarded the long, gleaming carcass for a moment, averted his eyes as if even the sight of the beast in death was too horrible to bear, and began to cry.

"Stop blubbering," Thamalon said. "The gods know, we have good reason to wish you ill, but we may forgo our vengeance if you tell us what we want to know."

Nuldrevyn shook his head. "I no longer care what happens to me, Uskevren. I weep because my son is dead."

Shamur peered at him quizzically. "Do you mean Ossian? What makes you think so? I gather he looked healthy enough when he left the castle earlier tonight."

"No," Nuldrevyn said, brushing ineffectually at his eyes. "That wasn't really him. He's gone. Marance murdered him."

Thamalon blinked. "You don't mean your brother Marance, whom I slew thirty years ago?"

"Yes," Nuldrevyn said. "He came back from the tomb to settle his score with you, and may the gods forgive me, I welcomed him." Fresh tears slid down his cheeks.

"Can this be true?" Shamur asked.

"I . . . think it may be," Thamalon replied, amazement in his voice. "I told you Master Moon's voice was familiar, and Marance always fought by whistling up beasts and demons to do his killing for him." He turned back to Nuldrevyn. "Tell us everything, and perhaps we will avenge Ossian for you."

Half mad with grief and the agony he'd endured under the cold, unblinking gaze of the snake, Nuldrevyn related the tale in a disjointed and only partially coherent fashion. Still, Shamur grasped the essentials. At last she fully understood how the masked wizard had tricked her into trying to kill her husband. But the Talendar patriarch's final revelation crushed such insights into insignificance.

"Midnight on the High Bridge?" she demanded, appalled.

"Yes," Nuldrevyn said.

Shamur looked at Thamalon. "It must be nearly midnight if it isn't already, and the bridge is halfway across the city." Even as she spoke, her mind was racing. If they dragged Nuldrevyn along with them, the old man could countermand the false Ossian's orders and call off the Talendar guards. But no, that notion was no good. In his present state of collapse, Nuldrevyn would slow them down too much. Nor was there time to locate another high-ranking Talendar, explain the situation, and prevail on him to intervene. All the Uskevren could do was commandeer a pair of horses, race to the High Bridge, and pray they'd arrive before the trap closed on their children.

Thamalon sprang up from Nuldrevyn's side. "Let's find the stables," he said.

CHAPTER 21

Shamur and Thamalon galloped through the streets at breakneck speed, never slowing. They veered around other riders, wagons, litters, and carriages. They scattered pedestrians, who shouted insults after them.

Shamur felt like cursing them in return, cursing them for idiots who ought to be home in bed, not cluttering up the avenues late on a snowy winter night, not impeding her progress when she was flying to her children's aid. The delight she often found in reckless escapades was entirely absent now, smothered by fear for Tamlin, Thazienne, and Talbot and an iron resolve not to fail them.

She wished she could think that Nuldrevyn had been mad, his tale, false, at least in certain respects, for there was a particular horror in the notion that the Uskevren's chief adversary was a dead man. But that comfort was denied her, for in fact, the Talendar lord hadn't seemed demented, merely distraught. Moreover, Thamalon manifestly credited the notion that Marance had returned, while Shamur herself had discovered in the course of her youthful adventures that the world could be a shadowy, haunted place, and the boundary between life and death more permeable than most people cared to imagine.

She tried her best to scowl her trepidation away. Mortal or wraith, judging from the way he always held back from the thick of the fighting, Marance was wary of his enemies' swords, and that ought to mean that she and Thamalon could cut him down and send him back to the netherworld.

Hooves thundering on the cobblestones, the stolen warhorses plunged out onto the broad thoroughfare that was Galorgar's Ride. From here, the Uskevren had a straight course north to the High Bridge, and Shamur prayed they would now make better time. She squinted against the icy wind now gusting directly in her face, straining for a first glimpse of the Klaroun Gate. Finally, after what seemed an eternity, the ornately carved arch emerged from the darkness ahead. A line of men, weapons in hand, stood across the opening.

Shamur knew the Talendar warriors wouldn't close up their end of the killing box prematurely, for then the children couldn't enter. Their present state of readiness could only mean that Tamlin, Thazienne, and Talbot were on the bridge, and that the other would-be assassins were closing in on them, if they hadn't done so already.

Though the guards were facing north, it would have been absurd even to hope that they wouldn't discern Thamalon and Shamur's approach, because, of course, the destriers' drumming hoof beats gave them away. The warriors turned and eyed the riders with an air of uncertainty. Shamur could virtually read their minds. They'd been ordered to hold the Old Owl's fledglings on the bridge, not to keep anyone off it. Still, the newcomers' frantic pace alarmed them, or else the guards reckoned they shouldn't allow anyone onto the span to witness their comrades committing murder. In any case, one of them waved a sword over his head, signaling the strangers to halt.

Thamalon had happened upon a rack of lances on the way to the Talendar stables and appropriated one for himself. He couched the weapon now. Meanwhile, Shamur drew her broadsword, and, recognizing the riders as a genuine threat, the warriors hastily readied themselves to receive a charge.

With his longer weapon and his steed a length ahead of Shamur's, Thamalon drew first blood. The lance punched through the torso of the warrior in the middle of the line. Thamalon dropped the now-immobilized spear and rode on. Other warriors lunged from either side, and he caught a sword cut on his battered buckler.

Shamur lost track of him after that, because her mount crashed into the line, and she had her own fighting to think about. She split the skull of the foe on her right, then cut at the man on her left. But across the body was the more difficult stroke for a rider, and the warrior managed to skip back out of range.

Shamur tried to push clear of the guardsmen. Had she succeeded, she could either have sped on up the bridge or turned and attacked anew with the momentum of a full charge to her advantage, but her horse suddenly balked. Something had evidently hurt or spooked the animal, but she had no time to wonder what, for now the surviving warriors were driving in from all sides.

Pivoting back and forth, Shamur slashed madly about with the broadsword. The destrier bit and kicked. One by one, the Talendar warriors dropped or reeled back with bloody wounds, until Thamalon, long sword in hand, rode back into the fray and dispatched the last pair of footmen from behind.

The Uskevren wheeled their mounts and galloped on up the High Bridge, past homes, shops, and a guardhouse where, according to Nuldrevyn, the sentries lay magically slain or at any rate incapacitated. Shamur peered into the gloom until she caught sight of the next contingent of men-at-arms, and then she felt a pang of relief, because the enemy warriors had not yet skulked all the way up to the tavern called the Drum and Mirror. The actual attack had yet to begin, and therefore, the children must still be alive.

Some of the warriors had evidently heard the hoof beats, cries, and clangor of blades arising behind them, because they were looking back in the couple's direction. Not giving them time to organize a defense, the riders charged them. A javelin streaked past Shamur and clattered down on the cobblestones behind her. Then she was in the midst of the foe, and, leaning out of the saddle, whipped her blade in a cut that tore open a warrior's throat.

She galloped on, dealing with any enemy who lunged or blundered into her path, but seeking one particular target. Assuming that Nuldrevyn had accurately described the trap, there should be a spellcaster here on the south side of the tavern, either Master Moon himself or a Talendar retainer, and said wizard posed a greater threat than any one of the men-at-arms. She wanted to eliminate him before he could do any damage.

Finally she spotted the mage. To her disappointment, it wasn't Marance but a tubby little man with a bald pate and luxuriant side-whiskers, clad in a checkered mantle. It was, in fact, Dumas Vandell, a jolly, down-to-earth fellow with a limitless supply of jokes, riddles, and humorous poems and ditties. Over the years, Shamur had chatted with him at many a social function, and rather liked him. Now, in the heat of battle, she couldn't afford to regard him as anything but an enemy, and judging by the alacrity with which, upon catching sight of her, he began to weave a spell, he was indeed resolved to kill her if he could.

She wrenched her destrier's head around and charged, hoping to reach the wizard before he completed his incantation. She didn't make it. A shadowy bolt of force, so indistinct against the night that she would never have noticed if not for the sparkling motes and whining sound, leaped from Master Vandell's fingertips. She swayed to the side, and the magic crackled harmlessly past her.

An instant later, she closed with the wizard. He threw up his plump white hands to fend off her sword, but her cut smashed through his defense and gashed his hairless scalp. He collapsed, and, perched on her stamping, chuffing warhorse, she watched him until she was convinced he was unconscious, then rode on. For a second, she rather hoped she hadn't killed him, and then, when another guardsman tossed a javelin at her, she forgot all about him.

She had to cut down two more warriors before she reached the entrance to the Drum and Mirror, and by that time her children were wandering out the door to see what all the commotion was about. Tamlin, exquisitely dressed as ever, although for some reason, he had an ordinary axe, a tool, not a proper weapon, slung across his back, as well as a pewter goblet of wine in his hand. Talbot looked unkempt as usual. Thazienne, eyes bright with curiosity and excitement was clad in a suit of dark, close-fitting leather.

Shamur had rarely been so glad to see anyone, and judging from the way the children's faces lit up when she careened out of the gloom, they felt much the same. Now, however, was scarcely the time for sentiment.

As Thamalon galloped up behind her, she shouted, "Mount up! Hurry! You're in a trap!"

Feeling eager and slightly melancholy at the same time, Marance strode through the fish market, an open space equipped with tables and stalls. With him marched a band of Talendar men-at-arms and Bileworm, cloaked in the flesh of Ossian. In another minute or so, Thamalon's get would be dead, and then, the wizard supposed, his soul could at last enjoy a measure of peace. But what a shame that he'd had to kill his own nephew to accomplish his purpose, and in so doing, forfeit his brother's good opinion.

Perhaps one day, after the Uskevren were extinct and

in consequence, the House of Talendar had grown more wealthy than ever before, Nuldrevyn would understand and forgive. In any case, Marance resolved that he wouldn't dwell on the matter, lest he cheat himself of his enjoyment of the slaughter to come.

Shouts, hoof-beats, and the ringing of blades sounded from the darkness ahead, jarring him from his reverie. He and his companions faltered in their advance.

"Those idiots attacked before us," Bileworm said.

"No," Marance replied. He pointed to a three-story cedar building still some distance ahead on the east side of the bridge. "That's the Drum and Mirror, and no one's fighting there yet. Someone has attacked our men."

"Should we run and help our lads?" asked one of Nuldrevyn's sergeants.

The warrior had actually been addressing Bileworm, or, as he imagined, Ossian, but it was Marance who answered. "Not yet."

After positioning his men and disposing of the Scepters in their guardhouses, Marance had elected to wait at the north end of the bridge, where it was absolutely impossible that the Uskevren would catch sight of him. Then, as midnight approached, he had created a magical implement that would enable him to see when his prey rode onto the span, and subsequently to survey the battlefield at need.

Though no one could see it, that small, spherical tool was floating above him now, following him about like a faithful dog. He focused his thoughts on it, and, abruptly, he was gazing down at his henchmen and himself, peering through the invisible orb instead of the eyes in his skull.

He sent the magical eye speeding along the bridge until he caught sight of the riders who had engaged his men. So far, it appeared there were only two attackers, but, mounted on destriers and fighting superbly, they were wreaking havoc even so.

As one of the newcomers cut down Master Vandell, Marance sent the eye winging closer, then twitched in amazement. Though the riders had made some small effort to disguise themselves, he recognized them, but how was it possible?

Bileworm sensed his master's stupefaction. "What is it?" he asked. "What do you see?"

"Thamalon and Shamur," Marance replied. He heard the quaver in his voice, felt himself shaking, and struggled to calm himself. "They evidently survived the demolition of the ruined fortress."

"How?" the spirit asked.

"I don't know," Marance replied, transferring his power of sight back into the eyes he had been born with, "anymore than I comprehend how they knew to come here to rescue their offspring. But it scarcely matters, does it? What does is killing the lot of them together." He gestured to one of the warriors, a burly fellow with a black mustache and a red scarf knotted around his brow. "Run to the north end of the bridge and bring up the rest of the men. Everyone else, attack."

The guards trotted forward. Marance turned to Bileworm. "You, too."

The familiar arched an eyebrow. "Me?"

"Yes. The soldiers may fight better with one of their patrons in the thick of the fray."

"Master, I'd really rather not."

"Don't be such a coward. Even wearing a corporeal body, you're all but invulnerable to any real harm."

"Still . . ."

Rage flared up inside Marance, and his body clenched with the effort to contain it, though he knew it wasn't truly his impudent servant who had so roused his ire, but rather these maddening Uskevren who had somehow frustrated his attempts to slay them time after time after time.

"You're my slave, and you will obey me," he snapped. "Go."

Bileworm sighed, drew Ossian's golden-hilted long sword, and scurried forward. He glanced back once or twice in the hope that his master would relent, but by that time Marance was already weaving magic, a candle held high in one hand and his staff in the other. Magenta sparks danced on the black, polished wood, and the cold air reeked of myrrh.

As Tamlin, Talbot, and Thazienne swung themselves onto their horses—destriers, Shamur noted approvingly, not palfreys, her children hadn't ridden out into the night completely unprepared for trouble—warriors in mufti came trotting down from the north. More of Marance's henchmen, joining the battle as expected.

Drawing her long sword, Tazi grinned at the approaching force. "Let's charge them," she said.

The wild, reckless part of Shamur's nature cried out in assent, but the portion that had loved and protected these children since their births demurred. "Not a wise idea," she said. "The guards will be receiving conjured reinforcements any second."

"All the more reason to punch through them now," Tazi said, "get within sword range of the masked wizard, and—"

"Your mother's right," Thamalon rapped. "We're getting the three of you out of here. Ride for home." Thazienne sneered, but when he turned his mount south, she, like her brothers and Shamur, did the same.

For a moment, as Shamur urged her war-horse into motion, she dared to hope they might escape without further difficulty, for the warriors behind them wouldn't be able to keep up with their mounts, and except for one or two survivors of the skirmish just concluded, the southern half of the bridge lay open before them. Then patches of soft violet light shimmered and swelled on the cobblestones ahead, and she realized that she and her family had run out of time.

"I suppose now we have to charge," Tamlin drawled. Even with enemies hurrying to engage him, he'd clung to his wine cup as he climbed into the saddle, and now he took a final sip, tossed the goblet away to clink on the pavement, and readied his sword.

"Insightful as usual," mocked Talbot. "No wonder you're the heir." Ahead, the purple lights died, leaving in their place a number of long, low, crouching shapes.

"Enough chatter!" Thamalon said. "Concentrate on the task at hand. Charge on my word, and . . . go!"

The Uskevren hurtled forward. One of the conjured creatures, ophidian but for the several short legs on either side of its scaly body, pointed its snout at Shamur.

She judged that she was still out of the beast's striking distance, but instinct warned her that it was about to attack her somehow, and she yanked on the reins and swerved her destrier to the side. A dazzling, crackling thunderbolt leapt from the reptile's head.

Shamur would have sworn that the flare of power missed her cleanly, but for an instant, her muscles clenched in agony. Evidently similarly afflicted, the war-horse stumbled, then balked. She kicked the steed, forcing it on at the behir, whose species she had belatedly recognized once the creature employed its extraordinary means of offense.

White radiance flickered and rattled on either side as other behirs assailed the rest of Shamur's family. The air reeked of ozone. The noblewoman's mount carried her into striking distance, and, unable to discharge a second lightning bolt just yet, the reptile that had attacked her reared up, its neck craning to place its head on a level with her own. Its crocodilian jaws gaped wide enough to snatch her from the saddle and swallow her whole. She thrust the point of her broadsword into the behir's neck, and, blood spurting from the wound, it fell.

A second behir scuttled into her path, running amazingly fast on its stunted legs. She disposed of that one with a cut to the skull, and then a pair of gnolls—hyena-faced warriors a head taller than a tall man—stalked out of the darkness, their poleaxes at the ready. Her eyes widened in surprise, for she'd been so intent on killing the behirs that she hadn't even noticed a second wave of Marance's agents materializing.

She rode toward the closer of the gnolls. When it thrust

its weapon at her horse, she knocked the spiked head of the poleaxe out of line with her broadsword, then dispatched the shaggy warrior with a rib-shattering chest cut.

Even as the gnoll fell, its compatriot rushed in and swung its poleaxe in a chop at Shamur's head. She barely managed to lift her sword in time for a high parry, and the impact jolted her entire body.

The problem with a weapon as long and heavy as a poleaxe, however, was that even a fighter as big and strong as a gnoll needed a moment to heave it back into a position for a second attack when an initial effort failed, and Shamur intended to exploit that. She grabbed hold of the poleaxe just beneath the wickedly curved blade.

Snarling, the gnoll yanked on the shaft of the weapon. Brawny as it was, it doubtless thought it could free the poleaxe from her grip with little trouble, and in fact, she shared its confidence. But she hadn't intended to immobilize the implement for long, just long enough to flummox the gnoll while she leaned out of the saddle and drove her point into its breast. The brute's pulling actually facilitated the action.

The gnoll dropped, and Shamur looked about. For the first time since the conjured creatures had begun appearing, she wasn't facing an immediate threat. She could spare a moment to look and see how her companions were faring.

For one ghastly moment, she felt a pang of fear, for she only saw three horses besides her own plunging and wheeling about the bridge. Then she discerned that although one steed had been lost, its rider had not. Tazi now sat behind Talbot on the latter's huge paint destrier, wielding her long sword to lethal effect despite the impediment of the broad-shouldered youth immediately in front of her. So far, except for superficial cuts and bruises, everyone in the family appeared to be all right.

Grinning, Shamur turned her horse toward the next foe blocking the path to safety.

Peering through the invisible eye, Marance watched the battle with growing incredulity.

His summoned creatures scurried among the corpses, human and otherwise, littering the cobbles. Nuldrevyn's troops, a pack of ill-trained dolts no braver than Avos the Fisher's hooligans, advanced warily from the north. Bileworm's leadership notwithstanding, they had yet to charge in among the wizard's more exotic agents. The astonished residents of the houses on either side of the roadway, roused from their beds by the clamor of combat, gawked from doorways and windows. At the center of the tumult, the Uskevren cut their way toward the south bank of the Elzimmer.

A fair-minded man, even with regard to his estimation of his most hated enemies, Marance would have freely conceded that each of the Uskevren was a formidable combatant in his or her own right. Now he saw that the five of them fighting in concert were little short of awe-inspiring. One foe after another fell beneath their bloody swords, until the wizard recognized that, impossible as it seemed, if he didn't undertake measures to hinder them, Thamalon and his family were likely to get away. Marance had better decide on his tactics forthwith.

He would cast the rest of his ordinary summoning spells, of course, but he couldn't assume that additional conjured servants would fare any better than those already sprawled and lifeless in the Uskevren family's wake. The same long, relatively narrow structure of the bridge that had made it seem a fine site for a trap likewise made it impossible for too many opponents to come at the riders simultaneously, and thus he couldn't count on overwhelming them with sheer numbers. Something extra was required.

Should Marance dive into the thick of the fray himself, throwing blasts of fire and the like? The memory of Thamalon's long sword ripping open his belly three decades before flashed unbidden into his mind, and his mouth tightened. Not that he was afraid, of course, for his death at the Owl's hands had been a fluke. He was confident of his ability to handle any man at close quarters. Still, it was foolish to fight in that manner unnecessarily. A spellcaster gave up much of his natural advantage when he allowed his foes into striking range, or, to some degree, even permitted them to lay eyes on him.

Of course, Marance could armor himself against ordinary arrows and the like, then fly above the Uskevren well out of reach of their blades, but even that might not be prudent. He had no idea what Thamalon and Shamur had been up to since he'd seen them last. He didn't know what sort of surprises they might have prepared for him, or what manner of puissant allies, wizards and priests, belike, might even now be speeding hard on their heels to the bridge.

No, all in all, it seemed best to destroy the Uskevren from a genuinely safe distance. Marance would do it with one of the great spells he carried in his memory, and never mind the drain on his vitality. After this encounter, he shouldn't need it any longer.

Should he then conjure the corrupt earth elemental? Perhaps not. Perched so high over empty air and running water, he might find it difficult to evoke and control the giant. Besides, somehow, Thamalon and Shamur had foiled the creature once already.

Smiling slightly, Marance decided another option was superior. Unless the Uskevren got off the High Bridge quickly, an improbability with the wizard's minions attacking them, the magic would inevitably kill them, yet, the true beauty of the scheme was that if he knew Thamalon, his old enemy might well stop even trying to depart.

Swinging his staff in intricate passes, the wizard turned widdershins and chanted in a rasping, grinding tongue never devised for a human throat. A knowledgeable observer might have recognized certain similarities to a spell employed by mortal wizards to invest themselves with the capacity to move objects by thought alone. But Marance's version, a secret he'd wrested from an ancient baatezu adept in Maladomini, the Circle of Ruins, was vastly more powerful. It could shift masses unthinkable for any earthly wizard.

The sky flickered red for a moment, and voices wailed and groaned from the empty air. Marance's body burned with purple flame as the power flowered inside him, and he stumbled with the glorious agony of the sensation.

The fire faded, or rather, withdrew inside him. In control of himself once more, he poised his hand above one of the fishmonger's cleaver-scarred tables. A toy-sized simulacrum of the High Bridge, made of violet phosphorescence, wavered into being between his fingers and the butcherblock beneath. After a second, he sensed that his creation had become palpable enough to touch, whereupon he took hold of it and began to shake it back and forth.

The bridge lurched, and Shamur's destrier staggered. Tamlin's mount lost its balance altogether, and the elegant young man, rather less elegant now that his lovely clothes were torn and soiled with the blood of his enemies, frantically kicked his feet out of the stirrups and flung himself clear to keep his leg from being smashed between the horse's flank and the roadway.

A second jolt followed hard upon the first. Shamur's terrified mount stumbled again. Realizing the impossibility of riding under these conditions, she scrambled out of the saddle and released the animal to look after itself. Talbot and Thazienne did the same. Thamalon, however, had to slay one of the remaining gnolls, magically compelled to attack even when it could hardly keep its feet, before he could dismount. Somehow he managed to control his panicky, staggering horse and wield his long sword at the same time, parrying a thrust of the gnoll's spear, then dispatching it with a chest cut. That accomplished, he jumped down onto the pavement.

Keeping a wary eye out for their foes, the five Uskevren blundered toward one another to confer. The shaking bridge rumbled beneath their feet. Houses on either side of the roadway swayed, their timbers moaning, and falling objects crashing inside them. A roof tore loose from its moorings, pitched backward, and plummeted toward the river far below.

"Quake!" declared Tamlin, raising his voice to make himself heard above the din.

"No," Shamur replied, "Our enemy's sorcery is shaking the bridge. Evidently he's willing to destroy the whole thing to kill us. I assume that either he's stepped off the north end already, or he has a magical way of getting off at the moment of collapse." She looked at the road before her, where cobblestones jarred loose from their bed and jutted like rotten teeth, and saw that she and her family had covered a good portion of the distance to the Klaroun Gate. "I think that if we keep moving, we have a fighting chance of getting off ourselves. However—"

Two more gnolls lumbered forward. Conversation ceased for a moment while the Uskevren cut the creatures down.

"You were about to observe," Thamalon panted, "that if we simply run away, everyone who lives on the bridge will die."

"Yes," Shamur said. Frightened and unaware of what was truly happening, most of the residents wouldn't even try to get off the span. Thinking to wait the strange rumbling out, they'd simply cower in their homes.

"Then we need to kill the masked wizard and hope that ends the shaking," said Thazienne impatiently. "Fine. That's what I wanted to do in the first place, but does anyone listen to me?"

Strands of sweaty black hair plastered to his face, his square jaw set, and a feral light in his eyes, Talbot nodded. "Let's have done with the wretch. Avenge Jander and Master Selwick here and now."

"And put an end to all this unpleasantness so we can go back to living like civilized people," said Tamlin, brushing futilely at a gory spatter on his sleeve.

"Come on, then," Shamur said. She and her family began to advance back the way they'd come, when the shaking stopped. For a moment, she wondered if her analysis of the situation had been at fault. Perhaps the High Bridge wouldn't break, perhaps the spell that threatened it had run out of power. Then spheres of purple glow swelled in the gloom ahead, and as soon as they birthed the creatures intended to block the way, the span resumed jarring back and forth. Evidently Marance was unable to rock it and conjure more of his minions at the same time, and so had elected to briefly suspend the one action in order to accomplish the other.

When Shamur approached close enough to see them clearly, she judged that the wizard's new servants had been selected specifically to operate on this precarious ground, for they all possessed more than two legs and a low center of gravity. One of them, a pallid creature somewhat resembling a centipede, its segmented body half again as long as a man was tall, scuttled toward her. Tentacles coiled and writhed between its round, black eyes.

From past experience, Shamur knew that a sticky secretion on a carrion crawler's flexible arms could paralyze at a touch. The tentacles whipped at her, she swept her broadsword in a parry, and the bridge jerked. She fell, her attempt at defense turned into a useless flailing, and one of the feelers brushed her wrist.

For an instant, a horrible numbness flowed up her arm, but then the sensation passed. Praise Mask for her sturdy gauntlet and sleeve, which had kept most of the crawler's greasy, malodorous poison from reaching her skin.

Though it might not matter in the long run. She was sprawled on the ground, and the insect-thing was still scuttling forward, chittering. She rolled across the heaving roadway with the carrion crawler in mad pursuit, and then, when she thought she'd widened the distance between them sufficiently to buy herself a moment, tried to scramble onto her feet.

Just at that instant, another tremor jolted her, but, fighting for balance, she refused to let it tumble her back down. She faked a dodge to the right, then darted left instead. Only deceived for a moment, the carrion crawler lashed its tentacles at her. A couple of them only missed by inches, but miss they did, and then she was behind the creature's head with its leathery natural armor and positioned to strike at its softer, more vulnerable flank.

She drove her point deep into the crawler's body, between the base of the head and the first pair of legs. The beast jerked spasmodically, then went down.

As she pulled her blade from the carcass, Shamur surveyed the battlefield. Thamalon was plunging his blade into the chest of what must surely be the last surviving gnoll. Talbot and Thazienne fought side by side against a trio of carrion crawlers. Tamlin, who had lost his sword, slammed the axe into the spine of an enormous, fire-breathing canine. The hell hound fell, and the youth crowed in delight.

"I told you this thing was lucky," he called to his embattled siblings, brandishing the gory tool as he spoke. Tazi sneered.

Shamur scowled in frustration. There were plenty of carrion crawlers and hell hounds still remaining, and the bubbles of violet and magenta light swelling on the roadway ahead promised even more adversaries. Meanwhile, the Uskevren had only succeeded in making their way a short distance north.

They were never going to cut through all of Marance's defenders in time to prevent the destruction of the bridge. They needed another solution, and perhaps, Shamur thought, smiling at the audacity of the notion that suddenly occurred to her, that meant it was time to stop behaving as if she were a mere earthbound warrior and start acting like the thief in the red-striped mask.

If she meant to try her idea, it had to be now, before she attracted the attention of another opponent. Leaving Thamalon and the children to keep Marance's minions occupied, praying they'd manage all right without her, she dashed to the facade of one of the swaying houses. Then, struggling to cling to hand- and footholds that constantly threatened to judder free of her grip, she climbed.

✧ ✧ ✧ ✧ ✧

For a man as orderly and intelligent as Marance, it was child's play to juggle the various elements of a complex task. He shook the bridge for a while, glanced through the magical eye to see how the Uskevren were faring, summoned some new opponents for them if it seemed necessary, and then repeated the sequence. Now seated on the table beside his magical simulacrum, he didn't even have to worry about the tremors knocking him down.

Nor need he fret over what would happen when the bridge collapsed beneath him. A single magic word would cause him to drift downward toward the surface of the river as slowly as a bit of silkweed fluff. Then, while his leisurely descent was in progress, he could either invest himself with the power of flight or, if, as he expected to be, he was absolutely certain that all five Uskevren were dead, he could simply click his iron thumb rings together and return to the netherworld. Perhaps the latter option was preferable, given that he'd pretty much worn out his welcome at Old High Hall.

If Bileworm was in the immediate vicinity, the magic of the rings would whisk him to the Pit as well, but Marance doubted the familiar would make his way back to the fish market in time. He supposed he might actually miss the scamp, his companion and confidant for nearly thirty years. But one must accept casualties in war, and, happily, the Nine Hells possessed an abundance of slaves.

A shout roused Marance from his musings. Turning his head, he saw that the strapping warrior with the red kerchief on his head had finally returned with the men-at-arms Marance had dispatched him to fetch. Three of them, anyway. The others had no doubt been too prudent to set foot on the quaking bridge.

"What are you doing?" the big man demanded, swaying as the vibrations rattled him.

"Nothing," said Marance, deeming the lie worth trying. "Go forward and help Master Ossian."

"Do you think we're stupid?" the guardsman replied. "We see that thing under your hand. *You're* shaking the bridge, and I know damn well that Lord Talendar wouldn't want you to do that. Stop it right now, or we'll stop you." He brandished his long sword.

"If you insist," Marance said. He took his hand away from the simulacrum, but naturally, the tremors in the actual bridge continued. It would take time for them to subside, if, indeed, that was still possible, if he hadn't already damaged the structure sufficiently that a collapse was inevitable.

"I told you to stop it!" the warrior barked.

"I understand," Marance said. "Evidently it's going to take a bit of countermagic."

He removed a scrap of fur, a piece of amber, and a paper of silver pins from one of his pockets, and then, manipulating the spell components, he began to chant.

When he was half way through the incantation, the men-at-arms somehow guessed what he was really up to, and frantically staggered toward him. But they failed to close the distance in time. A flare of lightning crackled from Marance's hand to the warrior with the scarf and blasted him dead.

Immediately the magic leaped from the importunate fellow's withered, blackened corpse to the guard behind him, then leaped twice more, slaying each man in his turn. Surveying the smoking, reeking husks, Marance sighed. "I regret that was necessary," he told them, then took hold of the bridge simulacrum once more.

Shamur waited for the present shock to subside, then leaped across the narrow gap between rooftops. Had she not chosen her moment properly, a fresh tremor might have staggered her and spoiled the jump. Even though the bridge wasn't shaking too badly, the houses still were. The vibration made her lead foot slip as it landed, and she fell and slid down the pitch. Grabbing for some semblance of a handhold, she managed to arrest her descent before it could fling her off the eaves into space. As she proceeded on her way, she reflected that if the shaking had made walking the roadway difficult, traveling the thief's path above verged on the impossible, even for a pupil of Errendar Spillwine.

Nor could she proceed cautiously. Unless she scrambled as rapidly as possible, risking a fall with every move she made, she stood no chance of finding Marance in time to prevent the destruction of the bridge.

At least her scheme was sound. The wizard hadn't thought to station any of his creatures up here, which meant that if she didn't plummet to her death, she could get at him without having to hack her way through dozens of defenders.

Off to the east, where the black river met the bay, she spied the myriad lights of the floating city. Had it only been last night that she'd bounded from vessel to vessel in pursuit of the tattooed ruffian? So much had happened since that it felt like a lifetime. She wondered fleetingly if the watermen could hear the tortured bridge grinding and rumbling, if they all were peering up at it, and then the section of shuddering roof she was currently climbing shed its shingles all at once.

The slates streamed down the pitch like an avalanche. She had nothing at all to cling to, and as the skidding, disintegrating shingles carried her relentlessly down toward the drop off, she could only scramble frantically, striving to reach something solid to grab onto before she plunged into space.

She seized hold of a piece of sturdy eaves just outside the slippage even as the loose shingles swept her lower body off the edge. She grunted at the jolt as her arms took her weight. The bridge lurched, and she gripped with all her strength to keep the shock from jarring her loose from her handholds. Then she hauled herself back up onto the roof.

Afterward, she would have liked nothing better than to lie still and catch her breath, but knew she had no time for such an indulgence. She forced herself to continue onward.

In a few more seconds, she peered down at the roadway. For the most part, Marance's minions were behind her now, but she still saw no sign of the wizard himself. She wondered grimly just how much farther she had to go.

Bileworm skulked through the shadows on Ossian's feet, the dead youth's beautiful sword in his hand. Or at least he tried. It was difficult to move stealthily when he could barely maintain his balance.

He was on his own now. As soon as the mock earthquake —perhaps he should call it a bridgequake—had begun, the Talendar troops under his nominal command lost all interest in combat. They only wanted to hunker down and wait out the tremors. Trust Master to initiate one strategy, then abruptly switch to another that entirely undermined the first one, and left the lieutenant charged with making the alpha plan work stuck in a precarious position.

Still, though Bileworm was now alone, Master had commanded him to fight, and fight he would, for he was far more afraid of the wizard's displeasure than the Uskevren.

His best course, he reckoned, was to pick out one enemy who had drifted away from the others, strike him down by surprise, slice off a recognizable trophy, and carry it back to Master. Surely then the spellcaster would concede that his servant had done his duty, and allow him to spend the rest of the battle idling safely at his side.

Bileworm spied Thamalon himself, finishing off a hell hound. The nobleman was at least ten paces from Talbot, his nearest ally, who was busy with adversaries of his own.

Placing his left hand over his breast, Bileworm glided forward.

Ironically, it was one of the tremors that saved the Owl, for by staggering him, it turned him around sufficiently to see the would-be assassin slinking toward him. He and Bileworm both came on guard, the familiar making sure to stand in extreme profile, angling the left side of his body well away from the human's blade.

"I know what you really are," Thamalon growled. "Nuldrevyn explained it."

"How nice for you," Bileworm said, then lunged.

Ossian had been a competent swordsman, and by inhabiting his corpse, Bileworm had inherited a measure of his skill. Still, employing his buckler, Thamalon deflected the attack with ease, then riposted with a head cut.

The nobleman's long sword sheared away the left side of Bileworm's face. The shock of such a grievous injury would have incapacitated any normal fighter. Bileworm, however, had no need to suffer discomforts arising in Ossian's flesh. He reflexively blocked the pain and renewed his attack.

The remise caught Thamalon by surprise, but, displaying the reflexes of a highly trained combatant, he twisted aside from Bileworm's point with not an inch to spare. Instantly he hacked at the spirit's extended wrist, slicing muscle and tendon and splintering bone. The blow didn't quite lop off Bileworm's hand, but it rendered it useless for swordplay.

Time to go, then. Hoping that Thamalon wouldn't see him depart in the darkness, Bileworm stumbled around, turning his back to the aristocrat, then exploded from Ossian's mouth. The lad's corpse collapsed.

His malleable form flattened against the cobbles, Bileworm slithered rapidly along, seeking another shell to inhabit. The first he came across was a behir carcass, and after a split second's hesitation, he passed it by. If a body wasn't manlike, it sometimes took him a few minutes to figure out how to make it move properly, and he needed a vessel in which he could fight immediately.

Next, he spied a dead gnoll with a gash in the side of its furry neck and its hide tunic tacky with blood. That ought to do. He poured himself between the creature's fangs, then jammed his substance into rough alignment with the gnoll's limbs. Rushing the possession this way, he might find that his new body moved a trifle awkwardly, but the violence of the bridge bouncing about reduced everyone to clumsiness anyway.

Bileworm stealthily turned the gnoll's hyena head. Thamalon was still poised over Ossian's mangled form as if suspicious that it was about to jump up and resume the battle. The familiar took hold of the gnoll's notched iron scimitar, leaped to his feet, and charged, once again hoping to take his opponent by surprise.

Alas, Thamalon sensed him rushing in on his flank, spun in his direction, ducked low, and extended his point at the gnoll's chest. Staggering as another tremor jolted him, Bileworm only barely managed to halt in time to avoid impaling himself, an injury that, though it might not have affected him at all, might also have inconvenienced him severely. Snarling, he hastily reverted to the fighting stance he'd employed before.

Struggling for balance as the bridge shuddered, the two combatants circled, until Bileworm discerned an apparent weakness in Thamalon's guard. He swept the scimitar in a brutal arc toward the outside of the human's sword arm.

Thamalon's blade instantly shifted back to the right, closing the line. Metal rang as the scimitar struck the long sword and rebounded. The nobleman cut at the gnoll's already damaged neck and severed its head.

Since the head couldn't fight, Bileworm elected to remain with the body. He plunged forward, slashing madly, hoping that sheer ferocity would compensate for the fact that he was now fighting blind.

His curved blade touched only air, and his leg gave way. Thamalon must have cut it out from under him.

As the gnoll fell, Bileworm streamed up from the stump between its shoulders. This time, Thamalon saw him leave, and thrust his point harmlessly through the familiar's shadowy form. Bileworm gave him a mocking leer, then darted away, shrinking himself so his foe would lose track of him.

Tottering, Thamalon pivoted this way and that, peering to see which of the corpses on the cobblestones would rear up and attack him next. Meanwhile, Bileworm circled, trying to decide the same thing. Which carcass would best serve his purpose?

After a few seconds, he noticed the dead Talendar guard slumped in a shadowy, recessed doorway at Thamalon's back. It was in the one direction that Thamalon hadn't glanced. Evidently he hadn't noticed it was there.

Swinging wide to keep the Owl from spotting him, Bileworm slithered up to the warrior's body and writhed his way inside. When the dead man's eyes began to serve him, he discerned that everything was proceeding according to plan. Thamalon still had his back to him.

Bileworm gripped the warrior's longsword and carefully climbed to his feet. He was resolved that this time, he would keep silent and succeed in attacking by surprise.

He assumed his fighting stance, crept forward, and aimed his sword to pierce Thamalon's spine. Then, just as he was about to thrust, his enemy spun around, lunged, and drove his point *through* the guard's heart and deep into Bileworm's form beneath.

Wracked by a shock and weakness he couldn't block out, Bileworm dropped his blade. Swaying, he told himself that this couldn't be happening. He, who had survived for millennia by dint of his cunning, couldn't perish at the hands of a dull-witted mortal man. Yet even as he denied it, he knew it was true.

"You aren't quite as clever as you think," Thamalon told him almost gently. "I pretended to ignore one of the corpses to induce you to occupy it, so I'd know from what quarter you'd attack next. And by taking such pains to protect your heart, you simply revealed where you were vulnerable."

The human sounded so smug that Bileworm felt some sort of mocking retort was in order, but with his mind crumbling, he couldn't think of one. His knees buckled, and darkness swallowed him.

Across the roadway, a four-story post-and-beam house rumbled, swayed, and collapsed. Shamur winced to think of the unfortunate family crushed or trapped inside, and then, at last, she caught sight of her quarry.

As she'd hoped, Marance was alone, in the center of the fish market. She realized that she'd unconsciously expected to find the masked wizard standing straight and tall to work his magic, his hands upraised and his dark mantle flapping around him. Instead, he'd seated himself atop one of the fishmonger's tables, where he was rocking a glowing violet miniature replica of the bridge back and forth.

The burnt black remains of four men who had apparently tried to interfere with Marance lay within a few paces of the butcher-block. A few pale, horrified faces gawked from the windows of houses adjacent to the market, but evidently none of these spectators could muster the courage to try to stop the spellcaster, even though they must realize that if he kept on as he was, his efforts were likely to kill them.

Shamur, of course, did intend to stop him, and this once, despite her natural inclinations, she had no intention of allowing her adversary a sporting chance, the better to challenge and revel in her own prowess. Marance was too formidable, and there was too much at stake, to opt for a fair fight as long as she had an alternative. If possible, she meant to slip up on him from behind and dispatch him before he even realized he was in danger.

Unfortunately, the fish market was one of the few sections of the bridge that didn't have buildings along the sides. It would have been easier to sneak around behind Marance if she didn't have to descend to ground level, but she reckoned that a skilled thief still should have a chance. It was night, after all, and she was wearing dark clothing, including a hooded cloak to distort her silhouette. She started to clamber down the brownstone wall of the last house south of the open space.

When she was halfway to ground, a tremor hit, and her poor, abused fingers, battered, wrenched, and rubbed raw by all the difficult climbing she'd already done, finally failed her. She lost her grip and fell.

She thought fleetingly that Marance was going to get

his chance after all, for he would surely notice her slamming down on the cobbles. Then she did precisely that. She tumbled into a forward roll to cushion the shock, but it was a hard landing even so, and knocked the wind out of her.

Though half stunned, she felt a pressure in the air around her, and when she looked up at Marance, she observed that the glowing simulacrum of the bridge was reshaping itself into a doll-sized image of herself. Knowing a magic that could shake tons of stone could surely crush her to jelly in an instant, she hastily scrambled several feet to her left. The feeling of pressure vanished, and her replica dissolved into a shapeless, shifting blob of purple light, from which she inferred that this particular spell couldn't seize hold of her as long as she kept moving. Good to know, though it still left her with all of Marance's other tricks to worry about.

She drew her broadsword and stalked toward him, noticing as she did that even though he'd stopped tampering with it, the bridge kept on shaking. That probably meant it wouldn't take much more abuse to make it fall; she only prayed it wasn't doomed to collapse regardless. Staff in hand, Marance rose and glided backward from the writhing ball of purple phosphorescence, maintaining the distance between himself and his adversary, interposing butcher-blocks between them.

"This is rather a pity," the wizard said. "If I have to fight one of you Uskevren face to face, by rights, it ought to be my principal enemy, Thamalon."

"I disagree," Shamur said. "You murdered my grand-niece and made me into your pawn, so I deserve the satisfaction of killing you. I've been hoping for a chance to confront you when you weren't surrounded with a horde of protectors."

"Then you're in luck," he replied, "for I've pretty much expended all my summoning spells already. But I really don't think I'll need them to dispose of you."

He reached inside his voluminous mantle. She sprang up onto a heaving table and charged him, bounding from one butcher-block to the next. He couldn't use them to impede her advance if she was running on top of them.

Still retreating, he brought out a feather, an article which she, who had known her share of wizards, recognized as one element of a spell of flight. She had to prevent him from casting it, or he'd soar up beyond her reach and magically smite her at his leisure. Reciting a rhyme, he twirled the quill through a complex mystical pass, and magenta sparks danced along its length. Meanwhile, still running, she transferred the broadsword to her left hand, drew her dagger with her right, and threw it.

She was grimly certain the quaking would hamper her aim, and in fact, the cast missed. But the knife flew close enough to his Man in the Moon mask to make him flinch, and the feather slipped from his grasp, disrupting the spell in progress.

Not allowing him time to attempt any other magic, she plunged into the distance and cut at his head, a hard, direct attack which, given that most spellcasters she'd known were not exceptionally skilled at hand-to-hand combat, she fully expected to land. But with the facility of a master, Marance slapped the broadsword aside with his staff. The two weapons were only in contact for an instant, but purple fire sizzled from the wooden one into Shamur's blade.

Wracked with pain, shuddering uncontrollably, she saw her opponent spin the staff to deliver another blow. Unable to parry, dodge, or counterattack in her current state, she floundered desperately backward and fell off the back of the table.

Once again, she crashed down with bruising force, but almost felt that the impact jarred some of the spasticity out of her, for her seizure abated somewhat. When, his staff weeping magenta flame, Marance scrambled around the table, she lurched to her knees and met him with a thrust to the groin. Since he halted abruptly, the attack didn't harm him, but it bought her a second to regain her feet. Then it was her turn to retreat and retreat while her twitching subsided.

Abruptly, catching her by surprise, Marance stepped backward as well, putting space between them, snatched something out of his mantle, and murmured another incantation. Voices moaned and gibbered from the air, and shadows danced crazily.

With terrible suddenness, bands of shimmering violet light appeared all around Shamur, thickening, meshing, rapidly combining to form a closed sphere. She lunged at one curved side of the trap and ripped at it, feeling the surface harden from a gummy consistency to steely hardness just as she forced her way through.

By that time, Marance was already completing another spell. A flare of dark power leaped from his pointed index finger. Shamur threw herself flat, and the magic sizzled over her. Even though it missed, for an instant, it made her jerk with agony.

She decided she couldn't allow him any more free shots at her while she was out of distance. Sooner or later, she wouldn't be able to dodge. She scuttled behind a butcher-block, then darted in his approximate direction from one such piece of cover to the next, scrambling on all fours, never presenting a target for more than an instant.

As she advanced, she heard him chanting in some bizarre tongue that was all grunts and consonants, but as far as she could tell, the spell had no effect. No destructive power blazed in her direction, nor did her surroundings alter.

Finally she was close enough to rush in and attack him. Somehow divining her location, he pivoted in her direction, settled into a fighting stance, and lifted the sparking, smoldering staff into a strong guard.

She nearly hesitated, for she was sure that last spell had achieved something, had set some sort of snare for her. But she couldn't very well retreat and permit him to strike her down from behind, then resume demolishing the bridge. She had no choice but to fight him, and so she bellowed and charged, trusting to her skills and aggression to see her through whatever surprise he had devised.

When she was nearly close enough to attack, her eyes met the strange, pale ones shining inside the sockets of the sickle-shaped mask, and Marance spoke a word of power. At that instant, Shamur's eyelids dropped, and her knees buckled, even as her mind grew dull and somnolent. She barely noticed Marance sweeping the staff around in a horizontal strike, and nearly failed to comprehend the significance as she did.

Nearly, but not quite. She dropped beneath the blow and bit down savagely on her lower lip. The burst of pain helped clear her mind of the unnatural sleep that had threatened to overwhelm her.

As she sprang up and came back on guard, she realized that Marance's last spell had given him a capacity somewhat like the basilisk that nightly guarded Argent Hall. He could now induce unconsciousness with his gaze, which meant it was perilous even to glance at his pearly eyes. In fact, she thought with a sudden, unexpected swell of her old daredevil's exultation, given all the wizard's advantages, this would almost certainly be the most challenging duel of her career.

Grinning, she feinted a thrust at Marance's foot, then, when the staff whipped down to club her wrist, she lifted the broadsword to cut his forearm. Retreating a half step, he spun his length of polished wood in a parry, and she snatched her blade back a split second before the two weapons could clash together.

He swung the staff at her head, and she jumped back out of range. At that point, he too tried to retreat, and she sprang forward to keep him from withdrawing too far away. She had to press him hard at all times, never allowing him a single moment's respite to cast a spell.

As they battled on, the crackling staff leaped at Shamur time after time, burning brighter and brighter, its corona of magenta fire burning streaks of afterimage across her sight. She ducked when the weapon shot at her head, jumped over it when it swept toward her ankles, sidestepped blows, or evaded them by hopping backward out of range, sometimes avoiding calamity with less than an inch to spare. Whenever Marance gave her a chance, she struck at him in turn, relying on compound attacks to draw the staff out of line and counterattacks to catch him at the moment he started to swing or thrust at her. She made sure above all else that whether her action succeeded or not, he wouldn't be able to bring his weapon into contact with her own.

Considering the handicaps she was laboring under, her mere survival demonstrated that she was fencing as brilliantly as she ever had in her life. But even so, she couldn't penetrate his guard, and soon, she would begin to slow down, for no one could fight as furiously, as she was, never pausing for an instant to catch her breath, without flagging fairly quickly. Meanwhile, if Marance felt any fatigue, he wasn't showing it, and she feared that such mortal limitations were meaningless to the dead.

If she didn't find a way to kill him quickly, he was going to do the same to her, and she could only think of one tactic that might serve.

Marance twirled the burning, crackling staff in a move calculated to draw Shamur's eyes to his face. He'd attempted the trick before, and, recognizing it for what it was, she'd refused to fall prey to it. Now, however, she intentionally did what he wanted her to do, praying that, having resisted the magical slumber once, she could do so a second time.

Marance spoke the magic word, and gray oblivion surged into her mind. Suddenly, everything was dull, distant, meaningless, and, her body numb and leaden. She simply wanted to collapse onto the cobbles and sleep.

Then some defiant part of her remembered Thamalon and the children, dependent on her to save their lives, and, biting her lip bloody, she thrust the lethargy away.

The magic had staggered her, and, pretending she was still in its grip, she continued to reel, meanwhile watching Marance through slit eyes. When he stepped in to bash her head with the staff, she lunged so deeply it carried her beneath the arc of the blow and buried the broadsword in his chest.

Now it was the wizard's turn to stumble, dropping the staff as he blundered backward. The sizzling sparks blinked out as the rod clattered on the cobbles. Shaking, he struggled to lift his fair, delicate hands, seemingly to bring his iron thumb rings together.

Shamur had no idea what that would accomplish, but, suspecting she wouldn't like it very much, she yanked her weapon from his torso, flicked off the thumb of his right hand, then cut at his head. The broadsword shattered the crescent mask and crunched deep into the skull beneath.

Marance collapsed. Believing that one couldn't be too careful with the undead, Shamur, panting, watched him for a time to make sure she really had destroyed him, and while she was so engaged, she noticed that at some point during the duel, the bridge had stopped shaking.

Apparently it wasn't going to fall.

CHAPTER 22

The Drum and Mirror possessed a verandah overlooking the bay, a railed porch warded against
cold weather by the same sort of enchantment that
protected the Wide Realms. Slumped there now,
filthy, sore, weary to the bone, yet actually feeling
fine, Talbot savored the warmth of the mulled wine
glowing in his belly and the splendor of the red
and golden dawn flowering above the Sea of Fallen
Stars. His equally grubby and battered parents and
siblings sat with him, likewise gazing to the east,
and amazingly, whether exhaustion or content-
ment was responsible, it appeared that no one in his
loquacious, quarrelsome family had a word to say.

After, as Talbot now knew, Mother had killed
Marance Talendar, the wizard's conjured minions
had fought on for a little while longer, then, one
species at a time, vanished back to wherever he'd

summoned them from. That, however, had scarcely been the end of the family's labors. Father had immediately gotten them started digging through the rubble of the several collapsed houses to rescue whomever might be trapped inside. In time, other residents of the bridge and a troop of Scepters had joined the effort, but the task had taken several hours even so.

It was finished now, and here the Uskevren were, all five of them basking in a rare moment of family amity. Then Tamlin straightened up a little, opened his mouth to speak, and Talbot winced, somehow knowing that his brother was about to spoil the mood.

"I did well tonight, didn't I, Father?" asked Tamlin, fatuously, in Talbot's jaundiced opinion.

Father smiled. "Yes, son. All three of you did."

"Then maybe this is a good time for me to tell you something," Tamlin said. "You know those dreary men from Raven's Bluff and wherever else it was?"

Father frowned. "The emissaries? Of course. What about them?"

"Well," the younger man said, "to tell you the truth, I sent them packing."

"You *what*?"

"Well, they just babbled on and on, and I didn't understand a word of it. I thought it would make life easier if I simply got rid of them, the better to focus on the effort to find you and Mother and catch the rogue who was trying to assassinate us. So I broke off the talks, trying to be nice about it, though I must confess, the outlanders seemed rather peeved even so. They said they would sail for home forthwith."

"You imbecile!" Father roared, his face ruddy with anger. "Do you know how much money that alliance would bring in?" He made a visible effort to rein in his temper, and Talbot could all but hear the wheels turning as Thamalon began to ponder how to salvage the situation. "I have commitments that absolutely preclude my leaving Selgaunt for at least a month, and by then some other House will have gotten in ahead of us. You, boy, must journey east in my stead. You'll apologize profusely for rebuffing the envoys, spread a fresh round of gifts and bribes about, and resume the negotiations."

Tamlin grimaced. "I told you, I wouldn't know what to say, and in all candor, I really feel that these past couple days, I've done my bit to serve the family already. Besides, I have commitments, too. I've already accepted invitations to any number of parties and balls."

"Fine," Father snapped. He turned to Tazi. "You'll go."

"No, I won't," she replied. "Tamlin's the heir, and if he isn't willing to shoulder the responsibilities of his position, I don't see why I should have to take up the slack, particularly now that I've just gotten over being ill. I'm planning to enjoy myself, not sit cooped up in a room and dicker endlessly over the price of knickknacks, or whatever it is you'd want me to discuss."

"So be it," Father said. He pivoted toward Talbot. "And what do you say, lad?" Tal could see the anticipatory disgust in the old man's eyes, the expectation that his youngest child, like the others, would disappoint him.

Rather to his own surprise, Talbot felt a momentary impulse to surprise his sire, to please him for once by undertaking this task and performing it well. But he knew he couldn't journey to a strange city. The full moon was coming, and it must find him locked in his cage backstage at the Wide Realms when it arrived. "I can't go either," he said. "Mistress Quickly has cast me in her current play and the two that will follow."

"You feckless ingrates," Father began, trembling.

Mother, looking utterly strange with her blisters, scrapes, bruises, and torn lower lip, her masculine clothing and short, dyed hair, laid her hand on his arm. To Talbot's surprise, the gesture sufficed to make the old man pause in mid-diatribe.

"You have a choice," Mother said. "You can take their recalcitrance to heart, or you can remember the valor they displayed earlier, and be proud."

The corners of Father's mouth quirked upward. "You have a point. For the moment, I will be proud, albeit grudgingly. Will you stroll with me to the far end of the porch?"

"All right," she said. As they walked away, Talbot wondered what they had to say that they didn't want their children to overhear.

For some reason, Shamur felt awkward and flustered, and it was worse when she looked at Thamalon. Hands resting on the railing at the edge of the verandah, where the enchantment of warmth gave out, she gazed out at the gorgeous sunrise gilding the rippled surface of the sea. The cold breeze smelled of salt water.

"I was just wondering," Thamalon said, a bit diffidently, "how soon you'll be moving out of Stormweather Towers, and where you'll go when you do. Obviously, you don't need to run all the way to Cormyr anymore, unless it's what you want. I'm sure Fendolac would welcome you back at Argent Hall."

Once again, a knot of emotion tightened painfully in her chest, and this time, at long last, she understood precisely what she was feeling, just as she knew there was nothing to be done about it.

"Perhaps Argent Hall would be a good choice," she said, striving to be austere, dignified Lady Uskevren, with never a hint of distress in her tone or expression.

And it was that very reflexive attempt at masking her true self that abruptly snapped her to her senses. Since Thamalon now knew who she really was, she didn't have to deceive him anymore. If she was willing to risk a bit more heartache and a wound to her pride, she could speak to him honestly at last.

She forced herself to turn and face him.

"Do you want me to go?" she asked.

His green eyes blinked in surprise. "No, milady. Despite all the quarrels and misunderstandings, I've always cared for you, and after these recent days, I think I love you better than before." He smiled for an instant. "Apparently I like it when a woman tries to kill me. I only asked about your intentions because I thought you wished to leave."

"At one point, so did I," she replied, "but gradually, I realized something. Somehow, by preventing you from truly knowing me for all those years, I likewise kept myself from perceiving you as you truly are. But the last three days have opened my eyes, and I see someone rather grand. I'd like to come to know him better, if it's not too late."

Thamalon beamed, an expression of such naked joy that it pierced her soul. "Even though he's an old man?"

"Yes. Judging from the way he handles a long sword, he still has a little life in him. So I ask to be your wife, my lord, a truer, fonder wife than I was before. I'll renounce swords and adventure and become my grand-niece once again." The declaration brought an upwelling of bitter anguish, and she swallowed it back down as best she could. She had made her choice, and must strive not to pine for all it would cost her. "I just hope I can resume the masquerade successfully. I thought I could hunt for Master Moon and still safeguard my secret, but it didn't work out very well. Nuldrevyn knows who I truly am, and even if he doesn't tell, any number of people have now seen the refined, weapons-hating Lady Uskevren brawling in the streets. It's possible that one of them will figure out that the Shamur of today and the thief of yore are one and the same."

Thamalon chuckled. "You do talk nonsense sometimes."

She peered at him quizzically. "What do you mean?"

"That if nobody else reveals your secret, we Uskevren will do it ourselves. Think about it. You committed your robberies almost a century ago. Nobody's outraged about them anymore. To the Selgaunt of today, Shamur the thief is a charming rascal in a series of amusing stories, not a threat to the common weal. Moreover, you're now the hero who prevented the destruction of the High Bridge. I very much doubt that anyone will want to arrest you for your past indiscretions, and if they should, we'll buy them off."

"Then I could live as I please," she murmured, not quite daring to believe it.

"Well, you can't go back to plundering our peers," Thamalon said. "That's simply not appropriate for the mistress of a great House. But I daresay we can satisfy your yen for mayhem somehow. You can fence, of course. Travel with our caravans and argosies and fend off brigands and pirates. Help stamp out the Quippers. Bear your sword against the Talendar, Soargyls, or our other rivals, the next time they take it into their heads to exterminate us. I only insist on one condition. Should anybody inquire, I always knew who you truly were."

"Agreed," Shamur said, and then, heedless of their dignity, of the eyes of their astonished children or anyone else in the tavern, she and Thamalon embraced.

THOMAS M. REID

The author of *Insurrection* and The Scions of Arrabar Trilogy
rescues Aliisza and Kaanyr Vhok from the tattered remnants
of their assault on Menzoberranzan, and sends them off on
a quest across the multiverse that will leave
FORGOTTEN REALMS® fans reeling!

THE EMPYREAN ODYSSEY

BOOK I
THE GOSSAMER PLAIN

Kaanyr Vhok, fresh from his defeat against the drow, turns to hated Sundabar for the
victory his demonic forces demand, but there's more to his ambitions than just one
human city. In his quest for arcane power, he sends the alu-fiend Aliisza on a mission
that will challenge her in ways she never dreamed of.

BOOK II
THE FRACTURED SKY

A demon surrounded by angels in a universe of righteousness? How did that
become Aliisza's life?

November 2008

BOOK III
THE CRYSTAL MOUNTAIN

What Aliisza has witnessed has changed her forever, but that's nothing compared
to what has happened to the multiverse itself. The startling climax will change the
nature of the cosmos forever.

Mid-2009

*"Reid is proving himself to be one of the best up and coming authors
in the FORGOTTEN REALMS universe."*
—fantasy-fan.org

THE KNIGHTS OF MYTH DRANNOR

A brand new trilogy by master storyteller

ED GREENWOOD

Join the creator of the FORGOTTEN REALMS® world as he explores
the early adventures of his original and most celebrated
characters from the moment they earn the name "Swords of
Eveningstar" to the day they prove themselves worthy of it.

BOOK I
SWORDS OF EVENINGSTAR

Florin Falconhand has always dreamed of adventure. When he saves the life of
the king of Cormyr, his dream comes true and he earns an adventuring charter for
himself and his friends. Unfortunately for Florin, he has also earned the enmity of
several nobles and the attention of some of Cormyr's most dangerous denizens.
Now available in paperback!

BOOK II
SWORDS OF DRAGONFIRE

Victory never comes without sacrifice. Florin Falconhand and the Swords of
Eveningstar have lost friends in their adventures, but in true heroic fashion, they
press on. Unfortunately, there are those who would see the Swords of Eveningstar
pay for lives lost and damage wrecked, regardless of where the true blame lies.

August 2007

BOOK III
THE SWORD NEVER SLEEPS

Fame has found the Swords of Eveningstar, but with fame comes danger. Nefarious
forces have dark designs on these adventurers who seem to overturn the most clever
of plots. And if the Swords will not be made into their tools, they will be destroyed.

August 2008

WELCOME TO THE

WORLD

Created by Keith Baker and developed by Bill
Slavicsek and James Wyatt, EBERRON® is the latest
setting designed for the DUNGEONS & DRAGONS®
Roleplaying game, novels, comic books, and
electronic games.

ANCIENT, WIDESPREAD MAGIC

Magic pervades the EBERRON world. Artificers create wonders
of engineering and architecture. Wizards and sorcerers use
their spells in war and peace. Magic also leaves its mark—the
coveted dragonmark—on members of a gifted aristocracy. Some
use their gifts to rule wisely and well, but too many rule with
ruthless greed, seeking only to expand their own dominance.

INTRIGUE AND MYSTERY

A land ravaged by generations of war. Enemy nations that
fought each other to a standstill over countless, bloody
battlefields now turn to subtler methods of conflict. While
nations scheme and merchants bicker, priceless secrets from
the past lie buried and lost in the devastation, waiting to
be tracked down by intrepid scholars and rediscovered by
audacious adventurers.

SWASHBUCKLING ADVENTURE

The EBERRON setting is no place for the timid. Courage,
strength, and quick thinking are needed to survive and prosper
in this land of peril and high adventure.

During the Last War, Gaven was an
adventurer, searching the darkest reaches
of the underworld. But an encounter with
a powerful artifact forever changed him,
breaking his mind and landing him in the
deepest cell of the darkest prison in
all the world.

THE DRACONIC PROPHECIES

BOOK I

When war looms on the horizon, some see it as more
than renewed hostilities between nations. Some see the
fulfillment of an ancient prophecy—one that promises
both the doom and salvation of the world. And Gaven may
be the key to it all.

THE STORM DRAGON

The first EBERRON® hardcover by veteran game designer
and the author of *In the Claws of the Tiger*:

James Wyatt

SEPTEMBER 2007